Romancing the Soul

ALSO BY SARAH TRANTER
FROM CLIPPER LARGE PRINT

No Such Thing as Immortality

Romancing the Soul

Sarah Tranter

W F HOWES LTD

This large print edition published in 2014 by
W F Howes Ltd
Unit 4, Rearsby Business Park, Gaddesby Lane,
Rearsby, Leicester LE7 4YH

1 3 5 7 9 10 8 6 4 2

First published in the United Kingdom in 2014
by Choc Lit Limited

A CIP catalogue record for this book is available
from the British Library

ISBN 978 1 47125 851 0

Typeset by Palimpsest Book Production Limited,
Falkirk, Stirlingshire
Printed and bound by
www.printondemand-worldwide.com of Peterborough, England

This book is made entirely of chain-of-custody materials

For Jamie. My Real Deal.

CHAPTER 1

Cassie Silbury fled down the plush-carpeted stairs, chanting over and over in her head the mantra, 'Stop freaking out. It wasn't real. *It. Was. Not. Real.*'

The sound of her heels hitting hard tiles heralded her arrival at the imposing reception hall. The relief that flooded through her at the sight of the exit was *very* real and there was nothing she could do about that; she was out of there.

Dashing through the doorway that she'd so confidently strolled through earlier, she hurtled down the stone steps fronting the Harley Street property. The normality of London's evening rush hour, with its cacophonous sights and sounds, enveloped and immediately soothed her. She cursed violently though as the biting wind sliced deep and she realised that she'd left her coat behind. Hugging herself tightly, she embraced her anger. Anger was good. For a moment there . . .

'Taxi!' she screeched, on seeing a yellow light. She vigorously waved her hand in the air to attract the necessary attention.

Cassie was in the back of the black cab before

it reached a full stop. 'Sixty-three Kensington Avenue!' she said, as she threw her bag and notebook onto the seat next to her. The cab manoeuvred into the right-hand lane, heading towards the sanctuary of home. And Cassie finally stilled.

But she was cold and angry and . . . would absolutely not think about the rest! She focused on her anger: *How dare he put those things into my head! How dare he make me think I was . . .? How dare he make me flee! And my coat! The evil little man!*

Cassie's restless eyes honed in on the open notebook next to her bag. She snatched it up triumphantly. 'Nevil L. Mann,' she'd written and underlined at the top of the page, alongside today's date, January 25th. Unsnapping the pen clipped to her notebook, she proceeded to scrub out the 'N' with a self-satisfied flourish that quickly became a furious obliterating scribble: 'evil L. Mann' it now read. She continued to eradicate his preposterous job title, which she'd jotted underneath: 'Past Life Regressionist to the Stars'. She stopped only when the nib of her pen wore through the paper, tearing up several of the pages underneath.

'*Stupid* evil little man,' she muttered. He knew full well who she was. He'd even told her that he was a fan of her work, before he'd proceeded to 'past life regress' her. She snorted at the ridiculous description of what had just occurred . . . before glaring at the taxi driver, who was observing her nervously in his rear-view mirror.

Beyond stupid, she further clarified to herself.

Who, in their right frame of mind, gave an investigative reporter a past life *from hell*? She desperately suppressed where that thought was going and forced a healthier focus. He was clearly deranged, along with the rest of his so-called profession. This piece was always going to be an exposé, just like so many she had written before, to prove his profession a sham. But things had just got personal.

And he'd been good, she ruefully conceded. She'd expected to imagine and 'manufacture' a past life. All her research indicated they were creations of the mind, with Cleopatra in the number one slot. She'd spent last night studying Elizabeth Taylor in the role so she could look damned good in her imaginings.

But she'd found that she had no control whatsoever over proceedings. Each time that evil man had voiced another one of his malicious, manipulative prompts, she'd sunk deeper and deeper into the horror playing out in her head.

And then he'd wanted her to talk it through with him, to apply context, to use the newfound knowledge to heal . . . *Heal? I had nothing to bloody well heal until I walked into that godforsaken building!*

No. Cassie needed a plan. A plan that would expose the profession for what it was. A sham. *That* and that alone would apply the necessary *context*. They had no right playing around with people's heads, making them think . . .

She grinned with self-satisfaction as it came to her. She might have been unsettled there for a moment, but Cassie Silbury was back on form. She knew what she had to do . . . just *after* she found oblivion through the bottle of vodka she was sure sat in the cupboard at home.

Three days later

'No way! Noooo way!' Cassie wailed the words over and over, mantra-style, while blindly fleeing the Tunbridge Wells town house. On automatic pilot, her feet followed the path and turned left after passing through the garden gate.

It was several minutes before she became aware of her surroundings. A park. A bench. She let herself collapse onto the bench and sat. Stunned.

Several more minutes passed before she allowed herself to think. And then it was to reflect: things hadn't gone quite to plan. It had been so simple; another 'past life regressionist,' planting a different past in her mind. The second couldn't possibly come up with the same as the first. She was supposed to have them by the short and curlies.

She let out a hysterical laugh at the question that flashed into her head: 'So Cassie Silbury – what did you do in a past life to deserve this?' Oh, she so couldn't go there. She urged her mind to cooperate, while her lungs released a shaky breath.

Cassie *knew* there was a perfectly rational, non-crackpot explanation for the two past life stories matching . . . exactly. She just had to find it. She groaned, hardly sparing a glance at the jogger who

4

found an extra burst of speed to lurch past her in a widened berth.

Concentrate Cassie. She shuffled awkwardly in her seat for several long moments before . . . enlightenment! Oh, it was a blessed, fanfare playing moment. *Of course!* She laughed delightedly, before shaking her head quickly. She'd never believed it, not for a minute!

It was so simple: The Conspiracy Theory. She'd come across enough of them in her work to know one when she saw one. And the NAPLR (National Association of Past Life Regressionists) – she couldn't help the snort – knew she was doing the piece. And they also knew her style. They would have known she'd go to another practitioner. The stories tallying had to be their attempt at credibility.

It wouldn't have been difficult, she realised, her mind warming nicely to the theme. There had to be methodology to their madness. The evil little people had, after all, studied past life regression and had qualifications on their walls to prove it. So, logically, there had to be an established method for planting a scenario into their victim's subconscious. All they would have had to do was ensure each of them knew the scenario to be placed and when to provide the necessary prompts. V*oila!* An idiot's guide to painting Cassie Silbury as 'bitch reincarnate.'

But I used a different name this time. How could this one have known what to plant? Cassie thrust

5

the highly unhelpful thought away. Conspiracy, she reminded herself. *Aaaand . . .*

Yes! They could have her picture circulating electronically on wanted-style posters. Although many would probably recognise her anyway as she was regularly in the press, not just through her critically acclaimed, high-profile written word, but because being the sister of Hollywood actor George Silbury hardly ensured anonymity.

Cassie quickly quashed the sinking sensation she experienced on thinking of George. *'Do you recognise anyone, Cassie?'* She wasn't going there. It was nonsensical.

Cassie realised another plan was required. A foolproof plan this time that took account of the conspiracy. She'd work on it on the way home. Standing up, on traitorously shaky legs, she looked around to gauge the most likely route to the train station. She had no idea where she was . . . other than a park in Tunbridge Wells. Cassie decided, once she was back in sight of home, she'd pop into Waitrose for another bottle of vodka. Just so it was in the cupboard.

Six days later

Cassie put the phone down and jotted the time and details of the next appointment in her diary. Casting an eye over the local newspaper advertisement before her, she grinned. Her plan was finally coming together. And Rachael Jones was a godsend.

Although qualified, Rachael Jones *wasn't* a member of the NAPLR, and therefore *wouldn't* be in receipt of the conspiratorial communications no doubt doing their rounds among members. Yet she did hold their approved qualifications. Indeed, she'd passed them all with distinction and, on qualifying last year, had received their most outstanding graduate of the year award. In an incredible stroke of luck that award had been presented to her by the NAPLR's Chairman. He'd provided, for the record, several glowing words on her abilities that couldn't be interpreted as anything other than an endorsement. How was he to know she'd not join the association? And how was he to know Cassie Silbury had her in her sights?

Cassie was delighted with herself. The fact Rachael Jones's 'flamboyant' newspaper advertisement indicated that she may well be a candidate for a padded cell and complimentary lobotomy, was simply the very sweet mallow icing on her meticulously planned cake.

Next Wednesday, Cassie mused, tapping the diary page with her pen. George would be back in the country . . .

She shook her head rapidly, urging herself not to even contemplate where that thought was leading. She reached for her glass and took a swift gulp of neat vodka.

But it was no good. George *would* be filming not far from where this Rachael nut practiced and . . .

what if he could come to the appointment with her?

Cassie was more battle-scarred than she was prepared to admit while sober and in control of her faculties. And ditto to the bricking herself about subjecting herself to the administrations of another head case. But George, despite his Hollywood heart-throb status, was sensible, grounded and her favourite and most protective older brother.

Cassie raised her glass to her lips. What was wrong with someone being there to hold her hand?

Two large gulps from her glass.

She wanted George there! He'd always been able to slay her dragons. Of course . . . If she could get *him* to past life regress, he could slay the most monstrous of all dragons to ever haunt her. With no crossover in their past, all those fears that kept creeping up on her would—

Stop! She dropped her head into her hands. There was *No. Such. Thing. As. Past. Lives.* Cassie wished with all her heart that she'd never started this story. Why couldn't they have had her as Cleopatra?

No! She raised her head in horror. She promptly downed what was left of her latest glass of vodka and desperately shook the empty bottle.

Hadn't Cleopatra killed her brother too?

CHAPTER 2

'Ummm . . .' Susie wasn't sure what to say. She slowly shook her head and replaced the newspaper on the kitchen table.

'It's brilliant, don't you think?' Rachael asked, bringing two mugs of coffee over, and curling her tall frame into the seat next to Susie's. 'I wanted eye-catching.'

Susie was truly lost for words. Rachael, her housemate and best friend in the world, had always been . . . she wasn't quite sure what adjective to put there, but *this*?

Rachael laughed at the look on her face. 'It's called marketing, Suse. Valentine's Day is coming up and I refuse to miss an opportunity.'

Picking the paper up again, Susie braved another look at the advertisement in question and silently groaned. It *was* eye-catching, but neither that or brilliant were the descriptions immediately springing to mind.

Firmly schooling her features, she attempted to form an opinion on the Casper-like ghosts shooting cupid's arrows around gravestones, surrounded by floating bulbous red love hearts. Subtly clearing her throat, she then tackled the words that were so clearly Rachael's . . .

No love or humping in this life?

Find out who you loved and humped in a past life! What did it for you then may do it for you now. Let the clues from the past show you the way to finding true love. Your Soul Mate is out there! Let a past life lead the way.

Contact Rachael, Past life Regressionist (bona fide) and This Life Guide for Love-Seeking Souls

While attempting to dispel the notion of Casper humping, Susie asked, 'Aren't there laws about this kind of thing?'

'Like what? The words are all mine.'

Not humping Caspers. 'No, I can see the words are yours love . . . About advertising and what you're implying.'

'I haven't *promised* to find their Soul Mate.'

'Look,' Susie was going to take the easy way out, 'I'm really not the person to ask. It's all very . . . *enterprising* of you.' She congratulated herself on both her diplomacy and for finding the perfect word for the situation, but paused as she realised that she had a responsibility here.

Groaning audibly now, she continued, 'But you know I'd rather see it come with a health warning.'

10

Rachael shifted awkwardly in her seat. 'That's not fair. I'm qualified now.'

'*Qualified?* I've never understood how someone as intelligent as you can have gone into something as . . . as—'

'You can hardly see me teaching snotty-nosed brats like you do!'

'I never set out to teach snotty-nosed bra— They *aren't* snotty-nosed brats!' Susie gritted her teeth. 'And I love teaching and I'm good at what I do. But you've a degree in economics, Rach, and have thrown away a successful career in banking to peddle—'

'My father's bank and I did my time. This is what I was always destined to do, Suse. I love it, too, and I am flaming good at it to boot!'

Susie couldn't help the 'humph!', but immediately regretted it as Rachael's visage shifted. Her cheeks, normally so pale against her dark hair, flushed and her amber eyes flashed. Susie's stomach lurched. *She wouldn't . . . surely she wouldn't.*

'You're going by something that happened before I was trained and I could make it all right if you'd simply let me regress you again!'

Susie desperately reinforced the locked box that stood in that darkened corner of her mind with heavy chains and padlocks. 'You are *never* getting into my head again. *Ever!* In fact, *nobody* is ever getting into my head again.'

How could Rachael have crossed the line? They never talked of that night.

11

'I accept things didn't—'

'Stop, Rachael,' Susie growled.

'No! This is the perfect opportunity to talk about it! It's time we stopped pussyfooting around your experiences that night.'

Susie snatched her hand back as Rachael reached for it and shuffled her chair several inches further along the table. She crossed both arms protectively over her chest. 'Don't do this, Rach.'

'I know things didn't go well,' Rachael said gently. 'But that was the drinks, the Ouija board, and . . . well, what we were all smoking didn't help.'

Loss. Such agonising, all-consuming loss. It was as if the locked box in Susie's head wept its abject wretchedness. No matter how many padlocks she applied to the box containing the memories of that night, the feelings she'd experienced always found a way out. They seemed to seep, as if they could soak into its very walls and escape as vapour.

There was nothing for it Susie realised, kicking her chair back and getting up from her seat, but her escape was hampered by Rachael grabbing the frayed and hanging pocket of her dressing gown.

'It's ten years ago now,' Rachael said softly. 'You have to let me put it right. I *can* put it right.'

Desolation. Susie closed her eyes, letting the sensation take its course. Ten years, ten days, ten seconds. Time was irrelevant here. It could never be put right. The moment she'd let Rachael into her intoxicated brain, for what had promised to be an *amusing* attempt at discovering a past life, the damage had been done. It was irreparable. She was irreparable. She stared at Rachael, incredulous at her naivety.

'Come on,' Rachael coaxed, before grinning and attempting to lighten the mood. 'I could be your "this life guide" and lead you to this Soul Mate of yours.'

'Rach,' Susie groaned, depositing herself back in her seat and holding her head in her hands. 'I didn't like you when I first met you and should have gone with my gut!'

Rachael actually chuckled. 'Despite your words though, you love me now. Once you got to know me you couldn't but.'

'More fool me. I should have followed my instincts. They told me you were dangerous.' Susie crossed her arms on the table. 'I will say this once again, in case you have any doubts in that warped mind of yours: *nobody* is ever getting into my head again. And you can times that exponentially when it comes to you!'

'Suse . . . What you experienced was—'

'Was *crap*, Rach! I know what you think it was, but it was crap. Playing with hypnosis or whatever the hell it was you did to me, in the state that we were in, was asking for trouble. No wonder my brain did what it did. You have chucked in your career to peddle crap. And the worst of it is that you don't see it for what it is. You genuinely believe in past lives, Soul Mates – in fact *any* spooky

13

dumb-arse thing. Oh, and did I forget to mention Fate, there? It's nuts. Completely nuts. You're nuts!'

'Kooky perhaps, but not—'

'*Nuts!* And I seriously worry about you! I mean the latest is so far beyond ridiculous it's . . . Who, sound of mind, could possibly think that their neighbour's cat was their Soul Mate!'

There was a sharp intake of breath from Rachael. Susie knew that had been a cheap shot.

'Look, I'm sorry. I know you believe it and consider yourself to be in a difficult situation, but it's just, it's just . . . nuts! I can't think of a kinder word to use!'

'You've already made your views on Matey perfectly clear, thank you. So how about you stop trying to distract me here, because I know that's what you're up to, and we get back to talking of—'

'He's a cat, Rach! A cat! Rob's cat at that!'

'Susie! I don't expect you to understand!' Pain flashed in Rachael's eyes. She continued quietly, 'I'm not sure I even understand it myself. It must be a blip. A definite blip in the system.' With resolve she went on, 'But I *can* help you, Suse. If only you'd let me!'

Not a chance.

'Why Rob didn't leg it out of the building as fast as he could that day, I'll never know,' Susie said. 'I'm pleased he didn't though because I like him. I did instantly. He's fun, even if he does humour you too much. But you wouldn't have seen me for dust. You gave the impression he was moving in to a building occupied by loons. I'll never forget that look on his face as his cat jumped into your arms and you started spouting total crap at it! Talk about first impressions. We hadn't even spoken to Rob at that stage!'

'You're so in denial.' Rachael shook her head sadly, refusing to be baited. 'How you can possibly not believe in past lives and Soul Mates after what you remembered that night, I don't know. Let me regress you again, help reduce your negativity towards it – at least recognise him for who he was. He was your Soul Mate, Suse. You lost him in 1826. He couldn't have been anyone else. And he could be out there right now, needing to be found.'

Betrayal. Complete betrayal. Damn it! 'For God's sake! I don't believe in past lives. I don't believe in Soul Mates. And I absolutely don't bloody-well want one! Especially if he's got four legs and fur!'

'I just knew you'd use Matey this way. I told you, he's a blip!'

'That changes nothing! Peter is—'

'As boring as shite! As I've told you on countless occasions. And totally not the one for you. *He's* not your Soul Mate. The one you remembered that night was. The one you lost when you were Hannah.'

Hannah. Too many feelings seeped out now. Susie was awash. *And* . . . She was *not* going to remember him! *Loss. Desolation. Betrayal.*

'It *wasn't* real!' Susie cried, desperately shaking

15

her head. 'Only you could ever think it was! We were all out of our heads. Nothing more, nothing less.'

'I *know* it was real. And I can help. *Please* let me put it right.'

Nobody could ever put it right, least of all Rachael. Why couldn't she understand that? Susie's life must now be viewed in two distinct phases: pre and post that January day a decade ago.

But Susie comforted herself with the realisation that she *had* learnt some important lessons from the experience: no alcohol, no recreational drugs, no letting anyone into her head. And absolutely no falling in love.

The latter was key to her ever achieving peace of mind. She could never risk experiencing for real the sensations her abused brain had thrown at her. Even that night, when their intensity had been excruciating, she innately knew they had been mere echoes, and what she experienced now, mere tasters of what such loss and betrayal would feel like for real.

She couldn't risk it. Peter was safe. He could never stir that depth of emotion within her. For that reason he was . . . perfect. *Why hadn't she seen that before?* He *was* perfect. She'd been procrastinating, held back by . . . she didn't know what. But he had to be the way forward.

She was brought out of her thoughts by Rachael giving her a hug. 'Okay. I give up. I'm sorry. I just got it into my head that now might be the time to try and broach things again, to offer my help. But you're never going to accept it, no matter how much you need it. Forgive me?'

Susie raised her arms to limply return Rachael's hug and gave a small nod. She knew Rachael was only trying to make things right. But she didn't know the half of it. But perhaps now *had* been the right time to talk about things? If they hadn't, she'd not have seen how perfect Peter was. 'I'm sorry too, especially about Matey. But not for calling you nuts. I have no choice but to stand by that.'

'You've called me worse.' Rachael grinned, releasing Susie to cross to the other side of the open-plan room. She now focused on the over-flowing bookcase next to the television. 'No more talk of that night. No more hurting each other. It's Saturday morning and it's about time we enjoyed it. You aren't seeing the bore until—'

'Peter.'

'That's what I said,' Rachael flung a bright smile over her shoulder. 'You're not seeing him until tonight. It's peeing it down outside. We can leave the supermarket until mid-week, *sooo* . . .'

She swung around with a huge beam on her face, waving around what she'd retrieved from the shelf. 'We can have a George Silbury day! Back to back films. I hold here, in my very hands, his latest DVD! I didn't think it came out for a few weeks, but there it was and I felt inspired. How good a friend am I?'

Susie felt like laughing hysterically and couldn't prevent the out-of-control, demented giggle. All the talk of that night . . . and now a *George Silbury* day! Why was this happening? Ten years . . . and now *this*. She already felt so battered and bruised. She didn't want any more reminders of how much of a mess she was, of just how close she was to . . . She'd called Rachael nuts. Rachael was nuts in a nutty way. Always had been, although Matey did take the biscuit. But she . . . She was nuts in the lock you up and throw away the key way.

Rachael fiddled with the DVD player, obliviously wittering away. Susie hardly heard a word.

They'd gone to see a film. The night after the night before. All the housemates: her, Rachael, Jen, Pip and Clare. It was the 11.00 p.m. showing. They'd still been hung-over. She'd been that *and* post-traumatic, the events of the preceding night still a gaping wound.

It had, appropriately, been a horror film. They'd screamed for England. She'd just stared. Stared at his eyes. George Silbury's eyes, she'd subsequently discovered. It was an early, minor role. Make-up, scars down his face. But his *eyes* . . . She'd become fixated. He was two-dimensional, acting a part. He was ripping people's throats out. But his eyes were beautiful. His eyes were trying to tell her something.

Her brain had been so screwed.

And the really desperately insane thing about it all was that his eyes still had that effect on her.

His intense, hypnotic eyes had the power to transfix her. She'd spent years watching his films. Knowing it wasn't remotely healthy, but somehow not able to stop. It was the most ridiculous, yet compelling sensation.

She'd never told Rachael why she watched his films. She'd played along when it was put down to the way he looked. Rachael would have applied some ridiculous mumbo-jumbo reasoning to the sensation. Anyone else would have had her committed.

But Susie knew it was simply down to his being caught up in the fallout of the most awful night of her life. If they'd watched another film . . .? In the state she'd been in, she'd have had the same reaction to Donald Duck!

Susie inhaled deeply. She was going to resist the pull. 'I'm going to pass.' She felt horrid at the hurt look in Rachael's eyes, but said, 'You go ahead, love. I'm going to pop over to Peter's. He was keen we do something and I've not been seeing enough of him. I'll catch up with you later.'

'*Peter?* You are going to see *Peter Boyles* rather than drool over *George Silbury?*'

Susie simply nodded, heading to her bedroom to get dressed. She tried to picture Donald Duck's eyes. But all she saw was Donald Duck with someone else's eyes . . . still trying to tell her something.

CHAPTER 3

George Silbury raised his eyes from the latest script changes and grinned broadly. He was instantly out of his seat and embracing the woman who had entered the room. 'Cassie, Cassie, Cassie!' he cried, lifting his sister up in his arms and swinging her round in circles.

Laughing, but batting him over the shoulder with her notebook, Cassie urged, 'Put me down, George. We're far too old for this!'

'Speak for yourself,' he chuckled, but quickly lowered her to the ground before they wiped out the unsuspecting girl who had entered the small room, arms piled high with make-up. Kara, he thought her name was. He addressed her, laughter still in his voice. 'Later. Come back later.' On seeing her anxious look, he quickly added with a reassuring smile, 'You've done your part, Kara. If they don't like it, blame me. I'll see you later.'

George caught Cassie's amused look as she watched the blushing girl leave the room. He ignored the raised eyebrows his sister sent his way. He hated the fact that women no longer acted normally around him.

Thank God Cassie still did.

Rubbing his shoulder dramatically, he teased, 'Don't you ever go anywhere without that notebook of yours? It's not much better than the sticks you used to beat me with.'

'I did not!' Cassie declared, laughing, and playfully batting him with the notebook again.

'Nice to see you too, Sis.' George dodged her book and grinned. 'And you *did* beat me with sticks. I despised you there for a while.'

He truly had, he realised guiltily. Their relationship hadn't started well. He had never understood why. Yes, she'd beaten him with sticks. Not that her efforts had hurt anything more than his pride – but he'd more than deserved it. He'd constantly set her up for falls and rejected her as she'd traipsed after him. She'd never given up though, determined to win him over. And she had certainly done that. He was closer to her now than he was to either of his brothers.

'I'm so sorry,' Cassie declared with undisguised feeling, shocking him from his nostalgia.

What on earth was she sorry for? He watched her slump down in the chair he'd earlier vacated and press her forehead. 'I've missed you so much.'

What the hell? George grabbed the only other chair in the room and positioned it before her so he could sit astride and look at her over its back. 'Cas?' he gently prompted.

'I'm fine. Really I'm fine. It's just so lovely to see you again.'

He was frowning, because he'd never seen Cassie like this. He'd detected something in their earlier telephone conversation but this was . . .? 'You talk like we haven't seen each other for years when we all spent Christmas together. It's not been much more than five or six weeks.' Attempting to make her smile, he said, 'I know I'm easy to miss and all that, but . . .'

He earned another bat with the notebook and took relief in the light-hearted intermission, but then continued, 'Are you going to tell me what this is all about?'

Cassie slowly raised her head and stared at him.

'You're beginning to worry me here, Cas.' He tried to keep his voice light, but he was alarmed at the almost haunted look in her eyes. 'What's going on? Is it a *man*? Has someone hurt you, because if they have . . .'

Cassie smiled and shook her head. He raised his eyebrows, not at all convinced.

'It's not a man. Well . . . actually one of them was. An *evil* little man, but the—'

'I knew it!' he exploded, leaping from his chair. He furiously ran his hands through his hair. 'Who is he and—' He abruptly stopped in his tracks as her words sank in. '*One* of them?'

Cassie started to laugh. 'It's not as it sounds. Sorry! I should have made myself clear. My mind is just not . . .' She paused, her laughter drying up and she looked at him through those haunted eyes. 'I think I need a favour.'

George crouched before her and squeezed her hand. 'Anything, Cas. Anything.' He racked his brain to think of any other time he'd seen his sister like this. But came up blank. She appeared vulnerable. And vulnerable and Cassie were chalk and cheese. He winced. At least in the adult Cassie. He remembered a little Cassie, blonde ringlets, hurt bubbling away in those dark blue eyes fixed so accusingly upon him; tears rolling down her cheeks and her bottom lip trembling. God, he'd been a shit! Fortunately, he'd come to his senses by the time she was five or six to his eight or nine, and he'd been able to spend the rest of his childhood making it up to her.

But Cassie protected herself. Always had done. Even as a child. The sticks in her tiny grasp, being a case in point. In fact, he'd go as far as to say that the adult Cassie generally controlled situations, never letting them control her.

He met Cassie's eyes with a reassuring smile. There were so many expressions flitting across her face. He just hoped he could help.

Slowly her visage settled into a much more familiar Cassie-like expression. He let out a sigh of relief . . . before it dawned on him exactly what that look meant.

Bugger!

Shaking his head, he attempted to clarify. 'When I said *anything*, Sis, I didn't necessarily mean . . .'

* * *

'You said "anything" George. In fact you said it *twice*,' Cassie reminded him, as they sat together in the back of the taxi.

She turned away from his accusing look. She would *not* feel guilty. She stared unseeingly out of the window as she attempted to stop that question from echoing around her head: *'Do you recognise anyone, Cassie?'*

The opportunity had presented itself. He *wanted* to help. She had to run with it.

'But I forgot who I was talking to there for a minute. I should have known your idea of "anything" doesn't remotely resemble a normal person's. I beg extenuating circumstances and—' George cursed as his mobile went off for the third time in the space of the five minutes he'd left the set.

'Yes!' he growled into the phone. 'I've already told him it's a family emergency and I'll . . .' After a pause, he continued coldly. 'I do have a family, Michael and this *is* an emergency.' He hung up and turned off the phone.

'I've never liked that man and I know the feeling's mutual,' Cassie said. 'Why don't you get another manager? You're in a position where you could choose anyone and—'

'Don't try and change the subject,' George interrupted, shaking his head and sounding weary. 'I do not wish to be past life whatever the bloody hell fool thing it is you're talking about. I don't understand why you're asking it of me, and why *my* doing it will make *you* feel better!'

24

'*Do you recognise anyone, Cassie?*'

'I've told you why, haven't I?' Cassie knew full well she hadn't. Responding to George's raised eyebrows, she said, 'I've done it twice and there's nothing to . . .' It was no good. Not if she was going to get him to do this. Quickening up her pace, so she could rush over words she wasn't comfortable admitting, let alone saying aloud, she said, 'I may have got a *little* spooked and—'

'*Spooked? You!*' He couldn't have sounded more incredulous.

'A little,' she said, returning her attention to the window. She was talking to George. It was hard not to be honest with him, harder than not being honest with herself, in fact. And he'd probably see right through her.

Her words tumbled out. 'All right! I'm cacking myself at the thought of being regressed again, but I have to do it! It's the only way I can prove that their whole rotten profession is a sham and stop the evil little people from playing games in people's heads and scaring their victims witless. I fled George. *Me! Bitch hack Cassie Silbury!* I *know* there's nothing in it. Absolutely know it! But—'

She applied the verbal brakes. There was only so much she could say here before he questioned her sanity. And she'd been doing more than enough of that for herself.

Recovering some composure, she continued more deliberately. 'Seeing you regressed, taking it in your stride, being told you were . . . Casanova or some such, is all I need. Then I'll be fine. Please George . . . help me out here.'

'Casanova?' George spluttered.

Cassie grinned. She knew George so well and was evidently not completely off form. She needed him distracted. He knew her too and had been frowning all the way through her semi-confession. Given half a chance he'd get to the heart of things, get her to spill all the beans.

But if everything went according to plan over the next few hours there would be no beans to spill. Then she would hang the evil little people out to dry for having done this to her. If it *didn't* go according to plan? She . . . *Anyway*, she had some diverting to do.

'You *are* linked to all your leading ladies.'

'You of all people know not to believe everything you read in the press. I'm fed up with—' George cut himself off with a curse. 'Stop changing the subject! I want to know what the hell has happened to make you—'

'You *were* with Harriet Brioche, Cleopatra to your Antony; Jenny Marks, Juliet to your Romeo—'

'Cassie!'

'Katie Smythe, Cathy to your Heathcliff. Please tell me you aren't going to be seeing Porsche Sutter-Blythe? I know she's your Elizabeth, but she's a complete—!'

'Cassie! Stop speculating on my love life and tell me *exactly* what's going on here! I've never known

26

you—' George stopped and narrowed his eyes. 'Why are you giggling?'

'It's just that you are still in costume. Did you know that? I don't think you did. And would Mr Darcy's trousers, or breeches or whatever they are called, really have been *quite* so tight?' She couldn't help the full-blown laugh, as George looked himself over and started tugging on his coat to restore his modesty.

Blushing, he muttered, 'I don't know why wardrobe keep doing it. As for you, finding amusement in my being in public—' He looked skywards. 'Bloody hell! You've done it again.'

Keeping George distracted may have been keeping Cassie's own mind occupied and providing some amusement to boot, but it wasn't enough to stop the butterflies in her stomach morphing into pterodactyls as the taxi turned onto Cromwellian Avenue. 198 . . . 196 . . . 194. Cassie looked frantically at the road before them. *Where was all the damned traffic when you needed it?*

George flung his head back to rest on top of the seat and let out a frustrated sound. 'You know the concept of past lives is ludicrous. So for you to be freaked out, means something else is—'

Cassie shamelessly broke in. 'You should get another manager. I don't trust Michael. And as for Porsche Sutter-Blythe – people call *me* a bitch!'

'Whatever they try and do to me,' George now said, resignation weighing heavily in his voice, 'it won't work. I tried hypnosis to give up smoking and they couldn't get me under. It's a waste of time . . .' He released a long-suffering sigh. 'But if you really think it will help, then so be it.'

She would *not* feel guilty. And he'd be fine, she'd make sure of it. 'I really do appreciate this George. More than I can possibly say.'

'I know. And that's what worries me.'

CHAPTER 4

Rachael glanced up from her position behind the small reception desk and nearly dropped the phone from her ear. Susie continued her conversation, unaware of Rachael's distraction.

'Rach? Come on! Lemon meringue pie or triple chocolate fudge cake? *Rach?* I've had a seriously bad day and am not going to spend all evening in the supermarket!'

'I'll call you back,' Rachael murmured, blindly lowering the phone. She couldn't believe who appeared to be heading her way. The profanities coming from the phone indicated that she'd failed to fit handset to phone-housing in her blind fumblings. She rapidly gave it the necessary attention, finally disconnecting Susie.

Looking back up to face the woman now at the desk, Rachael managed to croak out, with a forced over-wide smile, 'How may I help you?'

She couldn't stop staring at the man standing a few paces behind the woman, currently looking fixedly at his feet. *It couldn't be . . .*

'Cassie *Smith*. Five o'clock appointment with Rachael Jones.'

The man behind raised both his head and an eyebrow, and seemed to shift awkwardly. It *was* George Silbury! It definitely was. And . . . Rachael gulped. Those breeches looked like they had been melted onto him. They looked especially good with the knee-high black boots. Totally mind-bogglingly gorgeous in fact, she deduced, while her roving eyes continued up his long muscular legs. She deliberately skirted over his crotch because that *so* wouldn't be right, particularly with him in those breeches, but she let them travel over his evidently flat stomach, skim over his broad chest and continue up to his beautifully chiselled face, and the silkiest shoulder-length dark brown hair she had ever seen. And he was blushing. Oh bless.

Rachael reluctantly refocused on the woman in front of her, now impatiently tapping her false fingernails on the desk. Clearing her throat, she proceeded to say, as professionally as she could, 'Please take a seat.' She then leapt from her own, just managing to put the brakes on her sprint. She took a deep breath and attempted a more appropriate exit, involving the briskest walking she could manage. She probably looked as ridiculous as those marathon walkers you sometimes see on the news; only more so since she was in heels.

She comforted herself with the knowledge: this was meant to be.

Cassie turned from her position at the desk and smirked at George. 'It's the breeches, sweetie. The poor girl had no idea where to look.'

George shifted his coat again and tried to nonchalantly put his hands in his pockets. But they were too tight to even do that. Ignoring Cassie's chuckles, he let out an exasperated sound and collapsed onto one of the soft chairs distributed around two edges of the reception room.

It all looked very cosy – warm gold and ochre with accents of red and green – not at all like a waiting room. It was a shame he wasn't feeling cosy. He glanced at his sister. She looked pale . . . and scared. She wasn't telling him everything. 'Am I completely wasting my time here, or are you going to start talking?'

'Oh look, it's raining again. Pouring in fact,' Cassie exclaimed, moving quickly to the window. There, she raised a hand to the glass and point-edly kept her back to him. 'Your timing for returning to England was really off when you think what the weather must be like in LA right now.'

George sighed, leant back in his chair, and banged the back of his head repeatedly against the top of the soft padded seat.

'Susie! Susie!' Rachael hissed into her mobile phone. She stood in her consulting room, peeking through the gap in the door that afforded her a view of the two occupants of her reception area.

'Speak up! I can hardly hear you. Why are you hissing? I've given up on the supermarket and I'm coming home. If you can't be bothered to—'

'Listen to me. This is *really, really* important.'

'Can you please stop *hissing*? Actually . . . is it you or me? It could be me. There seems to be some kind of echo. It could be the line or I may—'

'Will you just shut up for *one* minute?' Rachael immediately scuttled backwards. Her raised voice had resulted in raised eyes in the reception area. Ignoring Susie's rant she proceeded from her new position in the corner of the room, farthest from the door. 'You have to listen to me. You would not—' Rachael stopped. She could hardly tell Susie *who* was sat in her reception room. Not if she was going to get her here. And she *had* to get her here. George Silbury was here – of all places! There was nothing for it. 'I'm not feeling good and I really need you here now.'

'Rach? Is that why you sound like that? Oh God! What's wrong?'

'Please Suse. Just get here as soon as you can.' *Groan.* 'I'm in my consulting rooms. I don't think I can make it upstairs to the flat on my own.' She added a moan for good measure.

'Rach? Ra—'

Rachael hung up her mobile and dumped it on her desk. Having second thoughts, she retrieved it, turned it off, and then placed it back on her desk with a little pat. If Susie had any questions, she could ask them right *here.*

Rachael strolled purposefully to the reception area. She couldn't get over the coincidence . . . No, it wasn't coincidence. Rachael didn't believe in coincidence. It was Fate. And she couldn't wait to see how things would play out.

'Ms Smith. I'm Rachael Jones. If you'd like to come this way?'

'My brother's coming along too if that's acceptable.' It was more a statement than a question.

'That's not a problem.' Rachael used her most professional of voices, wore her most professional of smiles as she bemusedly watched her client attempt to pull George Silbury from his seat. It was all very bizarre . . . until realisation dawned. 'I never considered the problems men had with the clothes of the day. I *know* women struggled with corsets . . .'

That comment trailed away for a moment as Rachael experienced an unexpected sensation. She shot a glance at Cassie, but now really wasn't the time to sort through what her head was trying to send her way. Frowning, Rachael attempted to refocus. Not that difficult when it was such a pleasant refocus. 'I never stopped to think how tight breeches might . . .' She'd *never* seen a man look so good in breeches. Actually that wasn't *quite* true, but she was getting distracted again. She shook her head to clear it. 'How tight breeches might . . . I mean how difficult must it have been to get on a horse if they couldn't even . . .?'

Cassie snorted, while George, having risen abruptly to his feet, looked menacingly at his sister. Through gritted teeth, he ground out, 'It wasn't

33

the breeches keeping me in the chair. It was me attempting to get answers from a sister who is—'

'Come *on*!' Cassie interrupted, propelling him forward. 'Consulting room.'

Susie bundled her mobile into her pocket, telling herself not to panic. Rachael would be fine. It was probably a migraine or . . . Why wasn't she able to talk properly? Taking in the busy high street she gauged she was probably fifteen minutes away. At this time of day it was quicker by foot than taxi.

Just how bad was Rachael? The more she thought about it, the more she worried. What if . . .? No, she told herself firmly. If she'd been choking, she wouldn't have been able to talk. But would she have been able to hiss? Should she call 999? Trying to instil calm, Susie reminded herself Rachael had called her. If she'd been that bad, she would have called 999 herself . . . Wouldn't she?

Susie ditched the few bags of groceries she'd bothered to purchase, repositioned her handbag so it was on her back, and ran.

'I don't mind regressing your brother,' Rachael told Cassie, sounding surprisingly calm. *She was going to be regressing George Silbury!* 'You're the last session of the day, so overrunning isn't a problem . . .' She paused as she looked over at the delectable man in question. He was standing with his arms crossed, frowning at his sister. She couldn't

34

believe what she was about to say. Clearing her throat, she said, 'Are you quite sure though, your brother *wishes* to be regressed? It's very important he's relaxed and happy to do this.'

'Of course I'll do it.' George sighed, raising both arms in the air as if in surrender. He then marched over to the black leather couch in front of the window. 'I rashly said I'd do anything, so here I am. You've not got a cat in hell's chance of getting me under though, but let's get this over with. And Cassie? Once we're out of here, you *are* going to talk to me!'

Susie was completely and utterly drenched. She would be, even if it wasn't pissing it down with rain, she thought disgustedly to herself. Sweat escaped her hot, puffing body in copious amounts. And it was no good. She had to stop. Bending down, with hands on knees, she firmly told herself not to die. Taking in air through ragged, noisy gasps, she attempted to ignore the pulsing pain in her head. She forced herself into action again; staggering now, rather than sprinting. Not that she was sure she had ever started out at a sprint. That had been the instruction her brain sent her body but . . . *God, she felt bad.*

Throwing herself across the road, dodging between stationary traffic, Susie wished for the millionth time that she was in shape. If only she had—

'*Accckkkkk!*'

Susie was forced to fling herself back to prevent

being mown down by a motorbike zooming past the traffic on the inside. If her already flat-out heart was capable of further racing, it would have done so.

She was still digesting the close call when the deluge hit her. After spitting out that which had entered her mouth, she took in the sludgy, scum-covered filth bubbling up from the overflowing storm-drain the motorbike had roared through.

For Rachael . . .

'Is he under?' Cassie scrawled onto the page with a shaking hand. She now held up her notebook and waved it to attract Rachael Jones's attention. She lowered her suddenly heavy arms, following the thumbs up.

This was a terrible idea. Cassie wondered what had ever possessed her to get George regressed? She should have just scrapped the story, admitted defeat – *had herself sectioned* – because nothing could be worth this. What if it had been him? What if they *had* been brother and sister in the past? What if she had destroyed him . . . *them*, and then . . .? She lowered her head to her hands. George was George. He had never been Freddie. Freddie had never existed. There was No. Such. Thing. As. Past. Lives.

'George. I'd like you to close that door you've just walked through,' Rachael instructed serenely to his reclining form upon the couch. 'Now turn back around. Take your time, allow yourself to acclimatise. When you are ready, could you describe to me what you see?'

Silence, although the sound of Cassie's own beating heart in her ears was thunderous. That door. It had been in a corridor full of them but that one had had almost painfully bright light behind it, escaping around its edges. It had almost pulsed as it compelled her to select and open it.

'Take your time . . . All in your own time . . .'

More excruciating silence. Cassie had found herself drawn to what she found behind it, swept along. Powerless to change direction, to stop what she saw herself doing. Dreading where it would lead, but innately knowing.

She felt nauseous now, but the physical sensation helped bring her to some sense. It had *not* been real. And she would intervene the moment any unacceptable or leading questions were asked of George. She was not going to allow them to screw him up as well.

'Do you feel able to share with me what you are experiencing, George?' Rachael's quiet, patient voice intruded. 'What do you see around you? Perhaps you are doing something. Or perhaps there are sensations you are feeling?'

There was a raspy sound from the couch. Cassie stared at George, her nausea stepping up a notch. But silence returned. Followed moments later by another such raspy sound. And then more silence.

It almost sounded like . . .? *No way!* 'You'll never get me under,' Cassie mimicked in her head as

37

another sound, suspiciously like a snore, was emitted. Well George, you seem pretty under to me! But the relief Cassie felt at this turn of events was immeasurable.

'Did he just snore?' Cassie scribbled on her notebook, holding her message up high, on now feather-light arms. Rachael's attention seemed to be trained on George though.

'When you are ready you can—'

Rachael's calm hushed words abruptly halted, and Cassie simultaneously screamed. An almighty crash had reverberated around the room.

CHAPTER 5

'Crap!' Rachael released with her breath. It wasn't that Susie had entered the room so dramatically, sending the door crashing and rebounding into and off the wall it was flung against, but the fact she had *staggered* into the room and looked . . .

Rachael wanted to weep. How was that possible? Susie looked *worse* than she'd initially given her credit for. Half-drowned . . . but in what looked to have been the filth of the Thames at low tide.

'I'm here, Rach,' Susie wheezed, bent double and gasping for air as she shrugged off her handbag. 'Barely, but I'm here. Are you okay? I think I might call 999 anyway.'

How could this have been allowed to happen? Rachael had had such a good feeling. One of those 'ring-a-ding-ding Fate is doing his thing' feelings.

Well things could still be salvaged. She evidently needed to get Susie out of here. She'd get her to the flat upstairs; hosed down; clothes, hair, make-up . . .

'Are you there?' Susie was more audible now,

but sounding seriously worried. 'Please be alive. Talk to me!'

Leaping from her seat by the couch, Rachael let out a horrified gasp and physically froze.

No. No. No. No. This wasn't happening. He had not just done that. He was out for the count and deeply so, having not reacted to the earlier crash. And she had *definitely* told him the eye stuff. *Your eyelids are feeling so heavy you won't be able to open them.* She distinctly remembered it. So . . . so . . .

Why had George Silbury just opened his eyes?

Rachael watched him rise from the couch and dive across the room to sweep a just-standing Susie into his arms. *What the—?*

He cradled Susie's face in his hands and stared into her eyes. 'I cannot believe you are here. It *is* you. It is *you*. Oh dear God, how I dreamed.'

His voice was ragged raw emotion. His words so heartfelt they were painful to hear. He covered every inch of Susie's face and neck in the gentlest, most tender of butterfly kisses.

'I'm never letting you go. Ever. Why did you lose faith in me, my love? I was true to you! How could I ever not be? Oh my angel, my dearest, darling angel.'

Rachael gulped, not one hundred per cent convinced this was happening. But her client was sat in what appeared to be a state of shock and her other client *was* currently *with* Susie! She couldn't allow herself to panic here, she really couldn't. She needed to be professional

40

and take control. She wondered if she should say something to her client – the one sat staring in horror – not the one . . . *George Silbury's tongue was down Susie's throat!*

What was she supposed to do? She had never come across anything like this before, never even heard of it. She watched Susie wrap her arms around George Silbury's neck and sink her hands into his hair. His hands were everywhere. There were moans and gasps. What the blazes was going on? She had to – *Susie! Her* hands were flaming well everywhere now, too and . . .

Rachael's eyes lowered, following the couple. They were—

'Hannah,' George sighed.

'Freddie,' Susie gasped.

They hit the floor, wrapped in each other's arms.

Cassie sat stunned. Completely and utterly stunned. Freddie and Hannah? This couldn't be happening. Her brain could not be expected to comprehend this. George *had* been Freddie? And . . . and . . . and . . . *Hannah!* That meant she . . . she . . . This was her worst nightmare. She needed someone to rush through the open door and cart her away because this could not be real. This had to be her cracking up. *Please let it be!* The alternative was simply too terrible.

Rachael's brain seemed to be on a loop. An incredulous loop. 'Hannah and Freddie united again?'

It obviously needed to be repeated because even Rachael was having problems comprehending the fact. And *George Silbury* had been Freddie? *Hannah's* Freddie? She'd known Susie had been Hannah and that she'd lost Freddie, but there was ring-a-ding-ding and . . . ring-a-*ding-ding*.

Crikey, she'd just reunited Susie with her Soul Mate! Because there was no question, in her twenty-first century Rachael Jones mind, that Freddie and Hannah had been Soul Mates. But *George Silbury*? And then she remembered sensible Susie's insensible obsession with the man. This just got better and better. Had she sensed him for what he was?

This was amazing and . . . Rachael dropped into her chair as she reached an ecstatic realisation. Oh. Thank you. Thank you. Thank you! How incredible was this? How long had she hoped to find a way?

She could *redeem* herself! *Finally* she could put things right. Not just all the angst she had caused Susie following that night ten years ago, because, as awful as that was, it was just the tip of the iceberg. She could actually make amends for the role she'd played in the past. When Susie had been Hannah, George had been Freddie. And she'd been Tessa. She could help put right what she'd help destroy then! This was incredible. This was Fate at his best. This was—

'They aren't moving!' Cassie cried out.

Rachael watched Cassie run to the two bodies,

lying entwined upon the floor, as if in slow motion.

'I can't have killed them again. I *can't*,' Cassie babbled, sinking to the floor beside them.

Rachael barely absorbed Cassie's words. It was as if she were observing events from a long way away. Susie and George lay motionless upon the floor. Half wrapped around each other.

Completely still.

Cassie knelt at their side shaking George, her attempts getting increasingly desperate . . . But he was just lying there.

Rachael somehow made her way across the room because she found herself knelt on the floor at their side. *Susie?* Oh God, Suse . . . She'd lured her here and – *Mother of Mary*. What had she done? She wanted to put it right, not destroy them all over—

'He's breathing, he's definitely breathing,' Cassie cried. 'And so is—'

'So is Susie,' Rachael gasped, seeing her chest move. She let the relief soak through her and took a moment to breathe again.

'What's the matter with them?' Cassie asked desperately. 'Is George still regressed? No. He ran across the room, so he can't be.'

'I don't know . . . He might be. I can't think properly.' Rachael clenched her eyes tightly shut and forced herself to take more deep, calming breaths. What the blazes was wrong with them? 'Umm. I haven't brought him around. Opening his eyes though and not bringing himself out of it – and the other – is . . . *unusual.'* What an understatement. 'But that doesn't explain Susie. We're going to have to call for an ambulance.' Rachael jumped up to grab her mobile from the desk.

'She could have passed out,' Cassie mumbled, as Rachael waited impatiently for her phone to fire up. 'George didn't give her much opportunity to catch her breath and she wouldn't be the first woman to do that around him. And George might simply . . .' Cassie's words died away to be replaced by a horrified, accusatory cry, 'Unless you've done something catastrophic to his head!'

Rachael, startled, turned in response to Cassie's cry and released one of her own. She was immediately back at Susie's side. She'd just seen her hand move. Taking it between her own hands, she started patting it. 'Suse. Suse, can you hear me? Did you see that? I think she's going to be okay.'

'What about George? What if you've done permanent damage?'

'I've not done anything to George other than hypnotise him.' She didn't see how she could have. She had to focus. One thing at a time. 'I'll try and bring him around in a moment. Suse? Suse?'

'Did he bump his head? Is that why he's—?'

'He's lying *face* down on *top* of Susie. I don't see how he could have done.' Releasing Susie's hand, Rachael said, 'We're going to have to shift him to give her some air.'

'Rach?' Susie's voice sounded.

Thank you! Oh, thank you!

Susie's eyes fluttered open.

Rachael stared down at her, anxiously. 'Suse? Are you okay? Please tell me you're okay.'

Susie's forehead creased into a frown. 'God my head is killing me. But . . . You're okay! Jeez I was so worried. What happened?' She let out a loud groan. 'That run!' Looking confused, she seemed to now take in that she was lying on the floor, and had managed to move the left side of her body, but was struggling with the right.

'Everything's fine. We're about to move him so—'

Susie screamed. She screamed again and again.

'It's all right. Don't panic,' Rachael reassured repeatedly, as she and Cassie rolled George off Susie and on to his back. He was like a deadweight. Rachael swallowed hard, rapidly dismissing that thought, but nevertheless her own breathing only resumed as she observed his chest move afresh.

As soon as Susie was freed, she scuttled top speed, backwards across the floor on her bottom. There she sat struggling for breath. 'What happened? Who is he?' she gasped out. 'Is he dead? Oh God! What happened?'

Susie didn't remember? Rachael wasn't sure if that was a good thing or . . . It was her turn to groan now. 'He's not dead, he'll be fine,' Rachael said quickly, as she watched Susie edge closer on her hands and knees. There was a frown upon her face. 'I'd stay over there, Suse. You've had a shock.' But it was no good. Using Rachael's shoulders as leverage, Susie got herself to her feet. Her head cocked from side to side as she looked at the man lying on the floor. She now turned her horrified gaze to Rachael.

And no matter how hard Rachael tried to magic up the perfect words to say in this situation, she completely lost her train of thought as Rob ran in through the wide open door, armed with a baseball bat. He'd obviously heard Susie's screams from his flat next to theirs, upstairs.

Rachael closed her eyes while thanking the heavens it was Rob. She found the presence of a friendly face more than a little reassuring right now. She was definitely going to have to rethink her business plan though. She'd been hoping to branch out, to specialise in a new area of business she liked to refer to as 'Soul Mate Recovery'. She'd been convinced that past life regression offered an invaluable source of information that could aid in the search and recovery of a Soul Mate. Well, it appeared she'd been right . . . kind of. But she really wasn't sure how much of this sort of happening she could take.

Susie's voice sounded, securing Rachael's full attention. She opened her eyes.

'That's . . .' Susie looked at Rob, while waving her arm vaguely in George's direction. Now turning to Rachael, she said, 'That's George Silbury. I *did* die. So did you. You must have been choking. I'm sorry I didn't save you Rach. I tried. If only I'd kept those New Year resolutions it could have all ended so differently. Didn't expect to see you here, Rob. How odd.'

Susie crumpled and Rob, ditching the baseball bat en route, crossed the room in a couple of bounds, catching her under her arms before she hit the floor.

Rachael screwed up her face and rubbed her eyes. When she removed her hand, she met Rob's confounded gaze.

'Rach. What *precisely* is going on here?' He looked down at Susie, currently propped against his crouching form, across to Cassie, bent over George, before returning his intent, piercing blue-eyed focus to her.

It was a fair question, but not one Rachael could answer quickly, or necessarily, believably. And just how distracting were those eyes of his, even in this flaming situation? She started to crawl around George, positioning herself beside his head, opposite Cassie.

'I'll try and explain. Just not right now. But thank you for being here to catch Susie. Can you make yourself even more useful and get her out of here? She'll only keel over again if she sees him. I just need to bring him back around. I'm hoping all I need to do is count—'

'He's *regressed*?' Rob sounded horrified.

'I'm not sure.'

'You're not *sure*?' Rob sounded even more horrified. She had to admit, it didn't sound good.

'I'm hoping that's all it is. I'm about to find out.

But can you *please* get Susie up to the flat and make sure she's okay? I'll attempt to explain later, I promise!' She now spoke to Cassie. 'I'm going to go through the usual process for bringing him back around. We'll see if that works and—'

'If it doesn't, I'll make it my life's work to destroy you!' Cassie vowed.

She sounded less traumatised now . . . and . . . definitely familiar. 'Right. Ummm. Well . . . if it doesn't . . . we call for help.'

Rachael spared a glance back to Rob, who'd managed to hoist Susie over his shoulder like a sack of potatoes. Being a fireman, he'd no doubt call it a fireman's lift. His T-shirt had crept up to reveal the bare skin of his toned stomach and a line of dark hair. She looked away quickly, but not before she'd experienced a snapshot to another time. No cravat. Top two buttons undone, bare skin at his throat and the top of his chest. There may have been dark hairs there and then too, although she couldn't be sure because of the physical distance that had been between them. She shook her head rapidly to clear it.

Their eyes met. 'I'll see to Suse,' he said softly. He glanced anxiously at George on the floor. 'But if he doesn't come around, call 999 and shout for me, too. I'm trained in resuscitation.' With that, Rob turned and walked out of the room.

CHAPTER 6

'Five, four, three, two, one. And now you're awake, George.'

George slowly opened his eyes and blinked several times. He felt disorientated. Then he remembered.

Turning his head, he found Cassie. Grinning, he said, 'See I told you they couldn't get me under. I'm sorry, Cas. But I'll hang around to hold your hand. Your turn!'

Raising himself into a seated position, he looked around . . . confused. He was on the floor. He looked to the couch and then back, but . . . He refocused on Cassie who had yet to talk and who, he now realised, was kneeling at his side. She wasn't looking at him though, but at the regressionist, Rachael something-or-other, kneeling on his other side. They stared at each other, motionless. 'Would someone mind telling me what's going on?'

They turned in unison to look at him, their expressions not at all easy to read.

But George now had other things on his mind. He was more than a little distracted. He patted his clothes down, and looked at the floor around him. He had the distinct impression that he'd lost something, but couldn't pinpoint what. He didn't like the sensation one little bit. He didn't have his wallet with him, he'd left that back at the film set, and his phone was there in his coat pocket, but . . .

He saw Cassie make a slight movement with her head in the direction of the door. Rachael cleared her throat before saying, 'We'll be back in a jiffy. Make yourself at home. We're going to . . . get another appointment in the diary!'

George looked at Cassie, surprised. 'You're not doing it now? Come on! It's a doddle, nothing to it. I'm here so what could possibly go wrong?'

Cassie seemed to pale before his eyes. She muttered, 'Not today, thank you,' before clambering to her feet and fleeing from the room in the regressionist's wake.

Looking around him, George patted his clothes again. They felt damp and actually looked . . . was that mud? He cursed, rubbing at the offending areas on his thighs, wondering if he'd brushed against the outside of the taxi. Wardrobe were not going to be happy.

He was definitely damp. Had he been sweating? Actually, thinking about it, he was feeling physically very . . . He glanced down at himself and cursed lengthily and repeatedly. *How was he supposed to cover that up in this costume?* He was going to have to sit here for several moments longer. He blushed furiously at the thought he may have embarrassed himself in front of Cassie and that regressionist woman.

Drawing his knees up before him and resting his elbows upon them, his attention was drawn to his hands. He raised them before his face. They were tingling and he had the strangest sensation that they had been in contact with something . . . precious.

'He doesn't remember?' Cassie spluttered, as she and Rachael reached the reception area and collapsed against the desk. She had just been through probably *the* most harrowing time of her life and her brother had woken up oblivious . . . and *grinned!* 'Just how is that possible?'

'Susie doesn't remember either,' Rachael said thoughtfully. 'And I'm not sure why. It could be shock I suppose; coming face-to-face like that. The circumstances . . . I need to think about it when I'm not so—'

'Traumatised?' Cassie suggested. Although traumatised didn't quite do it if Rachael Jones was feeling anything like she was right now. 'I'm going to need to see a shrink!' she suddenly shrieked at the realisation. 'And it's all your fault. I hold you and your whole damned rotten profession responsible for this!'

Rachael raised her eyebrows, frowning. 'I'm trying to work out who you are. I get it with your brother now, but you? We've met before. And I

51

don't mean having seen you on the pages of *OK!* magazine. You could have chosen something a bit more imaginative than Smith, don't you think? Couldn't you have been Seymour, Ballentine or Carrington, or even Smythe? I used to choose different names for myself as a child. My favourite was Rachael Fairbairn-Wyrd.' She paused before saying, 'Yes, we've definitely met before.'

Cassie didn't know what to say. Her plan had clearly failed on so many levels. She looked at Rachael through narrowed eyes. There *was* something familiar about her, but she couldn't pinpoint what. 'Believe me when I say I'd remember you if we'd met.' She was feeling even more disconcerted, if that were at all possible. And she didn't like it.

'You sound more yourself now than when you were babbling away about having killed them again. Would you care to explain?'

No. She wouldn't. She couldn't let herself think about any of this. She didn't have a hope of getting her head around it. It was highly likely she was going to end up in one of those padded rooms she'd imagined Rachael *bloody* Jones in. She needed a rewind button. Then she could go back and *never* have started any of this. She'd had a nice life, was fantastically good at her job, had won countless awards. Everything had been as it should be. But now?

'You're doing a story. But that stuff about killing them . . . You've been regressed, haven't you?'

Cassie couldn't deal with this. She needed . . .

vodka! That would do it. Perhaps being a lush was the answer? Permanently intoxicated she would never have to face any of this unbelievable madness that was now her life. And to think, before she'd started this damned story, she'd hardly ever touched the stuff. It was only in the cupboard to soften up her editor when he turned up to rant.

She was a calm, sensible, logical human being, she counselled, so how the hell was she supposed to give any credence to past lives? *Because of what just happened*, her brain snapped at her. And if she *did*, how could she ever live with what she'd done to George? No, Freddie! 'Arrrgggghhh! I don't want any of this!' she cried.

'Well, I'm afraid you've got it. Pretty incredible, really. Your brother and Susie: Soul Mates reunited! And I think it's safe to say they recognised each other. Not that I'd have expected anything else.'

'*Soul Mates?*' Cassie spat disgustedly. She was absolutely not in the mood for any more crap. This Rachael person was—

'Of course! The Real Deal ones, too. Not those phoney-baloney-interests-in-common crappity things people constantly misname. Denied their love as Hannah and Freddie, but finding each other again now. They are so lucky. Not all of us are so lucky . . .' Rachael's voice trailed away before she started up again. 'Anyway, the depth of feeling! I knew, of course, with how it all ended back then, but to hear him speak! And I know how much Hannah loved Freddie because of how

53

she reacted that night and then all that agonising loss stuff Susie's been going through. It has really screwed Susie up you know and I've felt terrible. She wouldn't let me put it right though, applying context, correcting her misconceptions. She has convinced herself it wasn't real, and that's it. But this is great! Your brother will sort her out. How exciting is that?'

'What the hell are you on? And how can you possibly call this *exciting*? This is catastrophic whatever way it's looked at. I'm almost certainly suffering a breakdown of some kind. And if I'm not, I tortured and killed my brother! This is so far from—'

'Yes! *Of course!*' Rachael interrupted, crossing her arms to fix Cassie with a smug look. 'It all fits. Kathryn Montague.'

Cassie had no idea how she stayed on her feet. And then it came to her: recognition. She clutched hold of the desk. 'You . . . you . . . Tessa Jeffries . . . *My maid!*'

But how? How *the hell* did she recognise her? No, she *remembered* her. She clenched her eyes tightly against whatever her head was trying to show her. She needed vodka. NOW! This was *not* happening. Absolutely not happening. There had to be a perfectly—

'Mmmm. We meet again. I don't know why *you're* looking so horrified. I should be the horrified one here. I can safely say, working for you is up there with the worst experiences of my so far discovered past lives. And I've been married to a turnip farmer. And got burnt at the stake! All your conniving, malicious ways and dragging me into your evil schemes ensure you pretty much get the top spot! But it seems we have an opportunity to put things right. To let Susie and George experience what was denied Hannah and Freddie. What you – no, God help me – *we* denied Hannah and Freddie in the past. Are you game?'

Cassie somehow found her way to one of the seats at the edge of the room. Her brain was mush and kept trying to get past her a load of— they were *not* memories. She seemed unable to get anything sensible out of her brain at all. She needed time to digest. To come up with the logical answer for everything that was happening. Conspiracy no longer fit, she knew that much. George would never be involved in something that would wreak havoc on her like this.

Speaking now from the seat beside her, Rachael said, 'We need a plan. They don't remember and that's got to be for a reason, so we have to decide what we tell them. I'm going to have to handle Susie with kid gloves anyway, with no mention of Soul Mates or Hannah. I'd rather she didn't discover my past role either so . . .' She shook her head. 'She's not going to take things well. In fact that's the understatement of the century.'

'You're incapable of talking sense, aren't you?' Cassie snapped incredulously. 'If you believe what you're saying, how *on earth* could your little friend

Susie *not* take things well? She'd have just landed herself my brother! Hollywood heart-throb. One of the most eligible bachelors in the world.'

'You so don't know, Susie,' Rachael said, shaking her head. 'In this life, in any event, but then I don't think either of us took the opportunity to know her before. If I had – if *Tessa* had – she wouldn't have fallen for what you – Kathryn – fed her.'

Although, on reflection, Rachael wasn't so sure about that. Tessa had been far more biddable than Rachael was now. She had been traditionally minded, too, and not at all in tune with herself. Far less . . . Oh just admit it – she'd been a wuss. Until the end that is when she had finally attempted to do the right thing.

'But anyway, Susie refuses to believe in Soul Mates, has no intention of ever falling in love because of the pain of loss she experienced when I regressed her back to Hannah – not that she believed it was a genuine regression, because she doesn't believe in that *either* – and is determined her future lies with a boring shite called Peter, whom I've never liked. To say he is—'

Rachael's words broke off when a frowning George walked into the room. He looked at Cassie for an overly long moment, before abruptly turning his attention to Rachael.

'Did you just hypnotise me?'

CHAPTER 7

'I did *what?*' Susie cried and promptly lowered her forehead to rest it on the kitchen table.

'Calm down,' Rachael urged. 'It's not bad. It's—'

'*Calm down? Not bad?*' Susie raised her head to stare at Rachael in horror. 'You're telling me I *necked* with *George Silbury*!'

George Silbury. George Silbury. Were he the last man on Earth she would still have to avoid him. She didn't react normally to him. And that was putting it mildly. And now she'd . . .

This was all too much. Susie had thought there was nothing more Rachael could do to screw her up, but she had seriously miscalculated. Her brain lapped this one up. Fresh fodder. Who needed that night of ten years ago?

'Yes! So tell me how that can be bad?' Rachael frowned. 'Although it was a little more than necking. I don't know the best way of describing it without going into details. Do you want me to?'

There was a guffaw from Rob on the sofa, which Susie chose to ignore.

Leaping from the table and pushing back her

chair, Susie cried, 'I hate you!' She couldn't help herself. She vowed there and then *never* to be led astray from first impressions.

Walking away to pace backwards and forwards across the room, Susie went over in her head what Rachael had said. She found herself saying, 'I don't believe a word. Don't you think I'd *remember* doing that to George Silbury?' A fresh stab of pain shot through her head as she attempted to recall what had happened.

Abandoning the exercise on a wince, she turned towards Rob. His six foot three inch sprawled-out form was overflowing from the sofa. His cat, Matey, was lying on his chest and he – Rob – wore a grin ear-to-ear.

'Rob?' she pleaded. 'Don't you think I'd remember doing that to George Silbury? I'd have to *remember*.'

'Don't look at me,' he said through his grin. 'I arrived for the worrying bit, and you did have me worried there, Suse. I clearly missed the good part. You'll have to give me the details later, Rach. It's definitely safe to say, living in the same building as you two . . . isn't . . . boring.' He seemed to sober as he spoke his last words, perhaps at the desperate look on her face. He shook his head and now continued more gently. 'I'm sorry, Suse. George Silbury *did* appear to be in the room, albeit unconscious. Rach says he was regressed, and he was definitely out for the count. You remember that, yeah? You identified him and then passed clean away. But what happened before that . . .?'

He shrugged his shoulders, raising his upper body in an action that had Matey leaping from him onto the floor, where he promptly started cleaning himself.

Now looking over the back of the sofa at Rachael in the kitchen area, Rob said, 'What I *do* know is that her story about him coming around and leaving with his sister adds up. I've checked and there's no body or missing rugs.'

A scrunched-up towel hit him full in the face before he could duck, as Rachael lobbed it en route from the kitchen. His resultant laughter fizzled out as she stood before him, hands on hips and glowering.

After a long moment of focusing on her, he said, 'Lord help me. Incredible as it is, I do believe what she's been saying.'

'Why would I make this up?' Rachael urged, turning to look at Susie. 'What possible reason would I have? If I'm lying, why did you come around with George Silbury on top of you?'

Denial was so much more preferable here. And Susie's body . . . She was still tingling *all* over. Her lips felt like they'd been branded, her breasts ached and as for her . . . Oh God. She was shameless.

'I'd regressed him,' Rachael continued patiently, repeating what she'd already said, but obviously feeling it was needed. 'You made your wonderful entrance into the room. You called out something like, "Talk to me. Please don't be dead", and then

59

he was all over you and . . . Do you know what? I *really* don't see why you're so upset here. This is George Silbury!'

'He was hypnotised!' Susie cried. 'Don't you understand? I seem to have taken advantage of someone,' – *but not just someone* – 'who was out of their mind, completely unaware of what they were doing. It's like . . . like . . . doing something to someone in a coma! It's like *necrophilia!*'

Rob snorted and immediately put his hand to his mouth and attempted to disguise it as a cough.

'I can safely say he was most definitely animate and *not* dead below the waist,' Rachael contributed. Rob coughed loudly and repeatedly. 'And he initiated things. You hardly took advantage of him. In fact, he didn't seem able to get enough of you. Even with you looking like you do and smelling like you do. And Suse, I hate to say this, but you really do stink.'

Susie knew. She still hadn't had a shower, and didn't want to consider what she looked like.

'All because of *you*, Rach! I ran all the way from the High Road in the pissing down rain for you. I even ditched the shopping! All so you could screw me up all over again. Why did you lure me here? What on earth did you think you would achieve? He would never—'

Susie stopped short as the most awful thought entered her mind. 'Tell me you didn't *do* something to his head? Tell me you didn't *make* him do what he did like they do on those hypnotic stage shows? Please tell—'

'Of course I didn't. He was simply regressed and, in fact, at one point I thought he'd fallen asleep.'

'You see I don't get this,' Rob said, sitting forward on the sofa. Matey rubbed himself against his legs. 'You hypnotised him and think he was regressed, so why did—'

'I don't think, I *know* he was regressed,' Rachael said defensively.

Rob blanked his face. He didn't believe in any of this regression and past life stuff and most definitely not Rachael's views on Matey. 'Okay,' he said. 'But if he was regressed, why would he suddenly launch himself at Suse?'

Susie observed Rachael shift awkwardly from one foot to the other. 'I'm not sure why.' She shrugged. 'Her words . . . perhaps . . . I don't know. Perhaps . . . they triggered a memory of someone . . .'

'So now you're saying I took advantage of him when he thought I was someone else?' Susie yelled. 'That's crap. Total, utter crap. So . . . you *must* have done something to him. What did you tell him to do? Did you suggest he—?'

'You really don't think very much of me, do you?'

'What do you expect when you—?'

'Girls!' Rob interrupted. 'This isn't helping anything. And Suse – Rach wouldn't do that to

61

you, you know that. We need answers though. They both zonked out, Rach. Why would they do that?'

'Who knows?' Rachael said, looking at her feet. 'There are lots of things about past life regression that . . .'

Susie had had more than enough. She took the opportunity offered by Rob's grilling to move to the farthest corner of the room. There she sank down onto the beanbag and rested her head in her hands.

What had she done? And to *George Silbury?* She knew Rachael was telling the truth. She could see it in her eyes; if her words weren't convincing enough. And there was no question her body was reacting to something, too. But she couldn't remember a thing. Why couldn't she remember? The fact she couldn't terrified her. Bearing in mind her erstwhile crazed reaction to the man, she couldn't help but wonder if encountering him in the flesh had sent her over the edge. If she'd snapped, had some kind of . . . episode? Perhaps that explained why she couldn't remember and why her head kept hurting her so much. Perhaps—

'I'm sorry,' Rachael said, plonking herself down to sit cross-legged on the rug in front of her. 'I was trying to be a good friend. You've liked him for years. I got one of my feelings and thought—'

'No, you didn't,' Susie said, shaking her head. 'You *didn't* think, that's the thing. You simply ploughed on, led by one of your loopy "Fate is doing his thing" feelings. And it's not Fate, Rach. The only thing we are fated to do is die. It's simply your excuse for forging ahead with some hare-brained scheme or other, sodding the consequences for anyone else that might be involved. More often than not: me.

'If you'd only asked me, I'd have told you I never want to meet him. Honestly, he's the last man on the planet I would ever let myself encounter. And now look what I've done? Do you have *any* idea how bad I feel right now? I acted like a sick, deranged, opportunist . . . hussy! I took advantage of him when he was out of his head. And if the guilt and humiliation isn't enough – it's assault, Rach: assault. He could press charges.'

'He can't remember either. And it wasn't like that.'

He couldn't remember? Well, at least that was one thing. The guilt and the humiliation could therefore be her own. She would have to live with herself though. And it did nothing to address the alarming possibility that her crazed eye obsession had graduated into something far more sinister.

'I did *what?*' George's outburst shocked the taxi driver into slamming on his brakes. He moved off again on a string of curses.

'Oh, for goodness sake!' Cassie exclaimed. 'You've been doing my head in. You just won't button up, will you? I told you I'd tell you, but not right now! I have serious things to consider

63

here, and all you keep going on about is: *did she hypnotise me? She couldn't have done, but something isn't right. You will talk to me, Cassie.* Well now I've talked to you.'

'Stop the taxi!' George cried. She would bloody well talk to him, and not the garbage currently coming out of her mouth. But *not* in the taxi. The driver was already showing too much interest in the goings-on.

As they reached a halt, George climbed out, marched around to the other side, opened the door, and escorted a reluctant Cassie out. Standing in a thankfully deserted bus stop in the pouring rain, he faced her. 'Tell me what happened. I don't for one moment believe what you just said, but tell me anyway.'

'I told you what happened! You leapt up from the couch, hurled yourself at a bedraggled, mud-covered woman, declared your undying love and set about having your wicked way with her. And then blacked out.'

'Cassie,' George said quietly. He didn't trust himself to speak any louder or he would be screaming at her. He had no idea why she was saying these things. The fact he had mud on his trousers, and his body felt the way it did . . .? There *would* be a sensible explanation for that.

'And her name was Susie, not that you bothered to introduce yourself. And you quite possibly called her by another name.'

'Cassie. Enough. I don't know what's going on

with you. You refuse to talk to me, and now you're coming out with the most ludicrous—'

'I don't want to talk. I have to *think*. I have to find the logical reason for everything that's happened, but you aren't giving me a chance here.'

'I'm not – because you haven't *told* me what happened!'

'I have!'

'God help me! You're saying I sexually assaulted a woman called Susie?'

'That's about right. You were all over her. Tongue down her throat. Hands everywhere. Then you took her down to the floor.'

'No.'

'Yes.'

'No. I wouldn't do that.'

'Well you did. So can you please now let me *think*. I'm sorry to have broken the news to you like this. I didn't intend to, and you don't deserve it. We can talk about it all later, when I've found the answer. Then I can explain all this away for both of us.'

George had been silently walking towards the waiting taxi as she spoke, and now opened the passenger door. He returned to Cassie, took her hand and marched her back to her seat, before climbing in after her and closing the door.

'Turn around,' he stated with deliberate calm to the expectant driver. 'Take us back to wherever you picked us up from.'

'We're *not* going back!' Cassie cried, shaking her head frantically.

'We are. If what you're saying is true, I have no choice.'

George was resorting to shock tactics. If this was the only way to get the truth out of Cassie, and hopefully get her to open up to him, then so be it. Because his sister was beginning to sound . . . deranged. 'If I've done what you say, the very least I can do is apologise to the woman.' He spoke quietly, determined to keep this conversation away from the taxi driver.

'That might not be a good idea.'

'Why?' *Come on Cas.*

'You don't react normally around each other,' she murmured. *Bugger.*

'It's time to come clean,' he pleaded, shifting in his seat so he could face her and hold both her hands between his. 'We don't need to go through with this,' he said lowering his voice further. 'You can simply tell me all this was a joke of some kind. I'll come around to yours. We can talk. I can help you with whatever it is you're currently going through. I'm here for you, Cas, but you need to open up. Start by telling me I didn't do those things and then we'll head straight back to yours, or mine, and we'll talk. You can tell me anything and everything and—'

'I can't,' she groaned. She shook her head and fixed him with those haunted eyes of hers. 'I wish I could. But you *did* do those things. It happened.

And I'm so sorry for having dragged you into this. I can't tell you how sorry I am. I should never have taken you there. Never started this story.'

George looked into his sister's eyes and could see she was telling the truth. *Bloody hell, she was telling the truth!* He'd assaulted a woman. He couldn't remember a damned thing, but he had *assaulted a woman!* He urged himself to stay calm and take several deep breaths in an attempt to slow his frenetic heartbeat. Deep breath. Deep breath.

When he finally felt able to talk, he asked in an urgent whisper, 'Did I hurt her?'

Cassie shook her head, no longer meeting his eyes. 'But she passed out too.' Her hushed voice sounded anguished. 'You weren't giving her much of an opportunity to breathe with your tongue down her throat and I think—'

George shot forward and hammered on the glass between themselves and the driver. 'Fifty quid if you get us there within sixty seconds.' To Cassie, as he sat back, he said, 'I don't have my wallet, so you'll have to sort it.'

George leapt out of the taxi before it fully stopped. The door to the building was closed. He pushed it hard a couple times, but it didn't budge. He pressed the buzzer. It was after office hours. He pressed the other two buzzers . . . and kept his hand on them.

'Sounds like someone's keeping their finger on the frigging thing,' Rob muttered.

67

Susie sat bolt upright and looked at Rachael and Rob in horror. 'It's not the police is it?' What if he had remembered and reported it and they'd come to arrest her?

Rob, who had headed over to the window to view the entrance below, started chuckling. 'It's all right, Suse. I'm sorry. I know I shouldn't be laughing right now but this is too much. It's not the police. George Silbury is trying to get in.'

Susie slowly turned to Rachael. 'You told me he didn't remember.'

'He didn't. I don't know if he does now. I'll go down,' Rachael said, standing up.

'I'll come with you,' Rob promptly said, already moving towards her. 'He's most likely not going to be happy with you.'

Susie was now on her feet, too. 'Don't. You. Dare. Nobody is going downstairs.' She spoke with deliberate calm.

With a grin, Rob plonked himself down on the sofa again, crossed his arms, and looked expectantly at Susie and Rachael.

'We're going to pretend none of this has happened,' Susie continued. 'We're going to pretend George Silbury is not at the door downstairs. We're going to pretend I have not brazenly assaulted him. And then he'll go away. When I know I can trust you to stay put, I will take a shower.'

Susie walked to the flat's main door, turned the key in the lock, removed it, and pocketed it. She went to Rachael's handbag, found her key in the midst of all her crap, and pocketed that, too. Rachael stood motionless throughout, her indignation evident from the sounds that kept escaping her.

Susie headed for the shower. Even if they buzzed him in, he couldn't get through the inner security door. *Sorted.* If the police were called, of course, that would be another matter. But she wasn't going to consider that right now.

As the water rolled over her she attempted to come to terms with what she'd done. And couldn't. She tried again to remember what had happened after she'd entered Rachael's consulting room. And couldn't. All it did was give her a blinding headache. She turned the flow of water down. It was too much for her overly sensitised body. She was beyond sick. Her body had reacted to her assault of George Silbury. She had a history of abnormal reactions to the man, but evidently she wasn't just screwed in the head: she was *dangerous*.

She could never see George Silbury again. In 2D or 3D.

'He's still down there,' Rob advised from his perch by the window. 'And he doesn't look happy. Drenched and smouldering more like. I'm surprised there's not steam coming off him.'

'I know he's still down there,' Rachael muttered. 'He's still leaning on the flaming buzzer! Can you believe she locked the bathroom door? She must have got the lock fixed. I can't even get in there and retrieve the keys. She has no right. This is *not* meant to happen. How are they supposed to get together if she does things like this?'

Rob swung around to look at her intently. 'They are supposed to *get together*? What are you up to, Rach? I can't make head nor tail of what's going on right now and—'

The buzzer stopped.

Rob abruptly turned to the window again. 'He's still there, talking to that woman you say is his sister. They look like they might be arguing. He's got his mobile out, is dialling a number and . . .'

Rob spun around as Rachael's mobile began to ring. He slowly shook his head at her.

'Yes! Yes! Yes!' she cried, scooting across the room. There was a yelp. 'Matey! I'm *sooo* sorry. I didn't see you there. Please forgive me.' What had she done with her phone? It had been on her desk downstairs. She'd had it to call 999. 'I gave my card and number to his sister . . . *Yes!*' She found her phone in the pocket of the suit jacket she'd been wearing, and immediately accepted the call.

'I have no idea what you did to me, but I do know I owe an apology to Susie. So will you *please* open the damned door?'

No introductions. Straight to the point. Assertive. He was angry and *definitely* smouldering. His voice was . . . Along with his looks, it was why half the planet lusted after him.

'I'm afraid Susie is indisposed,' Rachael said,

meeting Rob's narrowed eyes from his new position back on the sofa. She looked away quickly.

'Don't give me that. Open the door. You can't do something like this to me and then not let me attempt to put it right. You are dangerous. Playing around with people's heads and—'

'You have no right to take that tone with me. You were past life regressed, as simple as that. Your actions during that regression may have been . . . unusual, but had nothing to do with me. They were down to you. You got it into your head to launch yourself at my best friend and no one's to blame for that but you. I've never experienced anything like it. It was shocking. If you have some kind of . . .' *Dare she? Would this work?* '. . . repressed psychotic tendencies then—'

'*Repressed psychotic tendencies?*' he spluttered.

She couldn't believe she'd had the balls to say it, but hopefully it would have the necessary impact. She refused to look at Rob.

'I can't even remember what I did. I let you hypnotise me and the next thing I know . . .' There was a pause. 'Did I scare her?'

Rachael smirked and, signalling with her hands for Rob to move over, dropped onto the sofa next to him. She leant back to get comfortable, and absently stroked Matey who had leapt into the overly large gap that had formed between the two of them. Matey purred and moved on to her lap, while Rob sat with his arms crossed, shaking his head. Rachael focused on her hands as she

71

continued the conversation. 'I wouldn't worry. I doubt Susie will press charges. She wants to put it all firmly behind her. Her regaining consciousness to find you pinning her to the floor though was the stuff of nightmares.'

There was silence as he evidently absorbed the new information. 'Is she seriously indisposed, or is she avoiding me? God knows I don't blame her.'

'Both. But give it a few days and she may be more amenable.'

'I don't know what came over me.'

'You don't remember then?'

'No.'

'Could you put your sister on?'

'No.'

'Why?'

'I want Susie's number first.'

Rachael rattled it off with a smug grin and, after listening to his request that she relay his mortification to Susie, was put through to Cassie.

'I just blurted it out. I'm not thinking straight.' Cassie didn't sound good. 'He's beside himself. I just wanted him to stop going on, but didn't mean for this. All he needs is an opportunity to apologise.'

'No can do, I'm afraid. It didn't go too well this end either, but I'll work on her. Look, I know all this is freaking you out, but I can help. I've been there myself. I know we didn't hit it off in the past, but let bygones be bygones and all that malarkey. Getting Susie and George together will help us both, I promise. Just call me when you're ready to talk, yeah?'

As the call terminated Rachael sat for a moment with the phone resting against her mouth. She was still stroking Matey and took a moment to absorb the reassurance his presence provided. When she had found out Susie was Hannah . . . Holy moly, freaking out hadn't begun to go there. That night ten years ago hadn't been good for either of them. She'd had her suspicions, but confirmation had been something else.

Rachael took a deep breath and shook her head. *Finally* though, there was a chance to put things right. She caught Rob's eye. His intent gaze changed to a more quizzical one. No, make that suspicious. And disapproving. She wished he wouldn't look at her like that.

'What are you up to, Rach? What aren't you telling me?' His look changed to one of concern. 'I don't want to see Susie hurt. This talk of getting her together with George Silbury? He's *George Silbury*! While Suse is a looker, she was hardly looking her best earlier. And it doesn't even sound like she wants to get together with him. *And* he's connected with Porsche Sutter-Blythe.'

'You don't need to worry. I know what I'm doing. I don't want to see Suse hurt either. She won't be hurt. Quite the opposite. And now they've met, it should happen with or without me. It's down to what they are. But with Susie's hang-ups . . . I need to ease the process along and make sure all runs like clockwork. I owe them at least that much.'

He was frowning. Rachael refocused on her hands, still stroking Matey. She shook her head and smiled ruefully. She knew the answer, but asked the question anyway. 'Do you believe in Soul Mates, Rob?'

And yep. She'd glanced up and his face had blanked. Rachael sighed. 'I knew the answer to that one. And I also know you humour me. Past lives, Soul Mates, Matey – the lot. And I'm afraid if you don't believe in that stuff, you're not going to understand the explanation. You don't, do you? I'm right, aren't I? I know I'm right.'

His lack of belief in past lives was why she'd not told him they'd encountered each other before. There was humouring and then there was humouring, and the last thing she wanted was to risk their friendship. Her life had been so enhanced since he and Matey had arrived. Not everyone welcomed being told about a past life. And, in any event, it's not as if he'd come to her to be past life regressed. He knew where to come if he wanted to be.

There was a guilty grin on Rob's face as he fixed his eyes on his own hands. They rested together on his long muscular legs. With his head looking down like that, his blond hair had flopped over part of his face but she could still see his dimples. It's a shame she couldn't tell him she remembered him. She'd have happily described how he'd been admired from afar. How good he'd looked in breeches. How hot he'd been then . . . too.

Rachael felt heat rise to her face . . . and guilt. She snapped her eyes back to Matey who she began to stroke with renewed vigour.

'It's not humouring, Rach. It's for you to believe what you want to believe. It's not for me to judge.'

'Thank you,' she said. And it was heartfelt.

'But no, I don't believe in past lives, reincarnation, Soul Mates and . . .' She noticed his threaded hands upon his lap, clench tightly together. She thought he may have glanced up at her and then back down again. His upper body moved as he took in a deep breath. He raised his head to look at her. She felt obliged to meet that look. 'You *really* believe Matey is your Soul Mate, don't you? The one destined for you?'

She couldn't quite make out the expression in those eyes of his but it was disconcerting. She looked back down at Matey. She recalled the moment that he'd leapt into her arms and how she'd just *known*. It had been an OMG moment, just as she'd expected it would be. Of course things weren't *exactly* as she'd expected them to be . . . She swallowed painfully. 'I do,' she said quietly. 'I really do.'

There was a long pause from Rob as he concentrated on his hands which were now flexing and un-flexing themselves on his lap. He must have seen her watching them, as he murmured, 'Cramp,' before asking, 'Who was he?'

75

'I'm sorry?'

'Who do you think Matey was? Who is this long lost Soul Mate love of yours you are convinced has come back . . .' He inhaled deeply and audibly, '. . . as a cat?'

'I don't know.'

She felt his eyes drilling into her. 'You don't know?'

'No,' she confessed quietly. 'I've most likely not recalled that past life yet.'

'You don't *remember* him? So how on earth can you *know* he's your Soul Mate?'

She shook her head and smiled, raising her eyes to meet his. 'You don't have to remember your Soul Mate like that to recognise him for who he is. And you most definitely don't have to have been regressed. You simply need to meet. I've always known what to expect, but with Matey it's not . . . With Matey it's . . . complicated.'

'What had you expected?' Rob asked quietly. 'What had you always known to expect because I so get that Matey might be complicated!' He abruptly lowered his head again, this time, shaking it, too.

And Rachael knew how this was going to sound. Explaining about Soul Mates as she knew them to be was difficult enough as it was. She didn't understand why people seemed to struggle with the concept. Indeed, why everyone didn't know about them. She couldn't remember a time she hadn't. Her best guess was that everyone *did* know

76

about them – the potential for ultimate love – but that they simply didn't listen to their heart and soul. She took a deep breath and closed her eyes. Because with Matey on the scene it made such explanations . . . all the flaming harder! She didn't even fully understand Matey herself, so how could she possibly expect others to? And this was Rob. She really didn't want him to think she was mad. She took another deep fortifying breath and said, 'Thunderbolts.'

Rob remained focused on his hands. After a pause, he said, 'Go on.'

'You're asking what I expected, right?'

He nodded. 'Go on.'

'Okay. Thunderbolts as I've already said. But with Soul Mates we're also talking of the force of your reaction to each other, the depth of what you feel being so extreme it might not even be of this world. Soul Mates aren't like mates in an animal sense – or shouldn't be,' Rachael added defensively, pre-empting any reaction Rob might have felt inclined to give at that point. 'It's *beyond* that. But look what an animal will do to secure and protect its mate? And once you've experienced the total sense of rightness, the ecstasy, the bliss, the enhancement upon every one of your senses, the sheer joy in living and loving and being loved – a Soul Mate will attempt to overcome anything to keep it. Even death. It may take time. It may take lifetimes. Some may never find him. But you're not completely whole until you're united. And so often you don't know what you've been missing until you find each other again. It's so way beyond love per se. It's "*the* love". Love with otherworldly, supernatural cherries on top. Love between *the one* you were always meant to be with. It's ultimate. It's extreme. It's . . . The Real Deal. I've never been good at explaining it, but that's how it goes.'

Rob was silent. She braved a glance at him. 'I know what you're going to say,' she said.

'Just bear with me a moment,' he said, apparently struggling with his words. But he was shaking his head forcefully. He now raised it and said, 'It's no good. I've not a hope! I cannot *possibly* react to this diplomatically and humour you.'

'Rob—'

'You are saying you feel that for Matey? That Matey feels that for you?'

'Yes, No. Not exactly. I told you he's . . . complicated and quite possibly a blip. If he's not a blip, then it raises—'

'Have you *any idea* how you are sounding?'

'I know exactly how I'm sounding and just knew how this conversation was going to go. But please don't let Matey affect your belief in—'

'How can it not? I couldn't possibly believe in Soul Mates anyway, but with—?'

'I feel it, Rob. Don't you think it would be easier for me to deny it? I know how I sound. But I feel it, I do, and I can't possibly deny it. It wouldn't be fair on me, or him. What he's come back as isn't his fault. It's not as it should be, I know that,

78

of course I do. With what he is, the lack of recip-rocation, how can it possibly feel as it should? It's all so bittersweet and frustrating. So frustrating! But it's there. There's *no* mistaking it. Millions of Buddhists believe souls aren't just reincarnated into humans but animals too. It just never featured in what I've always *known*. But I felt the thunder-bolt, Rob. It was plain as day. And while this is difficult, what I feel is still so much better than nothing. I can't feel it all, of course I can't, but he comforts me. Emotionally, it's as if he supports me. I want reassuring right now because I don't want you to think I'm mad. Not you. And he's providing it. Right this very moment. I feel it. I feel what he is . . . here.' Rachael placed her hand over her heart.

Rob stood up abruptly. 'I've remembered I need to be somewhere.'

Matey promptly leapt from her lap to join him as he began to walk towards the door.

'Rob?' she pleaded. 'I know I sound eccentric, kooky – just plain mad! But I'm not, I promise you. I really don't want you to think that. It's all really confusing, but I can't deny how his presence makes me feel. And I'm right about Soul Mates. I so am!'

'I know you believe what you're saying,' Rob said softly, still walking to the door. 'And I don't think you're mad . . . although I haven't a clue why not.'

'Why don't you leave Matey here?' Rachael asked

hopefully. She could so do with the comfort. 'It would be good to spend some time with him. He's forever at your heels. I don't mind looking after him for a bit and—'

'Can't. Sorry. Vets.'

Rachael's stomach nose-dived. 'Is something wrong with him?' she cried, leaping up from the sofa.

'Not yet.'

'Not . . .?'

There was a pause. 'Not yet as in vaccinations, that kind of stuff.' He reached the door, Matey still at his heels, his back still to her. He raised a hand to clasp the wooden door frame. 'Rach . . . I couldn't believe in Soul Mates, with or without Matey in play so don't take it personally. All that love conquering all crap, even death? I'm not a roses round the door kind of bloke. I've never been able to believe in happy endings. Don't ask me why, I've just never been able to. I've always felt circumstances can intervene. Anyway, we're off to the vets so will you please stay out of trouble? And promise not to open the door to George Silbury if he returns?'

'Why?'

'It might not be safe and—' He cut off his words before continuing, 'Just wait until I'm around.'

With that he and Matey left the room. Rachael swallowed hard. She already missed Matey.

CHAPTER 8

George continued to watch the woman sitting in the corner of The Old Church restaurant. A shaft of sunlight was shining through one of the large stained-glass windows and the red-hued beam was making her hair, which he'd already labelled gorgeous: *glorious*. He wasn't sure how many prompts he'd been given before finally hearing Michael.

'What is it with you recently? Ever since you disappeared off with your sister . . . What was it by the way, the family emergency?'

Dragging his eyes away, George turned his focus to the much less appealing image of his manager: fifty-two years old, balding, but with a major comb-over issue. And he didn't like the way he'd just said 'family emergency'.

'You can't afford to be distracted, George. You have responsibilities and it's not as if Cassie isn't more than old enough to look after herself. That's one of the reasons I wanted this lunch. That and, of course, spending time with the divine Porsche. I've said it before, and I'll say it again: you two would make an incredible couple.'

George picked up a piece of cutlery to twiddle between his fingers and focus intently upon. It was more preferable, and at this point more appropriate, than looking at Porsche, who was sat to his left on the pew. Why did Michael have to continually harp on about this? He knew how George felt about Porsche. It wasn't just a lack of interest; it was active disinterest. He'd left Michael in no doubts about that, yet he still went on about the two of them. And despite the reports in the press, he and Porsche had never had a thing going. They never would. Not that Porsche necessarily grasped that point.

As Porsche's virtually bare thigh pressed against George's leg, he shifted away from her. She was dressed in a ridiculous creation, not at all appropriate for an informal Saturday lunch in a restaurant a few roads across from the set. With it being a converted church with stone walls and high ceilings, she must be freezing. No doubt he could act as a hot water bottle, but being chivalrous with Porsche was no longer an option. He'd been that once before, and that had marked the start of the problem.

'George,' she said in her Californian drawl, leisurely running her fingers up and down his arm. 'We're all worried about you.'

So sincere. George wondered for the umpteenth time why he'd agreed to do this film with Porsche in the equation. Come to think of it, that lake scene alone should have been enough for him to say no.

Michael, George remembered, clenching his jaw. 'She's moved on,' Michael had assured him. 'She won't be up to her tricks again. And the lake? Forget your fear of water. There will be body doubles and you'll be no more than knee deep.'

George shifted his leg yet again and pointedly removed his arm from Porsche's reach.

He wasn't presently in the right mood for either of his lunch companions. And Porsche was going to be a problem; he could feel it in his bones. As for Michael . . . He knew why his sister didn't like him. He wasn't someone you easily warmed to. Even George hadn't taken to him at the start, but Michael had stuck by him throughout his early struggling actor days when no one else would and George owed him for that.

George returned his eyes to the woman across the room. He was grateful that he could observe her at his leisure without alerting her to the fact. She was in a corner, near the old wooden doors at the front of the restaurant, while his party was at a table hidden away in an alcove off to one side. It allowed some privacy and would hopefully prevent the media turning up.

He was . . . drawn to her. No doubt about that. It didn't surprise him with the way she looked. Not at all the sort of girl he found himself in regular contact with, but there was something about her natural beauty that more than appealed. It was impossible to describe the effect she was having on him though. Physically, his heart was thudding and his body . . . tingling. All right it was *more* than tingling, an unfortunate fact bearing in mind Porsche's sidling up. The last thing he needed was her assuming his physical condition was down to her. But there was something else that was *exciting* him, and not just at a physical level. It was both disconcerting and compelling.

His extreme reaction to this woman was making him wonder . . . He couldn't help but think of Wednesday. His body hadn't behaved itself then either. Or on numerous occasions since as his thoughts returned to that day. Whereas his brain might not be able to remember what had happened in that consulting room, his body wasn't suffering with the same issue. And considering the circumstances, its response was mortifying.

He had not got much out of Cassie when she'd finally opened the door to him on Thursday night. Although she asserted it was less of an assault and more of a mutual attraction thing. But he'd been so far from a gentleman.

It had been more than physical then, too. He was sure of it. He realised he was making no sense here; he couldn't even remember what had happened. Yet he knew it. *Somehow* he *knew* that encounter had been . . . significant. No sense whatsoever.

He'd left countless telephone messages for the mysterious Susie. He'd sent flowers offering his humblest apologies, but she hadn't returned his calls. He couldn't blame her. Not with the way he'd behaved.

He didn't even know what she looked like. And Cassie hadn't been able to help there. 'You ask too much,' she declared. 'She looked like a swamp-land creature. I suppose she had longish hair, it looked lightish, but it was impossible to tell with the state she was in. Average height. Average build.'

'Eyes?' he'd prompted.

'Grey,' she replied, evidently surprised at herself for noticing. 'A striking grey.' She looked at George and frowned. 'Are you telling me, she's sparked your interest?'

He wasn't quite sure what to say. Had she? He had nonchalantly shrugged and hedged. 'Is it wrong to try and find out about the woman I'm supposed to have attempted to have my "wicked way" with?'

For some reason she'd looked stunned by his answer. He had to admit it hadn't come out as casually as he'd been aiming for, no matter how much he'd tapped into his acting abilities. Cassie had subsequently fixed him with one of her looks that he knew from experience saw too much.

'I don't believe this,' she finally murmured, shaking her head. 'She cannot be right about this. Yet . . .' She had stared at him again and discon-certingly appeared to find what she was looking for. With a shrug and a grin, she had then said, 'I take it she hasn't returned any of your calls?'

'No,' he had confessed, mumbling something about sending six bouquets of flowers. 'What's put that smile on your face?'

She had just shaken her head at him and her grin broadened.

He got nothing else out of her on that subject for the rest of the night. But when she volunteered her journalistic skills to find out more about Susie, he'd not said no.

George sat up straight in his seat as a man approached the woman at the table. He gave her a quick peck on the lips and sat down in the seat opposite. Siblings? Or something more?

'George! Snap out of it!' Michael demanded. 'No wonder I've had Francis on the phone about you. It comes to something when the director calls me. What has got into you? What are you looking at?'

George quickly looked away. *Who* was kissing her?

'And Porsche here tells me you've so far failed to get together to practise your one-on-one scenes. Men would kill to be in your shoes, yet you—'

The food fortunately arrived at that point and after the serving staff had departed, George focused on his plate with absolutely no intention of continuing that topic of conversation. George was having to psych himself up for any one-on-one time with Porsche. Moving his leg again, he realised it would have been too much to have hoped that Porsche could be similarly focused on her food. She wasn't touching her salad. It came with dressing, rather than without, she complained. Despite Michael's gallant attempts, she refused to ask for a replacement. Come to think of it, George had never seen her eat.

He spared a glance to the corner by the door. *Who* was kissing her? He could make out newly bare skin in the V at her throat. She'd shed her jumper. A *deep* V. George promptly choked on his mouthful of chicken. Shrugging off Porsche's hands from his back, he took several gulps of water, assuring everyone he was fine.

Giving up on his food and with glass of water in hand, he looked again. They were both eating. She appeared to be eating a salad of some kind and they were sharing a side order of chips. He still couldn't work out their relationship.

The more he reflected, the more he needed to see the colour of her eyes. It was mad, but he needed to see them. He glanced away quickly as he found his own eyes being redrawn to that incredible V. His anatomy didn't need that right now.

Susie was experiencing the strangest sensation; tingling all over. And Peter had finally arrived. Late. And despite their plans to see a film, he had announced that he needed to return to his mother's straight after lunch.

It was unfortunate he still lived with his mum at thirty-nine, but Susie understood his sense of responsibility. His mum was on her own, he the only child, and if he needed to take her to the hairdressers, rather than letting her catch the bus which stopped right outside both doors, he was obviously very . . . *caring*.

The tingling sensation wasn't caused by him, Susie knew that much. And it was beyond disconcerting. She was actually getting hot and flustered. She felt like she was being watched too; intently watched. But her few quick glances around the restaurant revealed everyone getting on with their own meals and paying her no attention whatsoever.

'Good week at work?' Peter asked.

'Yes thanks.' That wasn't strictly true. Wednesday had been particularly hellish. And she *was* talking about her working day here, not her personal life. But she'd tried sharing details of what she'd been doing with her class with Peter before: the bureaucracy, the parents, the idiosyncrasies of her kids, their funny moments, their misdemeanours – of which there had been plenty on Wednesday. But his lack of interest ensured it wasn't worth the effort of telling the tale. As for the rest of Wednesday? He'd asked about *work*. 'You?' she asked, with a catch in her voice.

As he spoke, Susie realised it was too much. Not what he was droning on about, although he was *droning*. But that sensation! She felt like she was boiling up. She had to shed her jumper. Once that was done, she continued to half listen to Peter while she returned to her food. Not that she tasted a single mouthful. She was too preoccupied with how her body was feeling. She looked up and gave

Peter a polite smile. But while his mouth continued to release its monotone words, he was actually looking at her boobs. She wished she could ignore that, but it made her wince. She glanced down at her chest. She hadn't been expecting to remove her jumper, and her top, although normally respectable, was a little too low bearing in mind the uplift bra she'd thrown on that morning. She gave her top a tug up, before continuing to eat.

She concentrated on her plate. Peter was *still* going on about work. Accountancy she couldn't understand; particularly when Peter was talking about it. He loved using long words that she supposed were meant to impress her. All it did was confuse and make her feel inferior. She'd never managed to get a handle on numbers; other than what she taught her eight-year-olds. She'd tried to explain that to him, but it had made no difference to the nature and tone of his explanations, meaning she'd no hope of contributing to such 'conversations'.

Taking a deep breath, Susie attempted to reorder her thoughts. She couldn't understand what the matter with her was. Her adverse reaction to Peter wasn't normally so extreme.

She sighed with relief as he ate his last pea and placed his knife and fork precisely together on his plate. She looked up at him to say farewell and yanked her top up again as it became evident he was saying goodbye to the boobs. She couldn't have him getting any ideas. He didn't believe in sex before marriage. She was counting on that.

As he departed, she called for the bill. He'd managed to avoid paying his share again. *So* canny with numbers, but on this occasion it was a price worth paying to see him disappear more quickly. She wasn't feeling herself.

Shrugging her coat on, Susie started to button it up while furtively scanning the restaurant. She was so sure she was being watched, but there was no one. Popping her pin number into the portable card-payment machine, she smiled and thanked the waiter. Retrieving woollen accessories from her bag, she pulled on her gloves, wrapped the scarf around her neck and popped the matching grey bobble hat on her head. It was freezing out there. It had sleeted the night before and there was sludge everywhere.

She left the restaurant without turning around.

George watched her dress. It was strangely sensual. She looked adorable wrapped up like that. A far cry from the scantily clad Porsche at his side. He saw her smile at the waiter. He gulped. It did things to his insides that a smile shouldn't be able to do. He ground his teeth as the waiter smiled back.

He was not going to miss his chance. He would catch up with her outside. He *had* to see her eyes. He watched her leave her chair. And there was the perfect excuse: she'd left her jumper behind.

George leapt up from his seat and quickly cut a dash through the restaurant. He'd already planned his route and only encountered one unforeseen obstacle – that damned waiter, who very quickly got out of his way. Snatching up her jumper, still warm, and which he couldn't resist holding to his nose, he was out of the door before it fully closed behind her.

And there she was. Standing with her back to him, repositioning her scarf against the elements and pulling her hat down further. George didn't feel the cold in this moment, despite being in shirtsleeves.

'I believe you left this behind.' He held her intoxicatingly scented jumper in his outstretched left hand. She slowly turned.

It seemed like time stood still while he waited for her to raise her eyes to him. And then he *knew*. It was her.

'Susie,' he whispered reverently, as he took in the most stunning eyes he'd ever seen. Deep, intense . . . warm grey. So warm. Dawn, he thought. A northern ocean at dawn. But that didn't begin to do them justice. He'd never seen a more heart-stoppingly beautiful sight . . . or had he? There was something disconcertingly familiar about this moment. He realised her eyes were growing larger as he held their gaze. Impossibly large. He reached out and instinctively grabbed her elbow as she stumbled.

Something precious . . . His heart jolted.

'Are you okay?' The colour had leached from her face. 'I'm sorry. I'm not here to assault you again. I didn't even know it was you . . . yet, somehow, I knew. I'm sorry. I'm babbling. And you don't look well. I'm so sorry. Come back inside and take a seat. I didn't mean to scare you.'

Susie couldn't remove her eyes from his. In the flesh they were . . . They weren't just brown. There was amber, and ochre and even tiny freckles of chestnut and mahogany. They were warm and alive and intently focused on *her*. They reached deep, deep within, wrapping themselves around her in a . . . familiar embrace?

And his voice . . . Her whole body, inside and out, was responding to its resonance. Thrumming. His hand on her elbow; it somehow seared through her thick winter coat to brand her flesh.

But finally she heard her head. She was face-to-face . . . with *George Silbury*!

George had extended his arm around her waist to provide further support. He was seriously concerned she would pass out. He shouldn't have shocked her like he had. He was an idiot. He hadn't thought. He'd been on a mission.

So pale, he thought worriedly as he looked down at her. But beautiful. Red-blonde hair. *Those* eyes. Dimples – although he'd only caught sight of them when she smiled at that damned waiter – a gorgeous curvy figure. He'd yet to hear her voice.

'I'm sorry. I've been meaning to thank you for the flowers.' Shaky, but husky. Sensual. *Come to bed* . . . He closed his eyes for a moment and swallowed painfully.

'Please come inside,' he somehow managed.

'No!' she cried, shaking her head hard. 'I need to go. Thank you again. Your messages . . . There is nothing to forgive. It was me. All me. You had nothing to feel guilty for. It's me that should have been asking for forgiveness. I'm so sorry. I'm grateful you're not pressing charges. I didn't deserve the flowers. I wanted to say thank you, but didn't . . . but couldn't . . . but . . . thank you.'

She was pulling away from him. He knew he had to let his arms drop from their hold, but his whole being cried out at the thought. 'Let me take you home,' he urged, desperate to continue their encounter.

She shook her head. 'Don't feel guilty or indebted. *You* shouldn't. I assure you there's—'

'I don't feel guilty or indebted,' he interrupted. Shaking his head, he corrected, 'Yes I do. And I'm sorry for interrupting. But that's not why I was offering to take you home. I shocked you and . . . God that sounds wrong too! I would just like to see you safely home.'

She closed her eyes for a moment, before slowly opening them. 'I'm not going home, but thank you anyway.' She pulled away more forcefully now and he had no choice but to let her slip through his hands. *No!*

'I'd like to see you again,' he said determinedly.

She stared at him for a few moments before saying, 'Why don't you believe me? There's *nothing* to feel guilty about.'

'Why don't you believe me when I say this isn't about guilt?'

'You sent six huge bunches of roses with cards expressing your mortification. And you're George Silbury.' Her eyes moved to focus to his right. Her expression hardened. No longer meeting his eyes, she continued, 'The person standing in the doorway behind you, freezing her tits off, is Porsche Sutter-Blythe. I'm Susie Morris. A thirty-one year old schoolteacher. Please know there was nothing to forgive. I'm more sorry than you'll ever know.'

Susie turned to walk away. She refused to let her body betray her. It didn't want to move. Her legs shook as they took her forward. She wanted to cry. And she had no idea why.

She wasn't right in the head. Not only had she wanted to fling herself into George Silbury's arms, clutch hold of him and never let him go – *literally* never let him go – she'd wanted to slap that look right off Porsche Sutter-Blythe's face. How dare she look Susie up and down in that way and then snigger! But she had a horrible feeling her violent urges had as much to do with the woman being *his* Elizabeth, as with the snigger. They were an item, according to the papers, and the look of blatant possessiveness in the woman's eyes and demeanour confirmed that.

Susie had no right to react to her the way she had. Even with her being one of the most beautiful women in the world.

Susie wasn't right. She really wasn't right. Her

behaviour around George Silbury was . . . She needed help. Psychological help. But how could she ever let anyone into her head again? It was just around him, she counselled. If she wasn't around him, it would be fine. She would be fine. She wasn't a risk to anyone else. She'd had ten years of . . . Except Porsche Sutter-Blythe. But she'd not see them again. She'd be fine. She would be. She'd be fine never ever seeing him again.

Susie refused to look behind her when she reached the end of the street. On turning the corner, she headed for the nearest wall. Bracing her back against it, she let herself slide down its surface. And then she sobbed. She hurt so badly . . . and had no idea why.

George stood and stared after Susie. She was walking away from him and he was being shredded. He didn't understand why, just that he was. He wanted to pursue her, but made himself stay rooted to the spot. The only way he'd get her to stop would be to manhandle her. Not the best thing to do after the way he'd behaved on Wednesday.

'George? Who on earth was that woman?' The drawl came from behind him.

He gritted his teeth.

'How women can let themselves go like that, I have no idea. No discipline. Do come back inside.'

He turned to fix Porsche with an icy stare as she posed in the doorway, tits indeed freezing off.

95

To think he'd once thought her vulnerable. But she'd only been seventeen back then. She'd not aged well. At twenty-four she was a bitch. In her little red micro-mini and with her forked tongue, she'd be much more at home in hell than standing in the doorway of an old church.

He started walking in the opposite direction to Susie. He couldn't trust himself to go in her direction. Realising he still held her jumper in his hands, he brought it to his face and inhaled. And that had not been a good idea.

He didn't react sensibly around her. Everything was extreme in her presence. His body. His mind. If he ever got her into his arms, God knows how he'd control his baser instincts. Not that that began to cover it. It was an extraordinary feeling. There was a connection there. Well, there certainly was on his part. For a moment he'd thought she felt it too, but then she'd rejected him. And now he was walking away.

CHAPTER 9

'How sad are we?' Cassie declared, taking her third piece of Hawaiian pizza from the box.

George grunted and opened another bottle of lager.

'Valentine's day and George Silbury, one of the world's most eligible bachelors, spends it at home with his spinster sister, eating pizza and swigging Peroni. The tabloids would have a field day. Perhaps I should tip them off, hey sweetie? It's about time you found *loooove* and they could put out some kind of appeal. Better still: a competition! You could provide them with three questions and choose the winner from the answers you like best?'

'Ho. Bloody. Ho, Cassie.' George was sprawled out on the rug on the floor of his living room, in front of the brown leather sofa his sister was curled up upon.

'Well it depends on the questions. I'm sure that between us we could come up with—'

'Enough, Cassie. Please. I'm really not in the mood.'

'Okay. So how about you tell me why you are in such a mood?'

'How about I don't?'

'Oh you are such fun tonight. Okay then, why aren't you at the Valentine's ball?'

'Why aren't you?'

'I didn't have a date! I was led to believe you were going to be in attendance with Porsche *Slutty*-Blythe?'

Despite himself, George chuckled at Cassie's play on the name.

'So, why aren't you?' Cassie pursued. 'With Porsche that is?'

'There is nothing between me and Porsche! For God's sake, give me some credit. And there was never anything between me and half that list of women you hurled at me the other day and I can't believe I'm having to say this, to my *own sister*!'

'I know and I'm sorry. But I would say, you might like to remind Porsche because all the stories have been coming from somewhere.'

He was fully aware of that. What was she playing at?

'Anyway,' Cassie continued. 'How did you know I wouldn't be at the ball?'

'I didn't. I was calling to say hello.'

'The mood you're in, I wish I hadn't picked up. What's the matter with you?'

'I'm fine.'

'Fine my arse!'

'So it's okay for you to tell me you're fine when

you're clearly not, and not for me? And on that subject, Cassie, will you *please* explain to me what's going on? Something got to you enough for you to ask for my help last week. You wanted reassurance and my reaction to the hypnosis could have hardly helped, but if you would—'

'Please, George, we aren't getting back to that. I'm presently okay, I think. I've been meeting with . . . an old acquaintance, and she's helped. Of sorts. And I have a plan, which if it works will help even more. Or, at least, I was okay until I came around here and encountered your misery-riddled presence. To think I was going to tell you what I'd come up with on Susie.'

George was up from the floor and deposited in the armchair across from Cassie before he knew it. Leaning forward, with his elbows on his knees, he looked at her expectantly . . . but then shook his head at the expression on her face.

'Priceless!' she declared, clapping her hands glee-fully, before she appeared to sober. She now shook her head and said quietly, 'This is unbelievable. This really—' She cut herself off and looked at him thoughtfully. 'I've never seen you like this before.'

'Cassie,' he warned. Why couldn't she just give him the information? Not that he was sure what he could do with it, bearing in mind he'd been rejected fifty-five hours ago and had yet to work out his next move. There *had* to be a next move.

'Susie Morris.'

He nodded. She said no more. 'Cassie, come on! Even I know that. Susie Morris, thirty-one years old and a schoolteacher.'

'Steal my thunder why not! And how do you know that?'

'She told me.'

'She *told* you?' Cassie said, choking on her latest mouthful of pizza and sitting up so abruptly that she managed to knock over her glass of wine on the polished oak floor by her feet. Ignoring it, she spluttered, 'Why didn't you tell me? I'm helping you out here and you forget to mention you've *talked* to her! So, she finally got back to one of your countless messages. I must say, she's taken her time.'

'We bumped into each other on Saturday,' he mumbled. She'd not returned any of his further messages since.

Cassie stared at him with a look of amazement in her eyes before it turned to confusion. 'How did you bump into each other?'

'We just did.'

'And . . .?'

George shrugged.

'Dare I ask what you thought of her?'

'You can ask.'

'A bit late to be coy. I'll make a deal. You tell me what you thought of her, and I'll tell you the other bits of information I have.'

'That's blackmail,' George ground out.

'Mmmm. A sister's prerogative.'

'Tell me if you have information on whether she's seeing anyone. If you have, I'll tell you what I thought of her.' Not that he was sure he even knew that himself.

Cassie grinned and raised her right hand for a high-five. He half-heartedly provided the required hand.

'She *is* seeing someone.'

George closed his eyes and attempted to brace himself against the pain that swept through him. It was beyond disappointment. It was—

Cassie reached across to touch his hand. 'But it's not serious. I have it under good authority that there is no love involved. My source referred to him as a "boring shite". Your Susie isn't at all keen on love. A . . . *bad experience* in the past. Hence her being with this man: Peter Boyles; an accountant who still lives at home with mummy.'

Dare he consider there was hope? He grimaced. But how could there be when she'd so clearly rejected him?

'She teaches at a primary school in Forest Hill. She's a humanities graduate from Nottingham Uni and, as you know, shares a flat with The Nutty Regresser. She has two younger brothers, who still live at home with her dad in Leicestershire. Her mum died when she was fifteen.

'I was going to give you a physical description, but now you've met . . . Just *how* did you meet, George? You didn't even know what she looked like!'

'I knew the colour of her eyes.'

'And?'

George held the bridge of his nose. How to try and explain something he didn't understand himself? He also considered it to be intensely private. Between him and Susie alone and perhaps something only the two of them might have a hope of understanding. He was making no sense these days. He sighed. 'I got distracted by a woman in a restaurant and it turned out to be her.'

'What do you mean, *distracted*?'

'I can't . . . She's very attractive and she caught my attention. We got talking and she turned out to be Susie.'

'Just like that?'

'Just like that.'

Cassie shook her head slowly. 'It's what you aren't telling me here. This is . . . So when are you seeing each other again?'

He looked away from Cassie's expectant face.

'No! She *didn't*. No way. Come on George, she didn't honestly say *no*?'

George rubbed his forehead. This was painful enough without having to hear Cassie's reaction to his rejection. 'What do you expect with the way I behaved? I don't blame her at all. I'm not sure any apology will be enough for losing my head that way and—'

'It wasn't like that.'

'As you keep saying. So what *was* it like, Cassie?

102

Mutual attraction you say, but she clearly regrets whatever happened.'

'You are just going to have to charm her, George. Is that the right time?' She tilted her head towards the clock on the marble mantelpiece.

He nodded, without looking.

'Okay. Time to go.'

'Come on, Suse! I'm not going to take no for an answer,' Rob insisted, arm outstretched.

'Ask Rach. She's over there and you've not danced with her so—'

His grin disappeared and he shook his head abruptly. 'I'm asking you, Suse.' He now raised his brows and smirked. 'And no is not an option.'

Sighing, Susie grabbed his hand and let him pull her up from her seat. 'I'm really not in the mood for . . .' She groaned at the track that started playing. She now shook her head at Rob and attempted to pull away. He chuckled and nodded back.

'No, *really* Rob,' she laughed, shaking her head more forcefully and upping her efforts to retrieve her hand. 'I've seen you dance to this before and I *promise* you, I'm not your girl here.'

'You are tonight,' he chortled, pulling her into his arms with one big tug, and manoeuvring them both on to the dance floor.

Why on earth had she decided to come out tonight? It was hardly getting her mind off . . . *someone*. She saw him again, standing before her in his shirtsleeves . . . before she'd walked away. And the pain was still with her. It hurt so much. The sensation bore more than a little resemblance to . . . She reinforced the box in her head. She couldn't go there. And she'd *had* to walk away. Before she'd done something seriously disturbing. Again.

Perhaps dancing this dance with Rob was exactly what she needed? If there was any hope of being distracted, it would be this.

She let Rob twirl her around and forced her mouth into an over-wide smile, no doubt exposing her gritted teeth. She braced herself for the moves she knew would be coming her way.

'What are we doing here?' George asked, climbing out of the taxi. He was facing the Saint George & Horn, evidently a popular nightspot, but not one he frequented when back in London. Anonymity was always an issue.

'There's a private party upstairs and that's where we are headed, so no worries. Just keep your glasses on for now. I'm sure they'll simply think you're a lookalike. Especially with that wretched look on your face. You've never been splattered across the press looking like that.'

'Cassie? Whose party?'

'Sorry. Can't hear you,' she shouted over her shoulder, as he followed her up the stairs, past the ground floor bar, evidently hosting a live band. 'And before you tell me you're not in the mood, check it out.'

'I'm sorry, Cas. I'm not—' George got no further, although he did whip off his glasses.

'Whoops,' Cassie released on a breath, evidently following his gaze. She attempted to propel him. 'George. We are heading to that table over there. *George?* We're heading over to the table Rachael is sat at. Will you *please* move your feet!'

George made a guttural sound, suspiciously like . . . a growl?

He couldn't remove his eyes from the dance floor. Susie was in the arms of another. Spot lit. The music from *Dirty Dancing* was playing. But it was the dirtiest dirty dancing George had ever seen. The man's hands . . . *his hands* . . . He couldn't think beyond the pain and *fury* that engulfed him.

He didn't know why seeing her with that man hurt so damned much. Well, yes, he did. He'd felt like this when she'd walked away from him the other day. And now that pain was combining with fury and . . . He had no right. But he wanted to beat the man to a pulp. Let him rut to the music then.

George was instinctively moving towards the dance floor, when he found his arm grasped. Shrugging it off, he vaguely heard Cassie in the roar that was now his head.

'George? George? What's the matter with you? George? For goodness sake! He's just Rob, their neighbour. I met him briefly when I went to see Rachael.'

He didn't care who the hell he was. Cassie stood in front of him. He carried on ploughing forward, so she was forced to move out of his way.

'Oh boy,' Susie thought. Rob was doing that thing with his leg between hers. She gasped when he grasped her bum again. Enough was enough. Pursing her lips, she gave him the look. He winked, but gave a slight nod, acknowledging he'd gone too far, albeit for the sake of the dance. He repositioned the offending hands. She knew what she'd been letting herself in for though. She'd watched agog as he'd done this dance before. His enthusiasm couldn't be faulted.

She smiled wryly at the thought of what her dad would say if he saw her now. It turned into a grin as she amended that to Peter and a chuckle when she put Peter's mother into the equation. And . . . *George Silbury?* That thought wiped the smile right off her face.

Damn! And she was feeling that tingling sensation again. This was not the time to get all hot and bothered and wanton. She even had that sensation of being watched. She was so clearly losing it. She released a huge sigh of relief as the track finished.

Standing with Rob's arms still around her, she looked up from his chest to tell him off for some of those moves, but got distracted on seeing Rachael.

'Hey.' Susie breathlessly exhaled, giving her a grin.

Rachael hardly acknowledged her before stretching up to talk in Rob's ear. Susie was pleased to note she wasn't the only one out of breath from the dance. Rob's heart was pounding.

He was looking over the top of her head as he listened to what Rachael was saying. His eyes widened and he paled. She caught some of Rachael's brisk words. 'I know you don't believe in this stuff. Yet. But trust me here. And if that's not enough, spare a glance at his body language.'

Rob rapidly dropped his arms, shooting a confused look at Rachael before they both focused on the same thing. 'Will you be okay?' he hissed at her. 'And Suse?'

Frowning, Susie turned to see what they were looking at.

George met the offender's gaze. The offender, after a moment's hesitation and a rushed conversation, fled. George's newfound instincts were screaming at him to follow, while his head frantically attempted to instil some reason into the equation. He was mid-internal battle, when he saw Susie stumble.

And then he was there. She clung to him and his arms wrapped tightly around her. She leaned against him, seeming to need the support. He manoeuvred backwards, moving them off the dance floor to a quiet corner. Cassie and Rachael followed. They were concerned. As was he. But every time he attempted to remove himself a little so he could get in a position to check how she was, she clutched him tighter.

That had to be a good sign, didn't it? She hadn't lost consciousness and . . . He shouldn't be thinking it, but her clinging to him felt good. Damned good.

As she appeared to stir, he loosened his hold but only a fraction.

Susie shook her head. The white noise which had been screaming around it was finally abating and her erratic breathing was normalising. How stupid – or nuts – was she? She could have sworn she'd just seen George Silbury. Opening her eyes to regain her bearings, she took a few moments to realise she was in someone's arms.

'I'm terribly sorry,' she breathlessly exclaimed, and looked up. But before her eyes had a chance to focus, her body told her whose arms she was in. And then her eyes *did* focus. And then he grinned. A slow, sultry, deliciously irresistible grin that transfixed her, while her body turned to jelly. His arms tightened around her.

'I think that last dance may have taken it out of you,' he said gently, his voice unmistakably shaky.

And the sound . . . It was doing that thing to her again, and leant up against him like this, the resonance thrumming through her was in perfect sync with the reverberations from his chest.

'It certainly had its effect on me,' he added quietly.

'Oh *please!*' she heard from behind. 'You were like a bulldozer and we will be having words.'

It was enough for Susie to recover herself. To be

aware it wasn't just the two of them in an intimate, intense, body-blowing, mind-numbing, *insane* vacuum! This was *George Silbury*. She couldn't admit how good it felt to be in his arms. She wasn't safe around him. And she was going to have to go through the inexplicable agony of walking away all over again.

Pushing against his chest, he dropped his arms. And taking a step back, she stood free of him. Her legs held her up. Just. But it didn't feel good. She wanted to be back wrapped in his arms, his body touching hers at every juncture. His broad chest pressed to her breasts. His powerful thighs against her hips. His . . .

'I'm so sorry,' she gasped, not intending to look into his eyes, but unable to resist.

Oh God! They seemed to be doing that connection thing. She shut her eyes tightly before she spoke again. 'I don't know what came over me.'

Her eyes snapped open again at his touch on her bare arm. 'Are you okay?' he asked. 'Your eyes shut and you looked—'

'I'm fine,' she managed, snatching her arm away, but instantaneously yearning for that lost touch. 'And calling it a night.' She had to get out of here. She turned to Rachael, who was talking into another woman's ear. She recognised her. The other woman looked up and smiled.

'We met briefly, but not in the best of circumstances. I'm George's sister. Cassie.'

Of course. She remembered her at his side when

109

he was . . . *unconscious in Rachael's consulting room!* The result of her throwing herself at his non compos mentis person! She had to get out of here.

Susie tried to smile back, but struggled. She didn't think she liked this woman, but didn't know why. She would have to think on that one when she was more capable of thinking.

'Rach? We're going, yeah.' *Now. Please.*

'Sure thing. I'll sort out a taxi. You wait here. Somewhere where you can sit down quietly. There's a lounge out back that will be cooler. You've gone from ghostly white to beetroot.'

Susie winced. 'It's okay. I'll—'

Her words were interrupted by those from the woman she had yet to make her mind up over. 'George, make sure Susie sits down. I'm going to touch base with Rachael while we get a taxi sorted.'

There was the answer. It required no thinking. She *didn't* like her.

And instantaneously someone's hand was on Susie's elbow, gently guiding her through the crowds. Oh God! This couldn't be happening. She was going to be really abnormal again. She could feel it in her bones. And she instinctively knew, walking away was going to destroy her this time.

CHAPTER 10

George led Susie to a table in one of the corners of the adjoining room. As soon as she was in a seat, he crouched down to her eye level. Not that she was looking at him. She appeared to be looking anywhere but. Resisting the urge to brush a particular strand of hair away from her face and tuck it behind her ear, he asked gently, 'Would you like a glass of water or something?'

She nodded and croaked, 'Yes please.'

'You sit quietly. I'll be right back,' he said, getting to his feet.

'And the something please,' she added, as he turned to go to the bar. 'Whatever you are having?'

'Whisky?'

She nodded repeatedly, still not looking at him.

George stood waiting for the drinks at the empty bar. Very few tables were occupied in this room and it appeared to be soundproofed, so little noise came from the dance floor next door. It was cooler too. Susie was notably flushed.

He turned to look at her afresh and his heart did that jolt. He shook his head. He hardly knew her, yet he was drawn to her in a way that defied description. And logic. He had the urge to stake his claim. To call her his. To never *ever* let her go.

But she wasn't his. He attempted to ignore the unfathomable burst of pain that fact dealt him. He turned to face the bar and pay for the drinks. She'd rejected him. She was only with him now because of Cassie's meddlings.

And she was in a relationship with another.

Did that man – Peter Boyles – touch her? His body screamed at the idea. *Did they kiss? Had they slept together?* He clenched his fists tightly and tried to rein himself in. He had no idea what was bloody happening to him here, but the idea of another man . . .

His head turned towards the door now swinging open, letting the deep bass beat from the music in the adjacent room seep in. His fierce gaze fixed on the man coming through the door.

'Shit!' that man appeared to exclaim as their eyes met. An admirably rapid about turn later, just the swinging door faced George.

Rob. Rob the neighbour. Rob the neighbour whose hands had been all over Susie. George took a deep shuddery breath. His baser instincts were clearly coming out and he never knew he had them. And it worried him. Was it dangerous? He'd clearly been dangerous in that consulting room. Psychotic tendencies or some such, Rachael Jones had said. Was he a danger to Susie? He'd not been aware of what he was doing then. He'd been hypnotised and would *never* let anyone into his head again.

He looked at Susie now as he approached the table with the drinks. He could *never* be dangerous to her. He knew that instinctively. Anyone who touched her though . . . *Bloody hell*! He really wasn't so sure on that one.

Susie focused on the flower she'd taken from the small display in the middle of the table and . . . massacred. Every one of its yellow petals was there on the surface in front of her. She had a serious issue here and, as if she needed any reminder of that, her body was innately reacting to who she somehow knew was approaching. And she wasn't even looking at him! But it was more than her body. It was her whole being. And where was the sense in that? It was an extreme reaction. Beyond extreme . . .

She closed her eyes for a moment. A decade-long crazed eye-obsession had graduated to this? Had she finally snapped? Was this what that night had inevitably been leading to? The thought of that night ensured the box in her head started seeping. She didn't bother reinforcing it. She didn't have the energy to fight what perhaps had been the inevitable. *Loss, desolation, betrayal.* They were all there. Beginning their leisurely, but oh so painful, meander through every cell in her body. Filling her with—

A blazing touch on her arm seared through her

body, blasting into her mind. Those feelings were *gone*. No dissipation. Just blasted. She snapped her eyes open in confusion, and came face to face with *those* eyes. So beautiful. So compelling. And seeking out their connection, as if invisible strands winged their way through her, instinctively finding their home and slotting contentedly into place.

When he wasn't there, those slots were empty. She was empty. *Nuts. Nuts. Nuts!*

'Are you okay?' That voice again. So concerned. His hand was still on her arm, providing that blasting – yet comforting, so comforting – blaze. A blaze that, if she was honest, was rapidly morphing into red-hot *lust* as it coursed through her veins. Her body throbbed in perfect synchrony to his voice. And his eyes . . .

She wrenched her gaze away, managing to squeak an affirmative. Her desperate wringing hands came into contact with a glass on the table. She didn't even think as she instinctively grabbed it, raised it to her lips, and emptied it in one tilt.

It hadn't been the water. 'Euuurrrgghhhhh!' she choked out, before hacking what felt like her insides up. 'Euuuurggggghhh!' she released on an uncontrollable shudder. Her insides were on fire, but not in a good way. Not in that incredible way she blazed when . . . She couldn't allow herself that thought.

As she finally stopped hacking, she became aware of a beautiful sound and someone pressed up close by her side, still spreading his blaze, shaking.

She focused through still watery eyes. He was laughing. It was deep, rumbling and completely mesmerising. It was the most amazing sound. It filled her with joy and made her want to laugh as if it was a compulsion.

'Susie?' he managed to get out while shaking his head. 'Why would you . . .?'

And then she was laughing too. She couldn't help it. He was contagious and in the moment it felt wonderful. It felt right. And his arm was loosely around her shoulder and another around her front, and . . . *Oh God, she was so aware of those arms.* His forehead lightly pressed to hers. His breath fanned across her face. His hand moved up and his thumb gently wiped away the tears still streaming from her eyes.

He moved back a few inches. 'You were flushed before but now. . .' He couldn't finish his sentence because of his laughter.

His eyes danced. They were meant to dance, she thought, and in that moment she wondered what it would be like to dance, too. To dance with the man she had no chance of acting normally around. The man she lost her mind around. The man she'd sobbed over as she'd walked away. The man she just wanted to wrap herself around and never, ever let go. The man she . . . *absolutely could not be around! Oh God!*

She had to go. She had to make herself go. She mustn't think of how badly it was going to hurt. She just had to . . . go. 'I thought that was the water,' she murmured, making an exaggerated shudder. His smile . . . How could it be reassuring, comforting, sympathetic – and hotter than hell – all at the same time? 'I must—'

'And it was mine,' he interrupted, apologetically. 'Mine was a double. I'm sorry. If I'd known what you were going to do, I'd have positioned the glasses differently.'

His grin . . . She was in so much trouble here. She'd been seeking Dutch courage, but it sounded like she was going to get oblivion. She hadn't touched alcohol for a decade. And . . . *Hell!* She hadn't eaten anything tonight. Oh God! She'd known she was going to act abnormally around him, but *now*? Go! Now, before the alcohol kicks in! What had she been thinking? She hadn't been thinking. That was the thing. Around him everything became jumbled and . . . Her panicked thoughts were interrupted by his voice.

That darned voice . . .

'You're going to say you need to go, I know you are. But there's something . . . There's . . . I . . .' His voice sounded remote to his ears, but George couldn't not act. It was a compulsion. It was as necessary to him in this moment as breathing. No. *More* necessary. If this was the last thing he ever did, then amen. Their eyes locked, reinforcing that incredible connection to his very core. 'Before the whisky takes effect.'

He watched the tip of her tongue moisten her lower lip and . . . he followed it.

116

The touch of his lips to hers was feather-light. It had to be. He couldn't give in to the pulsing need consuming his body; he *had* to keep himself in check. But *bloody hell*! It was as if that gentlest of touches unleashed the beast within. The dormant beast that awoke for Susie. A primal beast that had been rattling its cage around her, and now found its cage door flung open.

Oh God! His lips . . . Her body, her senses, her soul. She was being completely overwhelmed by their delirious response. *Ecstasy*. Her head was trying to break through, but . . . *Stop?* She wasn't *that* mad.

He groaned, knowing he had to keep himself in check. But as Susie responded, he surrendered. His tongue thrust forward and swept around her mouth, plunging as he pulled her into his arms in an embrace he prayed was gentler than his need. *Sweet Jesus*. Single malt whisky . . . and *ambrosia*. *Heaven*. Her taste awakened whole new sensations in him. Things were pinging all over the place. It was sensory overdrive. He'd never known anything like it. He was finally . . . *alive*.

Susie tried to press as much of her body against his. He must have instinctively known what she needed, because he took her with him so she lay over him as he straightened his whole body out, resting his head on the top of the soft padded seat, his legs stretched out with his heels on the floor. Not once did he release the fluid cage of his arms, not once did he release her lips.

She was powerless to stop. Stopping would kill her. She'd shrivel up and die; a barren husk when she could be so *alive*. She could feel his hardness pressing against her and she wantonly rubbed herself against him, gasping as he groaned and worked more magic upon her lips.

She moulded herself to him, embracing the sensation of feeling whole as their bodies wrapped themselves together; two pieces of a puzzle, always fitting perfectly in whatever configuration. Her hands were in his hair, grasping and tugging and she moaned into his mouth as his hand found her breast. She gasped when his thumb, working in ever decreasing circles, connected to its peak.

'Oh God. *Oh God!*' she exhaled, taking control of their mouths. Nipping at his lips and then moving to nip around his jaw.

'Susie,' he groaned, and her name had never ever sounded like that before.

This was her. Susie. A Susie she had never met before, but who she knew, instinctively, was *her*; who she was meant to be. Such pleasure, such excitement, such contentment, such comfort, such *completeness*. It should be scaring the hell out of her, but she couldn't think about that. Her body wasn't allowing her to think.

And in this moment, it wasn't thinking she needed.

'He won't be hurt, will he?' Cassie asked Rachael worriedly, as they descended the stairs on their hunt for a taxi.

118

Rachael turned with a raised eyebrow.

'I've never seen him like this before and Susie doesn't seem to be as . . . *enamoured* as George. How can they be what you insist they are if—'

'They've both got it bad,' Rachael declared, confidently. 'She's scared and fighting it. That's my legacy, I'm afraid. But now they've met, they're going to continue to be drawn to each other. It's the Soul Mate thing. It's Fate. They are meant to be together: the perfect match. And barring tragedy, they will be. I'm right, you'll see.'

They were outside now and observing the plentiful numbers of vacant taxis passing by. 'That coffee shop across the way looks tempting?' Cassie suggested, inclining her head in that direction. Their eyes met and they shared conspiratorial grins.

Rachael spoke as they headed across the road. 'It appears this time around we might be able to work together without my hating you.'

'I can certainly work with you. I want to see George happy. I've never seen him so caught up with a girl before.'

They'd reached the coffee shop and Rachael opened the door, holding it for Cassie to enter.

'But . . . this time around? Look our chats have helped a little, but I'm a logical person and a journalist by trade. What seems to be happening is just so . . . Look, my head – and *you* – are telling me the most ridiculous things right now. I—'

She broke off to order a tall skinny decaf latte.

At Cassie's prompting look, Rachael ordered, 'Large hot chocolate with cream, marshmallows and chocolate stick.'

'I need evidence,' Cassie continued. 'Proof. Something more than . . . *I just need proof.*' She wanted to say the comfort of proof, but in this case comfort would be the last thing it would be. 'I've decided to go to Worton Hall.'

Cassie had half expected there to be a Worton Hall, but finding the existence of the Wiltshire home she was supposed to have lived in as Kathryn Montague had not been a good moment.

'You found it then,' Rachael said, sounding not at all surprised. Cassie nodded slowly. 'I knew you would do this. And revisiting is just what you need. You'll realise you're not certifiable then. That all this is real. That you *were* Kathryn Montague. That Freddie and Hannah existed. That you really *do* remember me as Tessa. It will feel good.'

Cassie looked up from paying for the drinks, shaking her head as Rachael went for her purse. How could confirmation that she had been Kathryn Montague ever feel good?

'Believe me, it helps. Been there, done that. You too can be just like me.' Rachael grinned broadly.

Cassie shook her head. 'I wasn't looking forward to the trip. But now . . . God help me!'

'Being serious though . . .' Rachael continued.

'I was!' Cassie asserted.

'I know,' Rachael grinned. 'And I also know it's not easy coming to terms with things, but it has

120

to be the way forward. You're in no-man's-land at the moment. When I started recognising Susie as Hannah after my first regression, it was beyond crap. And it got worse before it got better. I needed to know she hadn't been Hannah to clear my conscience. So after several drinks, and more than one very large joint, I regressed her. Putting into practice what I'd learnt at an amateur evening class seemed like such a good idea at the time.'

'You *didn't*?' Cassie turned from the counter where they were waiting for their drinks, to stare at Rachael in horror.

Rachael nodded. 'And you can have no idea how much I've regretted it. The effect it had on Susie was . . .' Her voice faded away. 'Having my worst suspicions confirmed was . . . well . . .'

She needn't say more. Cassie knew all too well. 'You clearly believe all this so how did you come to terms with the guilt?' That was Cassie's greatest fear. If this was all proved, she wasn't sure she ever could. She was praying Worton Hall would provide some kind of miracle. If it could disprove everything, then she wouldn't have to live with the guilt. Yeah she'd have proven she had issues – perhaps she was having a breakdown? – but that would be treatable, and had to be better than feeling her insides wrenched out every time she so much as looked at George.

'You do come to terms with it. It isn't you, after all. It is the past. A past you – Cassie Silbury – were not in control of. And you can learn from it and ensure you don't make the same mistakes now as you did then. That's why it's a good thing. And you're forgetting that we are now in the amazing position of being able to make amends. There can't be a better way of detoxing the soul!'

Cassie shook her head at Rachael's terminology. They picked up their drinks and headed over to a table by the window. Rachael started to giggle as she walked. 'The look on Rob's face when he saw George . . .' Her amusement died away as she said, 'Although it served him right for dancing with Susie like that! He's danced like that with others, too . . .' She shook her head briskly. 'He will be all right don't you think? He will stay out of George's way?'

'If he's an ounce of sense in him,' Cassie said, placing her mug on the table and sitting down. Rachael pulled out a chair opposite and sat down, too.

Cassie raised a hand to her forehead and pressed it hard. It was if her head was attempting to nudge her in the direction of something. It had something to do with Rob, she was sure of it. She shook it hard and forced herself to refocus. 'I've never seen George like that before. It was caveman-esque!'

'Mmmm.' Rachael started to laugh delightedly. 'It was, wasn't it? And it's *exactly* what I would have expected. I know what's meant to happen but I've never seen two Soul Mates come together like this . . .' She fiddled with a discarded sugar wrapper that had been left on the table by previous occupants. She now said quietly, as if to herself, 'It's how it's meant to be. It's bound to be different with Matey.'

'Matey?' Cassie quizzed, before taking a sip of her coffee.

'You're not ready for Matey yet,' Rachael said with conviction. '*Anyway* . . . I'd say Susie isn't going to be too keen on the caveman antics. But then again . . .' She smiled. 'Who couldn't respond to George Silbury in one of those testosterone fuelled states?'

'Please! He's *my brother*,' Cassie cried.

'Don't worry. I just challenge anyone not to appreciate him. And yep, he is your brother . . .' She smiled smugly. 'Just as he was in the past.' Cassie narrowed her eyes at her. Rachael was shaking her head and laughing. 'And I'm betting you were all intent on writing one of your trademark exposés on past life regression, right? It's not really working out for you, is it? I'll be very interested to read what you finally produce. You can quote me if you like? It's got to be good for business.'

Cassie looked at Rachael incredulously now, before muttering, 'This isn't about work any more. I need proof for *me*.'

'You're a journalist. You won't be able resist writing about it all,' Rachael said, stirring her cream and marshmallows into the chocolate. 'And by the way, I strongly advise we remain shtum about Freddie and Hannah. Give George and Susie a chance to get their act together without that getting in the way. Suse wouldn't appreciate it and while all *should* slot into place, with Suse it's not going to be remotely that simple and—'

Cassie's eyes had wandered to the window while Rachael was talking and she had been absently watching two men get out of the car in front of the pub. 'I've zero intention of mentioning—' *With cameras*! 'Paparazzi!' she cried, leaping from her seat and gesturing towards the window. She now bolted towards the door.

'This is not good,' Cassie muttered, as she and Rachael rushed back across the road and started running up the stairs. 'They've gone up the stairs, too. Someone must have tipped them off! And I've a horrible feeling they're from *The Herald*.'

'We need help in the back room,' Rachael said breathlessly to the bouncer on the door. Making their way across and around the dance floor as quickly as possible, Cassie and Rachael finally reached the lounge.

Pushing open the door, Cassie froze. And just caught it on its rebound before it hit her full in the face.

'Wow!' Rachael exclaimed from her side, obviously not quite as frozen as Cassie. 'Susie, Susie, Susie,' she proceeded to tut, not that she sounded like she was admonishing.

'You – out!' Cassie cried, finally coming to her senses and launching herself into the room to stand before the photographer, blocking his view of the oblivious couple.

'And you!' Rachael demanded, wagging her finger in the face of the one speaking frantically into his mobile phone.

'Try and get their cameras and phones!' Cassie instructed as three bouncers entered the room.

George was vaguely aware of a disturbance, but it was somewhere a long way away. Somewhere outside of their cocoon. Their exquisite cocoon. A cocoon he never wanted to leave. A cocoon that felt so right. How could anything feel this perfect? He nipped Susie's lip back and smiled under her mouth. 'You taste amazing. I'm thinking you're like that moon dust stuff because every atom in my body is on the brink of explosion.'

Susie stiffened in his arms. She'd heard it too. She buried her head in his chest and groaned.

'George! George! Get yourself sorted! We need to be out of here *now*! *George?* For crying out loud! Please don't make me have to separate you.'

'Susie? *Suse!* Time to get yourself together here. You guys are playing to an audience and it's about to get much bigger.'

Awareness was invading and George had a horrible feeling he knew what was happening.

He attempted to push himself up in the seat. 'Susie?' he murmured. 'Are you respectable?' He started straightening out her clothing and buttoning up whichever of his shirt buttons he could reach in this position.

When she raised her head from his chest, he

took her face in his hands. So beautiful. Her lips swollen, luscious cherry-red, her brilliant grey eyes only now beginning to lose their sensual haze, her hair gloriously ruffled. What he wouldn't do to wake up to that every morning.

'Are you okay?' he asked gently.

She slowly nodded.

But out of the blissful cocoon, George was becoming furious with himself.

And a sense of dread took hold in the pit of his stomach. No matter how they'd physically reacted to each other, they should have been talking. He should have been gaining her trust, creating firm foundations upon which he could build. Just because he felt a connection, and a bizarre sense of familiarity and . . . rightness – God it felt so right! – didn't mean she did. And he couldn't settle for Susie short-term. Not now he'd found her. It made no sense . . . yet perfect sense all at the same time. It was so simple. He was following his gut here. And she was the one. He just *knew* it. And the thought of losing her . . . What had he *done*?

And in *public*?

CHAPTER 11

Susie sat at the kitchen table staring at the morning newspaper before her. She should have already left for school, but wasn't quite ready to face that particular challenge.

'Why aren't you returning George's calls?' Rachael demanded, heading out of her bedroom door. 'Cassie's been on the phone and says he's frantic.'

Susie winced. Not just at the words, but at their volume. She was nursing the biggest headache of her life, despite having consumed three mugs of coffee and a couple of paracetamols. No. The worst headache she got was every time she tried to remember those moments in Rachael's consulting room, when she'd forced an intimate acquaintance upon an unwitting George Silbury. She could remember their last intimacies.

Not that she needed to when they were splattered all over the front page of *The Herald*, in glorious multicolour.

The piece doesn't begin to do the experience justice. It was so beyond anything I . . . She stopped that thought right there, berating herself for such weakness after the talk she'd just given herself.

Practicalities. That's what she was supposed to be focusing on.

Like . . . why had she been wearing a skirt and *G-string?* She only had *one* G-string and she *never* wore it! That would teach her to get behind on the washing.

'George apparently worked all night trying to stop the story,' Rachael was saying. 'He called in every favour under the sun, threatened to sue, but they still ran with it. He's really worried about how you're taking it and needs to talk to you. I got the impression he was coming over if you didn't start returning his calls.'

That sounded like the incentive needed to get to school. She'd been toying with calling in sick; something she'd never before done. She really wasn't herself at the moment. She couldn't be here when—

Her stomach leapt to her mouth as someone rapped on the door. She frantically met Rachael's eyes, as she turned from the toaster she'd been re-filling.

'It's not him,' Rachael said calmly, heading towards the door with a slice of bread in her hand. 'But I know who it is.'

'Don't open—'

'Rob! And Matey . . . hiya you.' Rachael crouched down to let Matey lick the butter from her fingertips.

'He must have sneaked out behind me before I'd shut the door,' Rob muttered.

Susie caught Rob's eye and promptly groaned as the frustration on his face was replaced with a mischievous grin. 'And to think I was worried about you there for a while,' he said, as he crossed the room and came to a halt behind her. 'Not so anti-George Silbury now are we?' Draping his arms over her shoulders, he said, 'Oh Suse! You should have stuck to dirty dancing with me. Ours didn't make the front page.'

He grunted as her elbow made blind contact. She winced, wondering just where she'd hit, particularly when he sank into the neighbouring chair.

When he finally raised his head, he squeaked, 'I suppose I deserved that. Don't suppose you'd react well if I phoned in to claim the twenty grand price on your head?'

'God help me, Rob! Do *not* push me. I'm not in the mood.' Susie kicked her chair out violently.

'I'm sorry,' he said, reaching out for her arm before she could leave the table. 'I didn't mean to upset you. But you aren't half getting yourself into some right bloody pickles of late.'

'It's not as bad as all that,' Rachael observed, picking up the newspaper.

'No it's not,' Rob said. 'It really isn't. You've a lovely bum, Suse.' Susie no longer regretted using her elbow. 'I'm serious. Don't look at me like that. I was trying to say something nice to make you feel better.' No he bloody wasn't!

'Nobody can recognise you from this picture,' Rachael continued. 'It wasn't your face, facing the camera. In fact, because of what *was*, it's hard to see anything else. Nobody will recognise you, and nobody will be able to claim the reward for your identification. I suggest you talk to George and—'

'I'm going to work!' Susie snapped, finally making her escape and heading to her room to pick up her bag.

The last thing she heard before she slammed the flat door hard behind her was Rob's words: 'Just hit me with it, okay? Whatever *the hell* is going on, just hit me with it. Then I'll make up my own mind.'

George stopped pacing his living room the instant Cassie hung up the phone. 'How is she? What did Rachael say?' he demanded.

'How do you think she is? You're hardly taking this well either.'

George brushed his hands repeatedly through his hair and resumed pacing. This was all his fault. He knew the risks of being in the public eye and yet he'd exposed Susie. And in such a fashion. He'd been weak. Unable to resist. Somehow, deep down, he'd *known* how kissing her would feel. He'd been craving it. And, dear God, it had *blown* his mind!

'I must say,' Cassie said, picking up the newspaper from the coffee table. 'From a journalist's point of view, the name of the venue couldn't have been any better: the Saint George & Horn. It's a sub-editor's wet dream. There are so many headline possibilities and I'm afraid they're all going to be out there in the coming days. I didn't expect the best play on words from *The Herald*, and clearly we didn't get it. I mean, "*George gets his horn out?*"'

George grimaced again. 'But I didn't! And it's the picture!' he blustered. 'Susie splashed around for all to see. Filthy perverts getting off on her.' He felt the growl rise. 'She's there in a double page spread with the, "Do you know this woman?" appeal.'

'And then there's Porsche's contribution,' Cassie murmured.

Yes. Then there was Porsche's contribution. George got his phone out and switched it on again. He had countless unanswered messages waiting for him from Michael, Francis, his mum, his brothers, Porsche – God help him, he'd throttle her. What the hell did she think she was playing at?

But none from Susie.

He paused from his pacing and called her number again. Voicemail. He left yet another message. 'Susie. *Please* call me.' He was as desperate as he sounded.

He hung up and switched his phone off. He was supposed to be on set. Filming had been scheduled to start two hours ago and they weren't going to abandon their efforts to track him down. They'd already sent people around to hammer on his door. Well, they could hammer away.

He stood motionless. His fears firmly taking hold.

'She's not going to give me another chance. I know it. We should have talked. I should have gained her trust. I should have reassured her that this wasn't a quick romp. But no. I acted like a rampant, adolescent school boy.'

And then it hit home.

'Bloody hell, Cassie. I think I've *lost* her!' He sank to the sofa, with his head in his hands.

Cassie was at his side, trying to prise his hands from his head. 'George? George? Look at me. She probably just needs time.'

'Why does Susie make me feel like this?' He turned his face to meet Cassie's, but she'd looked away. It made no sense at all. He hardly knew her for goodness sake.

But it didn't *feel* that way. It felt like she was *his*. *The* one. Not that he'd ever believed in that before. But he did now! Last night, with her in his arms . . .? He had never felt anything like it. And it had been so much more than physical. Oh, his body had reacted to her, there was no question about that. It had reacted to her like it had never reacted to another. But he'd felt . . . at peace. At journey's end. Whole. Complete. That this woman was the purpose of his entire existence. It was insane. But it had felt so damned right. And no one had ever made him feel like that, physically or emotionally. He'd always enjoyed women. But *last night* . . .? She'd ruined him for anyone else. Not that he would ever want anyone else. He wanted Susie. No other. And he'd just cocked everything up! And the idea of losing her was excruciating.

Cassie finally returned her gaze to him and said, decisively, 'If you're serious about Susie, prove it. Don't give up at the first hurdle. The best things in life are worth fighting for. *God almighty!*' she exclaimed. 'You've got me quoting proverbs. I'm an award-winning journalist and you've got me . . . the things I do for you! And if you can't win her, then she isn't worth it, George. Do you understand me? If you're meant to be together, and you've given it your all, then you will be. But who said life was easy? Again and again! You're killing me here.

'I've a good feeling though, sweetie. I really do. But it doesn't look like she's simply going to land in your lap, no matter what might be—' Her voice stopped abruptly, before starting up again. 'Of all the girls in the world, you had to choose one who isn't after you because you're George Silbury. That makes her worth fighting for. So what is it? Give up and hit the bottle like I did a while back, or fight for someone truly worth having?'

He reached out and hugged her. He needed the comfort. And he had to snap himself out of this. He had to find a way forward. But what? He had no idea how he was supposed to win Susie. Did she even want to be won? But last night . . . Last night she'd felt it, too. She must have done. It was too damned powerful to be one way.

'I suppose now is not the time to tell you Mum's on the case?'

He groaned.

'Mmmm. She considers you were careless, let your guard down and that such "uncharacteristic distraction" might mean there's finally hope of seeing you settled.'

He groaned again.

'I told you it wasn't really the time, but it's nice to have her off my case for the foreseeable future. If you want to get your own back on Porsche by the way, you might consider introducing her to Mum. I never knew Mum's vocabulary included such words. I was rather proud of her. Oh! Greg and Mark called to offer you their support, too. They've aborted trying to contact you directly. I won't tell you the rest of what they said. But clearly our brothers would have made damned fine sub-editors! I *obviously* gave them the appropriate ear bashing. But they both seemed to be impressed that Saint George, never before caught in a compromising situation, finally appears to be human.'

Susie pulled her hat lower and wrapped her scarf around most of her face, as she climbed onto the bus. She was going for the Invisible Man look. She couldn't risk being spotted.

Nobody seemed to be looking at her she noted on taking a seat, but it was worth the precaution. If she was ever identified she could lose her job. But that thought hardly got a look in with everything else going through her head.

It had felt so right . . . In the moment, the *delusional* moment, she'd felt there couldn't be anything righter. As if he awakened her and only now could she start living. As if they were made for each other. As if . . . *he felt the same!*

She closed her eyes and shook her head at her own stupidity. And it was a good job it wasn't right, she counselled. Because she would have been laid bare, exposed to the risk of experiencing all that loss, desolation, betrayal stuff for real. Which could never happen. Ever.

He'd zapped those haunting feelings for pity's sake! And she knew why: what was the point of her brain relying on all that manufactured pain from ten years ago, when with George Silbury, the risk was for real. There was something about George Silbury that . . .

Enough she ordered herself. What she had thought had been between them in those moments, so clearly hadn't been. Oh yeah. They'd physically done what they'd done, but as for him feeling anything more? The connection between them? It had all been in her screwed up head!

Porsche Sutter-Blythe's quote in the newspaper ricocheted around her head, hitting the bull's eye yet again.

'It's something we'll laugh about. Overweight, cellulite-infested bimbos shamelessly *throw* themselves at him all the time, *taking* what they can get. You'll note his eyes were closed. They had to be. But his eyes aren't always closed. Not to those he *actively* seeks. And not with whom he discusses the future. Let's just say, with that photo, this one has got her *comeuppance*. Please don't make me say any more.'

She should never have let her get away with that snigger. She should have marched into the restaurant, picked up a fork, marched back outside and—

'No!' Susie cried, evidently aloud, because when

she reopened her eyes everyone on the chock-full bus was staring at her. She slid down in her seat, repositioned her hat and wrapped her scarf up so she was mummified with only her eyes visible. Why were they still looking at her?

It had all become clear with Porsche Sutter-Blythe's quote. He was with Porsche. Susie had been entertainment. They were going to be laughing about her together. And she'd got her just deserts.

Susie couldn't forgive herself for taking advantage of, and violating, a non compos mentis George in Rachael's consulting room, so how could she have ever expected *his* forgiveness? All his apologising . . . it had been part of the plan. He'd not involved the police. No doubt that would have been problematical for someone in the public eye. No, he'd sought his own revenge, doubling it up with entertainment for him and Porsche to boot.

Overweight, cellulite-infested bimbos shamelessly throw themselves at him . . . taking what they can get. His eyes aren't closed to those he actively seeks. This one has got her comeuppance.

No matter how hard Susie tried she'd been unable to come up with an explanation for last night. Why George Silbury would have . . . Oh God . . . with her! She'd repeatedly asked herself *why?* Because it made no sense. How could he possibly be interested in her? He, who was dating Porsche Sutter-Blythe, one of the most beautiful women in the world – and had been linked to all the others – interested in *her*?

She *did* consider herself overweight. She *did* have

cellulite. And she *had* acted like a bimbo. Totally mindless. But around him she was incapable of thought. Around him the only thing she knew was an overwhelming need to be in his arms, joined with him any which way she could. Whether he was willing or not!

But all was clear now. And she deserved it. She did.

Her phone went. Rooting it out of her bag she saw his number flash up. She turned it off. She was not providing any more entertainment. She could imagine him and Porsche having a giggle about it in bed. Oh God! Fork. Fork. Fork.

It cut to the bone. It tore her up. Oh God. It was killing her. She was going to cry again. Why had she ever had to encounter him? She'd had Peter.

The crying reached sobbing stage.

Peter could never have made her hurt like this. She would never have been extreme and lost control around him . . . except to bash his boring brains out if he hadn't stopped droning on about his mother!

She'd . . . *lost George*. Not that she'd ever had him. *Loss, desolation, betrayal.* She was insane. Help. She'd get help.

The tears fell faster. She pulled up her scarf to cover her eyes, too.

George walked away from Susie's building. She'd gone to work. He could go to her school. But his turning up could blow her anonymity. He'd come back later. He'd come back again and again.

Whether she agreed to see him was another matter.

CHAPTER 12

Cassie finally found the courage from somewhere to enter the grounds of the Montague family's private chapel.

She had meant to visit yesterday, but had fled as she reached the ornate wrought metal gate at the graveyard's entrance. As the gate now closed behind her, she reaffirmed her need to do this.

She'd spoken to Rachael on the phone. Well, no, she'd *bawled* down the phone at her, wailing about how the places, the dates, *everything* matched, and how horrifyingly familiar everything was. And then there were her memories – Kathryn's memories – which now, triggered by the setting, or perhaps her final acceptance, flooded her head.

Put it to bed, Rachael counselled. Learn from it. Redeem where possible. But look forward, not back.

Forward, not back, Cassie reminded herself. What had her life become having to rely on the counsel of Rachael Jones? And Cassie Silbury didn't *bawl*! Although that's exactly what she felt like doing all over again.

She took a deep shaky breath. Forward not back

was sensible. But it was so much easier said than done. Because Kathryn was becoming more and more a part of her . . . and she hated her! Each thing she remembered made her loathe her all the more. And she'd been her. She'd done those things. Manipulated, conspired, plotted, hated . . . and ultimately destroyed. How was she ever going to live with the guilt?

Cassie took another deep shuddery breath and made her eyes focus on the inscription upon the stone tomb now before her.

Lord Frederic Montague
Son of the Earl and Countess of Worton
Died 1826. Aged 22 years

She sank to her knees. 'I'm so sorry, Freddie,' she murmured repeatedly over the course of several minutes, all the time fighting to regain control.

She finally reached a better place where she told herself again and again: I am Cassie Silbury; *not* Kathryn Montague.

Cassie took a deep breath and relinquished the bowl of soft peach roses she clutched to her chest. She placed them on the wet ground. She then stroked a hard, cold cherub's face; one formed each corner of the tomb.

'I promise you now, Freddie, I will do everything in my power to see you and Hannah reunited. You've found each other again, you know. There can be no more denial. I watched your reunion in that consulting room. Heard your words . . .' She swallowed hard. 'You're George now. I see that. And I love you so very much and I think he's already in love with Susie – your Hannah.

'I'm not like Kathryn. I promise you I'm not. I'm on your side. So is Rachael – Tessa. And getting you and Hannah back together . . .' Cassie released a shaky sigh, 'might just get me through this mentally intact.'

With one last gentle stroke of the tomb Cassie determinedly rose from the ground. She spared a glance around her. The beautifully kept grounds, surrounded by their short curving brick-built wall and with the small Norman chapel at their heart, were all familiar to her, thanks to Kathryn.

As she focused on the chapel's porch, she experienced Kathryn's latest snapshot from the past: Freddie's funeral. Cassie inhaled sharply at the subject matter . . . and nearly choked on that breath as her eyes clashed with those of the man standing framed in the doorway, a distraught woman at his side.

Matthew Argylle.

He appeared to be looking straight at her and the look in his cold blue eyes . . . so, so icy cold. No emotion. He may have been the past and long dead and gone, but his gaze seemed to slice through her. Cassie shivered, instinctively wrapping her arms tightly around her body.

Kathryn had thought herself in love with this

man, although as far as Cassie was concerned, it hadn't been love – more being in love with the idea of having him, with finally getting what she'd made up her mind to get. Cassie could find no love within Kathryn, despite all her desperate soul-searching. Only hate.

Such cold, cold eyes . . . He had been her partner in crime. *No! Kathryn's* partner in crime. The two masterminds. Tessa, aka Rachael, just did what was ordered. Although the knowledge Kathryn had of Tessa's yearning looks at a man, had served her – *Kathryn!* – well. So, so easy to manipulate. They had all been.

Cassie frowned as her head attempted to intrude, to point her in the direction of something. But it hadn't a hope with those eyes fixed upon her . . . and the memories of the even colder Kathryn.

Kathryn hadn't cried. Her brother was dead and she hadn't even *cried*! Dead because of her and Argylle's efforts to prise him away from Hannah. Freddie was to marry Prudence. *Not* Hannah. That was the plan. So simple.

Cassie attempted to divert her gaze to look at the sobbing woman to Matthew's right: Prudence, his sister. But Cassie's eyes seemed frozen to the frigid depths of Matthew Argylle's eyes. She couldn't move them no matter how hard she tried. It was like that time George got his tongue stuck to the frozen door mirror of the yet to be defrosted family car. She desperately clutched at the memory. A Cassie memory. She wasn't Kathryn. She was

Cassie Silbury. Such memories made her who she was. *Not* Kathryn Montague's!

George had decided to lick the frost. He never made that mistake again. In fact none of them would. He may have only stayed like that for a matter of minutes before Mum came to the rescue with warm water, but he was terrified. As was she. Their brothers didn't help. Telling George any movement and his tongue would be ripped off. The hysterical tears streamed down his face. Cassie was what four, five? She recalled standing on tiptoes and stretching up to use Molly the dolly's dress to wipe away his tears. This was her life. *Not* Kathryn Montague's. But she still couldn't quash Kathryn's memory! The bitch was determined to have it play out.

The Montagues and Argylles had long hoped for a union between Freddie and Prudence. Not that Freddie ever played ball. But Prudence loved him and had done for years. How much Matthew artificially fed that love with lies about Freddie's own feelings towards Prudence, Cassie could only guess at. But it was in character. In the event, Prudence would have done anything to secure Freddie. And that proved useful.

But Matthew and Kathryn didn't plot just to see Prudence happy. They'd been incapable of such selflessness. For Matthew it was about money, nothing more, nothing less. He was after the money the union between his sister and Freddie would afford him access to. And once that was secure, he'd continue in his own longer shot pursuit of some foreign heiress. Not that he'd told Kathryn the latter, of course. She'd not discovered that fact until the end. No, Kathryn had believed his words that a union between the two of them would follow that of Freddie and Prudence.

For Kathryn . . .?

Cassie physically retched as she thought of what it had been about for Kathryn. The action ensured she finally managed to snap her eyes away from Matthew Argylle's. Oh, she had wanted Matthew Argylle, but she had also wanted to see Freddie – the golden boy – suffer. She had yearned to see him struggle. To be denied. And along had come Hannah. He could be denied the one thing he wanted above all else.

For Kathryn had despised her brother. A sentiment fuelled by jealousy and resentment. And as far as Cassie was concerned: mental imbalance.

Cassie sat down on the cold gravel path and hugged her knees to her chest.

Freddie could do no wrong. Freddie could charm and had done so since the cradle. Freddie possessed looks and charisma that guaranteed whomever or whatever he wanted was his. Bar the love of his sister.

Kathryn was the eldest, yet Worton Hall, *her* home, would be Freddie's. Kathryn could only ever do wrong. Kathryn alienated rather than charmed, not that she tried the latter and she rather enjoyed the former. Kathryn's looks weren't even deemed passable. And when they had both been ill, it was *she* that had been left with pox marks across her face. Not *he*! Oh no, nothing would mar that beautiful face. Except pain.

While Freddie didn't have the love of his sibling, Kathryn *did* have the love of hers. Despite all she had done to him over the years. So forgiving! So perfect! So stupid! *She* had been the intelligent one!

It had taken what had happened at the end to finally alienate that love.

Cassie hugged her knees yet tighter to her chest. How could a sister hate a brother so much? And George had been Freddie!

How could anyone hate George? Cassie *wasn't* like Kathryn. She'd never hated George and never could, even when he'd made her cry as a child. She'd always loved him. In fact she'd always loved him best. George undoubtedly possessed looks and charm that neither she nor her other brothers had a hope of matching. And he could pretty much have whatever or whomever he wanted. But she didn't hate him for it! She loved him! Okay, Cassie never faced what Kathryn had; the restrictions on women of her day. Cassie would be pissed. Definitely. But it wasn't Freddie's fault! Kathryn had been sick. She had to have been. Otherwise, Cassie was going to have to label herself as evil-reincarnate.

She swallowed painfully, and tentatively braved another glance around her. Matthew and Prudence still stood in the doorway, but they were fading. She tried to find Tessa – Rachael – among the other attendees. A friendly face would be *really* comforting right now . . . but she wasn't there.

Cassie shut her eyes and urged the flashback to disappear completely. She focused on the present. Her: Cassie Silbury. George, Susie, Mum, Greg, Mark, her nieces and nephews, even the Nutty Regresser. Then there was her editor and all her newspaper colleagues and her work and . . . She took a few calming breaths and forced her eyes open. Matthew Argylle was gone. They were gone. She closed her eyes again and thanked God, or whoever the hell she was supposed to thank, for such mercies.

Cassie made herself stand and ordered her now numb legs to move. She wasn't finished here yet. She walked slowly past the tombs holding Freddie and Kathryn's parents. Numb. She felt nothing. She wasn't surprised. Kathryn cared for no one but herself.

Cassie now stood before a smaller, less elaborate tomb.

Kathryn Montague
Died 1827. Aged 27 years

She stared. And stared.
And then spoke the words she needed to say.
'You nasty, scheming, malicious, evil, psycho-bitch! How could you have done it? How could

you have done it to Freddie. To *George*! To *my* George! You killed him. You killed them! It may as well have been by your own hand.'

Cassie finally stopped physically beating the cold hard stone and let out a string of curses. She should have brought a sledgehammer with her. Her bare fists were futile. There was no crumbling. Not even a crack. But her knuckles were bruised and bleeding. She nursed them by crossing her arms and placing them under her armpits.

She wasn't remotely satisfied. But took some comfort in knowing that Kathryn had never secured Matthew Argylle. After Freddie's funeral he'd gone to the Continent, not at all interested in marriage to Kathryn. Her dowry had never tempted him and the Hall and title would eventually pass to a male cousin. Cassie very much doubted, however, any amount of money would have tempted Matthew Argylle into marrying Kathryn. They'd worked together. He would have seen at least a glimpse of what she was. And Kathryn had thought she was the intelligent one. Had thought she'd known about manipulation.

The last news Kathryn had of him before she died was that he was engaged to a Spanish heiress. There had been no broken heart, just raging anger.

Cassie spared one last disgusted look at the tomb. She was wasting no more time on the dead and buried Kathryn Montague. She refused to allow her to live on.

She knew what she must do. First there was

George and Susie to sort out. Rachael called it redemption. No, she had a feeling, it was love.

Then there was her writing. Perhaps Rachael had been right? Would the journalist in her be able to resist this story? She had it in her power to prove the existence of past lives. She might even be able to prove the existence of Soul Mates, although she needed to give that one significantly more thought. But it was potentially huge.

Cassie turned and walked along the winding gravel path and through the metal gate.

There had been no Hannah to see. Hannah and Freddie hadn't been buried together. Separated in life and in death. Until now, Cassie vowed.

Hannah's was a grave within the grounds of the village church. Cassie had been there this morning, while not yet ready to visit Freddie and Kathryn.

Hannah Marsh
Daughter of Sir Gerald and Lady Jane Marsh
Died 1826. Aged 17 years

Cassie left her a matching bowl of roses. They were her favourite.

She now knew Freddie had regularly raided Worton Hall's rose garden. He picked Hannah her blooms in the dead of night. During their secret meetings, he presented them to her. He loved to see the look on her face during those precious moments. To be in receipt of such a look, he believed, made him the most blessed creature on earth.

Freddie considered Hannah his. And his alone. *Forever.*

Cassie had so far read only one of the letters between Freddie and Hannah. She had been loaned a bundle of them by the present day Montagues who had kept them in a cupboard in the impressive library at Worton Hall. The only change Cassie could discern to Kathryn's time living there was the computer on the desk, the electric lighting and the family photographs. Even the furniture was familiar.

The present day Montagues viewed Freddie and Hannah's relationship as a tragic love story. The extent of Kathryn's role – and Matthew Argylle's – had been found out upon her death, when her own correspondence was discovered. Cassie declined their offer of borrowing those letters, too. She possessed far too much insight into the evil mechanics of Kathryn's mind as it was.

Zapping her car remote with her bruised right hand, Cassie climbed into the driver's seat. Glancing at her mobile on its housing, she noted thirteen missed calls. She knew who it would be. She'd missed a series of deadlines over recent days for promised stories and her editor was on the warpath. She'd get right back to work tonight. Rachael was right. This *had* helped.

As Cassie put the car into reverse and twisted in her seat to look behind, she spotted the bundle of letters sat next to her handbag on the back seat. They'd been penned by both Hannah and Freddie.

She had never expected to find anything Freddie wrote and sent to Hannah, but Hannah's family had discovered Freddie's letters upon her death and emotively returned them, blaming the already devastated Freddie for her demise. As if he'd needed any more twists of the knife in those final days before he, too, died. After all, Kathryn had been self-appointed chief knife-turner.

Cassie put the car into first gear and her foot heavily on the accelerator pedal. She was going to leave Kathryn Montague where she lay. But learn from her. She would read all of Hannah and Freddie's letters. She had to know. And no. There was no forgetting the journalist in her.

She just couldn't brave reading them today.

CHAPTER 13

George hated appearances on television talk shows such as this. And this one was a biggie. Michael was all hyped up, reminding George of all the things he needed to mention: the films about to come out; the one he was currently filming; future projects. Then there was the live broadcast warning. Etc. Etc. Etc. George didn't need to listen to Michael's words. He knew what he was meant to say. He'd played this part a hundred times over.

But tonight was going to be different.

Susie wasn't returning his calls, was never in or refused to answer when he went to her building and he was desperate.

There was a flurry of last-minute activity around him. The presenter was doing the usual blurgh. The orchestra burst into music. That was his cue.

Don't balls this up George.

He walked out onto set, remembered to smile at the applauding and whistling audience, moved to shake hands with the now standing presenter, then sat down.

The audience was still whooping away. Blushing,

George raised his lowered head to provide a small smile of appreciation. It was all he could manage in the circumstances, and finally things quietened down. The presenter looked at him with intent.

George took a deep mustering breath. Here we go.

'Oh. Dear. George!'

The audience laughed. Predictable really and George shook his head with what was hopefully a wry smile on his face, rather than a grimace.

'You've been in the press a lot this week!'

More laughter.

'But your people have given me strict orders not to talk to you about that. So I suppose we're going to have to talk about the new film. The reason why you're back on your home turf and . . . getting *entertained* at the local nightspots!'

More laughter and George forced another smile, while clasping his hands tightly together on his lap. He took a very large intake of air and raised his head to face the presenter.

'I don't mind talking about that night, Jonathan.'

Loud applause and whoops.

'Susie! Susie! Get your butt in here!'

'For crying out loud, Rach! I was about to get in the shower! What on earth is—?' Susie froze mid-hop in her bedroom doorway, instinctively grabbing the door for balance. She stood motion-less, dressed in a T-shirt, off-white panties, and with her jeans hanging off one foot.

Rachael frantically pointed at the TV, while

pulling cushions off the sofa and sending them scattering across the room, her usual method of hunting for the remote control.

But Susie needed no direction. She could see exactly who was on the screen. And her whole being cried out.

'He's just volunteered to speak to Jonathan James about Monday night!' Rachael squealed. 'I can't find the remote. I need to record this. Will you get in here *now*?'

2D, 3D . . . she couldn't do it. How could she have thought she could feel no worse? It was Sunday night and she'd been a wreck all week. No amount of self-counselling lessening the impact of the separation. The pain threatened to submerge her now. She closed her eyes.

What was he going to say? Was he going for name and shame? Had the newspaper piece not been enough? It was her own fault. She should never, *ever* have been in his actual presence.

She felt physically sick. She should go to the bathroom, but was rooted to the spot. If she could get herself there, she could even surrender to that part of her that yearned to sit on the cold tiled floor, hugging her knees, slowly rocking herself backwards and forwards.

The Addams Family theme tune entered the pitiful pulp that was once a functioning brain. No sooner had it sluggishly processed, then it silenced as Rachael answered her mobile.

'Cassie! *Yes*, it's on now.' Rachael still scooted

around wreaking havoc with her free hand. 'Are you recording it? I can't find the remote and . . .'

Covering the phone, she yelled, 'Susie! *Help me out here!*'

He felt physically sick. So much rested on him getting this right.

'George. Just for the benefit of us all here. Did you just say you *will* talk about that night?'

'Absolutely. You have the exclusive straight from Saint George's mouth . . . although the horn isn't coming out. And for the record, it didn't then either.'

Laughter and clapping from the audience.

'Very good.' Jonathan James chuckled.

George pretended not to see Michael in the wings, although he had a clear view of him from his seat. Michael was repeatedly doing the cutting sign across his throat. It was pretty easy to read his lips, too. George returned his eyes to the presenter before him.

'Wow. I won't be needing the autocue then. Can someone get me a pen and paper? I'm going to need to scribble some questions. But here's one for now. Tell me . . . was it *worth it?*'

More laughter.

Deep breath and a prayer. 'At the time it was. At the time it blew my mind.'

'I bet!'

More laughter.

George felt the blush sweep across his face. 'It

did.' He shook his head and looked intently at the presenter, 'But it wasn't what it looked like. This really isn't easy for me to talk about. I've never spoken about my private life before, but in this instance, where another person is involved like this, and there's even a price out on their head, I feel I need to.'

In his peripheral vision, George could see things getting heated. Michael was being restrained. He'd known he wouldn't be happy. Image and all that, but he hadn't expected him to get this upset. But he was doing this, whatever.

'Such an intensely private moment should never have happened in public. That was my fault and I will never forgive myself for the position it has put the woman concerned in. It was a private party, but that was public enough.' He looked at his grasped hands upon his knees. 'It was a very, very intimate . . . incredible moment. It wasn't cheap and tacky like the papers have portrayed it. I was with the most beautiful, compelling woman I have ever met. I forgot myself.' He looked at the presenter with a wry smile, 'I kind of do that around her. I don't act remotely normally. It's scary. The extreme . . .'

He was rambling.

He shook his head and looked at his hands. 'I knew I was going to muck this up. I don't have a script. I tried to come up with what I needed to say, but it's not coming out right!'

Laughter. He liked to think it was sympathetic.

'Ummm.' He leant forward, his forearms on his knees, hands grasped, head down and staring blindly. 'It's scary as hell but she makes me feel . . . She does something to me. I kind of feel . . .Well, I can't say how I feel because it will sound crazy, but . . . we haven't spent enough time together. She's kind of addictive. I'm not sure there would ever be enough time to . . .'

'Because of work commitments?'

'No. Because there's not enough time in the world to . . .' He took a deep breath and sat back in his seat. 'We haven't spent enough time together because I screwed up. I would like to be able to talk to her but she's . . .'

'She's *dumped* you?'

'Don't sound so surprised. I messed up big time. I haven't secured her trust and I want that more than anything and . . . I'm probably scaring her with the way I'm sounding . . .' He met the presenter's eyes. 'Do I sound mad to you?'

He laughed. 'No, you sound like you've got it *baaad* mate!'

Laughter and a few claps and a few *aaaahhhs*.

'I'd settle for anything. Anything she felt able to give. We could take it slow, quick, whatever she wants. I'm game. I want us to talk though. To talk until the cows come home. I want to find out every tiny little thing about her. I want to hear her laugh again and . . . I'm so setting myself up for a fall here! I feel like I'm baring my soul. And I've just realised my family are going to be watching

155

this – and *my mum!*' He rubbed his forehead. 'But what have I got to lose? My pride I suppose. But I've got more than enough of that on set at the moment.'

'*Pride and Prejudice*, ladies and gentlemen. George Silbury is the next Mr Darcy. And of course, Porsche Sutter-Blythe is your Elizabeth. We were under the impression you two were an item?'

George looked pointedly at the presenter. 'You, of all people, know not to believe everything you read. You've had your fair share of coverage in the gossip columns recently.'

'Bollocks the lot of it!'

Laughter.

'Exactly. You have to understand as well that leads are always linked.'

'Porsche's on record as saying—'

'I can't talk about what Porsche may or may not have said. I don't believe what I read. She's on your show in a couple of weeks, so no doubt you can talk to her then. She's a great actress and is doing a fantastic job as Elizabeth, but our relationship has only ever been professional.'

'So where did you and this mystery woman meet? I'm assuming you're still keeping her a mystery? You don't feel like enlightening us?'

'What do you think?'

Laughter.

'It was worth a try. Well, where did you meet?'

'In unusual circumstances, but I won't say any more than that.'

'I'm afraid we have to wind up here. George
. . . you've put the record straight there. Whoever
she is must be very special because that took
some balls. Once you guys have got your act
together . . . remember me when writing wedding
invites!'

'Yes. Yes. Yes and . . . if only.'

'Ladies and Gentlemen, *George Silbury!*'

'Suse? Susie? *Flaming Nora!* Will you stop staring
blankly like that and get up from down there! We
have things to talk about and there's *no* way you
are avoiding them.'

Susie's eyes began to focus again and she realised
she was sat on the floor in her bedroom doorway.
Rachael was standing before her and, as she raised
her head, she took in the hands on hips that
accompanied her words.

'I'm putting the kettle on. Then you and me are
going to talk.'

None of it made any sense. She couldn't grasp
what he appeared to have been saying. 'Rach?'

'Mmmm.'

'What did I miss?' He couldn't have been talking
about her. He must have been involved in another
sensational story of some kind. But . . . *he wasn't
with Porsche Sutter-Blythe?*

'I'm sorry? And will you get up off the *floor?*'

'What he was talking about . . . What did I miss?'

'You aren't making any sense here. He was
talking about you! *You,* you silly mare! Do you

157

have *any* idea how lucky you are? I get Matey and you—' Rachael cut herself off. 'Kettle.'

Nothing was making sense. And now she was losing all sense of reality. 'Rach. I need help; professional help. I've crossed that line.'

Rachael was suddenly there, plonking herself down on the floor in front of her. 'You don't need professional help, Suse,' she said gently. 'You just need to remove the blinkers and see what's happening here. You met a man. In unconventional circumstances, but you nevertheless met. True or false?'

Not *any* man . . . And he wasn't with Porsche? And they weren't laughing together? He wasn't seeking revenge?

'Suse. True or false?'

'True . . . I think. Oh God, I'm so confused.'

'You have chemistry going on between you. A *lot* of chemistry. True or false?'

'I don't know what it is or if he—'

'He's just announced to the world he loses control around you. That he finds you compelling. That it's extreme. Therefore he feels it. Do you feel it?'

'I feel something but . . .' He couldn't feel it too. How could he feel it too? 'It's not normal and—'

'And thanks be it's not, otherwise you and he would be launching yourself at everyone! Instead you both react to each other. What's wrong with you guys not being able to keep your hands off each other? And you can hardly tell me you don't enjoy it. And he's just told everyone how good it is for him. So, I ask again, you have chemistry going on between you. True or false?'

'It's not that—'

'Yes it is! He reacts to you. You react to him. End of. So, true or false?'

'I can't think! It doesn't make any sense. Just *look* at me!'

'I'd rather not thank you.'

'Exactly! He's got Porsche Sutter-Blythe . . . *no . . . not now.*' She knew she was frowning. 'But he's got all the beautiful—'

'He wants you!'

'That makes no—'

'Did he or did he not just call you the most beautiful, compelling woman he has ever met?'

'He can't mean it. He can't . . . I'm losing any sense of reality here. If he really said that then he's as mad as me, but—'

'He feels it too! You can call it mad, call it whatever you want. Just don't ignore it! Tell me why the blazes you can't be mad together? What harm can come of it?'

'This is doing my head in. It's nonsensical, it's—'

'I don't know how you can say that, Suse. You hardly look like the back-end of a bus. Okay, you might not be in the Sutter-Blythe league, but who is? You have lovely red-blonde hair, gorgeous eyes, appealing impish dimples and a stunning smile. You are *beautiful*! You've got a lovely body to boot, too. So what that you wear size twelve clothes rather than size six . . .'

'Fourteen,' Susie murmured. 'The last jeans I bought were a fourteen.'

'No! Seriously? No wonder you kept that quiet. But so what? You do it for him, Suse. You do it for George Silbury, you lucky cow! I know you're scared, but you can't honestly tell me you'd prefer to be with the boring shite?'

She could *never* be with Peter after she'd felt this way with George. She'd ended it. How could she ever be with *anyone* else? She was ruined. She was going to die an old desiccated maid.

'George is scared too. So why can't you be scared together?'

She wanted to believe he could feel this way so much. Although her pitiful mushed up head wasn't as remotely keen as the rest of her. It was haemorrhaging those awful sensations again. It seemed to want to remind her why she couldn't go there. Frantically remind her, as if it saw George Silbury as the biggest threat Susie Morris could ever face.

'I know you're anti-love, Suse, but there is nothing stopping you simply testing the water. Nobody is saying plunge straight in at the deep end. He said he'll take whatever you're prepared to offer. Don't you owe it to yourself, to both of you, to just see what you have here? What harm can it do? If it goes wrong, then you're just back to where you are now. And anyway, I think you're forgetting about the sex here. Sex with George Silbury!'

She *so* wasn't. Her body wasn't letting her. She

closed her eyes. She needed her head here. But . . . firstly it made no sense. Secondly . . . it made no sense. Thirdly . . . *Jesus!*

'I need to get my head around this. To try and . . .' She trailed off.

She had to do something with herself, but didn't know what. She pushed herself up from the floor and aimlessly revolved. She paused as her eyes took in her bed. That would be something. And perhaps she'd wake up in the morning and everything would make sense. She'd likely find she had been living in some bizarre parallel universe. In the morning she would find herself back in a pre-George Silbury in the flesh existence and . . .

Her whole being, minus her head, wailed at the idea. She needed sleep. She needed oblivion.

'Umm. Bed. I'll be gone early in the morning. School trip to Canterbury. Night, night.'

George wasn't listening to Michael, although it was evident that he was furious and he'd been vaguely aware of him on the phone to Porsche. He'd attempted an escape, bypassing the limo, but Michael caught up with him just before his taxi pulled away.

George was reflecting. He had done what needed to be done. He'd said his piece. And he prayed it had more of an impact than his countless phone messages and fruitless ringing of Susie's door buzzer. He had never felt more helpless than during this past week. Neither had he ever wanted anyone or anything more. But he was frustrated at every step. It was like repeatedly banging his head against a brick wall – hard, really hard – and not stopping until it was bloodied and . . . it was currently pulverised.

What if she didn't respond? He let out a shaky breath. He couldn't allow himself to contemplate that.

The taxi turned the corner onto his road. 'Up by the black car,' George directed the driver before they came to a stop.

'See you tomorrow, Michael,' he muttered, climbing out of the taxi.

'Not so fast!' Michael blocked the door George was slamming shut with his chunky leg and a grunt. He followed him out. 'We've things to talk about.'

'Not tonight. Tonight—' George spotted Cassie rushing towards him.

'Cas? What are you doing here?'

'Come here big broth. I think you deserve a hug. I've brought some liquid refreshments and just wanted to . . . well, give you a hug!'

'You can't drink tonight, George. You've an early start in the morning.'

George grinned as Cassie broke away from the promised hug to give Michael her 'you are a slug' look. It really couldn't be good to be on the receiving end of that. And it had the desired effect because Michael was now back in the taxi and closing the door.

George watched with relief as it pulled away. He started moving towards the house with the carrier bag Cassie had brought with her.

'Cas?' She wasn't following, but standing motionless, staring after the taxi. 'Cas?'

'Sorry . . .' she said, frowning and rubbing her hands up and down her arms as if she were cold. 'It felt like someone walked over my grave. I'm . . .' She shook her head. 'I'm fine.' She now turned to smile at him and started following.

George reached for her hand with his free one, stopping short as he felt bandages. 'Oh God, Cas, what have you done?'

Cassie lay in her bed later that night. Well, the early hours actually. The clock was currently reading 3.17. She couldn't sleep. Her mind refused to switch off. It seemed to be seeking some kind of answer through its frenetic activity. It wasn't to do with work, she was sure of it. She'd nailed her latest piece on the arms trade. Rachael had been right. She was finding a place for the past and managing to get on with the present. More than managing. And the idea that George was on the cusp of happiness felt great. It went a long way to nullifying the guilt she couldn't help but feel for Kathryn's actions. It was Kathryn, *not you*, she urgently reminded herself.

Yes George and Susie had yet to get their act together, but they would, she was sure of it. It wasn't Rachael's talk of Soul Mates that told her that because she was still struggling with that one, or more specifically, the *details* of that one: *love but with supernatural cherries on top?* Rachael couldn't even point to the source of her information. 'I just *know*. Born with it. A gift. Call it what you want but I reckon we all know about them, but just aren't listening.' Cassie sighed. No, it was seeing George. He had it seriously bad. And according to Rachael, so did Susie. It was just a matter of time before they sorted themselves out.

So what was preventing her sleep? Not having the remotest idea what her mind was trying to piece together, Cassie rolled over and turned on the bedside lamp.

She reached over to retrieve a letter from the top of the bundle on her bedside table. It was one from Freddie.

Thursday morning

My dear Miss Marsh,

I beg you will read this letter and pray that the fact you were not walking upon your usual paths was as a consequence of the unseasonably wet and stormy weather and not because of any wish to avoid me.

No doubt you will have heard of my visit to The Grange on Tuesday last, made with the excuse of inviting your father to a shoot. Whilst hoping to encounter you at your home gave me temporary respite from the elements, I was disappointed. The only comfort I seek Miss Marsh (or may I be so bold as to call you Hannah?), is that of being in your presence.

It has been my desperate desire to speak with you, after what happened, but I now have no recourse but to resort to pen and paper. I am far from an accomplished letter writer, however, and would therefore urge you to make allowances for this. My no doubt rambling, possibly insensible and almost certainly indecipherable attempt follows.

I am sorry! I am sorry! I am sorry! Never before have words been used with such heart-felt sincerity or with such desperate need for forgiveness. I am speaking them aloud as I write them upon the page. I am furious with myself for having put you in such a position, more furious than any man can ever have been with himself nor ever will be.

I am at least able to provide you with some peace of mind by assuring you that your identity remains a secret. You have my word no scandal will befall you or your family.

I beg you will send me some indication of your forgiveness!

Yours, in hope,
Frederic Montague

'Oh Freddie,' Cassie murmured fondly, repositioning both herself and her pillows in order to sit up. With the benefit of Kathryn's memories, she knew what he was referring to. Cassie giggled.

It had been at a private ball at the Fitzwilliams's. They held one every summer, although none before or after could have lived up to that one of 1826.

After the first several hours of dancing in hot, stifling conditions, the four hundred or so guests had answered the summons to the cooler gardens for a firework display in a near stampede. As that first firework whizzed and banged and then provided its dramatic flash . . . it hadn't only been the sky that was lit up.

But also a seat amongst the shrubbery, housing a couple in a most compromising position.

Freddie and Hannah's saving grace was the momentary nature of the illumination and they took full advantage of the restored cover of darkness. For with the next flash, only one person, Freddie, appeared upon the bench – much to the disappointment of the erstwhile gleeful audience. Indeed, a collective groan sounded.

But the speculation. Hannah had been obscured from view during the illumination, but illumination was what buzzing society desired. Wagers were even placed on the betting books of gentlemen's clubs across London as to the identity of the mystery woman. But keeping a low profile, Freddie and Hannah managed to save her

166

reputation. Not to say that, as time went by, people didn't begin to put two and two together. But society couldn't be sure, and by then Freddie had made his intentions abundantly clear.

And that had been the problem.

On that sobering note, Cassie continued reading the next letter.

Thursday afternoon

My dear Miss Marsh,

As I have had nothing by way of a reply to my letter to you of this morning, I am in despair. However, it occurred to me that perhaps you have not yet found the means of conveying a message to me. I therefore thought it best to write again to inform you that by the gate leading into the watercress meadows, there is a large oak tree. Whilst hoping to encounter you, I discovered a hole in the trunk some six hands up on the west side, hidden under vegetation growing from a knot above. If you were to be kind enough to write to me, the hole is large enough to hold a letter and appeared dry, despite the then torrential rain. I will visit it daily, in the hope of a word from you. I pray you take pity upon me and leave me a letter!

I can only reiterate my apology. My conduct was wholly unpardonable and so much beneath that of a gentleman, I can no longer refer to myself as such. The faculty of rational thought deserted me the moment my eyes rested upon you again.

On seeing you so pale after your energetic dance with Mr Richard Barratt, a gentleman in possession of sense would have sought out your mother or the Misses Barratt. I, however, felt compelled to follow you into the gardens instead. I had to assure myself as to your well-being – and to be near you, if only for a brief moment.

I then compounded my faux-pas. On satisfying myself as to your health, I remained, taking un-gentlemanly advantage of your being alone. I did not grasp this, the most precious of opportunities, of conversing with you, as I should have done. Indeed, my head is beyond full, Miss Marsh – Hannah, of questions as to your likes, your dislikes, your dreams, your fears. Alas, they remained unsaid.

My only excuse being that, in that moment, holding you within my arms was as necessary to me as the air I breathe.

My regrets about what happened are merely with regard to the consequences my actions have had for you and of your possible opinion as to my character and intentions. Not of the moment itself. For it was the most precious of my now miserable existence. Out of your arms, I am the most wretched of creatures.

My dearest – and you have unquestionably

rendered me yours – I am at your command. I fervently hope that you will not feel compelled upon any course of action as a result of my abominable failings. Your identity is safe. But should you so desire, I would most willingly call upon your father to ask for your hand in marriage.

I am aware enough of my failures to realise that you may wish never to set eyes on me again. Should that be the case, I concede you have every right to feel thus. But please do not think for a moment that I will resign myself to such a fate. For I intend to win you. You occupy my thoughts to the exclusion of all else, as well as all my dreams, as has been the case since that first encounter in church.

There I watched your every move, both your fond smiles and where necessary, frowns for your young brothers; the raised eyebrows for your father. Then there were the dancing eyes for the Misses Barratt – and their brother – and the well practised politeness for the Reverend.

The moment your eyes were raised to mine as I returned to you your shawl, I believe I became yours. You awakened within my being something so staggering in its intensity, it is both awe-inspiring and terrifying. To ignore it would, however, be to condemn myself to the most barren and desolate of existences. A hell not worth living.

Would that you felt just the tiniest degree of that which you inspire within me, I would cry from the rooftops, 'I am the luckiest man alive for Hannah Marsh adores me!'

You have in your power my destruction or my salvation. I beg of you to look within yourself. If there is any return of sentiment, no matter how small, please grasp it!

For I am free to wed Hannah, would you but have me. I am aware that my name has been linked with that of Miss Prudence Argylle. Since we were babes in arms, our families have talked of a union in order to strengthen the two estates, but this has never been my intention. There are no feelings involved on my part and the lady in question is aware of my sentiments. I will ensure that my position is made publicly clear as well.

Before I send this via a trusted messenger, I would just like to add one thing – if you should hear of an unfortunate public altercation, know that it was but a result of my inability to have our moment together cheapened. Rest assured, your identity remains secure.

Yours, dearest Hannah, I am yours should you but have me.
Frederic (Freddie) Montague

Cassie smiled as she refolded the letter and placed it on the bedside table. God Freddie had

it bad. Just like George! And an unfortunate altercation? Freddie basically called Lord Alistair
Granger out in front of most of the Ton – society's
elite of the day – on overhearing his comments on
the notorious indiscretion. If their relationship had
not been strong and sense reached, Freddie would
have found himself duelling one of his closest
friends at dawn.

Cassie reached out for another letter. But
stopped.

The next letter might . . . She wasn't up to that
tonight. She promptly switched off the light. But
why was her head doing that damned nudging
thing again?

CHAPTER 14

'Ronald,' Susie groaned. She now addressed the child sat next to her at the front of the coach. 'In the bucket, sweetheart. In. The. Bucket.'

She held the plastic wastepaper basket, lined with a carrier bag, in position and turned away as her own stomach heaved.

Ronald Wittering was child number five to succumb to travel sickness and the coach wasn't currently the most pleasant place to be. They were out of buckets and baskets and there were three seats no longer fit for purpose. Fresh air was a long distant memory.

They were on the way to Canterbury, Susie counselled. This was not a literal journey to hell, but she didn't see how it could get much worse than this. She'd have struggled with this coach journey at the best of times, but hadn't slept a wink last night. And the past couple of weeks had been little better. Once upon a time she'd taken a good night's sleep for granted.

Susie turned instinctively on hearing suspicious giggles from several rows back. '*Joseph Robinson!*'

The bloody child had his trousers down, evidently about to moon out of the window. He met her eyes. He instantaneously pulled up his trousers, spun himself back around in his seat, plonked himself down, fastened his seat belt, and now sat like a little angel.

Okaaaaaay. Her eyes were obviously reflecting her mood rather well.

Susie swallowed hard as her physical senses sent the most horrible, *horrible* scenario to her brain. There was a feeling of warmth on her hand and then that which now seeped through to her lap. She slowly turned back around. Yes. Ronald had missed the bucket!

Hearing a sympathetic sound to her left she met the eyes of a parent-helper across the aisle. That sympathetic look was going to be her undoing. Susie meekly smiled back. She couldn't open the floodgates. Not here and now.

But she was so tired.

And her life no longer felt real. For the past eleven days it had been either – thinking of this journey it was particularly apt – *hell* or heaven. Extremes, with nothing halfway normal in-between.

And George Silbury was at its heart. A Hollywood film star: a man it should have been impossible to ever meet; a man whose appearance in 2D alone incited a reaction in her that had had her questioning her state of mind for a decade.

But George Silbury in the flesh . . .

Susie gulped and closed her eyes, urging her body to behave.

Rachael's consulting room: hell. Her body, not suffering her head's amnesia, strongly protested. *It* voted for heaven.

Discovering what she'd done in Rachael's consulting room: hell.

Lunch with Peter: hell . . . except for that incredible tingling sensation. Susie snapped her eyes open. It had been *him*! George Silbury had been in that restaurant. It had been *him* making her all hot and needy. She groaned at the strength of her reaction to him while not even knowing he was in *the room*.

Coming face-to-face with George Silbury outside the restaurant. Her body all but purred at the recollection. But it had been so much more. The way he made her feel simply by looking at her with those eyes. And the touch of his hand on her elbow and then his arm around her waist. And his voice. And then he asked to take her home. And hadn't he asked to see her? But then there was Porsche Sutter-Blythe. And that walk away. Heaven *and* hell. She dared her body to dispute that one.

Susie shifted in her seat to allow repositioning of the bucket. Its weight was causing cramping in her hand. Holding it now with two, she found herself face-to-face with a green-looking Ronald Wittering. She closed her eyes.

Coming face-to-face with George Silbury on the dance floor: *No!* Had he seen that dance with Rob?

She half choked. That was a terrible thought and one she refused to consider right now.

'Miss Morris . . . You're not going to. . .?'

She shook her head, her eyes still closed. 'No Ronald. *I'm* not going to be sick on *you*.'

Finding herself in George Silbury's arms when she'd ailed on the dance floor: heaven, but then hell when she'd come to her senses and stepped away.

Hearing George Silbury laugh: heaven.

Laughing with George Silbury: heaven.

Kissing and being kissed by George Silbury: heaven.

Touching and being touched by George Silbury: heaven.

That feeling that being with him was so right. That only with him could she be complete and truly alive. Heaven . . . but so nuts!

Surrendering to the moment in George Silbury's arms: heaven, although it was hotter than hell.

Susie was now boiling hot. She didn't have any arms free and couldn't take any layers off. Why hadn't she taken her coat off before she sat down? Then she remembered what was currently in her lap and was grateful for her long coat. She was damned if she did and damned if she didn't. She blew through her lips in an attempt to cool her face and forehead.

She deliberately thought of what she knew would dampen her ardour: the newspaper article and thinking George had been in league with Porsche Sutter-Blythe. *Worse* than hell.

Telling Peter it was over: hell, although he hadn't taken it too badly. It was her; she'd felt awful.

And then there was George's declaration last night. And she had no idea how to label that. Because . . . Oh God, she wanted it to be heaven. She wanted it to be heaven so much. Well, at least her body did. No it was more than that. Her body and soul did. In fact all of her did, except her head.

Her head kept telling her it all made no sense. He couldn't possibly be attracted to her. That he couldn't be feeling it too. And anyway . . . George Silbury was danger.

She knew why her head saw him as such. There was no question, Susie realised on a shaky exhale of breath: George Silbury had the capacity to destroy her. Her head was just making sure she didn't forget it.

'Miss Morris?'

'It's okay, Ronald. I just sighed.'

She sighed again. Every time she used her head she was right back there in hell: confusion, turmoil, fear and that was forgetting the questions over her sanity. Although . . . if he felt it too? Jeez, *if* he felt it too, then she wasn't dangerous, was she? It would mean it was mutual. God, she couldn't get her head around this.

Perhaps she shouldn't use her head? What would happen if . . .? Her head kindly resorted to high pitched shrieking alarm calls.

But when she didn't allow herself to think and

surrendered to what she instinctively seemed to need . . . then it was so heavenly she wanted to cry.

But how could she dismiss her head? That was like asking her to be a bundle of mindless cells. In her case, from the erogenous zones and they'd have to be complete with nerve endings . . .

She cleared her throat. 'I'm fine, Ronald,' she said, pre-empting what she knew would come.

But she wasn't being fair here. How George Silbury made her feel went way beyond her erogenous zones. He reached parts of her she'd never known existed. Made her feel . . . If she let herself feel it, there was everything there anyone could ever desire. Attraction, so much attraction, yet comfort and peace, too. It felt so right. No wonder her head was protesting so strongly.

Susie needed a middle ground though. Not, 'to think or not to think'. But was there a middle ground where George Silbury was concerned? It appeared to be extreme all the way. Like roller coasters and she'd always hated them. And she could really have done without the reminder of sick here.

She opened her eyes. Was it safe to move the bucket away? Probably not. She heard the driver speak. Glancing out of the window she saw they were nearly there.

'Ten minutes or so,' he said.

She groaned. They appeared to be closer and she'd got her hopes up.

'I know you want off here as soon as possible, love. I reckon you're thinking of changing jobs. Join the club. I've got the window open, but you'd never know for the effect it's having on things in here. I'll get us there as soon as I can, but they've closed off some roads for something or other. I can't use the usual drop off on Saint George's Lane.'

Saint George's Lane?! *Saint George's* Lane?! Her life was one big joke at the moment. On her. There was bound to be a horn in there somewhere, a hunt with herself as the prey and a price on her head.

The driver continued and she paid keen attention to prevent herself thinking anymore of Saint George and how he had *sooo* not been a saint. He'd been . . . That was the point she started listening keenly.

'I'm going to have to take you to the coach park. It'll be another ten minutes or so walk from there along the river. I'm sorry, love.'

She channelled back into her thoughts, refusing to focus on how the day was panning out. But she couldn't make head nor tail of them. She knew one thing though.

She was going to have to call George Silbury.

Being on location today was not what George needed. He took the phone out of his pocket and checked again to see if there were any missed calls.

Susie hadn't called. It was only 10.00 a.m., the

178

day after the night he'd bared his soul in front of millions . . . but she hadn't called.

Had she seen the show?

If she hadn't, she'd have seen the papers, the TV, or the internet. The fact was, if she didn't call then . . . He couldn't let himself go there. He was completely out of options. It was only ten, he told himself firmly. There was time yet.

He was sure she'd felt it too . . . Cassie had even hinted at it. She was in communication with Rachael Jones, who had suggested this wasn't one way. That Susie was no longer seeing the accountant, but that she had 'issues to resolve'. Despite his urging, Cassie had categorically refused to elaborate.

And he wasn't meant to be thinking of Susie! He and Graham, one of the cameramen, had escaped for a cigarette break. But, as if he needed a reminder, even having a cigarette led to thoughts of failed hypnosis attempts to quit and then the hypnosis eleven days ago . . .

He would have been better off never having met her. But that wasn't true. Those moments in her arms were the most incredible of his thirty-seven years. The only time he'd ever felt truly fulfilled. Not that he'd been sexually fulfilled . . .

He should never have started these thoughts. He shifted uncomfortably. But the fulfilment had been far, far deeper than that. Without her, he felt . . .

Enough! He stubbed out the cigarette against the wall and popped it in the bin. He turned to

179

Graham. He'd evidently been talking and George had heard not a word. 'Sorry,' he said.

'It's all right mate. A girl's involved so I understand. They're having to re-jig things big time for the next scene, so I reckon we've got at least an hour. I'd murder for a proper cup of tea and not out of them paper cups. And the bitch is on the warpath so . . .'

That was enough for George. The very mention of Porsche was enough to make his blood boil. He was barely in control around her, hence his making sure he was only ever in her presence in front of the camera. That way he was less likely to lose it. Darcy, being a repressed character with all that simmering nearing combustion stuff going on under the surface, was allowing him to act the part pretty much instinctively.

Even the aftermath of Elizabeth's rejection had seen him thinking of Susie and . . . *More* than enough!

George refocused on Graham. 'Right. A decent café. Let's start the hunt!'

'You know, you've caused me a right headache,' Graham moaned, as they sauntered along one of the roads cleared of traffic for filming. They headed towards the business-as-usual one up ahead. 'If you'd warned me about last night, I'd have made sure Jeannie didn't watch the show.'

George shot him a surprised glance. He really liked Graham's wife, Jeannie. She was one of the few women who didn't go all giggly on him.

'You had her in tears, mate. Sobbing away she

was. And then she just turned rabid on me. Demanding when *I* last did anything romantic for her. The long and the short of it, she decided I'd *never* done anything romantic in our nine and three-quarters years together and stomped off to bed, wittering away about how me and the kids view her as domestic staff and didn't she deserve some *respite romance*!'

If his actions had to be labelled George would have used desperate, rather than romantic. He glanced at Graham as they started across the road. 'When *did* you last do something romantic?'

'Don't *you* bloody start!'

'She's worth—'

George's words died on his lips as he and Graham were forced to sprint across the last few metres of road as a coach, evidently desperate to reach its destination, revved its snarling engine and headed straight for them.

George turned to stare at it as it passed. It was full of school children and . . . it made him think of Susie. He followed it with his eyes, scanning the rear-end writing. It was a London coach firm . . . and his body was buzzing.

He took a deep breath. Doing what he was thinking of doing was crazed.

'This way,' he muttered to Graham. And started to jog.

'Keep up!' George shouted, putting on another sprint. He was fit, he had to be in his line of work, but this was one mean coach. It hurtled through orange lights and weaved in and out of traffic as if possessed. But he refused to lose sight of it.

'What do I look like?' he asked himself, having spared a glance behind him. Graham was trailing miserably. But it was all the people stopping from going about their business to stare after him that raised the question. He was out in public in Darcy's costume again. Yes, he had his winter coat on, but it was undone and flapping behind him . . . George groaned . . . like Batman's cape.

He *was* Batman. He was set to film the sequel next year.

And then there was that little matter of running after a coach like a madman. The only saving grace was that this was Canterbury. In London he'd have a pack of paparazzi in pursuit and helicopters scrambled.

Hurling himself around a corner so he could pick up sight of the coach again, he looked skywards in thanks. It was pulling into a coach park.

CHAPTER 15

As the coach finally parked, Susie experienced the overwhelming urge to run down the steps, take a huge breath of fresh air and kiss the tarmac. The journey from hell was finally over. But then she remembered she had the journey home. She couldn't think about it. She'd think about . . . the ten-minute walk along a river bank with twenty-nine eight year olds!

'We'll get the kids off the coach while you get yourself cleaned up,' one of her teaching assistants came over to murmur in her ear. Susie smiled wanly and nodded. She must have been tightly clutching the bucket on her lap because she felt her fingers being loosened and the thing removed, to be replaced by a pack of baby wipes.

Susie sat motionless in her seat as the kids piled off the coach. She needed these few moments. She was at work. She couldn't let any of this get to her. She *would* get through the day. Blindly pulling out a baby wipe, she started scrubbing at her hands and then eased herself out of her now revolting coat, which she rolled in on itself and stuffed into one of the empty carrier bags she always carried with her. She tied its handles into a tight double knot.

Looking down at herself, she realised she was going to freeze. Although she was wearing a long-sleeved top, it was only thin because she'd expected her coat to do all the hard work.

As if seeing the perfect opportunity to get away with it, her body started warming up. Why did it keep doing this? But this time its timing wasn't half bad. She would be outside in freezing temperatures, so getting all hot and steamy might stop hypothermia setting in.

She would have preferred the tingling not to have started, she reflected, as she used more baby wipes to scrub at her face and her neck, in fact any exposed skin she could find. She knew Ronald Wittering hadn't reached behind her ears, but it was psychological. She needed the memory erased. If only the troubles in her personal life could be so easily scrubbed away.

Surprisingly though, she realised she didn't mean that. The idea of not seeing George again . . . *loss* . . . The last week had been agonising. If there was a chance . . . .? How she'd felt with him had been incredible. How she felt without him was . . . hell. There was no two ways about that. Her head started screaming at her again. Why was nothing simple?

On a sigh, Susie popped the used baby wipes in another carrier bag and threw her handbag strap over her shoulder. It contained all the details she needed for their entry into the cathedral. She walked up and down the coach aisle, checking that the kids had taken all their belongings and then, on a deep breath, prepared to descend the steps.

She gulped. White noise. Lots and lots of white noise. She clutched the handrail for support.

'Hi.'

She was staring. She could feel herself doing it. And her body was responding which meant he really was there before her and this was not her head playing sick games with her. And his eyes, his eyes were doing that thing and . . . She found herself letting them. She needed to feel that myriad of sensations they induced. In this moment, it was comfort, so much comfort and the promise of so much more that she felt. It was what her body currently craved. And that connection of his provided it. She was in so much trouble here.

But how could George Silbury be in front of her? It made no sense that he was . . . *Oh God! Seeing her like this!* And her body dared to feel *comforted*? Okay, she'd cleaned herself up, but she'd just been covered in Ronald Wittering's sick! And no, no, no – she so hadn't dressed for George Silbury. She was in her practical work gear and had just scrubbed away any make-up she'd been wearing . . . No! She didn't have *any* on! She'd not bothered with it this morning after tossing and turning all night. And her hair was hanging in rat-tails because of the baby wipes she'd used on her neck and hairline.

And look at *him*. Standing there, so beautiful. With his dark hair and gorgeous deep brown eyes with those incredible long lashes – and the body of a god. He truly was beautiful, and that wasn't just her verdict. He'd been voted the most gorgeous man on the planet countless times.

No wonder he was frowning.

'I was . . . just passing.'

She'd known last night that he'd been out of his senses, his eyes metaphorically closed. Well it appeared he'd just opened them. He was going to walk away. And who could blame him? What must she look like? And she hadn't returned any of his calls even after all those lovely unfathomable things he'd said on the television.

I was just passing? George couldn't believe he'd just said that. He had been aiming for casual as he braced himself in the doorway of the coach, battling the urge to enfold her in his arms and never let go. He hadn't seen her in a week and it had been the longest week of his life. She was so damned beautiful, it was . . .

Susie dropped herself down to sit on the top step and lowered her head to her hands.

'Susie? Are you okay?' he asked, immediately concerned.

'I'm fine,' she whispered. 'I'm fine. It was . . . good to see you.'

No! She wanted him to go? 'I shouldn't have . . . I'm sorry. I didn't mean to . . . Look, I'll go if that's what you want. I get it now, okay, so I'll . . .'

Her head shot up and she looked at him in apparent confusion before holding his gaze. God, that connection. How could she not feel it? How could she possibly turn her back on this? She . . . she was shaking her head. 'I . . . I . . . don't want . . . Oh, I'm so confused. I've just had the coach journey from hell and you've . . . surprised me and . . . I was going to call you, but haven't had a chance yet and I didn't sleep a wink last night and I'm at work and have got to get the kids to the cathedral and we are already running so late and Ronald Wittering was sick all over my coat and now I'm going to freeze to death and I've no idea why I'm telling you all this. I'm sorry. I was going to call, I promise.'

George gingerly lowered himself onto the step below hers, forcing himself not to sit too close or he wouldn't be able to stop himself from providing the physical support his body was screaming out to give. *She was going to call him?* 'Hey,' he said gently. 'It's okay. I'm sorry you're having such a bad day. I won't delay you any further, but can I do anything to help? I don't know what I can do, but name it. I'm good with kids. I've got nephews and nieces and . . .' His voice petered out as she looked at him . . . astounded? 'Silly, sorry. You need to be approved these days to be in the company of children so . . .'

She was shaking her head again and seemed to be struggling to get her words out. Finally she said, 'Thank you.'

'What for?'

'Offering. You're right, you can't, but it was incredibly kind—' She shook her head hard. 'Why are you here? I'm sorry. This is Canterbury and . . . this is the last place I'd have expected to . . . encounter you.'

George looked pointedly down at his attire

'You're filming! Oh, I'm sorry. You've enough on your plate and . . .' She looked around frantically before asking quietly, 'Where's Porsche Sutter-Blythe?'

'She's back on set.' A gust of icy wind swept up the coach steps and he frowned as he absorbed what she was wearing and what she'd said earlier. He *could* make himself useful.

Standing up, he started to remove his coat. That thin top Susie was wearing at another time and place would be inducing far different thoughts. He gulped. *Another* time and place. This was not remotely appropriate. He had to focus.

'What are you doing?'

'I'm giving you my coat.' And he really liked the idea of this. There was something primal about her wearing his clothes. 'You can't go about Canterbury dressed like that in these temperatures. You'll catch pneumonia.' And that was an awful thought. 'In fact, you'd better have my shirt, too. It's thick and long . . . look.' He pulled the tails out of his waistband to demonstrate. 'You can wear it like a long jumper and—'

'*Stop*!' she cried.

His hands stilled at a shirt button as she hurtled

188

down the steps. She came to a full stop on the tarmac before him. There she raised her hands in a stilling gesture. Her gaze was frantic. She glanced over his shoulder, and then returned that gaze to him.

'Please stop. I'm absolutely fine. I don't need your clothes. You will freeze.'

He shook his head. 'There are clothes back in wardrobe I can have. You absolutely cannot walk around Canterbury like that and . . .' He was undoing the next button, but paused on a frown as she started to frantically wave her hands up and down.

'Please,' she begged.

Susie could *not* have George undressing. Not only because of what the idea of that was doing to her . . . and jeez, what that idea was doing to her! She could recall how it felt to be in his arms, the firm contours of his chest under her hands, his scent, his . . . clearly her body no longer craved comfort! And she was at work!

But that wasn't the only reason. George had *not* gone unnoticed by the women supervising the kids. She got that. Of course she did. Who could help but notice George Silbury? *But now he was proposing to remove his shirt!* She gulped, then dared a glance in their general direction again. Yeah, they'd all morphed out of mummy-mode and were now staring at him goggle-eyed. Every last one of them! She couldn't have them seeing him like that. Definitely not!

'If you won't take my shirt, will you please take my coat? You can hardly go about like that and I really need to help here.'

'Your coat will be great.' Anything to stop him removing his shirt in front of . . . She saw their looks. The hussies!

'Please put it on before you catch your death,' he urged, taking his mobile and wallet out of his pockets and holding it out to her.

'What about you?'

'Honestly, I'll be fine. *Please.*'

Susie pulled on his coat and was immediately engulfed by his scent and enveloped in his body heat. This was such a bad idea. How the hell was she supposed to be Miss Morris wearing this? Her whole body was . . . Oh God! And he was grinning that grin . . . She gulped again and attempted to shake herself free of the heated haze that could only result in her doing something really stupid.

She looked down at herself. That would cure her. And sure enough the arms went at least four inches below the end of her fingers and the coat was floor length on her. She looked like a damned hobbit! She was rudely reminded they were in company as she heard laughter, sniggering, excited chattering, whispering and heckling coming from her class. She was never going to live this one down. And she was going to be walking the streets of Canterbury looking like this.

She hated being the centre of attention at the best of times and today was evidently going to be a day of public humiliation. *Another* day of public humiliation.

She looked at George with a grimace and flapped her arms up and down.

'Cute,' he said quietly. 'Very . . . cute.'

And that look in his eyes. There was heat there. But there *couldn't be*. She had to be reading him wrong. There's no way he could be looking at her like she thought he was.

But she was a goner, she realised as she wallowed in his scent and body warmth. And that grin. And his kindness. She'd never had a hope of denying her reaction to him, no matter what her head shrieked at her. Although her head was unexpectedly quiet at present. Intoxicated, no doubt, like the rest of her. It was just too powerful a pull. And a simple choice between heaven and hell. Yes hell would invariably result, but at least she'd have taken as much of heaven as she could get.

This was ridiculous. He had no doubt come to his senses. This was George Silbury for pity's sake. And one look at her today and he would have been shocked back to reality.

'Ummm. Thank you again. I'll obviously get your coat back to you. I don't know the best way of doing that. But if you let me know what's best for you then—'

'Susie?'

He'd taken a step forward and almost completely closed the gap between them. Her body . . . But he'd lost that earlier look and was frowning. Her heart seemed to stop. Here we go.

'Tell me please. I said it how it was last night. I very much want to spend time with you, to get to know everything there is to know about you. To earn your trust. I am more sorry than I can put into words for the position I put you in with the press, but I am not sorry for what happened between us. I think we have something here. A spark and a connection, which I don't want to abandon. But if you don't feel it, if you aren't interested in finding out how we could be together, tell me now.'

Her heart made up for all those lost beats.

She vaguely heard another male voice. 'Guys . . . unless you want to give the game away here, start acting like you've just met. And hello. My name's Graham. George forgot to introduce us.'

Susie blinked. George cursed and she was aware of him taking a step back because she felt the loss.

She shook her head and forced herself to focus for a moment on the blond-headed man who obviously owned the voice. 'Susie. Sorry. Good to meet you.'

He was still *interested*? She couldn't not do this. She couldn't. She raised her voice slightly, for the benefit of any audience. 'You've been incredibly kind and thank you. I saw you on the telly last night and I'm one hundred per cent sure she'll call. She'd be mad not to be interested. She may just be a little . . . scared and need to take things a day at a time perhaps?' Who was she kidding?

Her head wasn't stupid enough to fall for that one. She knew what she'd just signed up for. But she couldn't say no to heaven, however short it lasted.

She dared a glance at his face and it took her breath away. His eyes were dancing again. And the smile he gave her went straight to her heart . . . and lower. She forced herself to look away. 'Well, I'd better get . . . going. And thank you.'

'It was a pleasure meeting you Susie Morris. And . . . she should know, I'm more than a little scared, too.'

'Cute,' Graham said, as they walked back. George turned to glower at him. Graham smirked. 'I believe I've twenty grand in my sights.'

George took a deep breath. Graham was one thing. But the last thing they needed were any of those women helping out with the kids suspecting and calling the press. George would not have Susie hunted down. 'I saw you talking to them, what did you say?'

'I didn't lie.'

George came to a full stop and stared at him in horror. 'What the hell did you tell them?' he hissed.

'I said we'd been looking for a café but don't know Canterbury very well and ended up there. Oh and that we responded to a damsel in distress who is borrowing some clothes. Silly not to when we have a wardrobe department on hand and all that crap.'

George closed his eyes for a moment and let

himself calm. That actually sounded pretty good. 'I'm impressed. Thank you.'

'No problemo.'

Walking again, George said, 'Twenty grand to keep shtum, twenty grand for keeping out of the way, twenty grand for sorting out the women. Umm. Jeannie still hasn't got her kitchen extension, and you're in her bad books because of me, and then you could also take her away for that "respite romance" so let's make it a round hundred grand and—'

'George! I was jesting about the twenty grand!'

'I know you were. But I'm in a good mood and if we hadn't been hunting down your cup of tea, I'd never have known Susie was in Canterbury and—'

'I'm not taking your money! While the mad dash through the streets of Canterbury nearly gave me a coronary, I'm glad to have helped.'

'Fine. I'll give it to you and Jeannie for your tenth wedding anniversary. I owe you, Graham. And if you won't accept the cheque, then I'll schedule the builders and book up the romantic break myself.'

One-handed, Cassie added milk to her tea, picked up her mug and, walking to the sofa, began reading the letter in her other hand.

Friday morning

My dear Mr Montague,
It is with horror that I write, knowing in what a wretched state you have just seen me! The

194

full extent of my appearance only became clear upon my return home. I am putting pen to paper post-haste, before my maid has even had a chance to remedy matters, as I am anxious to apologise.

Should this morning's debacle have resulted in a retraction of those sentiments so beautifully expressed in your letters of yesterday (they were truly wonderful letters Mr Montague – or may I call you Freddie, as I am more than happy for you to address me as Hannah? – and I now hold them to my heart and treasure), I would fully understand. Coach travel, it would appear, is most disagreeable to the youngest of my brothers and he was upon my knee when he took so violently ill. You obviously came upon us as we attempted to provide him with refreshing air.

But Freddie, should your sentiments remain – oh my dearest Freddie – should you still think of me as you did when you penned your glorious letters, then sing it from the rooftops. And I will join you. I would cry, 'I am the luckiest woman alive, for Freddie Montague adores me!'

But we must not. If we could wait until the interest in our firework display dies down, Mama and Papa need never suffer the knowledge of my indiscretion.

It was not your fault alone, Freddie, and being in your arms was the most wonderful moment of my existence so far. For should you still hold me in the esteem of which you wrote, then I truly feel the rest of our lives will be as wonderful, if not more so.

However, I cannot but question why you should see me thus – if indeed you still do. Miss Prudence Argylle is extremely beautiful and with family connections I lack. But Freddie, I would have you any which way I could.

Your riding coat, so gallantly lent, will be cleaned before being returned to its most knightly of owners. It is still upon my person as I write. It holds your scent and reminds me so of being within your arms. I shall hold it close upon my pillow as I sleep. For I dream too, Freddie. Would that my dreams come true!

I intend to walk tomorrow to the north of the meadows. I will be there at around four of the clock and very much hope to encounter you there.

I am yours, Freddie, if you will still have me – and for as long as you wish.

Hannah

Cassie quickly retrieved the next letter from the pocket of her cardigan . . .

Friday evening

My dearest Hannah,
Of course I will still have you – and forever, my darling!

As an aside, may I be so bold as to ask that you keep my coat upon your pillow, until I have the honour of taking its place? As for your own cloak which fared so ill today – it must be replaced. But, my dearest darling, my wish is that you wear the new garment publicly whilst upon my arm! I beg you will go to the draper's and choose a suitable fabric. Or would you allow me the honour of surprising you? If so, please give me the name of your dressmaker and I will have her make one to your measurements as soon as possible.

Yours,
Freddie

CHAPTER 16

'Will you get that goofy look off your face and stop that dreadful sound? I definitely preferred suicidal.'

Susie ignored Rachael's words and continued humming as she made her morning coffee.

'The least you can do is *tell* me why you are acting distinctly "un-Susie" like. I know it's to do with George Silbury, you lucky, lucky cow. I'm your best friend and *deserve* an explanation. May I remind you, it was *moi* that introduced you?'

Susie continued to hum.

'I won't beg, you know. You've been like it since you got home on Monday night. And I know it's to do with him because you came home dressed like a victim of some kind of deranged shrinking experiment. Or worse. A hobbit.'

Susie's humming suffered a momentary glitch.

'It was his coat. There's no question. Not that I've studied his physique *of course*, but it was a *very* good match. And it was Versace, whom we know he models for, because I checked the label. Then there were the pockets. Did you know there was a serviette in one of them from Café de Paris,

198

with the words "Call Me" on it? The signature could *not* have been from the lady it purported to be because that would be *beyond* sensational.'

Susie's humming died a death.

'But he'd evidently used it as a tissue. Very evidently, but it was a useful clue.'

Susie began humming again, albeit a little less self-assuredly.

'How you managed to go on a school trip to Canterbury dressed in one thing, and come home dressed in George Silbury's clothes is mind-boggling. You were in charge of children, Suse. I don't get it. Cassie and I have our theories. Of course, the things she's heard in the press room – unsubstantiated reports that his manager keeps suppressing – add to the intrigue. That stuff about sprinting after a coach . . .'

Susie stopped humming. But immediately started up again in order not to betray her interest. He ran after the coach? He'd not told her that. They'd talked. And they'd talked. And they'd talked. Every night on the phone. He was stuck in Canterbury with a punishing schedule; never off set before 10.00 p.m. He was quite prepared to head back to London in order to meet up, but by the time he got back it would be at least 11.30 p.m. and he had to be back in Canterbury by 6.00 a.m. It wasn't fair on him, and neither would it give her time to do him justice, of that she was sure.

So they'd talked every night, conversations they never wanted to end. From childhood television programmes through to politics and the humanitarian conflicts in the world. They'd talked of her day at work. All those things it was good to unburden or simply share, but which Peter had never shown any interest in at all. And George *was* interested. Genuinely interested. And they'd talked about his day. A world she couldn't begin to imagine, yet he somehow made her feel a part of it. And so much else. They'd speak for hours and she'd look back and not necessarily remember the specific content of what they'd been saying, but just the sheer pleasure and sense of joy at their interaction. On Monday they'd obliviously talked through the night, their only being alerted to that fact when George's alarm clock went off. The other nights they reluctantly, but practically, imposed a curfew. But then had never kept to it. How either of them was still functioning, she had no idea. It must be the high. Because George's beauty was most evidently not just skin deep. And it felt as though she had known him forever.

But it was Friday today; hence her exceptionally good mood. There was no filming or school tomorrow. And he was back in London tonight. And . . . She sighed as she contemplated her evening. But she'd got somewhat distracted. *He ran after the coach?*

'I've told you something you didn't know,' Rachael cried.

Not good.

'Ha ha! You tell me and I'll tell you!'

Did she honestly think she was that stupid?

'There was talk of Porsche having a hissy fit?'

Oh for goodness sake. That really wasn't fair. Susie aborted humming. There was no point in keeping up the pretence. She turned to face Rachael. 'He ran after the coach?'

'Oh yeah, if the unsubstantiated reports are to be believed. Cassie's questioned George and she's convinced it's for real, although he's being as obstructive as you. She even went over to Canterbury to interrogate him, but he was like a clam. But I'm not telling you any more until you tell me what happened.'

'I've ten minutes before I go to work. Tell me what you know and I'll tell you what happened when I get home.'

'No deal. What do you take me for? You give me the potted version and then I'll tell you what I know – all in ten minutes. And then you can give me the *juicy* details when you get home.'

'Cassie,' George muttered into his mobile, silently cursing at the thought of yet another interrogation.

'Susie spilled.'

'I'm sorry?'

'Susie spilled the beans. Do you know how that makes me feel? She tells her friend, not a blood relative, all about what happened, before you – my brother, my own flesh and blood, my favourite brother at that – even acknowledge the existence of a dicky bird!'

George sighed and rubbed his brow, before quickly removing his hand. He mouthed sorry to the woman currently touching up his make-up. 'What did she say?' He wondered what ploy Rachael had used to get it out of her.

'No. You'll end up telling me you've got to be back on set before you utter a word. We're lacking the details. And then I've some questions I need answers to. So come on! Spill!'

'I've got to go.'

'No. I refuse to let you—'

'Goodbye Ca—'

'Mum's coming to see you!'

Cassie now had George's full attention as she had known she would with those words. He signalled the make-up artist away and sat forward in his seat. 'When?'

'She's really worried about you. I know you've been putting her off, but ever since she saw you on *The Jonathan James Show* she's been frantic. She says she has to see you're okay. She's worried you're attempting to put a brave face on—'

'*When* Cassie?'

'This weekend.'

George groaned. 'Where's she planning on staying?'

'At yours, of course. You're the one with the six-bedroomed house. I've a one-bedroomed flat. Well two, as you know, but *she* doesn't need to know that. I keep that door firmly closed. And if you tell her I will *never* forgive you.'

'*When* is she arriving?' He had a horrible feeling.

'Tonight.'

'*No way!* She's not coming tonight. I mean it. There is no way—'

'Anything planned then, George?'

Bugger. Bugger. Bugger.

'You spill and answer my questions, and I'll keep Mum away tonight,' Cassie bargained. 'But I'm not having her for the weekend. Neither am I giving away the existence of a second bedroom. So I need your credit card number to foot the bill for a hotel. And a meal. Throw in a show, too. And then I'll keep her out of your hair. But for that you talk to me. And right this very minute!'

'You were *vomited* on?'

'Will you stop saying that, please,' Susie urged, feeling queasy at the recollection. 'And I really don't appreciate you getting straight on the phone to tell George's sister our conversation.'

'By Ronald Wittering?'

'Why do you think I think twice before telling you anything? Now will you *please* tell me about Porsche?'

Susie was finding it hard to digest what Rachael had already said of George chasing the coach through the streets of Canterbury. There seemed to be enough independent reports from stunned onlookers to make it possible. The description of the clothes he was wearing matched, too. But why would he . . .? It was . . . it was . . . The very idea was beyond lovely! It was totally unbelievable, but beyond lovely! It made her feel . . . Oh God. Trouble didn't begin to go there.

She had a horrible feeling her heart had become involved. Her whole being, even her mind, had fallen under his spell. It seemed that with each word he had uttered this week, it became more charmed. He was intelligent, challenging, funny, kind and it was seriously impressed.

And if his words weren't enough, there'd been that gesture, too. When she'd got back from school on Tuesday there had been a parcel waiting for her. And inside . . . cashmere, grey, three-quarter length, tailored, stunning . . . designer! She'd never heard of the designer before but had looked them up and had difficulty comprehending the financial worth of the coat she'd then had cradled in her arms. A year's pay, give or take a few cans of baked beans, and she might have been able to afford it herself. But it was the most beautiful item of clothing she'd ever seen. And it was a perfect fit. And felt so wonderful to be in. And then there'd been his note which had accompanied it . . .

Please keep mine. I like the idea of that more than I perhaps should. But if you are in need of one, this may be more suitable for public use? I doubt dry-cleaning will ever eradicate the memory of Ronald Wittering from your coat, just as an eternity will never erase the memory of how you looked wearing mine yesterday.

I won't be offended at all should you want

to change it. I just couldn't take the risk of you catching pneumonia. Fortunately they were able to make it in that fabric over night.

Yours, George

Susie closed her eyes. So much trouble . . .

But while her whole being was unquestionably charmed, it hadn't stopped the alarm calls sounding from that part of her head designed to protect. That part of her was evidently resistant. But she couldn't heed them. It was too late. Running screaming from George as it seemed to want her to do, would cause the very pain it was seeking to protect her from.

'If rumours filtering out are true, then George has refused to spend any time at all off camera with Porsche. She's gone to the director insisting that she needs to work through scenes with George on a one-to-one basis. George has said any work that needs doing can be done while the cameras are rolling, increasing the chances of getting the perfect moment on film. He's not budging and has told Francis he'll walk. She, in turn, has said she'll walk. But Francis is apparently so impressed with some of the performances George is turning out, he's told Porsche to get over it; they're getting to rehearse, albeit on camera, so there shouldn't be an issue.

'She's livid. She even threw into the pot the "George and the Horn stuff", saying he needed to be controlled and shouldn't be able to call the shots. Francis apparently laughed in her face. The studio is delighted with all the publicity. George Silbury has never been a hotter commodity and therefore interest in his films is sky high.'

Susie sank into the armchair. George was actively avoiding Porsche? She was a total utter goner.

'I thought you needed to be off to school?' Rachael queried. 'You said ten minutes, that was like twenty minutes ago.'

Shit! Susie leapt from her seat and dashed to fetch her bag. She was supposed to be on playground duty first thing. Collecting her bag from her bedroom, she smiled. That beautiful, beautiful coat was currently nestled in tissue paper within its box under her bed. She so wanted to wear it, but what was between her and George seemed so . . . personal. Between just the two of them at the moment. And then there was what Rachael's reaction would be!

Susie quickly repositioned her duvet, pulling it up to cover George's coat that sat upon her pillow. She didn't want Rachael getting her grubby mitts on it. She couldn't stop smiling. She couldn't help it. She was seeing him tonight. She turned to run out of the room . . . and froze when she spotted the empty hanger on her wardrobe door.

'Rach!' she screamed. 'If you've borrowed my dress, I'll hang, draw and quarter you!'

★　　★　　★

'Yes Cassie, I ran after the coach. Sprint? Yes. Satisfied? And yes, I surrendered my coat and was very happy to do so. No, there was no further clothes removal . . . from either of us. Cassie!'

He sighed and forced himself not to visualise that scenario. 'Rest assured that if there had been, I would not be telling you. And yes, to the Porsche stuff. Who are your sources? Michael will blow a gasket if he knows so much of this on-set stuff is getting out.'

'How the hell did you know she was on that coach?'

'I have no idea how I knew. I just did. I've answered more than enough of your questions to honour our deal. So you keep Mum away. Tell her I'll call her next week to arrange meeting up. I'm in London again tonight. If you let me down, I'll tell Mum about the second bedroom.'

'You *wouldn't!*'

'Try me. Book yourselves in wherever you want, in whatever kind of suite you want – for the weekend. Not just tonight.'

'I'm not entertaining Mum for the weekend.'

'Neither am I. Not this weekend. So—'

'And just what is happening this weekend, George?'

'Goodbye Cassie.'

Susie stomped into her bedroom. She'd ended up leaving work late because Joseph Robinson had managed to get his head wedged in a hole in a tree after school. How he'd done it, she still didn't know. It seemed to be a physical impossibility, but his parents needed calming down and it wasn't right leaving the other staff to deal with the fire brigade, particularly when members of her own class, keen to see the mooning tradition continued, kept insisting on pulling the helpless child's trousers down.

And then she'd gone to the dry-cleaners to pick up her dress. The dress she was supposed to be wearing tonight, but which Rachael had borrowed last night and got covered in ketchup and mustard and which, under threat of painful death, she'd been ordered to drop off at the dry-cleaners first thing. Of course, with the way the day had gone, the dry-cleaners couldn't find the damned dress. After nearly slapping the woman behind the counter and then the subsequent panic attack, Susie had had no choice but to hit the shops.

She was brought out of her painful reminiscences by the sight of her dress, hanging in its dry-cleaning film upon her wardrobe door.

'Arrrrggggghhhhhh!' She flung her bags down and stomped her feet.

'What?' Rachael asked from her doorway.

'Out! Out! Out!'

'By the way, I picked up your dress to save you some time.'

Susie slammed the door.

It was 6.45 p.m. now and she was due at George's at 8.00 p.m. She had to have a bath, do her hair and make-up, shave her legs and underarms, and address the major deforestation required down below. No man had seen her down below for, mmm . . . three years. She hadn't let Peter anywhere near it.

Susie groaned and sank to the bed.

She was terrified. How could she possibly please George Silbury? Oh she'd go through the beautifying motions, but what was the point? She was dreading him seeing her with no clothes on. How could she have ever thought he'd seen her looking bad on Monday?

He'd dated the most beautiful women in the world. Of course he had, because he was so darned beautiful himself. He'd done love scenes with countless more. She clenched her fists and firmly dismissed such a horrid thought. The idea of George naked with other women. . . . And she *was* overweight, at least when compared to those body-beautifuls he'd dated. And she did have cellulite. Thank you Porsche Sutter-Blythe for pointing out the painfully obvious.

Seeing her naked would most certainly restore George to his senses. He'd run screaming. Perhaps she should cancel. But God she wanted him: body and soul – and partially sighted. She was so screwed. Lights off. The lights would have to be off. Because the moment he caught a glimpse of her, the George and Susie Roadshow would be no more.

★   ★   ★

George sped along the M2 in his BMW 6 Series thinking he would no doubt get caught for speeding. Michael had waylaid him and he was only now driving back. He was not in the best of moods and was furious with Michael, not only for delaying him, but for what he had said.

Apparently Michael had received countless calls about Canterbury and very much hoped it wasn't anything to do with 'that bint' George had publicly humiliated himself over. She was most definitely not worth ruining his career for. And it would be ruined, should he choose to settle down with someone not in the business. Anyone outside of the industry couldn't take the media pressure or stomach the filming schedules.

Not that any of that really mattered, Michael continued to say, because she was clearly playing the hard-to-get card and that was the only possible reason George could be interested. He suggested George hurry up and 'fuck her' so she was out of his system and he could get back on track. It was at that point George had given him two black eyes and left.

He was still livid. Some of the stuff had hit home, such as the media pressure. But if Susie couldn't cope with the media then he wouldn't hesitate in moving out of the public eye. It was that simple. He had made an obscene amount of money and never had to work another day in his life.

And then there was the Porsche stuff that Michael had started off their ill-fated meeting with.

She'd evidently got Michael on board and the man had put considerable effort into encouraging him to spend more time with her: publicly to aid publicity for the film; privately to help her with the role she insisted she was struggling with. And then he'd said, yet again, how good George and Porsche would be together!

Rumours getting out of the rift between him and Porsche wasn't good, George knew that, but to be honest – so what? Her public comments about Susie were inexcusable. And it could only be down to a bruised super-ego. He was probably the only man to have ever turned her down. There was clearly no accounting for taste.

George winced as he recalled that night seven years ago. She'd appeared so vulnerable. His rejection had been as kind as possible, yet, somehow, she'd been even worse since, particularly in recent weeks. It made no sense. He should never have accepted this role. And that was Michael again.

George was going to have to sack him. Michael had already left countless messages apologising for what he had said, but the damage was done. Not only with what he had said about Susie. He was beginning to wonder whether Michael was even acting in his best interests anymore. George had never wanted to do this film. What they were paying was ludicrous, but he didn't need it. But did Michael? In hindsight, he'd been seriously railroaded and Michael's cut for George doing the film was as ludicrous as the sum being paid to him.

George took a deep breath. He'd deal with it all on Monday. He refused to have anything impinge on his time with Susie.

Which brought him to tonight. And . . . He clenched his fists around the steering wheel. He was terrified. What if he messed it up? Their conversations this week had revealed Susie to be perfect – completely and utterly perfect. Just as he'd *known* she would be. She was intelligent, witty and he was so under her spell. He could just imagine what their arguments would be like. She was strong-minded, as was he, and they would challenge each other. But dear God . . . the making up.

Everything about her brought out feelings so extreme their force was staggering. She had him hook, line and sinker. Mind, body and soul. He was laid wide open and that was a vulnerability that scared him to hell.

But there was nothing on this earth that would keep him from her. She was the one. He knew it. There was a connection there . . . soul deep, and with her fears, he was sure it went both ways. It was too strong not to. But that hadn't stopped her dumping him. He had to attempt to rein himself in. He mustn't scare her off. He was scaring himself with the depth of his feelings, so he was going to have to keep himself in check. If he lost her again . . . he couldn't allow himself to contemplate it, not if he was going to keep sane. But the fear of losing her . . . haunted him.

What he *could* contemplate was whether he would be up to scratch tonight. George momentarily shut his eyes and let his head rest on the steering wheel as his car came to a stop at a junction. He was experienced, he couldn't deny that and should be taking comfort. He'd never before had a complaint. Quite the contrary. But he might as well be a virgin when it came to Susie. He had *never* been with a woman where his feelings were involved like this. He never knew such feelings existed. He'd thought himself in love once, but had clearly been delusional. What if he disappointed her?

Why didn't he just cut to the quick! He was like a horny teenager around her, and they were hardly known for their control and staying power. Perhaps they should just talk? But he knew from their reaction to each other that it wasn't likely to stop at that. He'd been imagining slowly undressing her and taking in the view all day. He was going to disgrace himself tonight, he just knew it.

As he headed through London, George passed the turning he would take should he be going to Susie's. He instinctively slammed his foot down on the brakes. Cursing, he belatedly checked his rear-view mirror. He was normally a safe driver, but there was nothing normal – or safe – about his reaction to Susie Morris.

If he continued driving he could just about be home for 8.00 p.m. He could call Susie and tell her he might be a little late, just in case he hit

traffic. On the other hand . . . he'd already show-
ered and changed at the hotel before checking out.
If he took that turning, he could be with Susie in
two minutes rather than thirty.

George did a U-turn.

'Rach? Rach? Can you do something with my hair?
I've used half a bottle of anti-frizzing serum and
it's still—'

Susie froze in her bedroom doorway. Much as
she had when she'd watched a 2D George Silbury
say all those lovely things about her on the television. Today he was *most definitely* 3D.

Why didn't she learn? Hot and flustered and
tingling all over meant George Silbury. Next time
she felt it without him in her sights, she was going
to have to immediately rectify her appearance – or
hide.

Okaaaay . . . the calm side of her brain said. It
could be worse. She wasn't standing in her greying
knickers and jeans hanging off one leg. The less
than calm side of her brain reminded her that she
was standing before George Silbury in her fluffy
grey dressing gown and . . . Oh God! She had
those ridiculous Bagpuss slippers, courtesy of
Rachael, on her feet. And her *hair! Shit Shit Shit!*

And he was grinning and his eyes were dancing.
But, of course. Because that just meant she lost
any ability to sound remotely coherent and . . .

'Hi,' he said, in a way that should be illegal. Oh
yeah. He'd just added his voice into the equation.

Needing a little support she put her hand on the door frame, attempting to look casual.

'Hi,' the frog in her throat croaked, because she clearly wasn't capable of speaking for herself quite yet. Realising what she sounded like, she sent it packing and had a go herself. 'Hi.' That sounded gushy and girly and breathless.

She gave up, unable to do casual in the circumstances. She'd never be able to do casual around him. 'I can't believe you've seen me looking like this. I was going to attempt sophisticated tonight and . . .'

He took two strides over and was now . . . If she reached out, she could touch him. She'd had to stop speaking to gulp.

His eyes were looking that way . . . Heated, no . . . ablaze. And she was clearly combustible because that look seemed to be setting her alight from the inside out. Evidently her body knew *exactly* what it wanted tonight. What it had always wanted. What it had always needed. To be joined as one with George Silbury.

'Susie,' he said, in a way that made her feel so precious she wanted to start crying. She wanted to say 'George' in the same way and just cling to him and never ever let him go. Seriously . . . never ever let him out of her arms. And just how nuts would that look? He gently pushed a strand of her treacherous hair from her face and tucked it behind her ear. 'I was passing by and . . . it was the right decision.'

'Susie! George is here!' Rachael yelled from the direction of her room. 'Oh!' Her voice was nearer, evidently now in the main room. 'Sorry. I had to take a call . . . you can see for yourself.'

George leaned forward and spoke in Susie's ear, his warm breath whispering across her skin in a way so deeply erotic, foreplay became pointless. 'I've missed you. And red is now my favourite colour.'

She tried to get her head functioning. He'd missed her? That was so lovely. So, so lovely . . . But red? Why would red . . .? It was taking way too long to process the question but . . . No! She'd long ago lost the cord of her dressing gown and, standing as she was, it was gaping open and revealing her new undies. She used her free arm, the one not holding her up, to try and close the gap before he saw any more of her imperfections.

'It was the best decision I have ever—' *That voice.* But it cut off.

Susie became vaguely aware of another male voice, calling out. 'Rach? Suse? I'm heading down the chippie. Do you—?'

George was suddenly taking control of her dressing gown situation. Indeed, he wrapped it around her gently, yet more tightly than she could have ever thought possible, and then positioned her arms so they acted as clamps, keeping it firmly closed.

Rob. It finally came to her. He must have let himself in and be after takeaway orders. Not that

216

she could see him, as she was now faced with the wall that was George Silbury's back.

The very broad, muscular wall that looked incredible in the charcoal T-shirt, stretched taut across his shoulders. She itched to reach out and touch, to wrap her arms around his slim waist, to bring their bodies together. She would rest her cheek on his back, feel his warmth and strength and his life force. It was almost a compulsion.

Instead, she found fortitude from somewhere and took the opportunity to dive back into her bedroom to get dressed. George had been more than eager to cover her up. Lights off. It would be fine with the lights off she desperately reassured herself.

As she closed her door she heard Rachael call out, 'Chips and jumbo sausage for me. Oh! Where'd he go? *Ahhhh.* I forgot about you. So . . . did you really get propositioned by . . .?'

CHAPTER 17

George turned the ignition off. They'd hardly spoken in the car, the ease of their conversation on the phone seeming to have escaped them both.

He'd attempted to put the record straight about that bloody serviette though. When he'd taken out his wallet and mobile from his coat, he simply hadn't thought – which didn't surprise him in the circumstances. But it hardly put him in a good light. He prayed Susie believed him.

And then there was the fury he'd felt when the man known as 'Rob' had so casually entered Susie's home. She was half-naked, for God's sake. Looking a million times more provocative and alluring than any woman in any state of undress ever could. How he'd won the struggle to keep his shaking hands from her body, he had no idea.

But then 'Rob' didn't practise such restraint. George couldn't allow himself to visualise him, yet again, dancing with Susie. He wasn't before him so his fury was impotent. And it was a very good thing, bearing in mind what he currently felt like doing to him. But the thought of him seeing her like that . . .? But he *hadn't*, he counselled. She was with him tonight. And every other night if he had his way.

And now they were at his home and . . . he was terrified. It wasn't just his body crying out for her. It was him. His whole being and it was over-whelming. This wasn't going to be mindless sex, so far from it. This was going to be him, serving himself up on a platter, with his heart completely exposed in the middle. A heart he questioned ever fully beat until it encountered Susie. And which he doubted could ever function again without her.

And what if he was a disappointment? He sat for a moment clutching his steering wheel.

'George?'

He turned. Oh Susie. She looked as he felt. 'I'm scared,' she said, in a voice that gripped his heart in a vice.

His seat belt was off and he gently cupped her face in his hands. He let his forehead drop to hers. 'So am I, sweetheart, so am I. I can take you home right now if that's what you want.' He'd do what-ever she needed here. 'Or . . . or we can slow things down, and help each other through this?'

His intoxicating breath brushed across her face, gently stroking, while his thumbs moved tenderly upon her cheeks. Her body wept for him. Her whole being, bar that troublesome part of her head. Susie unclasped her hands from her lap and moved them up across his shoulders, tenta-tively feeling his muscles play beneath the thin fabric, before she curled them into his chestnut, softer than silk hair at the nape of his neck and let it run through her fingers. He was scared too. They were both caught up in this insane need thing . . . Although he'd soon recover his senses; she was going to be such a disappointment to him.

The nearer they'd got to his home, the more terrified she'd become and the louder those alarm calls she was trying so hard to dismiss. She knew she wasn't going to be good enough for him. Yet she could never want anyone else.

She *must* take this opportunity and have of him what she could. What her whole being was crying out for. And then when she lost him . . . She needed to be in his arms. In his arms she couldn't think.

And she needed to be as one with George.

'Tell me why you're scared,' he urged gently.

She simply shook her head.

'We're going to talk this through, sweetheart. We're going to take this slow.' He spoke against her lips, before kissing her so tenderly she wanted to cry. He groaned in response to her tongue travelling the velvety smoothness of his lower lip.

'No.' She followed the seam of his lips, teasing herself with his taste. It was addictive, compulsive, heavenly. She wanted heaven. She took a deep breath and prayed he wouldn't reject her, not now. Not yet. 'No talking. No thinking. Our bodies joined. Sex. I need you George . . . Please?'

George slowly moved his head back to stare at her. His heart pounded. His body screamed.

He managed to find some semblance of his voice. 'We don't need to—'

'I need you . . . in me,' she whispered, so huskily, so seductively.

Those words . . . *those* words . . . *from Susie!* That beast that only Susie stirred, roared and George's whole being shook with the force. If those words weren't enough, there were her eyes. They promised a fulfilment incomparable to anything upon this earth. And that promise travelled straight to his core before it exploded, touching every cell within his already screaming body. To deny those eyes would surely render a man insane. And they were looking at *him* like that. No man could ever have been so blessed . . . or incited.

He gulped, striving to rein himself in. He had to clear the roar from his head. They should talk. He turned his face to kiss the palm of her hand. But it was primal, relentless. That look in her eyes: irresistible. He prayed for restraint.

'Unless you don't want me. I'd understand.'

Unless I don't want *her?* The beast within beat his chest. There was only so much a man could take. Screw prayer.

George was instantaneously out of the car and at her door. *Unless I don't* want *her?* He grasped her hand, had her out of the car and was leading her towards the house. He attempted to slow his stride, but she still had to run. They were up the steps.

His shaking hands – God his whole body was shaking with the force of his need – somehow got the key in the door, they were through the door, the door was slammed shut and . . .

'You're sure?' he choked, their eyes connecting. He had to be sure, even in this state where neat testosterone pumped through his veins. Because it was Susie. And even now he was terrified of losing her.

She nodded her head, moistening her lips with the tip of her tongue.

The roaring beast snapped its leash and liquefied to course through his veins.

He closed the distance between them. With two fast driving steps she was back against the wall.

'Unless, I don't want you?' he murmured incredulously, his fingers entwined in her hair as his body pressed her against the wall and he moved against her so she could feel how rock hard he was for her. She gasped, and he swallowed the sound, claiming her mouth with the full force of his need. *Her taste!* He saw dots in every spectrum of the rainbow. He was in the mind-blowing sensory overdrive that was his with Susie. Only Susie.

He wanted her! And she needed him so much. Susie clutched the hair at his nape pulling him down as she stretched on tiptoes, incredibly deepening the kiss. Their tongues parried and plundered while her body . . . *Oh God!* She was *all* erogenous nerve cells. His hands wherever they touched sent sparks of neat ecstasy straight to her core. She clutched his shoulders as her legs turned to jelly.

His leg was between hers, keeping her standing and the feeling of his thigh just *there* . . . Her body was in raptures, while her whole being recognised him for who he was. He was *hers*.

He lowered his forehead to her shoulder and . . . stilled, bar for his ragged breaths. *No! Don't stop! Please don't stop.*

As if he heard her his thigh pushed even higher against her and his mouth found hers in an onslaught that had her seeing stars. His hands travelled in a frenzy and she felt her dress being wrenched up, but then he slowed, stroking the bare skin of her thighs in excruciating, feather-light touches.

She found the bare skin of his back. It wasn't enough. She tugged at his top and he knew what she needed almost before she did. He moved back just enough to yank it over his head and drop it to the floor. He was back against her in a heart-beat. Her hands travelled across the contours of his chest with its thin scattering of dark hair, down to his hard flat stomach, his abdomen. He seemed to hold his breath, but let it out on a long groan as she followed her hands with her mouth, her lips, her teeth, her tongue. His taste. She lapped as if it were her lifeblood.

He captured her head, his lips travelling over her whole face and jaw. As he imprisoned her mouth, his hands moved to the fabric at her neckline. It wasn't cooperating. He ripped. She gasped and gasped again as he dragged down the cups of her bra to expose her breasts. He stood still, breathing hard as he stared at them. Then his shaking hands, torturously slow and gentle, brushed over them. Just as she was ready to throttle him, he lowered his head. He teased with his mouth, his tongue. Mercilessly he circled, nipped and then suckled. She flung her head back, arching herself to push more fully into his mouth. His hands on the small of her back pulled her closer still. She clutched at his head, holding him in place.

Susie's moans reverberated through him, fuelling a wild inferno that blazed with a white-hot heat and intensity that he'd no hope of controlling. He raised his head so he could pull her to his bare chest and feel them skin to skin. She moved against him so erotically. He released his groan into her mouth. She was his. *His*.

She wasn't close enough. He wasn't sure she ever could be. His hands worked between her and the wall and grasped her bottom, pulling her tightly against him. He could feel the shape of her as he pressed himself hard against her core. He replaced the contact with a hand. The feel of her through her moist panties had him swallowing both her moans and his own.

Her hands found the waistband of his jeans. She unbuttoned, her fingers at each strained then . . . popping button. God help him. He should make her stop. But he couldn't. He couldn't stop.

He raised her up and her legs wrapped around his waist. She rocked herself backwards and forwards against him. It had to be now! He braced her back against the wall as he sprung free, and he yanked those red panties that had so taunted him under her dressing gown, barely registering the sound of their tearing.

He was poised at her entrance. He was going to be joined with Susie. This was his life's purpose. Their eyes locked.

Simultaneously he plunged forward in one rapid thrust. She cried out and he may have roared. He was so lost in the moment, he didn't know. He stumbled, but recovered. He was not going to blank out. The sensation of her wrapped around him and knowing this was Susie, *his* Susie, completely overwhelmed. He'd never known pleasure like it. How could anything this sublime exist? How could he survive such staggering ecstasy?

He opened his eyes, as did she, and they relocked. They were connected now, body and soul. He was in so deep. There was never a question of that. And he fully embraced it.

He lowered his head to her shoulder in an attempt at regaining control. But the scent from her skin drove him crazy and her hands in his hair . . . The power of their connection urged him on. But if he went with his primal need, he'd be pummelling into her with a force that scared even him. He wouldn't allow himself to hurt her, no matter how much it cost him. This wasn't how he meant to love her.

'Don't stop,' she whispered and he felt her tender kiss upon his lowered head. 'Please don't stop.'

He raised his head to meet those stunning eyes. They were so beautiful he felt tears stinging. They reflected his need. Could they possibly reflect his love? 'I'm going to hurt you,' he gasped out, 'I need a moment to—'

She pressed two fingers gently upon his mouth, shushing his words.

'Don't stop,' she urged, thrusting her hips forward against him.

He began to withdraw.

Susie frantically clutched at him, 'Don't go!' she pleaded.

She met his gaze. His dark sensuous eyes seemed to glow from within. That glow travelled down through her body, revisiting all their connections.

He thrust home.

She cried out and couldn't help but fling her head back against the wall. He followed. 'I'm not going anywhere,' he vowed in her ear, before withdrawing again and driving forward to nip at her ear lobe.

She clutched his shoulders, her nails digging into skin. She was completely consumed by sensation. Completely consumed by George. He withdrew while his mouth travelled from her neck, down to her breasts. He plunged home again to suckle and tug with his mouth.

She literally climbed the wall with each driving thrust. She'd never ever, ever experienced anything so staggeringly, overwhelmingly . . . *right* in her life. It could only be this way with him. They were a perfect fit, two pieces of a puzzle finding their connection. Had she perhaps known it for years? Had sensed who he was from his eyes?

There could be no more reflection. Her hands around his shoulders, clenched into fists as she met his increased pace. The pleasure was getting too much. Her whole body was on the brink of explosion. This was nuclear. This was . . . He went faster and harder and *deeper*. Oh God! Oh God! Oh God!

And then she was braced tighter against the wall and his hand . . . *No!* She tried to shake her head. It was going to be too much. But she couldn't stop her flailing. His hand was there between them and his thumb was at *that* place amidst her deforested curls. He applied pressure in exactly the right spot while he pounded within. She was light-headed as her senses overloaded. He adjusted their position a fraction. Then thrust into her again.

She urged herself not to black out.

'Look at me, Susie. Look at me,' he rasped in her ear.

She was fuzzy but as their gazes locked, all was crystal clear. Those connections that slotted so perfectly into place were pushed truly home. She could almost hear the clunks. She exploded with a shattering scream and he filled her with a roar.

Filled that one last gap within her being, the one she hadn't known even existed until this moment. And she wanted to cry. To cry at the force of pleasure ripping through her; to cry at the sense of being totally at one with George. He was hers. She was his. Whether he knew it or not. This was meant to be.

As Susie's senses finally began to return, she heard his gasps for air, felt the heaving of his chest under her hands. He dropped his forehead to the wall to the side of her head and turned to face her. She couldn't quite reach him in that position. She wanted to cradle his head in her hands. He just stared at her as he recovered his breath.

This hadn't been sex. This had been an earth-shattering joining of body and soul. This had been . . . George Silbury. Had he felt it too? Oh God! Please let him have. *Please don't let this have all been me!*

He simply carried on staring. And she felt the need to babble, to break the silence she prayed wasn't awkward. It didn't feel awkward but . . . 'I knew you'd be good. But . . . but that was out of this world.'

'How are you able to talk?' he gasped. 'You shouldn't be able to talk.'

Oh, she could talk, she could more than talk. But then she remembered he was holding her up. No wonder he was struggling.

'You can put me down.' She winced. 'I'm amazed you managed to hold me up at all.'

He shook his head.

'George? Put—'

'Did I hurt you?' he suddenly groaned, clenching his eyes tight and shaking his head. 'I should never have taken you up against a wall . . . and the moment I'd got you in the door! I'm so sorry.'

'You're *sorry*?'

'More sorry than I can put into words.'

'Why would you be sorry for—?'

She stopped and closed her eyes against the pain. She'd expected her euphoria to last just that little bit longer. Her glimpse of heaven she'd desperately hoped would continue beyond . . .

'Susie?' he asked, anxiously, seeing something was very wrong. He moved to stroke her face. She opened her eyes, but wouldn't meet his. She forced a smile.

'I'm sorry, you're sorry. It was really good for me and I'm sorry I didn't do it for you. I—'

'Susie?' he shook his head, incredulously. 'Sweetheart, I'm not sorry for what we just shared . . .' How could she ever think he was sorry for that? 'Look at me. I'm sorry for taking you so quickly and like a bloody animal and . . . *without protection*! I'm clean. I promise. I've never not—'

She abruptly silenced him with her mouth before breaking off with an earth-shattering smile. She stroked the side of his face. 'I've got the other covered,' she assured.

'I lost control and . . .' How was he supposed to tell her how it was? That she was still in his arms because he didn't want to put her down? He didn't ever want to put her down. Not now that he'd found her. Not putting her down meant there was no chance of losing her . . . Because if he'd thought he worried about that before . . . 'You were incredible, Susie. You blew my mind. You always blow my mind. But I now have no mind left to blow. And I'm trying to hold back on telling you how I feel because I don't want to scare you and . . . You're *grinning*?'

She reached up to cradle his face in her hands. 'How could I not? You think you'd scare me away after *that*? I may regularly question my sanity where you're concerned, but I'm not *that* crazy.'

'You have no idea what you do to me, do you?' he asked, shaking his head.

'If it's a fraction of what you do to me, then I'll be happy.'

'I suggest you scrap happy and try out deliriously ecstatic for size. I was trying to apologise for losing control. I was concerned I'd hurt you and—'

'You didn't,' she reassured. 'You were incredible.'

He grinned . . . before frowning. 'What did you mean, "unless I don't want you?" Have you *any* idea what those words did to me? You weren't saying it to provoke a response, I know that.' Although, boy, had it provoked a response. He was constantly having to battle his urges around Susie, attempting to rein himself in so he could act like a rational human being, rather than being driven by the instincts that raged through him. Yet those words . . . He'd had no hope. No hope whatsoever. 'How could you possibly think I didn't want you?'

Susie was so not going there. Despite the blip, she'd never felt so wonderful, so blissfully contented, so . . . *whole,* in her life. She refused to ruin it with the reminder he'd not yet seen her body properly. She glanced down at what she could see of herself. Jeez, he'd destroyed her dress. She remembered the rip and grinned, but it quickly disappeared as she took in her boobs still hanging out. She blushed and quickly popped them back into her bra. At least that had survived. She knew for a fact her knickers hadn't. But at least he couldn't see her bum or her thighs like this. And if lights were off, she'd be fine. Or if they did it against walls . . .

She looked back up to meet his eyes. He was still waiting for an answer. 'We're not having that conversation with you holding me like this,' she fenced.

'You forget about me still being inside you.'

She hadn't forgotten that. She felt him stirring deep within. She smiled slowly and moved her hips a tad, meeting his warning look with a too innocent one of her own.

'You still haven't told me what you meant and we can have *every* conversation like this.'

'Fine,' she grinned, broadly. 'Then I'll do this . . .' She rotated her hips and . . . gulped. That had somewhat backfired. She suppressed the moan and after swallowing hard, managed to gasp out the end of her sentence, '. . . every time you insist on having conversations like this.'

'Fine,' he replied, turning and walking towards the stairs, Susie still in his arms, wrapped around him, them still connected.

'George put me down. What are you doing? Put me down.'

If he could keep them together like this . . . He groaned, incapable of continuing any more thought. Every step was proving agony. Susie's earlier play had already stirred things to life and the jarring movement was causing significant issues. Evidently he couldn't get enough of Susie, despite having just experienced the best sex of his life. Not that sex remotely covered it.

As the latest jolt had its effect, George was forced to question how much further he could go. He could *not* take her on the stairs. He couldn't. He was supposed to be taking her to his room and they were going to talk . . . For God's sake! He'd just taken her up against a wall and . . .

She moaned quietly, aggravating the issue. That sound . . . Her head dropped to his shoulder and he could feel her quickened breaths against his skin. He took another step up. They both cried out.

'Susie . . .'

He moved up another step and she squealed.

'I'm going to have to stop.' He couldn't believe he was going to do this. But the choice was letting her go or . . .? There was no choice whatsoever.

'I'm so sorry,' she groaned. 'I must be breaking your back here. Put me down.'

Not a chance. 'I will put you down, but not because of that. I need you. Again. Now. I'm sorry – *not* for needing you,' he said pointedly, to prevent any further misunderstanding, 'but . . . *Bloody hell*! Have you ever done it on the stairs?'

'No. Have you?'

If he could press the rewind button . . . But he would always be honest with her. 'Yes. But not these stairs and nothing is ever going to have been like this.'

Her head was off his shoulder. 'Who did you do it with on the stairs?'

'Susie . . .'

'Was she beautiful? Of course she was. I bet—'

'Susie.' That was a growl.

'She was thin wasn't she?'

Give him strength. He kissed her to both silence her and because his self-control had expired. The last clear thought he had before Susie literally brought him to his knees, was that he was going to have to talk to her about her beautiful body. Perhaps he might do so while kissing and tasting and nibbling every delectable pore of it.

And his shopping list was growing. Her bra was proving . . . tiresome.

CHAPTER 18

'I can't believe I found my jumper in your bed,' Susie giggled, now under a sheet within that bed and snuggled up beyond contentedly, to a 'jaw-droppingly spectacular in the noddy' George Silbury. She thought of that coat of his in her own bed and giggled again. She rubbed her feet up and down his long muscular legs, revelling in the sensation of the hairs rubbing against her skin, while running a hand over his unbelievably perfect torso. Being in his arms felt so right.

Which was wrong. Because this was George Silbury! How on earth had this happened? She'd never been a lucky person, always having to work hard for everything. Life simply couldn't be this good – or wrong! She was *not* a glass half-empty person, just a realist. There had to be a catch. And she knew what it would be . . . *bugger off, head!*

'As I recall you didn't provide me with an opportunity to return it.' His arm, draped over her back, held her to his chest and his fingertips ran gently, but distractingly, up and down her spine. She couldn't believe her body still had the energy to respond. They'd been at it all night. It was well into the next day.

She'd been so wrong to go with her head and to have thought the worst of him. So wrong not to have taken heed of what the rest of her was crying out for. While being in hell herself, she'd hurt him. Hurt him badly. He cared! George Silbury cared! For her! Susie Morris!

'For *now* he cared,' her head corrected. Well she'd take it. She could not, would not think of what lay ahead.

'I'm so sorry for not returning your calls. It was just all so confusing and—'

'Scary?'

'Yes. But . . . I really am sorry.' And she had to change the subject here. She refused to mar this time with George. 'George . . .' She drew slow circles upon his chest. 'I've probably got the wrong end of the stick, but . . . have you ever run after a coach?'

His hand on her back stilled. There was a long pause before he groaned. 'You know, first the jumper . . . now the coach. Really, my humiliation is pretty much complete. Yes Susie, I ran after your coach.'

How could he make her feel any more precious? 'That's not humiliating. That's so lovely. Thank you. Thank you so very much.' She snuggled up closer to him, hugging him rather than herself – because she could.

'And that scary conversation you've just tried to

avoid,' he continued. 'You were right to because it wasn't the time. If you remember, we have such conversations with me inside you.'

Susie squealed as in one mind-bogglingly quick move, George had her on her back, pinning her down with his body. Ohhhhhh. Myyyy. Godddd. That felt . . .

'You can't possibly be up for—'

Susie swallowed her words as George moved his hips to ably demonstrate just how prepared he was for such a 'conversation.'

He grinned and cocked an eyebrow. 'You were saying . . .' But then he frowned and immediately rolled off.

Noooo!

Breathing raggedly as he lay on his back at her side, he said, 'I've no chance of thinking, let alone talking in that position.'

Susie reached out to touch him, but he grasped her hand to hold it still against his chest and rolled onto his side to look at her. He pulled the sheets up to her chin, tucking her hand in too, after pressing a kiss to her palm.

'A rain check. We're going to talk.'

Susie attempted to snuggle up again with the purpose of diverting, although that wasn't the only purpose.

George released a sound that could have only been described as a whimper and looked at her pleadingly. 'Please Susie? This is really important to me.'

Why did he have to play that card? And that look on his face. How could she deny him? She slowly, tentatively, nodded.

'We work together physically, would you say?' He let a piece of her hair run between his fingers.

She grinned. How could she not?

'I'll take that as a yes, but perhaps you could not grin and distract me here?'

Susie giggled as she found a pillow shoved between their lower bodies.

'We've established we work together physically, so . . .'

Susie was laughing now. 'I lost count of the number of times you made me—'

George groaned and another pillow found its way between them. God his eyes . . .

'*Please?*' Those eyes now pleaded. 'I need to know. Do I still scare you?'

Susie diverted her look to his chest. 'Do we really have to talk about this?'

'I know you don't want to,' he said, leaning over to give her a stunningly tender kiss. 'But if we talk about it, then we've got a chance of resolving it. I don't want you scared or worrying about things. I want you happy. Blissfully happy. I don't want anything getting in the way of me and you.'

Those words. And *his eyes* . . . She'd made the mistake of looking up again.

'I'll go first if you like?'

She pursed her lips and nodded.

'Thank you,' he whispered over her lips, before

leaning back and taking a deep breath. 'I confessed to being scared last night . . .'

Susie reached out to stroke his cheek and he turned his face to kiss her hand.

'Are you still scared?' she asked, not wanting him to ever have to be scared about anything. He kissed each finger before threading his own fingers between hers and cradling her hand upon his chest.

'Of course,' he sighed. 'I thank you for being satisfied with my performance so that has eliminated that worry, but—'

Susie couldn't help the snort of laughter. '*You* were concerned about *your* performance?' That was mad. He was having her on.

He raised a wry eyebrow before chuckling. 'Laugh all you like, but anticipating being a disappointment to you was not remotely laughable at the time. It was seriously—'

'You are not serious? You seriously can't be serious! How could you possibly think *you* could disappoint *me?* Look at you, George. Just look at you. You are, yet again, officially the sexiest man in the world this year and you have this knack of just being near me and I get all hot and needy. Even if I don't know you're bloody well there! How could you possibly think—?'

'Well how could you possibly think I didn't want *you?*' he countered, very cleverly, she thought. 'And that's what you implied last night.'

She knew he wasn't stupid, but he didn't have to prove it. In fact, being stupid now and again might come in highly useful. Actually, why did she ever think his intelligence was attractive?

'I react to you in exactly the same way you just described, Susie, with an addition that's down to gender.'

How could he feel it too? It made no sense whatsoever. He was as deranged as she. 'How could I think anything else, George?' she asked quietly, gently prodding his chest to help demonstrate the point. She shook her head. 'You are so far out of my league. You have dated the most beautiful women in the world and rolled around naked with the rest of them in front of the cameras.'

The thought of him being with those women made her so jealous. Coupled with her own insecurities, she couldn't keep it from her raised voice. 'They all parade around on tropical beaches, in non-waterproof bikinis, so they can appear on the pages of *Hello!* magazine and make people like me feel even more inadequate. How could I *possibly* think *you* could be happy with *me*? Porsche's description was bang on and you are going to run away screaming when—'

George growled. He *literally* growled, and the pillows were gone and he was pulling her onto his chest and hugging her in his arms. 'I will never, ever forgive Porsche for what she said. She is a—'

'She wants you George, I can see that, but it isn't just Porsche. I didn't need her to tell me I've not a chance of securing you and—'

He interrupted her with the foulest string of curses

she'd ever heard. Some of them were . . . wow . . . and together they were really impressive.

He shifted their positions so they were both sat and gently lifted her chin. She found herself looking into the stunning depths of his eyes. So earnest. 'You *have* secured me, Susie, completely, totally, overwhelmingly. And *you* are the most beautiful creature to have ever walked this earth. Your body, your hair, your eyes, your mouth, your mind – you! You have no idea how beautiful you are, do you? You're a natural. You don't have to contrive it. You just have it, yet you don't see it. But believe me, others do. I do. You seriously are the most beautiful woman I have ever encountered. I'm surrounded day in day out by women whose beauty is engin-eered. Who work hard at it – too hard. But that's not beauty. It's a mask. What's before me now is the real thing. You are incredibly beautiful, Susie. And I am being one hundred per cent honest.'

Oh my God. *I love him.*

'And shall I tell you what scares me? Scares me stupid?' And he couldn't believe he was confessing this, but perhaps it would help reassure her. 'Losing you. Because having found you, I feel like the luckiest man in the world, the luckiest man to have ever been upon this earth.' *And I'm plagued by that damned fear.*

'You aren't going to lose me, George,' she said, stroking his face, not remotely understanding how he could possibly feel this way. He looked so vulnerable. '*I'm* going to lose *you*! And how you've managed to get me to tell you my worst fear, I don't know. But you *will* come to your senses. You will. And I'm going to be left behind suffering the consequences . . .'

'Who was he?' George spoke so quietly she almost didn't hear him as he shook his head, his eyes closed.

'Who?'

'The one you loved and lost. Cassie said you had had a bad experience in the past and have sworn off love.' He opened his eyes now and she felt the pain she saw there. 'Is he why you won't believe me? Why you don't accept my assurances?'

Oh George. She was torn between hugging him and reacting to her anger. She chose the latter and extricated herself. She flopped down onto her back and crossed her arms over her chest.

How *dare* Rachael blab to Cassie! And with the reference to that night . . . those damned feelings were at full force. She closed her eyes as they engulfed her and – they were gone. George had reached out to touch her face. He'd zapped them. The relief . . . but then, of course, she knew why he had that power. So it was hardly reassuring.

'Talk to me,' he gently urged, now lying at her side, facing her. 'I promise I'll tell you anything you ask of me and I will never lie to you. I vow that now.'

With a bent arm across her forehead, she revealed bitterly, 'There wasn't anyone. It was just a terrible experience at the hands of Rachael.'

He remained quiet, but sneaked close enough to pull her into his arms again. He was too good to be true. But was clearly expecting her to continue.

'It was a decade ago,' she confessed quietly. 'We all had too much to drink, too much dope and Rachael attempted one of her "past life regression" things.' Her disgust at the very concept was clear. 'It wasn't real, but my brain freaked out and gave me a taste of . . . some not very nice sensations. It didn't feel at all good and those feelings . . . loss, desolation, betrayal . . .' She attempted to say them flippantly. 'Well, they regularly come back to haunt me.' She was so not telling him about the eyes! 'So I've avoided situations where I might become exposed and at risk of feeling that way. Unfortunately, you're now on the scene . . .'

He made a spluttering sound.

'*Fortunately* you're on the scene,' she corrected, shifting to stroke his chest reassuringly. 'But *unfor*tunately I am now completely exposed. And I am George, completely exposed with you and no doubt going to suffer all that stuff for—'

He'd raised her chin so she could meet his eyes. 'I will never leave you and I will never betray you.'

'You can't say that.'

'I just did and I have never meant anything more.'

'You can't! And you haven't seen me with the lights on!'

'What on earth are you talking about?'

'I don't look like those women George and when

you see me with the lights on, you are going to take one look and—'

'You haven't taken on board a thing I've said, have you? I don't want you looking like those women. Not one of them is a patch on you. Susie? Sweetheart, how can you possibly feel this? You don't think I've seen you as we've made love? Seen you and worshipped you and loved you? I don't know what else to say to reassure you. Actually, you know what? I will put myself through torture. I will *force* myself to make love slowly to every part of your body . . .' He shut his eyes for a moment before taking a ragged breath. 'It will be torture because clearly your body doesn't do a thing for me. But I'll go through the torture, if I must.'

How could he make a joke about this? She raised herself up to punch him on the arm a bit too hard to be playful.

He grinned. 'Can't you see how ridiculous you're being? And incidentally, it will be torture because I started off with this very intention several times last night, but lacked the staying power to get past the early hurdles! But if it must be done, my torture will begin the second we've finished talking and I've minimised the chance of *you* leaving *me*.'

'I will never leave you!' Susie cried, never ever meaning anything more. Although she continued on a mutter, 'Unless you carry on taking the piss out of my legitimate concerns.'

'I'm not taking the piss,' he said gently. 'You are just so far off the mark with how I see you. And the way you see yourself, too. You are gorgeous, Susie, totally and utterly gorgeous. My words aren't helping, so perhaps a bit of action will. See what I'm prepared to do for you? The selfless sacrifices I'm prepared to make?'

She punched him again, repeatedly, and laughing, he grabbed hold of her wrists. Pulling her back down by them, he said, his mouth just beneath her lips, 'You are gorgeous, Susie. Now say that thing about never leaving again and add the bit about betrayal.'

She shook her head and couldn't help but match his grin. 'I will never leave you and never betray you.'

'Thank you,' he said, sounding so sincere. And his eyes . . . He kissed her nose. 'I will hold you to it. I may just need you reminding me now and again.'

As he released her wrists, she used a hand to stroke his face while he threaded his fingers through those of her spare hand.

'Can you still not remember what happened when we first met?' he asked.

She shook her head, playing with a dark flop of hair over his forehead. 'No. I just get the biggest headache and—'

'You too?' George raised himself up, concerned. 'Don't try and remember then, baby.' He kissed her forehead so tenderly.

She could get used to this. Not that she should.

'It doesn't make any sense,' George mused.

'When Rachael did her regression thing on you . . . you can remember?'

'Unfortunately, but I won't,' she ground out. Never. She added a few more chains to that box in her head for good measure. 'It wasn't real. None of it is. Loopy, but not real.'

'I suppose we could have banged our heads or something . . . But . . .' There was a long pause.

'George?' Susie prompted, gazing into his eyes. 'Move in with me?'

CHAPTER 19

Cassie loved her mum very much. But she was going to get lockjaw if she was forced to grit her teeth for much longer.

'Mum. As I've explained, George is going to call you and arrange to meet up. It would not be appropriate to just turn up on his doorstep. He's got plans and I don't think—'

'Cassie, the taxi is basically going to go past his door, so—'

'No, it's not. You asked the driver to take a detour en route to the hotel. The *detour* is going to go past his door.'

'I'm just going to ring his bell and see if he's there. I'm worried about him. When you *finally* have children of your own you will understand. His reassurances on the phone didn't hold true. If I ever get my hands on the girl that hurt him like this, I will not be accountable for my actions.'

'The same girl you had such high hopes for? The one you had such a good feeling about because she drove him to lose his head in public?'

'She hadn't hurt him then.'

'I have it on very good authority that they've patched things up.'

'Perhaps I'll get to meet her then, and be able to gauge for myself whether she's got the potential to break his heart again.'

'*That's* what this is all about!' Cassie cried, turning to glare at her mother accusingly. She shook her head. 'You suspect she's what he's got planned this weekend and you want to meet her! Mum, that isn't fair. That really isn't fair. I won't allow you to do this.'

'And just how do you propose to stop me?' Addressing the taxi driver, she instructed, 'Just over there behind the black car please.'

Cassie bolted out of the taxi as soon as it pulled up. There was no way she could let this happen. On reaching George's front door she pretended to ring the bell. After a moment's pause, she announced, 'He's not in, so let's go.' She turned with the intention of heading back down the steps.

Unfortunately her mother was right behind her. How could she move that quickly? And no way! She had just magicked a key from her handbag. 'Where did you get that from? You can't do this, Mum!' Cassie cried, pressing herself tightly against the door to prevent her mother getting to the lock. In so doing she accidentally rang the bell. If George had a shred of sense he wouldn't answer the door.

'Cassie . . . Do you wish me to continue to pretend I do not know you have a second bedroom at which I could stay *every* time I come to London with little or no notice?'

She *knew?* And boy did she choose her moments. The scheming . . . And George was going to kill her – *her*, Cassie, not Mum, although it was her he should be throttling!

Cassie scooted around in her own handbag to retrieve her phone. 'Mum, let's just see if we can get hold of him on the phone rather than breaking and entering, shall we?'

'I don't believe a mother using the key her son gave her to access his property "whenever she wanted" is breaking and entering.'

'The intent you have Mum is not innocent, so don't try and play it with me. It won't work. I know exactly what you're doing here.'

George had to move, although he could lay with Susie sleeping in his arms forever. He lowered his face into her hair and absorbed the sensation. The soft silkiness against his skin, her scent. This was heaven. There was no better word for it. And she'd said yes. He couldn't help the grin that appeared on his face . . . And to think he was supposed to be taking things slowly! He'd never been more nervous of asking a question before in his life. In fact, he'd never before asked that particular question of anyone. And her pause had been agony.

But she would be the first, the last and the only. He'd make sure of it. And those haunting fears? Susie had them of a sort, too, although hers were down to another awful experience courtesy of Rachael Jones. He really hoped he'd managed to reassure her. If he hadn't succeeded quite yet, he would make it his priority.

As for his . . .? He shook his head at himself. He wasn't sure where the hell his fears came from. Did everyone experience this fear of loss when they'd found 'the' one? Whatever. He was going to work on getting a grip on them. He'd get them under control . . . somehow.

Forcing himself to move, George very carefully extricated his limbs from Susie's and sidled out of bed. He paused to watch her snuggle into the space he'd left. She was so beautiful. How could she possibly think she wasn't? Lying with her glorious hair, blonde but with those amazing red tinges, fanned out around her on the pillow . . . She actually looked like an angel. He smirked as he recalled the passion that had led to this point. Perhaps not so angelic – but definitely his heaven.

And she looked perfect in his bed. Right. Righter than right. He wanted to wake up every morning with her as the first thing he saw. Her breath and her voice, the first thing he heard. And forever had a good ring to it. But first things first.

Food. He'd invited her into his – *their*, he grinned – home, and had offered her no food at all. He pulled on his jeans in order to head to the kitchen and cursed silently as the door buzzer rang again. He had no intention of answering it, but glanced anxiously at Susie to make sure she'd not been disturbed. She snuggled down deeper into the pillow and he gently pulled the sheet up to cover her. As George headed out of the bedroom door he retrieved his mobile from his pocket and switched it on. He'd not been able to find his watch to check the time. It lit up: 5.00 p.m.! He frowned. He *really* needed to get some food going.

Absently scanning through the messages received, he clicked on Cassie's to hear what she had to say. He froze as her panicked voice sounded in his ear. *Bloody hell!*

Cassie stood in George's entrance hall nervously shifting her feet. She had absolutely no idea what to do. She'd at least made it into the house first, managing to pick up and stuff into her handbag those garments littering the floor. Garments, she was quite convinced, George would not want their mother to see. She winced, trying not to think of the shredded item of clothing she'd found and what had evidently taken place in the entrance hall.

Mum was currently in the living room off the hallway. Cassie was standing guard to make sure she didn't wander any further. Cassie had already tried to convince her George was not at home, and even pretended to have checked upstairs. But her eagle-eyed mother had spied his car outside and insisted on waiting for a few minutes, as he had 'most likely just popped out.' Cassie explained

250

the concept of taxis and limousines, but the scheming witch was refusing to budge. How long had she known about the second bedroom?

Cassie had called and left a message for George and rung the door bell again, but failing actually going upstairs – which she was absolutely *not* doing – she didn't quite know what to do to tip George off to the predicament.

George walked down the stairs, pocketing pieces of Susie's bra en route and some black shreds of fabric – God he'd annihilated her dress. He met Cassie's relieved, but frantic eyes.

She shook her head and pointed repeatedly to the living room. She then partook in frenzied gestures before reaching into her handbag, producing underwear and his T-shirt, before shoving it back in and dramatically rolling her eyes. As he got closer, she mouthed, 'I'm sorry.' It graduated to urgent whispers when he was before her. 'I tried George. She diverted the taxi and then produced a bloody key on the doorstep. And do you know what? She *knows* about the second bedroom! She shamelessly used it against me.'

George knew what his mum was like. He loved her desperately, but when she decided on something, there was no way she'd budge. He bent down and kissed Cassie on the cheek. 'Thank you for trying.'

'You forgive me?'

He chuckled. 'Of course. And thank you. I'm just relieved you kept her away until now, but I need her out of the house before Susie wakes up because Mum is the last thing I'd inflict on her at this stage.'

'She says she can't wait to get her hands on the woman that hurt you so badly.'

George raised an eyebrow. 'Help me get her out, yeah?'

'Deal,' Cassie declared, high-fiving his raised hand.

'Well I must say you don't look any worse for your ordeal,' George's mum declared as he walked into the living room.

'I'm not, Mum.'

'A shirt wouldn't have gone amiss, though.'

'I wasn't expecting visitors.' She knew exactly what she was doing here George realised, noting the sparkle in her far too alert blue eyes. She was seventy-three, had borne four children, but didn't look a day over fifty. And her brain, he knew from experience, was as unmarked by the years. Cassie had it spot on in her message: Mum wants to meet Susie and nothing will stop her. Well, it wasn't happening. Not yet. Exposing Susie to his mum was not a good idea; it wasn't fair on her. And while he'd yet to control that fear of his, he was not taking any unnecessary risks.

'So it's serious,' she stated. Not a question, just a statement. 'Has she moved in yet?'

She was uncannily perceptive, always had been. He'd never been able to hide anything from her.

George cleared his throat awkwardly and looked

to Cassie for support. She shrugged her shoulders and winced.

Susie rolled over, stretched and grinned. She couldn't help it. She didn't think she had ever before felt this content.

Betrayal . . .

If she could lop off her own head and still function, she'd damned well do it!

Susie continued with her body roll, intending to return the favour George had bestowed upon her. But instead abruptly sat up in bed. Where was he? She didn't at all like not waking up next to him.

'George?' she called. Perhaps he was in the bathroom. Dragging the silk sheet off the bed to wrap around her, she ventured to the adjoining room. Empty. But such a stunning room. And she couldn't wait to explore the sunken plunge bath, the size of a small swimming pool. And look at that! There was even a hook for a bathrobe right there at the steps into the thing.

Grinning, she moved out of the bathroom and George's bedroom, to tentatively explore some of the rooms upstairs. 'George?' She really didn't feel right nosing around his house like this. It was gorgeous though. Other than his bedroom . . . and the shower room, how could she ever forget that shower . . .? she hadn't really noticed anything but the entrance hall and the staircase last night. And even then she'd been . . . distracted. She blushed at the memories and let her body do its heating and tingling thing before she attempted a refocus.

The house was huge, but very tastefully decorated and despite its size and George spending so much time in the States, it still felt like a home. She stopped in an upstairs corridor to look at what must be family photos. She played 'spot George' in some of the 1970s images full of children wearing striped jumpers. She was sure she had it right. One hundred per cent sure. It was his darned eyes.

She wondered where he could be and, as her stomach grumbled, thought she'd found the answer. She was starving. It had to be the kitchen. And she would kill for a coffee. But that could wait until she'd wrapped her arms around him and held him tightly for a while or so; there was nothing so wonderful as that feeling of being in his arms.

Holding onto the carved wood banister of the sweeping staircase she held such fond recollections of, she descended, being careful not to trip over the sheet. It was trailing behind her too and for a moment she felt like a fairy tale princess. She couldn't believe she appeared to be . . . in a relationship with George Silbury! And he thought she was beautiful. And he didn't want to lose her. He was mad, truly mad.

At the bottom Susie pondered as to the direction of the kitchen. George could help. 'George?' she called. 'Where are you? Could you perhaps come and ravage me again? Actually it's my turn to ravage. When I find you, I'm going to suck your—'

254

She stopped as George dived out of a room off the entrance hall. She grinned. God she'd missed him. He grinned back. That incredible lopsided smile that hit her soul deep, and *his eyes* . . . But his expression changed to a frown as the door he was attempting to close behind him, refused to shut.

He rolled his eyes and was instantaneously before her. 'I am so sorry,' he murmured, before kissing her. That kiss did things . . . But he'd moved his head back on a curse and a frown. 'I'm so, so sorry!'

Amidst her confusion he moved to her side, wrapping an arm around her waist. She looked up to his face for clarification, but was distracted as a woman emerged from the room he'd exited. Tall, dark-haired, elegant, very beautiful . . . Why was . . .? Susie's brow furrowed. She looked similar to the woman that was in so many of the pictures upstairs that she'd always assumed to be George's—

'Susie . . . may I introduce you to my mother?'
Nooooo! No! No! No!

George tightened his hold around her waist before his hand moved down to grasp hers. He squeezed reassuringly.

'She decided to pay me – *us* – an impromptu visit, while letting herself in with the key she should never have been given and which will now, of course, be confiscated. I believe she wanted to meet you.'

His *mum*? His *mum*? She was standing meeting his mum in a bed sheet and . . . Oh shit! Susie groaned as she recalled her words and it had evidently been audible, because George squeezed her hand afresh and pulled her closer. She looked up at him and he gave her a reassuring smile. She could see the concern in his eyes though. And a heartfelt apology.

Susie turned to look at the woman again. His sister had now also appeared from the room and, looking at her sympathetically, mouthed, 'I'm sorry.' Perhaps she wasn't too bad after all.

Susie said the only thing that could be said in the circumstances. 'Thumb. I was going to offer to suck that splinter out of your thumb.' Turning to George, she asked, 'Have you got the splinter out, George?'

He grinned at her and raised an eyebrow in that amazing way of his, before lowering his head to say quietly in her ear, 'Clever, very clever. Not so sure it worked though. I am so sorry. I had no idea she'd turn up. If it's any consolation, I've been standing in front of my mother with an almighty hard-on thanks to your earlier suggestion.' Susie couldn't help the giggle. 'She will be physically removed if she hasn't left in one-minute flat.'

'It's a pleasure to meet you, Susie,' his mother said, interrupting their intimacies.

Susie turned her attention to her, noting with satisfaction that George pulled her back against the front of his body and wrapped his arms around her front. She closed her eyes momentarily; she could feel the problem he had.

'I can see I'm intruding though and must leave you to attend to my son's . . . thumb.' George cleared his throat behind her, while his sister had her head in a hand. 'I won't disturb you a moment longer. We will have our opportunity to talk properly. My apologies for the intrusion.'

She reached out to grasp Susie's hand with both of hers. Susie looked up to meet . . . was that a twinkle in her eyes?

As she turned away and headed towards the door, she said, 'Cassie – return their clothing, please.'

That night Cassie collapsed in relief upon her sofa. Snuggling under the duvet she'd dragged from her bedroom, she looked contentedly into the relaxing flames of the log fire she'd lit.

She owed Mark big time. He'd finally agreed to summon Mum on the pretence of needing help with childcare. She'd happily scuttled off to Kent to rescue her eldest son, having completed her mission here to meet Susie. And to drive Cassie up the wall. Mark could have been in no doubt as to Cassie's desperation, but she wondered just what her oldest, very shrewd brother, would insist on in terms of repayment.

Sighing, she reached out for her mug of tea. That was one thing she could say for her mum's visits: Cassie appreciated her life all the more when she'd gone. And George and Susie seemed to be getting their act together. She'd never before seen that sparkle in his eyes. Yes. Life, bizarrely, despite the horrors of previous weeks, was good. Popping her mug down, Cassie stretched out to pick up a letter from the unread pile on her coffee table. Freddie's, she noted from the handwriting as she snuggled up again in the duvet. She was actually managing to view these letters objectively now, she realised, for what they were. The past. A painful past, yes, but she could clearly differentiate the past from the present now.

As she unfolded the letter she wondered what this would relate to. They were in chronological order, so things had yet to get nasty. The Argylle family still expected Freddie to marry Prudence, despite his past assertions to the contrary and the unmistakeable interest he was showing in Hannah. Although intent on riding out the post-fireworks storm, no observer could miss the way they looked at each other, or the chemistry between them.

The venom Cassie experienced in Kathryn's memories caught her by surprise. Why she was surprised she didn't know. It was in character. Swallowing, Cassie reassured herself exactly who she was.

It was pretty evident though, had the Argylles not enlisted Kathryn's help with separating Freddie and Hannah, she would have acted independently to the same end.

In the event, they'd approached her for assistance when the extent of the Hannah problem became obvious. When Freddie had given Matthew Argylle two black eyes on his suggestion he satisfy his lust for Hannah, but marry Prudence.

My dearest angel,
Pray forgive me! You should never have encountered my mother thus.

Rest assured, she will never reveal the compromising nature in which we were found. She wishes to see me happy, Hannah, and I could never be happy without you.

Your using a splinter of wood by means of explanation was very clever and —

Cassie dropped the letter from suddenly shaking hands.

No!

Flinging off the duvet, she ran through to her bedroom and opened her bedside drawer to retrieve the letters she'd already read. She opened the one she'd read at random in Wiltshire, and scanned the contents. Freddie's flower garden raids. *Yes!* George didn't have a flower garden. She dismissed the number of bouquets George had sent Susie when she hadn't returned his calls because . . . it wasn't helpful. She picked up the next. Church and a forgotten shawl. Okay! She collapsed on the bed in relief before scanning through the next. Not good, really not good. She was beginning to feel ill. She knew what the next letter held.

This was impossible. Totally impossible. And she was *Cassie Silbury!* Cassie Silbury couldn't possibly even contemplate . . .

She dashed out of her room to grab her bag. Finding her mobile, she dialled.

'We need to talk. Now.'

CHAPTER 20

It was 1.00 a.m. and Rachael could not believe she'd got herself out of bed to traipse across London at Cassie's beck and call. A bed she'd only just collapsed into having consumed far too many cocktails with Rob. A Rob who, tonight, had seemed intently focused on drinking himself into oblivion.

She'd not managed to get to the bottom of his low mood at all. It wasn't to do with what she'd told him about Susie and George the other day, she was sure of that. With the proviso that he keep shtum because Susie wouldn't appreciate him being given the details quite yet, she'd, as requested, 'hit him' with the pertinent facts: they were Soul Mates from the past and had recognised each other during George's regression – the aftermath of which he'd witnessed – and were now coming together.

He simply let her talk and afterwards appeared stunned. But following a *very* long silence, he finally said, 'I can only hope they get their happy ending and things start running more smoothly for them because Susie deserves a break.'

'You believe what I'm telling you?' Rachael had urged.

'I was on the receiving end of his look, remember?' He had then turned to her in that intent way of his and murmured, 'I never thought you were mad, Rach. Although on occasions I wish you were.'

He then told her a funny tale about work.

So his low mood hadn't been about that. Nor work. Nor a girl. He'd been most adamant about that. It had all been more than a little frustrating and worrying.

Just like the rest of her night was proving.

Hadn't she done enough of all this beck and call stuff in the past? But there had been a desperate edge to Cassie's voice that had her concerned.

It was bloody freezing, but no sooner had Rachael rung the buzzer than she was hauled inside and through an inner door. Now in the living room of Cassie's flat . . . *very* nice, she was about to demand what the blazes was going on when she caught sight of Cassie's face. She stood with her back against the closed door and looked . . . She could look no more worried were she watching the grim reaper approach.

'Cassie?' Rachael tentatively asked.

Cassie flung herself across the room to disappear through another door. There was some banging around before she re-emerged with a full bottle of vodka and two tumblers.

Rachael shook her head. 'Not for me.' She'd had more than enough tonight.

261

Cassie continued to pour the drink into both glasses which she'd placed upon the dark wood coffee table. The table was positioned in front of the Victorian fireplace that currently housed a roaring fire. Rachael winced and moved as far away from the flames as she could with furniture in the equation. Open fires were something she had never been able to stomach even before she'd been regressed. It had all made sense when she had learnt of that burning at the stake once upon another time.

'You're going to need this,' Cassie said with surety, before promptly downing the contents of her own glass.

Rachael frowned. 'How about you tell me what this is all about?' she ventured, moving herself over to the sofa, kicking a duvet out of the way, and sitting down.

But Cassie had disappeared again! Rachael flung herself back into the cushions of the sofa in frustration.

Seconds later a pile of papers landed in her lap and Cassie slumped down on the sofa next to her.

Rachael glanced from Cassie, who now had her head in her hands, to what looked like . . . old letters . . . *Letters?* 'Are these Freddie and Hannah's?' she cried, unable to hide her excitement. She snatched one up, absorbing the aged paper and the fancy writing. She'd known Cassie had been given the letters, but this was the first time she'd seen them. 'Have you read them? We're talking *serious* love here, aren't we? With the cherries on top? Can I read them when you're done? The more I learn the better. I can't help but feel that the Soul Mates thing might be a tad more complicated than I've always considered it to be.' Rachael shook her head. Now wasn't the time to consider all the questions Matey had wrought and what else she might not know . . . She necessarily refocused and prompted, 'Are you going to tell me what this is all about?'

Cassie remained silent. And Rachael had had enough. 'Flaming Nora! You have to tell me what's going on here. I can't help if I don't *know!*'

Cassie slowly raised her head and looked at her with a haunted look upon her face. Rachael's stomach plummeted.

Cassie's eyes blinked before she asked quietly, 'What do you know of . . . history repeating itself?' Her voice had cracked halfway through that question before she continued to say, 'I'm talking of multiple events someone experiences in a past life playing out in their next, not the world history and whether it's cyclical debate.'

Rachael stared long and hard at Cassie as she thought through what she'd just asked. When she had completed that process she slowly shook her head. It was becoming apparent that the fresh bottle of vodka Cassie had produced was not the first of the night. She knew Cassie had been drinking far too much a while back. Not that she herself could really talk with the amount she'd consumed tonight, but social drinking was a far cry from this. Even *if* Rob hadn't been particularly sociable.

'History would seem to be repeating itself,' Cassie continued in that quiet, cracking voice that might just have been an attempt at matter of fact. 'Or at least some of it is. There's no denying the evidence. It's there in the letters. Not everything tallies, which I'm attempting to clutch on to, but if I look at what's there I've no choice but to consider it. To more than consider it. I thought you should know what I've found. To be told what appears to be happening to George and Susie. I also thought you might be able to help. You seem to have theories on pretty much everything. And for obvious reasons it's not something I've ever contemplated so know nothing about—' Her regularly breaking voice broke off completely and she swallowed audibly. 'I just need to know why and how it's happening so I can make sure it stops. I'm sure you'd like it to stop too because . . .' She focused those haunted eyes on Rachael and any attempt at matter of fact that might have been there went straight out of the window as she cried, 'Because taking it to the logical conclusion, if it continues to repeat . . . my brother and your best friend are going to *die!*'

Just *how* much had Cassie had to drink? Rachael needed to calm her down and get her to bed so she could sleep it off. She'd crash out on the sofa tonight to make sure she was okay. Perhaps in the morning when her own head was completely clear of alcohol – although she could safely say she was finding the present situation sobering – they could chat about her drinking? Not an appealing prospect and one that sobered Rachael up yet further. But someone had to have that talk with her.

'George and Susie are *not* going to die,' Rachael reassured, patting Cassie's hand. She couldn't believe she was having to say this. And to Cassie! 'Well they are. Of course they are. We're all fated to die. But not yet, anyway. Or at least I hope not. How beyond tragic would that be? That would be a real nasty twist from Fate.'

'Your people skills are second to none!'

Rachael shook her head and continued to say, 'History does *not* repeat itself like that, Cassie! What you are talking of is impossible. I have no theories on the subject because it's a ridiculous concept. Why would you ever think *I'd* have theories on it? So how about we—'

'I need you to listen to me.'

Rachael met Cassie's eyes and promptly flopped back in her seat with a sigh. She'd taken in her determination, and it was highly evident she'd not a hope of calming her down until she'd got this out of her system.

'Thank you,' Cassie said before releasing a sigh of her own. Although hers was shuddery. She then took a deep breath and began.

'Hannah and Freddie made a public spectacle of themselves at the firework party.'

Rachael remembered. It had been the hottest gossip of the season.

'Hannah's identity wasn't known,' Cassie continued. 'But Freddie publicly called out Lord Granger over his comments, refusing to have what he and Hannah had going demeaned.'

Rachael nodded, but failed to see where this was going.

'Don't you *see?* George and Susie were caught at it in public. Susie's identity has to date remained a secret. And there's even a price on her head! Hannah had a price on her head too with all the bets being placed. *And* George has made a public declaration on national TV refusing to have their encounter cheapened!'

Rachael shook her head. 'You can't possibly consider history is repeating itself on the basis of that. I really think we should look at getting you to bed and—'

'I am not finished,' Cassie cried.

Rachael closed her eyes and sighed again.

'Hannah encountered Freddie after her little brother threw up on her. Freddie gave her his coat. She'd been on a coach. And I wouldn't be a bit surprised if Freddie hadn't chased after it!'

Rachael slowly opened her eyes.

'Hannah and Freddie were caught in a compromising situation by Freddie's mother. Hannah produced a lame excuse about a splinter. I've been with my mother today. George's mother. We encountered George and Susie in a compromising situation . . . and Susie produced a cock-and-bull story . . . about a *splinter*!'

Rachael sat forward in her seat and stared at Cassie.

'The only thing definitely not matched is an encounter with a shawl in church. The flowers I'm not sure about. George hasn't got a flower garden so . . . He didn't send roses did he? But Susie isn't religious is she? You'd never get George in a church. And surely she doesn't own a shawl?'

Rachael had stopped listening. It had to be coincidence. But then Rachael nearly choked at the thought. She didn't believe in coincidence. Fate. She believed in Fate. Ring-a-ding-ding, Fate is doing his thing. But this couldn't be Fate. George and Susie would have their own fate. It couldn't be the same as Freddie and Hannah's. If that was the case, it would be a continual cycle of history repeating itself over and over. That didn't happen. She knew that. She'd had completely different past lives. She'd yet to discover them all, but those she knew about *were* different.

'You don't think their meeting during George's regression, while he was reliving the past, could have in any way linked the two?' Cassie was asking. 'I'm a sensible person – I am! But it was as if they were Hannah and Freddie for those moments before they passed out, or whatever the hell it was they did! Could it have possibly . . . muddled things up? I can't believe I'm asking this, but I have to! Because of what I've found, what's there

267

before me, because of what seems to be happening and because I have to make it stop!'

'This makes no sense,' Rachael mumbled. And you didn't 'relive' the past when regressed, you *remembered* it! 'History doesn't—'

'You believe in *every*thing else yet won't even *consider* this? With everything I'm telling you?'

'Because despite what people think, Cassie – I'm left of centre. Not clinically insane!' This *had* to be coincidence. She couldn't allow herself to think it could be anything else. Not with how Hannah and Freddie had ended up.

As she reached a realisation, Rachael let relief flood through her. She declared delightedly, 'In any event, history *can't* repeat itself. Even if technically it could. They only ever ended up dead because of us. And we are out of the equation. You're no longer plotting their downfall, I'm not assisting you . . . In fact, it's quite the opposite. We're working to unite them!' Rachael was feeling rather pleased with herself and worryingly relieved.

'There were *others* working against Freddie and Hannah! Not just us. There was Matthew and Prudence Argylle—'

'It makes no difference. History cannot repeat itself like this.' Rachael was absolutely not prepared to consider the possibility.

'Something is happening to allow it to repeat. We're out of the equation, but the other factors must still be in place.'

'Cassie, will you stop this! History is *not* repeating

itself! There are bound to be some similarities going on. Their personal characteristics aren't that different this time around to what they were then, so they are bound to make similar choices and that could lead to similar patterns. But it doesn't mean history is repeating itself. And you yourself pointed out there are things that are different. If history was repeating itself, which of course it isn't and can't, there wouldn't be differences! Things happened in the past that have not happened in the present and vice versa! It's simply . . . similarities. Will you just pause to listen to yourself for a moment?'

'I'm trying not to because I know how I'm sounding. But something has to be the same for this to be happening. Personalities may be a factor, but I can't see how that's enough. It can't be down to location being the same or us being the same so . . . What if we aren't the only ones around from the past? We're here. So are George and Susie. What if others are? What if other people are the other factors and that's why history is repeating itself? What if they are behaving just as they did in the past and that's allowing—'

'Cassie! Susie and George are not going to die as they did in the past. Which is what this is all about, isn't it? The similarities are simply playing to your fears, don't you see?' Rachael shook her head. She hadn't realised Cassie was still struggling so much. She'd thought she was finally coming to terms with things. She continued gently,

'I know it's hard, but it's the past, Cassie. The past. Forward, remember?'

'It's impossible to look forward with what appears to be happening! What if there *are* others around? What if—'

'Others *will* be around. We are all surrounded by people we've known in the past, but not all from *one particular life*! There's a spread across the ages which no doubt ensures history can't repeat itself in the way you're talking of.'

'What if Matthew and Prudence are around? What if they are plotting to—'

'They're not! I just knew that's where you were going! Will you please stop this! Actually, thinking about it, the presence of so many of us from the same time in the eighteen hundreds – you, me, George, Susie, Rob – may be why we're seeing such similar patterns emerging. We're all having an influence on things going on around us, as we did back then. But it makes no difference because none of us want to see George and Susie separated. And even if Matthew and Prudence *were* around – which they aren't! – they wouldn't necessarily be baddies. We've turned good.

'And do you know what? Even if the similarities continue – and that's all they are – they're going to cease because we aren't going to be turning things nasty this time around. Correct me if I'm wrong, but up to this point Kathryn and Tessa's actions weren't having much of an impact on things. Kathryn had got Tessa to befriend Hannah's maid so we knew her whereabouts and the such, Kathryn had started planting that seed within Tessa, and no doubt Freddie too, that there was more between Hannah and Richard Barratt than there was. But other than that, at *this* stage . . .'

Rachael's words died away as she took in Cassie's confounded gaze and the words that now accompanied it.

'Rob? *Rob* was—'

Rachael screwed up her face as she realised what she'd done. She hadn't meant to let that slip out. It was so much easier when you identified people yourself and in your own time.

'Richard Barratt!' Cassie cried. 'I *knew* there was something but . . . I see it now! Does Rob know? Does he—' Cassie broke off to stare at Rachael, aghast. She whispered, '*The energetic dance with Mr Richard Barratt.*' She now shook her head slowly. 'Freddie watched Hannah dance with him. Just like George watched Susie and Rob dirty dance! How many "similarities" do you want before you consider that history might just be repeating? And . . . *Oh my God!* You look at Rob just like Tessa used to look at Richard Barratt!'

'I do not!' Rachael cried indignantly. 'I absolutely do not.' She didn't! Yes he was as attractive this time around as he had been that time, but she had Matey! 'Rob's a friend!' she cried. 'And you cite that as another *similarity*? If things were "similar" I *wouldn't* be friends with Rob like I am now. Tessa and Richard never even spoke! She just watched him from afar. She was a maid for crying out loud and he was a member of the gentry. They had no chance. And *I know* that Rob and Susie are just friends. Nothing more. And neither do I remotely resent their friendship. Not like Tessa who struggled with Hannah spending so much time with Richard! And neither do I have you – Kathryn! – feeding me lies about the nature of that relationship, fuelling jealousy and envy and using it to get me to do your dirty work. Unlike Tessa! So how about you take that history repeating theory of yours and stick it up your—'

Rachael broke off on a gasp. *No!* 'And before you say a word!' she cried, 'I wasn't at all jealous that Rob danced like that with Susie!' And she wasn't! She *wasn't*! It had to be because she was a woman, Rob an attractive man . . . and Matey was . . . not. *Damn the blip!* 'See? History is not therefore repeating itself,' she said weakly.

Rachael now watched Cassie's face pale before her eyes. Flaming Nora, what was she going to say next? 'Rob is *not* going to be plotting against George and Susie!' she pre-empted. 'He's—'

'I thought of who I know . . .' Cassie's voice was so quiet Rachael could barely hear it. 'No wonder I had such a bad feeling and started going down this route. I knew there had to be other factors . . .' Cassie's haunted eyes held hers. 'They're here. *They* are here. Matthew and Prudence are here.'

CHAPTER 21

'I don't need feeding, George,' Susie giggled, nevertheless opening her mouth to receive the piece of fresh pineapple George held poised on a fork.

'I know, but this is rather fun.' He leant forward to kiss her gently on the lips and to expertly – *soo* expertly – lick up some pineapple juice that had managed to escape. 'I think every Sunday morning should be spent like this. And humour me; I've never handfed a woman before.'

Susie gently pushed George's hand away as he attempted to provide her with more fruit. She giggled and raised a brow. 'That's because we can feed ourselves. And I'm sorry, but I couldn't possibly eat any more.' She leant forward and gave him a lingering kiss before sitting back in her chair so her overly full stomach felt less uncomfortable. She took the opportunity to let her eyes wander around the kitchen again. So tasteful. Gorgeous actually. Understated, but *very* evidently *very* expensive. It was all a far cry from her and Rachael's flat. Well, her old flat, she realised on a frown.

'What's put that look on your face?' George asked, wiping his fingers on a piece of kitchen towel, sliding the plates forward on the table laden with enough food to feed an army, and resting his crossed arms upon the cleared surface.

'Just how strange it will be not sharing the flat with Rach.'

'You'll miss her?'

'Mmmm. We've been living in digs or sharing places ever since Uni. It will be strange. I'm not quite sure how she'll fend for herself. She's not the most practical of human beings.' George was frowning now, she realised.

'Are you having second thoughts?' he asked tentatively and intently watched his index finger brush croissant crumbs around the table.

Oh George. She leaned forward, placing her own arms upon the table now and inching them forward. When they made contact with his, he looked up and she shook her head and grinned.

He reached out to pick up her hand with one of his own and play with her fingers before joining their palms. 'I can't believe I'm saying this, I really can't. But. . .' He sighed. 'There's a whole suite of rooms on the top floor which if, for the short-term at least, you . . . If you would feel better you could offer her those?'

'Not a chance.' Susie smirked, shaking her head. 'She would drive you up the wall, I promise you that. But thank you. Thank you so much for offering. I'll talk to her. It'll be fine.'

He shrugged, but his relief was more than evident and Susie started giggling again. 'What would you have done if I'd said yes?'

Grinning and chuckling in that totally irresistible way of his, he said, 'I really don't know. But evidently I'll put myself through anything for you! We didn't exactly hit it off. I think the accusation of my having repressed psychotic tendencies following whatever it was *she* did to *me* that day, may have had something to do with it.'

Giggling uncontrollably now, Susie managed to get out, 'She didn't! I'm so sorry.' Then archly, she added, 'What *did* you do, George?'

He laughed. 'That's the million dollar question!'

'Whatever it was my body kind of liked it.'

'Ditto,' George murmured, with *that* look in his eyes as he held hers.

Susie decided there and then that it was impossible for her body to run at normal temperature around George. She released some air from her lips to blow it up over her face. But God it felt good. Deliriously good. As did George simply holding her hand.

'We should pop over and pick up some of your things later?' he suggested. 'And we should sort out the best way of getting you to work from here.'

'I'll bus it,' Susie said, before real life intruded. She groaned at the realisation. 'I've got marking to do later. I forgot all about it.'

'Perhaps I could run a bath for when you've finished?'

She met his grin. She knew just where he was going with that suggestion and that sounded like a pretty wonderful incentive to get the marking done pronto.

'About the bus though . . .'

'Mmmm,' she said, it being her turn to play with his fingers. His hands were huge. She raised one up and placed her palm to his again. Wow. She should have known. He was what, six foot two to her five foot four, well *possibly* three? And his fingers . . . How could someone have sexy fingers? She felt herself blush as she remembered recent occurrences. There was her answer.

'I would drop you off at work myself if there wasn't the risk that I'd be spotted and your anonymity blown. But I could arrange a car and that way . . .'

She shook her head. 'It's no issue at all. I always get the bus. I like going to work on the bus. It gives me time to gear up for it and, if I'm lucky and end up nabbing a seat, to read.' He was still frowning and clearly had something on his mind. 'What is it?'

'You know I will do everything I can to protect you from the media, but there's always the chance they could find out about you. That whole fiasco with *The Herald* . . . And if they do, there will be no warning. I don't want you to have to tackle it alone.'

'I'll keep a low profile. Believe me, the whole idea of appearing in the press again, or God forbid

276

having my photo taken . . .' She hated photos of herself, even when they didn't involve G-strings, 'means I'll be careful. Very careful.'

His frown deepened. 'Susie . . .'

He seemed to be struggling to find a way to best choose his words. He shook his head firmly and started afresh. 'Susie, I'd like to get you some bodyguards.'

She blinked. 'I'm sorry?'

'You heard me, sweetheart.'

She shook her head. 'Bodyguards?' She looked into his eyes and took in the determined look on his face. *Bodyguards?* She shook her head adamantly now and spluttered, 'No way! *Absolutely* no way!'

'I think it would be prudent. If the press got wind of you, then all hell will break loose and—'

'Don't be ridiculous, George. You I get but *you* don't have them!'

'Sometimes I do and it would make me feel better here. It's just a precaution and—'

'No! No George, no! I don't need *bodyguards*. I'm a teacher! And nobody knows about us. I can't believe you've even suggested it.'

'What about . . . What about when, or if, we choose to go public?'

Susie knew she'd blanched. Shit. 'Look we'll deal with it then. But in the meantime – no way! If I keep a low profile there's no reason to think the media will find out about me. There is absolutely no need for bodyguards. I don't need them and I won't have them!'

George silently cursed. He'd known this would be a sensitive subject, but hadn't expected Susie to be quite so adamantly opposed to the concept. But he *needed* her to have bodyguards. If the media got wind of her, it would be a frenzy with her right in the middle of it, all alone and unguarded.

But it wasn't just the media. He winced at the realisation.

The idea of her being bodily guarded appealed too, thanks to that damned haunting fear which he'd yet to get a grip on. Rather than lessening, it was bloody well growing and was unnerving him big time. Yes, she might leave him, but alternatively, she might get hurt and . . . He couldn't finish that thought. Bodyguards would be a comfort. He'd work on her. And himself. Because he knew he was being illogical and needed a healthy dose of rationality.

Yet rationality seemed to regularly go out of the window where Susie was concerned. He could keep his head in any damned situation . . . unless it involved Susie. With her, instincts kicked in. Extreme instincts. Deep rooted, hunter-gatherer, protect what's mine instincts. And trying to control it . . . particularly where her safety was concerned . . . Jesus.

But there *must* be a way to reach a happy compromise here that worked for them both.

As for the media . . . He'd do whatever it took to protect Susie from the public eye. Whatever it took.

'I believe we need to work on a mutually agreeable

compromise,' he said, raising his eyebrows. And how rational had he just sounded?

Susie frowned before breaking out into a wide grin. And that look . . . straight to his groin. 'Feel free to *work* on me whenever you like, George. If you think you're *up* for it, of course?'

'I am Cassie Silbury,' Cassie asserted out loud as she sat at her desk in her second bedroom where so much of her work was done. She was saying that, not because of fears she was Kathryn Montague, but *because she was Cassie Silbury: top investigative journalist and bitch hack!* She needed to get a grip on herself and if it meant going into full-blown professional mode to do so, then that's exactly what she'd do. Because God help her . . . personal mode was a bit of a mess right now.

She took a deep fortifying breath. She would look at everything objectively and not allow panic to enter the equation as it had done last night, despite her best efforts to the contrary. Rachael had been spot on when she had said Cassie's fears were being played to. Of course they were! The whole idea that George might—

Cassie Silbury, she urgently reminded herself as she abruptly sat forward in her seat and grabbed her pen. She was going to be calm and rational. She repositioned her notepad so it was squarely in the middle of her desk and directly before her. See. She could do this.

'What' and 'Why' she quickly wrote on either

side of the blank facing page to form headings for columns. And then underlined both words rapidly rather than allowing herself to add, 'the effing hell is happening?' after the first word and 'did I ever start this damned story?' after the second. She promptly added question marks after each word to close down the possibility of additions and drew boxes around each to further contain and isolate. She continued adding to the bulk of those boxes as she pondered the appropriate title to go at the top of the page. She concluded she didn't need one. She was hardly going to be able to forget what all this related to.

She sat back in her seat, the top of her pen against her front teeth. What *was* going on? *Why* was it happening? She let all of Rachael's words and reassurances play back in her head. Which she promptly shook because her life was such that she had no choice right now but to give serious consideration to what The Nutty Regressor had to say. While she would concede that on a personal level she'd found herself warming to Rachael, what came out of her mouth . . .?

But Rachael *did* know about past lives. Cassie's investigations often involved talking to experts in their fields and . . . She categorically refused to apply that label to Rachael! But she was her best shot right now. The internet had proven a joke on this subject. Cassie recalled what Mark Twain had apparently said, 'History does not repeat itself. But it does rhyme.' Clearly he'd never been in

Rachael's consulting room because rhyming didn't quite hit the spot here. Taking a deep breath, she forced herself to focus.

Similarities? History repeating itself? It seemed like semantics to Cassie. Surely they were much the same? She sat forward to scribble 'ACTION' on the blank left hand page, and added 'Gaps?' and 'Monitor and Compare' underneath the new heading. She'd try and find out from George whether more had been happening than she was aware of. Perhaps the fewer gaps there were, the more likely things would fall into the history repeating camp? But to be honest, she didn't care what label was applied to what was happening – but that it seemed to be happening at all!

Monitoring what George and Susie were up to in the present and comparing with the past was essential though. She swallowed painfully. She'd read the remaining letters this morning . . . She clenched her hand tightly around the pen. *Grip Cassie. Get a grip!* Some of their contents Kathryn had known about. Some she hadn't. Monitoring would ensure Cassie could gauge whether whatever was happening was still happening . . . because if it was, it absolutely had to be stopped.

She now wrote 'HOW???' in the centre of that main page and circled it forcefully. She presently hadn't a clue what to put under that, but refused to let her panic rear its head again. Hopefully this would all stop all by itself and she'd never ever need to come up with an answer for that one.

So . . . 'Why?' She raised a hand to her forehead and pressed. All those reasons Rachael had suggested could stand. Perhaps the circumstance of their meeting was having an effect too? But it was no good. She couldn't help it. *How often did she use that gut feeling in her work before allowing it to lead her to—?*

'Matthew and Prudence' she wrote and felt decidedly ill as she took in that she'd written it where the title would have gone. She rapidly added a question mark . . . no, *four,* and then added their names right under the 'Why?' column, too. It took a moment but she managed to refocus. They were the answer. If they'd come back good then she could stop worrying about any of this. How could nasty events repeat with all the nasty drivers out of the equation? And who cared if good events replayed? That would be fascinating rather than . . . terrifying.

Cassie added under her 'ACTION' list: 'Investigate Michael and Porsche'. She refused to let herself think of how she'd never liked Michael and that Porsche was a prize bitch. That was not at all helpful right now. Instead, she reminded herself of her primary rules of investigation: don't jump to conclusions. Let the evidence speak.

Cassie threw her pen down on the desk and, pushing her notebook out of the way, placed her elbows where her pad had been and lowered her head to her hands. She could not believe they were back! But all would be fine. It had to be! She thought back to the letters and to Kathryn's memories.

What were the chances of anything happening with a horse in London? And she and Rachael *were* out of the equation so that couldn't happen anyway . . .

It was Saturday morning and Susie stood watching Darcy on his horse. Was there ever a more spectacular sight? Incredibly she could think of several as she recapped over the past blissful, heavenly week. Whereas it wasn't appropriate to think such things in public, it didn't stop her body's response.

George was laughing with Mr Bingley, Alexander Devereaux. And the sound of George's happiness rippled through her. She closed her eyes and let her body wallow . . .

'You are good for him, my dear.'

Susie snapped her eyes open and gripped the top of the wooden fence in front of her.

'I'm sorry for startling you. He does look rather dashing, although, of course, I'm biased. He did turn out rather well though, don't you think?'

Blushing profusely and attempting a broad smile, Susie turned to face George's mum. Caught red-handed. Again.

'Mrs Silbury. How lovely to see you again.'

'Do call me Jennifer.'

'I didn't know you were in London . . . Jennifer.' Susie managed a genuine smile.

'Neither do George or Cassie yet. I'm going to

surprise her later. Presently, I'm incognito.' She chuckled and signalled to the spade she'd leant against the fence. Susie did a double take.

'Don't ask,' Mrs Silbury said. 'Then you can't be an accessory. Let us just say the opportunity was there and it was too good to miss.'

This didn't sound at all good. What was she up to? Susie glanced over to George, but the cameras were now rolling and she couldn't make eye contact.

Despite her concerns, though, Susie couldn't help but warm to George's mum. She evidently caused George and Cassie issues, but how nice would it be to have someone around to interfere in your life? Susie missed her own mum. She'd been without her a long time now. Her dad . . . well Dad was Dad. He'd found the strength from somewhere to bring her and her brothers up, but he wasn't who he used to be. Susie called and visited, but it was never the other way around.

'I'm delighted to hear you've moved in with George,' she was continuing. 'I've never known him so happy. Although he still seems to be keeping you under wraps. It's difficult, I know. But you *are* going to the premiere next week?'

Oh, she was good. Susie narrowed her eyes and their target held her hands up. 'Guilty. And George would not be happy should he know I mentioned it.'

Susie sighed, returning her focus to George. She knew he wanted her to go to the premiere. Not that he'd put pressure on her at all. He knew how she felt about the media, but he *had* spoken of how proud he'd be with her standing by his side. Not that Susie could possibly accept that. And then there were the photographs, and all the speculation that would come with her attendance: was *she* the girl George had 'got his horn out' for?

George reassured any coverage on that could only be speculation. They could prove nothing. He had a team of top lawyers on it and nothing libellous or slanderous could ever go into print. Not one newspaper would dare. After a glass too much wine last night, George had even said, how, if it was just the once, he would love to be able to cry from the rooftops that she was his. She loved him for the sentiment, extraordinary as it was, but was terrified of what coverage might result. As much for George as for her.

Michael, his manager, had introduced himself this week, waylaying her on the bus to school. He'd said how George's career could be ruined by the wrong image and he'd made it clear that Susie was the wrong image. And she'd always known that. And then he'd warned of the media scrum. That no matter the intentions, there could be no protection. Photographers would be everywhere. He'd also insisted that she'd have to give up her job. The media would be too much of an issue, even if she wasn't deemed unsuitable to teach because of her G-string centrefold.

Susie released a shaky breath. She hadn't warmed to the man at all, but then she wouldn't have warmed to anyone pointing out the painfully obvious. And neither had she felt able to tell George of the encounter, in case he gave the man further black eyes. He was blinded when it came to her, Michael had explained, and wouldn't listen to sense.

Because he was presently out of his senses.

'I can see it weighs on your mind. Did George tell you he's planning on giving up acting to protect you from the limelight?'

Susie swung around. 'He's *what?*'

'I didn't think so. Don't get me wrong, I'd be delighted to see him settle down, lessen his work-load, not be in the States all the time. But to abandon it? He's good at what he does. And he adores it. He doesn't like the accompanying para-phernalia, but he loves acting. Always has done. He wrote his first play when he was six, roping everyone in to the lesser parts. It was about a cowboy who ate too many baked beans.' She chuckled at the memory. 'I recall his brothers and sister were the baked beans.'

Susie couldn't suppress the smile as she pictured a six-year-old George, just as he appeared in some of those photographs on that upstairs wall at . . . home. God, it was home. It *felt* like home, too!

But he *couldn't* give up acting. Not for her. She wouldn't allow it.

'The media won't be easy,' his mum continued. 'But George will do everything he can to protect you. And the novelty will wear off. Did you know he even has a designer on standby to make you a dress, should you decide to go to the premiere? But he won't push it. He refuses to push you into anything you're not comfortable with. I'm rather envious about the dress though. I can just imagine the creation. I believe he has reserved a particular fabric, just in case. You are a very, very pretty girl Susie and you make an incredibly handsome couple. I very much think he wants to show you off. He's not happy with you sneaking in and out of the house with that cleaner's overall on.'

George *knew* about that?

'I believe the premiere is next Saturday. I might be convinced to hang around in London until then. It would, of course, depend on whether someone would let me come along to a few dress fittings with her? George would be the happiest man alive with you at his side. Perhaps . . .'

'Arrrgggghhhhhhhh!'

Mrs Silbury calmly stopped talking while Susie spun around in the direction of the ear-shattering scream.

'Cut! Who the hell was that? Coffee break everyone.'

'Time to go. Perhaps I could call for you after school on Monday?'

Susie absently nodded as she watched the flurry of activity and people running. When she turned again to clarify things, Mrs Silbury had gone, although she could distinctly hear her voice.

'Oh deary, deary me. How unfortunate. Did you slip over in that horse manure? How could it have ever got there? And so much of it! Everyone, everyone help poor Miss Sutter-Blythe here.'

She hadn't? Susie spun around in an excited circle, not quite able to stop laughing aloud.

'And what's made you so happy?' that voice rumbled in her ear and reverberated through her body as her waist was grasped in a pair of wonderfully strong hands and she was pulled against someone's wonderfully strong body.

'Nothing,' Susie giggled, before biting her lip and swinging around in George's arms to look up and meet his gorgeous dancing eyes. 'I like your mum. And I'm not even an accessory.'

'My mum? What's . . .?'

The words, screamed in that affected drawl, got closer and had evidently got George's attention too. 'Away! Away! Don't touch me. Find that damned horse and put it down!'

Susie could feel George trying to keep his laughter at bay. He very kindly turned her around in his arms, to share the view.

'Away! Away! What are you all staring at? Haven't you got jobs to do? Start by finding that horse!'

Susie turned to hide her response in George's shaking chest and he turned them both around so their backs were to Porsche as she stomped past.

'My mum you say?'

'Did I say that? But I do like her. And the horse. Which reminds me . . . . can you teach me to ride?'

Susie had been toying with the idea all morning

as she'd watched George on horseback. How wonderful would it be if they could go riding together? He was already teaching her to fence, something he did to help keep fit. And just how good did he look in that get up? She got very hot and sweaty during fencing. Next time she might actually try some of the moves.

Fencing was certainly preferable to the run she'd insisted on accompanying him on. She'd forgotten about the running bit. But then she wasn't ruling that one out again either because there'd been that kiss of life . . . She was exaggerating, but when she'd lain gasping for breath he'd . . . She gulped.

'I believe you ride exceptionally well,' George rumbled in her ear.

'George! *Horses*. I'd love you to teach me to ride.'

'I don't want you learning to ride,' he stated categorically, but then frowned.

'Why?'

'I don't know.' He seemed as surprised as she was by his words. 'I just don't like the idea of it.' He shook his head. 'It's probably because I used to be scared stiff of the things. As a kid you couldn't get me near one. It was my father who made me confront the fear and learn to ride. But I don't like the idea of you riding. Really don't like it.'

Susie took a step back so she was out of his arms, and crossing her own. 'George? *You* ride so . . .'

'I know!' he said, holding his hands up. 'I know

what I sound like. I'm sorry. Of course I'll teach you. But only if you take it seriously and . . .' He caught her look. 'Bugger! Let's go find a horse.'

George was not happy doing this. In fact, that was a major understatement. He'd been scared witless of horses when he'd been a kid, and seeing Susie on one now, reminded him why. She could be hurt. People died from falling off horses.

'Will you *please* stop frowning down there, George?'

She wasn't worried at all. It was him. She was loving every second and he should have been loving seeing her loving every second. But he wasn't.

She had a hard hat on. The horse – the oldest nag he could find, used as a cart horse in front of the cameras – was only walking. But his fears were screaming at him. It was both ridiculous, and alarming.

His phone went. Blindly removing it from his pocket so he could keep his eyes firmly focused on Susie, he accepted the call.

It was Michael and he needed them to meet over coffee to chat. Doing so would be the perfect excuse to get Susie down from the horse. This was perhaps the only time in recent history that he'd welcomed Michael's call.

George still hadn't sent the man packing. He'd apologised profusely for his comments about Susie. He'd simply not understood how George felt about her. Now he did, he would support

George wholeheartedly and do his utmost to ensure Susie had as easy a time with the press as possible. There was that little matter of feeling bad about giving him the panda eyes, too.

'Hang on, Michael,' he said into the phone, while moving over to Susie.

'Time up, Tonto. I've got to get back.' He brought the horse to a standstill and began helping her down, realising too late that lowering her so slowly down his body was not a good idea considering the revealing nature of the lower body attire he wore. He handed the reins over to the person acting as groom and they exchanged a covert glance. Tom. One of the new bodyguards that he'd put in place as of today. Tom knew what he needed to do.

'We'll catch up later,' George said against her lips.

'Promise we'll do it again!' she cried. Her little jumps against his body doing nothing to help his situation.

Evidently seeing the glint in his eyes, she clarified, 'Riding. Lessons. You. Me. *Horse*. Promise?'

Against his better judgement he did.

Susie was bored. They were filming again and it didn't matter where she stood, she couldn't see George. She wondered if she shouldn't go off and see if she could borrow a horse. She could surprise George with what she'd learnt and they'd be a step closer to all those sunset rides together . . .

Her mobile rang and caller display showed

Rachael. Rachael and Cassie were currently driving her and George up the wall. But Susie was bored. She started walking in the direction of the stables, and picked up. 'Rach? What's up?'

She instantly regretted it. 'Will you *stop* asking me to account for my every action? I'm only picking up because I've nothing better to do. *Butt out* will you? There's interest and there's freaky obsession in the relationship. What is it with you and Cassie? Why do you need to know *everything* we do? Actually, don't answer that. I really don't want to know. She's there with you, isn't she? I can hear her in the background.'

Rachael clearly hadn't covered the mouthpiece well, because Susie heard her hiss to Cassie, 'Flaming Nora! Will you be quiet she can hear you! Stop reverting to type and telling me what to do. We *cannot* tell her not to do something because the moment I warn her off something, she *will* do it. It might even give her the idea. And then where are we? We agreed.'

And Susie thought she and George were mad. There was clearly something doing its rounds. They could all perhaps share a wing, have neighbouring cells.

'So have you been up to anything exciting?' Rachael asked, innocent as pie.

'I'm not telling you anything.'

'Come on. I miss you Suse. Since you've moved out we don't catch up. We used to tell each other everything.'

And there was the guilt card. She should have seen that one coming. Rachael had used everything but that all week. Including blackmail. And no, Susie hadn't relished the idea of George finding out she'd been a fan for the past ten years. There was such a thing as self-respect. She was going to have to choose her moment for that one. Thank God Rachael didn't know about the eyes. But in any event, threatening Rachael with tipping her father off to the night they'd spent in the police cells removed that threat rather nicely.

But Susie did feel guilty. They *weren't* catching up like they used to. And she did miss her. A little. When she was bored and George wasn't around. And when she wasn't being blackmailed. 'Okay, I give up! I've taken up fencing and had my first riding lesson today. George is teaching me and—'

'No! No. No. No!'

'Excuse me?' Susie asked, both astounded at Rachael's response and more than a little indignant. 'What the hell do you mean by no? What gives you the . . .?'

Susie's words trailed away as it became evident Rachael wasn't listening to her, but was instead conducting her own urgent conversation on the other end of the phone. She couldn't make out all the words, but heard Cassie cry, 'Oh dear God! Tell her she *cannot* get on a horse again. *Tell her now!* And she *must* stay away from Michael and Porsche! *Tell her!* Do you believe me now? Or are you still insisting on the damned church? It's still repeating! It's not stopped! This shouldn't be happening. Not at all! Not without us! It's them! It's them!'

'You are not to ride, Suse,' Rachael now said urgently into the phone. 'Promise me you won't ride! And avoid Michael and Porsche like the plague. It's better to be safe than—'

Susie had heard more than enough. 'You both need help.'

She closed her phone and switched it off before popping it into her pocket and proceeding to the stables.

Getting a horse was proving difficult. The groom that had been so helpful for George was proving not at all helpful for her. In fact he was insisting every last one of the horses was needed on set any moment. Frustrated, she turned to walk away, but spun around delightedly when she heard a familiar voice.

Graham. George's friend. She'd first encountered him in Canterbury, but George had introduced her to him properly this morning. It was lovely to see a friendly face, especially after the burly attitude of the groom.

'They're not being very helpful, are they?' he said, leaning against the outside wall of the stables having a fag.

'You could say that.' She moved over to lean beside him. 'I was bored and it seemed like a good idea.'

'You ride then?'

'I love riding.'

'Never understood it myself. But you're talking to the wrong person. I've never seen that bloke before today. It's Jo you need. Come on. We'll get you sorted.'

Okkkkaaaaay. She was on the frigging horse. Getting on it hadn't been remotely as easy or pleasurable as when George had helped her up, but the part with Graham shoving her up with his shoulders on her arse was thankfully over and done with. And she'd eventually convinced Graham she knew *exactly* what she was doing and had most *definitely* been on a horse before. And she'd finally managed to shoo that burly groom away, too. He didn't look like a groom. He was so damned big and butch he'd flatten a shire horse.

So . . . Susie just needed to get the horse moving. She made a bit of a clicking noise, rattled the reins around in her hands, did the giddy-up bit while jiggling around. Mmmm.

Aha! He was finally moving. Oh, this was good. There was nothing to this riding malarkey. 'What a lovely horse you are.' She would walk around like this and then she might brave a little trot.

The sound of approaching hooves had her twisting around carefully in the saddle. *No!* The bitch. Riding like a dream. And she'd spotted Susie and was no doubt coming over to gloat. One of these days she'd wipe that smirk off her face. Picturing Porsche how she'd looked earlier, courtesy of

George's mum, with a few forks embedded here and there, Susie returned the smirk.

'Helllloooooo,' Porsche drawled, on drawing nearer.

Susie grunted.

'I saw George teaching you earlier. He's a fine teacher, very fine indeed. He seemed focused on the task in hand. Which was good. Personally, I find he can be so easily distracted. Particularly when giving private lessons. And demanding, so very, very demanding. Not that that's a complaint, of course. Such sessions are *sooo* invigorating and . . . mutually satisfying.'

Betrayal . . .

Susie beat her head into submission, firmly reminding herself of the falsehoods Porsche had fed the press, implying a relationship with George. She thought of sharpened pitchforks.

'I'll race you,' Porsche challenged.

Yeah, right. And Susie was going to risk falling flat on her arse in front of her. There was no way she was going to give her that satisfaction. She would choose her moment to . . . *Oh . . . shit!*

Porsche had circled Susie's horse before suddenly tearing off and the action and sound of galloping hooves had spooked him and . . . the challenge was on! Susie had only been casually holding the reins and one had slipped through her hands and – nope, both. Oh God. She desperately clutched the horse's mane, shut her eyes . . . and prayed.

★   ★   ★

'Go!' George ordered Harry, another one of the bodyguards he'd hired, as he mounted his own horse and followed.

Harry had just reported that Susie was giving herself a riding lesson. George had no idea how she'd managed to pull it off, particularly in front of three damned bodyguards, one of whom was acting as an impromptu groom. Attempting to rein himself in, rather than the horse, he counselled himself to remain calm. Rational. He needed more rationality where Susie was concerned. Rational would be very good right now.

George rounded the corner of the makeshift paddock to see Porsche on horseback, circling Susie. *Great!* He wondered just what venom . . . His thoughts froze as he focused more clearly on Susie. She was on the same horse as earlier, which was something, but with her up there like that it looked neither old or nag like enough for his— *And she wasn't wearing a hat!* He attempted to repress the panic, but there was zero chance of being rational here. He and Susie were going to be having serious words. Porsche was leaving and . . .

George watched in horror at what happened next. Then he was sinking his heels into the side of his horse. He noted three other horses joining the chase, each approaching from a different angle, but equally keeping their distance in order not to frighten Susie's horse any further than perhaps it already was. She'd lost the reins, he could see that much. He couldn't let his emotions click in here.

He'd release them when this was over and she was safe and sound. She *had* to be safe and sound.

Realising he was going to have to attempt to take control of Susie's horse, George approached in an arc. Drawing alongside, he uttered a prayer to the heavens, as he gathered his own reins in one hand, and reached across with his other hand to retrieve Susie's. It took several attempts but he managed to keep his own horse under control and, when he finally had her reins in his grasp, he gradually pulled them up to bring the horse to a measured stop, rather than one which would see Susie catapulted through the air. The other three riders circled, helping to contain the horse. It was slowing, slowing. It had stopped. And Susie was still in one piece.

Only now did George's body start to shake uncontrollably. That fear that plagued him . . . He could have lost her. She could be dead. He could have lost her because of her own *stupid, bloodyminded foolishness.*

The horse had stopped. Oh thank God. She wasn't going to die. She was going to see George again. How ridiculously tragic would that have been? To have died now, just as she'd found him. It would have been just her luck. And he wouldn't have been happy with her. He presently seemed as scared of losing her as she was of losing him. Perhaps it was catching?

He need never know. If she told him, he'd never

teach her to ride. Not that she felt like riding again at this precise moment, or indeed on this precise horse. It was all the bitch's fault. If Porsche hadn't turned up and issued the challenge to her horse, then none of this would have happened. But it was over now. And she wasn't dead.

Susie concentrated on the task in hand. It would be good to remove her hands from the horse's mane and unclench her eyes right now. When nothing happened, she decided on taking things more slowly . . . Mmmm. Perhaps she'd just stay in this position a little longer and let her heartbeat slow down a smidgen and give her traumatised brain a tad longer to send the message through to her hands and eyes.

'Susie?' There was that dreamy voice. The one that reached so deep. She really wasn't functioning properly. Shock, which no doubt accounted for the tingling, too, although just thinking of George could set that off. Or perhaps she'd fallen asleep on the bloody horse. It was, after all, taking an inordinate amount of time to get her body working again.

'Susie? Let go of the mane, sweetheart.'

'What exactly do you think I'm trying to do? Or do you think I'd choose to sit here frozen to the spot on this big, stinking . . .' and he really stank, 'beast that just tried to kill me? Why don't you try and ask me to open my eyes, too?'

A pair of wonderfully strong hands wrapped themselves around hers and began to pry each of her fingers from the mane. Ah ha. Who needed your own body when someone else's was at hand? Particularly one that managed to make her body go all . . .

And what do you know? That thought was enough to make her eyes snap open. She immediately shut them again.

'Not happy to see me, sweetheart?'

Those hands wound their way around her waist and she found herself being pulled off the horse and set to the ground. It was a good job they wrapped themselves around her so tightly because her legs were not performing. She wanted to wrap her arms around him, too, but they weren't performing either. She rested her head against his chest, inhaled his scent and felt his chest rise and fall. It was rising and falling very rapidly. His heart was pounding, too.

'Don't *ever* do that to me again!' he urged in her ear. Despite his voice sounding shaky, it had the force behind it of an order.

'I don't intend to,' she squeaked, knowing what was coming next.

But he took his time. She was impressed. But no matter how nice it was to be held like this, it wasn't at all nice to anticipate what was coming next.

'Go on!' she cried. 'Tell me how bloody stupid I am! Shout at me, please. I'd rather we get it over with because you're killing me here. This calm before the storm stuff is worse than anything you could scream at me!'

His arms clenched tighter around her. Gently, but in a voice threatening to break, he said, 'You weren't even wearing a hat.'

'I forgot. And I'm sorry. I'm really, really sorry. If I'd known how it would all turn out I wouldn't have . . . I just wanted to surprise you with how good I was getting.'

George raised her chin and stared into her eyes. Oh, that connection. It was there pretty much all of the time now, even when she wasn't looking into his eyes. But the extra kick was incredible.

'You terrified me,' he confessed and she could see it there in his eyes. 'I have never been more scared in my life. Promise me you will *never* do that to me again.'

'I'm not planning on it,' she said, attempting to lighten the mood, but his eyes only darkened.

'That's not good enough, Susie. Promise me here and—'

His words cut off as a gun sounded. They must be doing the shooting party scene again. Susie felt a breathtaking blow to her back. She was falling to the ground. And then pain shot through her head.

'Susie? Susie? Sweetheart can you hear me?'

There was that voice again, but it was sounding desperate, so desperate. Oh George. She hated him sounding like that.

'Get the medic now!' it screamed.

And there were those hands. They were stroking

301

her face so gently. But owwwww! Her back was killing her and her head felt like Mike Tyson had been let loose on it. She gritted her teeth against the pain and made to sit up. Her eyes were shut. She opened those, too.

'Susie? Dear God. Don't move.'

She was being pushed back down, but didn't want to be down. She was lying on her back and it hurt and . . . what had just happened? She started shoving the hands away, even though she knew they were George's. She didn't want him to start thinking she was some kind of invalid or something.

'Let me up. I'm fine. My back hurts, I have a bit of a headache, but I'm fine. What happened?'

'Susie.' Despite the warning note to that voice, it still reverberated through her doing that X-rated thing.

'Don't Susie me. Let me up!'

'You were knocked unconscious and you've blood streaming down your face. You're going to do one bloody thing I ask here without arguing or God help me—'

'Or God help you what, George? You're going to need more than God's help if you don't stop pushing me back down again. Please! I'm fine.'

'Or God help me, I'm going to have to tell you how much I love you and ask you to marry me!'

Oh George. And there was nothing for it. Nothing at all. 'I love you, too, for what it's worth and yes please. Although, are you really sure? Divorces are expensive. And before I black out, I'm coming to the premiere.'

Everything went black.

George sat by the bed staring at a sleeping Susie. Possible concussion, severe bruising to her back and ribs, but the doctor insisted she should be fine. Both times she'd lost consciousness was for less than a minute, but each time George thought he'd lost her and it had been pure, unadulterated *agony*. No wonder the fear haunted him. If he lost her, his heart couldn't . . . He could honestly say, it would kill him.

Susie was playing it all down, not at all happy with the attention. But she hadn't been standing where he had. Hadn't seen the horse – his horse at that – panic at the shots and rear up. By the time he saw what was happening and covered Susie, while the other men brought the horse under control, the hooves had done their damage.

And she'd lain there, so pale, so still, blood pouring down her face from a head wound. He'd doubted he could live through that again. And then she'd damned well done it to him again. The bloody woman! After saying she loved him and would marry him.

But *divorce?* They were definitely going to talk. He knew her fears but – Jesus! He could never leave her. Never betray her. He thought he'd re-assured her on that front.

Unless of course she was talking about leaving

him? Fuck! They would talk as a matter of urgency. Straight after he'd covered every square inch of her in the tenderest of kisses to remind himself she was still alive.

George poured himself another coffee from the flask. The doctor had suggested observation for twenty-four hours. He wasn't going to take his eyes off her, not for a second.

And he'd been right about the bodyguards, despite feeling guilty as hell for employing them. Call it a sixth sense, call it a simple response to his irrational fear, call it – God he didn't know what to call it – but without them today, he'd never have been there and . . . he couldn't allow himself to think of what might have resulted.

George ran his hand through his hair and rubbed his forehead furiously. He was going to have to call Cassie, too. He'd picked up a message from her earlier. Made *before* the accident it seemed. She'd insisted it wasn't safe for Susie to ride.

And he needed to know *just how the bloody hell she had known that?*

Saturday

Vow to me now Hannah, you will NEVER put yourself at such risk again – if not to save your own neck, but mine!

My darling, I can stand it no more. My place is there at your bedside, not beside myself with worry and helpless here! No

304

more secrets, I beg of you. I will manage the talk and your mama and papa.

Promise to marry me now! The Montague Ball is a week away. Be on my arm, my love. Let me finally cry from the rooftops, I beg of you!

Yours forever, Freddie

My dearest darling Freddie,
Yes! Yes! Yes! Let us be wed now, my love, so I can be in heaven upon this earth every second of every day. Our separation is too big a price, together we will stand tall.

Be reassured, I am quite well and not remotely lost to you. Nor will I ever be. My love for you is so great that should we ever be parted in this life, I will find you in the next. We will always be together, my Freddie.

Pray forgive me my utter foolishness? I only hoped to surprise you with my improved seat upon a horse. The encounter with Miss Argylle and her brother's shots were merely bad luck. And the vow is yours. I will now ride only with you at my side, for I would do everything with you at my side.

I will be at your ball, Freddie, but cannot help but fret about everyone's reaction. I know I can never be good enough to be seen upon your arm. Pray for me, Freddie, so that

I may not disappoint and that I may make you proud.

Do we meet as planned on the morrow? I need to hold you again within my arms. It is a necessary medicine and will revive me as nothing else. You are my life tonic Freddie, and I am much in need of my missed doses. I am quite, quite well and beg of you not to deny me our lesson. Fencing feels so daring and you look so very dashing.

Eternally yours, Hannah

CHAPTER 22

'I can't keep avoiding his calls! *What* do I tell him?' It was Monday morning and a desperate Cassie watched George's number flash up on her mobile yet again.

'I don't know,' Rachael said, taking a bite from a golden-syrup smothered cream cracker. She sat mirroring Cassie's position at the other end of the sofa, her back resting against the side of the arm, her feet up.' I really don't,' she continued through her mouthful.

'Will you watch the crumbs?' Cassie snapped. 'How you got past thirty living on that crap I don't know.'

'Suse. She did the cooking. But I'm afraid George's calls are pretty inevitable after you warned him off the horse.'

'You warned Susie, too!'

'Yep. But, it's not Suse calling is it? She never asks me for any explanations. And note how much notice she took of my warning.' Rachael released a frustrated sounding sigh before haphazardly brushing off yet more crumbs from her person and reaching down to pick up a large plate from the floor by the sofa, which she proffered. It held a number of crackers with an extraordinary array of multicoloured toppings. Cassie rapidly shook her head. Particularly as she'd seen what went on them.

'I've got to tell him,' Cassie groaned. 'I've no choice. They have to be warned. But . . . but . . . Just how the hell am I supposed to tell him history is repeating itself and that if it continues to do so . . .? Oh God! And this is all happening because of me! If I hadn't started this story . . .'

Rachael shook her head and abandoned the crackers. 'You can't tell him all that and you know it. And you have to stop jumping the gun here, Cassie. You're worried, I get that. But it *will* stop. *Very* shortly. Because it *has* to. You could warn him off Michael and Porsche, tell him what you've found out.' She looked pointedly at Cassie's phone; on silent mode, it was flashing up George's number again. 'But that would of course involve talking to him. And in any event, from what I gather, he already knows your views on those two. As for the rest? Providing the explanation he's no doubt after? Even I'm struggling with history repeating itself so imagine what his reaction will be. He'd most likely never listen to a word you say to him ever again. And all over something you don't know has or is happening.' Rachael shook her head rapidly as Cassie went to interrupt. 'You don't know! And before you suggest it, I've not a hope of talking to Suse. She wouldn't even give me the time of day on this. We reached an agreement on that front a long time ago. A decade ago to be precise.

'And here's the thing. I'm not even sure it's *safe* to tell them about this stuff. Look what happened in the consulting room. They don't remember Hannah and Freddie and that's got to be for a reason. And with Susie's hang-ups? Whose to know she wouldn't still run away screaming and never come back?'

Cassie again saw George lying unconscious on the floor of Rachael's consulting room. She felt her accompanying terror afresh. It hadn't been down to the regression because Susie had lost consciousness too. Could that happen again? Could telling him be dangerous? And could Susie leave him? What would *that* do to him?

'This is hell!' she cried, clutching her head in her hands. 'I'm powerless and . . . and . . . I'm *never* powerless! There has to be something I can do!'

If only she could find a way to remove Michael and Porsche from the equation. But she'd found nothing in her investigations to date that could secure that. Which was the only thing that would give her peace of mind right now.

'I'll grant that what you've found isn't good,' Rachael said.

'Isn't good?' Cassie shrieked. 'Isn't *good*!'

Rachael had the good grace to grimace. 'No. Not good. Not good at all but—'

'The parallels between the past and the present are horrific, Rachael. We already knew Porsche wants George, as Prudence wanted Freddie. All those things she said in the press about Susie are a complete giveaway. But just as Prudence was fragile, Porsche has seen shrinks galore! She's exactly the kind of person Matthew – or Michael! – would have a field day with.'

Cassie had a hunch there was more to find out about Porsche. Some kind of history between her and George that Cassie's research hadn't revealed. If only she could talk to George. Not that it would change a damned thing. The woman wanted him, just as before. And look how that had turned out!

'George *has* got her sussed though, Cassie. He's refusing to spend time with her so is already on to her which—'

'But what about Michael?' Cassie wailed. 'He's been his manager for years. And he's a master manipulator just like Matthew was!' She took a deep breath as she recalled what she'd found out about Michael's failed marriage and the psychological games he'd played. His ex-wife was still in counselling nine years on! And as for his motive . . . Cassie pictured her notepad. Under the heading of 'Matthew' she'd scribbled down what Kathryn knew had driven him in the past: gambling debts; significant financial losses from the 1825 crash; *in desperate financial straits*. She'd been forming a list entitled 'Michael' this week, adding to it as she discovered more. She swallowed hard. She'd been forced to write: 'gambling debts' and 'significant financial losses from a series of overseas property investments due to the recent global crash.' His bank balance was in the red to the tune of millions and the banks were calling in their loans.

She'd also had to add 'drugs' to Michael's list. His expensive drug habit was only compounding his financial difficulties. But no matter how hard she'd looked, she'd found nothing on that front that was capable of getting him locked up. She took a deep shuddery breath because what her searching *had* revealed was the nature of some of the underworld characters he owed money to. They would soon start baying for more than their money, if they weren't already doing so.

'We don't *know* Michael is acting on things,' Rachael said. 'Just because he's—'

'He's *got* to be as desperate as Matthew was! He's in dire financial straits. And if George reduces the number of films he does to spend more time with Susie, then—'

'Cassie! Will you *please* stop this! We don't even know they were involved in what's just happened! It doesn't look good and the two of them being around is . . . *unsettling*, but—'

'It still played out!' Cassie cried. 'Without us! Why else—?'

'We don't *know* it's played out! It may simply have been Suse wanting to learn to ride, just as she did in the past; a personality trait that has carried through into this life which would make it . . .

coincidence. Stop looking at me like that. We don't *know* what happened so there's zero point in panicking. You've been avoiding George so can't get the facts from him and Susie refused to elaborate when we spoke. In fact, I got very little sense out of her. It was all about a "bloody stinking horse" and something about shire horse flatteners.'

'We were so involved,' Cassie murmured, slowly shaking her head and raising her eyes to meet and hold Rachael's. 'Tessa reported back that Hannah was out alone and giving herself a riding lesson. Kathryn and Matthew decided it would be the perfect opportunity for him and Prudence to have a little chat with her, to warn her off and no doubt play to her weaknesses. As we know . . . it went further than that.'

Rachael sat up and moved to sit conventionally on the sofa. It was clear she was remembering the past, too. 'I don't know what he was thinking,' she whispered.

'I do. He was desperate. And Kathryn knew it and gave him the gun. She gave him the damned gun! She and Matthew shared a look as she removed it from the cabinet at Worton Hall. "Could you not be out shooting?" she asked. I remember it word for word. "You *must* possess a reason for being there . . ."'

There was a long silence before Rachael spoke. Putting her hand on Cassie's knee, she said, 'We *weren't* involved, Cassie. Things *are* different now. Susie was hurt, yes. But how could it have played out? And if that isn't reassuring enough, George is ahead of us here. Not only is he avoiding Porsche, but he must be sensing some innate need to protect Suse, perhaps because of how it all ended last time? It's fascinating really. He can't yet remember Freddie, but there's something that's driving him right now. According to Suse's furious telephone call this morning – and boy oh boy was she livid – George has got her safety well and truly covered. He's in some serious doodoo, but as long as Suse is safe, they both are. It's different, Cassie. Very, very different. Freddie didn't act in this way. Why would he have felt the need to? Whatever similarities there are *will* stop.'

Cassie gave Rachael's hand a squeeze in thanks. She had to get a grip on herself here. Rachael was right. Things *were* different. So different. How *could* things play out? And she had to look at the facts. *Facts, Cassie! First rule of investigation!* She didn't even know Michael and Porsche had been involved and . . . *Oh God!* She loved George so much. He had it covered. Whatever may or may not be happening. Whatever Michael and Porsche may or may not be doing or have planned, he had it covered anyway! And she knew from experience how protective he could be. Overly so sometimes. A wry smile appeared on her lips as she recalled his reaction to one of her past boyfriends . . . He was going to do Susie's head in.

'I made all the right sympathetic noises as Susie explained her plight, but I believe your brother is one of my favourite people right now,' Rachael said, grinning broadly in response to Cassie's small smile. She quickly added, 'Simply because it's better to be safe than sorry, of course. Not because I think Susie needs protection because this is going to stop very soon. It might already have! Look, try and buy yourself some time with talking to him. Because I honestly don't think they are meant to know quite yet. If he starts turning up at your place, feel free to hide out here. It's all way too quiet without Suse . . .'

Rachael gave Cassie's hand another reassuring pat and sat back in her seat.

Closing her eyes for a moment, Rachael took a deep comforting breath. Before taking another because the first really hadn't worked. *Unsettling?* Her words had been about reassuring Cassie and hopefully herself in the process. But *unsettling?* After what had just happened to Suse, that hardly went there. Why the blazes was this happening? She normally put things down to Fate, but she couldn't let herself consider him right now. Coincidence was so much more preferable because . . . *Why* hadn't it flaming well stopped with her and Cassie out of the equation? It should have done! How could things still be—?

She was snapped away from her worried thoughts by the quick rap on the door, which was then promptly flung open.

Rob. And *Matey*! She leapt up and scooped Matey into her arms before returning to the sofa

314

where she sat with him on her lap. She really needed him right now.

'I was just after news on Suse,' Rob said quietly.

'She's fine, Rich— *Rob*!' Cassie spluttered. 'Just . . . bruised.'

Rachael shot her a look and promptly winced. This was the first time Cassie had seen Rob since she'd identified him as once being Richard Barratt. If her voice and words hadn't been a big enough giveaway of the fact, how she was now looking indicated that her mind was awash with Kathryn's memories of him.

Rob looked at Cassie uneasily before shooting a furrowed-brow look Rachael's way. She watched his eyes lower to Matey before his frown deepened and he shut them. He shook his head before reopening them. Still focusing on Matey, he said, 'I won't crash in here. But I just wanted to say . . . if you'd like to spend more time with him, then I'd . . . I can see the Soul Mate thing must be . . . *Okay* . . . I realise you must find the situation you are in difficult with him being what he is and . . . *Bloody hell!* Look, just know that I have no issue with you . . .' He turned away and started to head towards the door. 'With you spending more time with him. And I'm relieved Suse is okay. I'll be seeing you. Stay Matey,' he commanded, seeming to know without turning around that Matey was attempting to leave her lap.

'Wait! That's lovely. Thank you. I'd love to spend

315

more time with him. But please don't go,' Rachael cried.

A strange sound escaped Cassie. She was evidently struggling with something. Those memories could come thick and fast on first recollection.

Rob paused and shot an anxious look in Cassie's direction before continuing even more quickly towards the door.

'Don't go Rob . . . I've *cream crackers!*'

Rob paused and she heard his low chuckle. He turned and looked at her for a long moment, before shaking his head. After what seemed like an age, he slowly smiled. 'Mustard?' he asked, with a raised brow.

'American!' Rachael said, matching his smile. *His eyes!*

'You make things so difficult,' he murmured as he walked over and sat down on the floor next to the plate, now positioned on the stack of books to the side of the sofa. He picked one of the yellows.

'And now you're here, and because you're one of us, so to speak . . . I'd be really interested to know what you think of history repeating itself.' Rachael spoke casually, but all the time watched his reaction closely. 'Not in the sense of historic world events and the cyclical debate, but as in events that have happened to someone in the past repeating themselves in the next life.'

From the way his hand halted on the way to his mouth and the blank look that appeared on his face, Rachael could tell that that question was having much the same effect on him as Cassie's had had on her. But to be honest, Rachael was pretty much coming to the view that she and Cassie could do with all the help they could get on this subject, and really welcomed the opportunity of talking it through with him. A trouble shared and all that.

Rob opened his mouth to say something, closed it again, but before he could say anything, if indeed he yet knew what to say, Cassie exclaimed, '*Matey?*'

Rachael turned away from Rob to face her, and saw that she was staring at Matey who remained on her lap, purring away as she rigorously stroked him. *Flaming Nora!*

'I've been thinking through past conversations we've had,' Cassie continued, in that voice she used when she was attempting matter of fact but failing. '*Matey?* You mentioned him before. I clearly recall it. And with what Ri— *Rob* has just said, and you there with . . . It's a namesake, right? *Please* tell me it's a namesake or I swear I'm . . . Do you have *any* idea how close you had me to being on board with the Soul Mates stuff. So close.' She'd lifted her right finger and thumb up to indicate how close. 'Even the damned cherries! I just wanted one thing sorted in my head. Just one thing! And *now?* Tell me – *please* – that I've got completely the wrong end of the stick here? God knows I'm not myself right now.'

Rachael returned her focus to Rob. He gave her

a sympathetic look. Rachael swallowed hard. She liked to think she and Cassie had some kind of mutual respect thing going on and didn't want to threaten that. And she liked her, too. Neither, of course, did she want her writing a story about her and Matey because that *really* wouldn't be good for business. And neither did she really want to have to deal with this right now. *Crap!*

She smiled weakly back at Rob and took a healthy dose of reassurance from Matey. There was nothing for it. 'Well you know how millions and millions and *millions* of Buddhists in the world, including the Dalai Lama himself – and you *know* how wise and well respected he is – believe souls aren't just reincarnated into people . . .?'

'Why?' Susie asked from the foot of the stairs, where she stood with arms crossed and her foot tapping rapidly.

George paused for a moment in the front doorway. God she was gorgeous, even with that furious look on her face, but he knew he was in trouble here. Things had not panned out at all well today. But what choice had he had? He closed the door behind him and moved forward to take her into his arms. Unfortunately, she side-stepped him and moved to lean against the wall, still with her arms folded.

'What are you doing on your feet?' he asked gently, attempting to mask his frown. He moved to lean against the wall opposite so he could face her. She looked pale. 'You're meant to be resting. You didn't go to school today, which is good, but . . .'

'No, George. I didn't go to school today.'

'Susie . . .'

'I *wanted* to go to school! And I told you *no* bodyguards! We agreed to revisit as and when we go public. Instead you go *behind my back* and employ a crack unit of ex-SAS ball-breakers who'd make mincemeat out of Arnold Schwarzenegger in *Terminator* mode!'

'Sweetheart—'

'Don't you *dare* sweetheart me! You had *no* right. They kept me imprisoned George! They wouldn't let me out of the house. As you well know because it was on *your* orders! I couldn't get hold of you all day – funny that – and they refused to be reasoned with. *We follow orders,*' she mimicked. 'But not mine! Never mine!'

'Baby—'

'You have *no* right to baby me! And Tom . . .' George knew what was coming and chose to focus on his feet. He hated Susie being angry with him. 'Odd that he bears such an uncanny resemblance to that obstructive shire horse flattening groom I had the unfortunate experience of encountering on Saturday, isn't it George?'

'I'm sorry things got heavy-handed today, truly sorry. Will you please sit down rather than stand?' He gestured towards the bottom steps of the stairs. She should not be on her feet like this.

She glowered at him and shook her head.

'In my defence: it was a good job they were there on Saturday and here today. You said you wouldn't go to school. If you'd done what you *assured* me you would do, and which the doctor insisted on, you wouldn't have even known they were—'

Her look silenced him. That flash in her eyes – it was like lightning across thunderous skies. It was incredible. And the effect it was having on him, not at all appropriate. Damn. He looked at his feet with added urgency.

'I changed my mind, George. Which last time I checked was not an *imprisonable offence!* Why? Why did you do it? I thought we'd talked it through.'

And they had. And there was hurt in her voice now, not just anger. Bloody hell! But how could he possibly explain the depths of his fears? She knew he worried about loss, just as she, but no matter how hard he'd tried to apply logic and common sense, his fears had continued to grow. And after Saturday they no longer seemed to simply haunt, they all of a sudden seemed horrifyingly *real.*

'I know you worry about me,' she was saying. 'But I worry about you, too. Do you see me stopping you going to work because I don't trust that bitch of a co-star of yours? Do you see me—?'

'I'm not the one being so blasé about my own health and safety! *You changed your mind?*' And he hadn't meant to raise his voice here. He had been determined on cajoling, reasoning . . . apologising.

But this was too much. She was under doctor's orders to stay at home. She'd told him she would. Yet she'd *changed her mind!* Had been intent on putting herself at risk – again! 'Your actions today, just as on Saturday, were stupid and reckless and—'

'Stupid and . . . You are calling *me* stupid?'

Yes! 'I'm sorry,' he said, rubbing his forehead. 'I don't want to argue with you, but you have to admit—'

'You call *me* stupid when *you* employ three body-guards knowing full well what my reaction will be? You dare to call *me* stupid? Have you any idea how humiliating today has been?'

There was that hurt again. And the guilt that he'd been experiencing all day, that refused to go away no matter how much he told himself he was doing the right thing, now engulfed him.

'And their names, George, why? Why would you do it? Was it to make my humiliation complete because if it was you've succeeded. I bet you've been having such a laugh at my expense and—'

'Susie!' he cried, shaking his head and sweeping his hands through his hair. She was infuriating. How could she possibly think that? 'I employed them because they are the best! You think this is about humiliation and *having a laugh*? It was – is – about keeping you safe because *you* seem unable to do that yourself! The doctor said rest. *Rest. Not* go to work! I never set out to humiliate you. You know that. You must know that. And believe me, there is nothing about this that I find remotely amusing; my need for you to have them, or your reaction to them. Do I look amused here? No Susie. I'm tearing my hair out because the last thing I meant to do was upset you, but you gave me no choice! I couldn't be here when you were intent on setting off to school, no matter how hard I tried. So I did what I had to. How about you tell me why *you* did it? Why you showed such a blatant disregard for your well-being when you know how much I worry about you? Particularly after Saturday!'

She said nothing, but did at least have the sense to look awkward.

'And for your information, they *are* a crack unit and their company is called Tom, Dick and Harry. That's their names. What else could they have called themselves?'

'Hulks R Us? Grunt, Grunt and Grunt?' And there was no trace of her earlier awkwardness as lightning again flashed. 'And you had a choice. As should I. Worry is one thing, but what you did today went way beyond what I can possibly—'

'Susie—'

'Anyway, I reckon they should rename themselves,' she announced, crossing her arms afresh and looking pleased with herself. 'Tom and Harry? No, best make it The Dickless Duo.' At his frown, she continued, 'I bet they didn't tell you that they lost Dick for a while today, did they?'

They had what?

'Dick pushed me too far and I found his weak spot. It was pretty obvious really and it caused enough of a diversion to get me out the door and into your mum's waiting taxi—'

'You went *out*?!' George was instantaneously before Susie. And what the hell had his mum been thinking? Susie had nearly died on Saturday!

'Trouble in the ranks, George? I had a dress fitting. For *your* premiere! I tried to contact you to call them off, but you've been un-contactable – to me at least – all day. Why I went to the trouble I have no idea when you treat me this way.'

George was speechless, completely and utterly speechless and his head beyond a mess. Fury, terror, guilt, helplessness all blindly rampaged through him. Fury at Susie, his mum, at Tom, Dick and bloody Harry, at himself for not having been here to ensure this couldn't have happened – and for his feeling the need for any of this in the first place. Terror at what could have resulted; he could have lost her like he'd so nearly done on Saturday. Guilt. So much damned guilt. Her hurt was bubbling away and he'd caused it. And she'd gone out for the dress fitting for *his* premiere. The problem was with him and he had no idea how to remedy it, how the hell to get a hold on these gut-wrenching fears. And it was Susie paying the price. Helplessness, total and utter helplessness because . . . what was he supposed to do? It was as if he sensed a *need* to keep her safe.

'George?' Susie prompted and she sounded concerned now, rather than angry.

He shook his head not knowing what to say or do. He turned away to sink down on one of the lower steps of the stairs, where he held his head in his hands. If he carried on like this he'd drive her away and lose her anyway.

'George?'

He felt her hand on his arm. She'd joined him on the step.

'George?'

'I'm sorry. I'm so sorry,' he said, the words coming straight from his heart. 'The way I handled today.' Taking a deep breath he raised his head to meet her eyes. She looked so concerned. 'I panicked. And I know I'm not being fair on you. But after Saturday—'

'I'm fine, George,' Susie whispered, moving her hands up to stroke the side of his face.

'But you might not have been! And if something happened to you . . .' His words broke off on a choke. He couldn't lose her. He couldn't. Not now that he'd found her.

'Oh love. It's not going to.' She held his face between both her hands and met his desperate gaze with those stunning eyes of hers. 'You have to stop worrying. I had no idea you were worrying so much. Why didn't you tell me?'

He lowered his head to rest his forehead upon hers. 'Worry doesn't begin to go there and I've no idea how to explain it to you.'

It doesn't feel like fear anymore, rather a sixth sense that if I don't act something terrible is going to happen to you.

'After Saturday, everything has gone into overdrive.'

'Saturday was an accident George and today . . . Look, nothing is going to happen to me. I'm sorry I worried you, but you've got to stop this. We have to enjoy what we have now, don't you see that? What we have is magic. But too much thinking will ruin it. Stop worrying. Please? Start enjoying what we have. It's the only way.'

He closed his eyes and lowered his forehead to hers again. *Please God, let these fears be irrational.*

'I'm not happy with bodyguards, you know that, but if it will help you here, we'll sort something. Would that help?'

He moved back to stare into her eyes. She meant it. And relief immediately overtook his body. So much relief. He didn't deserve this. Didn't deserve her.

'The things I do for you,' she murmured as he pulled her to him, wrapping his arms around her tightly.

'Thank you. Thank you,' he said, as he buried his head in her hair. 'And I'm sorry. I'm so sorry, sweetheart. I'm going to work on things, okay?'

'Damned right you are. I'll help you with that because I cannot believe what I just agreed to.'

'I love you,' he whispered.

'So you should. I love you too, evidently more

than is healthy. There is a condition though. That you now stop acting like a caveman and keep your troupe of Neanderthals under control.'

'You think I'm a caveman?' he murmured, moving back so their eyes locked.

She moistened her lower lip, holding his gaze. 'No. Yes. Today, yes. You aren't worrying at this precise moment in time, are you?'

And he couldn't help the grin. They were so attune.

'Put me down!' she shrieked as George picked her up and flung her – albeit gently, and really less of a fling than a gentle placement because she was still bruised – over his shoulder.

'I'm giving you caveman here,' he said, walking up the stairs. 'Although this Neanderthal apologises profusely for things getting out of hand today and is beyond grateful for your understanding and forgiveness and I promise to get a grip. We will talk and reach a compromise, but not when you're standing on your feet. And I'd like very much to show you how badly I've missed you today. Being out of contact has been hell . . . *Please*?'

He was met with silence. *Bugger*. Had he more apologising to do?

'Will you fling me on the bed, rip off your clothes and uncontrollably ravage me?'

George groaned. If he could make it up the stairs this time. But he had to. Because it would be gentle lowering, *sooo* gentle, rather than flinging; she was still recovering from Saturday.

Not that he was sure he ever would.

CHAPTER 23

Susie stood before the mirror not believing what she was seeing. How had they managed to make her a dress that . . .? It was a miracle. An optical illusion. She didn't know how they had possibly managed to do it. She looked . . . She looked . . . God her boobs looked amazing, her stomach 'looked' flat, her waist small and . . . turning around for a moment just to triple check . . . her bum didn't look humongous. They were geniuses. And the colour, a stunning deep grey with an almost metallic, silvery sheen, but with an underlying . . . something; it didn't look grey, despite *being* grey. In fact: it was stunning.

'It had to be that colour,' he said.

She moved her eyes so she could see George in the mirror. He was leaning against the door frame, watching her intently. He was in his formal tux, bow tie hanging loose and untied around his neck; the top few buttons of his shirt undone. His dark hair was ruffled in that way she loved. He was . . . breathtaking. And for now: he was hers.

'Susie . . .' His eyes almost glowed and they transfixed her. 'You are . . . You look stunning, but

327

that word – *no* word – could do you justice.' He shook his head. 'The dress, the colour . . . It's exactly that of your eyes as they look at me, while your lips are swollen, your cheeks blushed, your hair mussed and . . .' He cursed before breaking off and crossing the room in a couple of strides.

Now standing behind her, he pulled her back against him, the length of his body pressing tightly against hers. She leant her head back to rest on his chest. How could he make her feel like this? She continued to hold his eyes in the glass.

'Thank you,' he said. 'Thank you for being by my side. Thank you for agreeing to marry me. Thank you for making me the happiest man the world has ever seen. I love you. I will *always* love you.'

And that look . . . The sincerity, the depth . . . Susie could feel the tears welling. 'Don't get all soppy on me,' she said, her voice full of emotion. 'You're going to make me ruin my make-up.'

She turned around in his arms to clutch his shirt and to bury her now wet face in his chest. 'I love you too. If I managed to explain how much you'd realise just how nuts I am. And it's me that should be thanking you. Oh God, I've got to stop crying. I'm *so sorry*! I've got mascara all over your shirt! And I can feel my eyes going all red and blotchy and puffy and—'

He kissed the top of her head, holding her tightly. He chuckled in that way that reverberated through her whole being. 'So now isn't the time to get

328

down on one knee and give you your engagement ring?'

He had the ring? Oh God she was seriously going to lose it here. 'George!' she wept, clutching his shirt tighter and shaking her head profusely.

'We can hold the ring,' he said gently, stroking the small of her back. Lowering his head, he rumbled into her ear, 'But don't deny me the chance to go down on one knee. There's something I want to do down there.'

Susie's tears seemed to freeze in their tracks. *No!* He *wouldn't?* Not when she'd spent hours getting ready and . . .

But her body was singing ecstatically and her temperature rising alarmingly. And then there was all that tingling . . .

She slowly removed her face from his chest to meet his eyes: dark, intent and . . . that glint. Coupled with that grin . . . Oh God, he *would* and she was wanton mush.

Her head managed to secure a moment's airtime. 'But we can't! I'd have to re-do my make-up and . . .'

While she'd been talking, he'd been inching up the skirt of her full-length dress and . . .

Her head wasn't meant to be used around George anyway.

There was something to be said for the natural look, Susie conceded as she stared, stunned, at the morning newspapers before her. She couldn't comprehend that the person in the pictures was her.

She'd gone with her hair loose and tussled (having spent three hours in the hairdressers getting it put up); her lips cherry-red and swollen (who needed a Paris Lip, George had quipped, unashamedly); her cheeks naturally blushed rose-pink . . . And her eyes! They were the *exact* same colour as her dress. The only make-up she'd worn was a smidgen of eyeliner and some mascara . . . and, okay, the *odd* spot of concealer.

Who needed make-up and hairdressers with George around? He made her *feel* so beautiful and cherished and . . . loved.

And George . . . She couldn't help but focus on George in the images. He looked as heart-stoppingly beautiful as ever. Oh, she loved him so much. He looked happy and . . . *proud.* Proud to have her at his side. How did this happen? And how perfect did the man get?

Yes, that day he'd unleashed Tom, Dick and Harry on her, had been . . . difficult. Okay, it had been more than difficult. But they'd reached a compromise of sorts. He had been acting out of worry, she could see that now. Irrational worry, but worry nonetheless. And she knew how powerful fears could be. Not that hers were irrational, of course. Hers felt way too real for that. Hammering on a few more securing batons to that box in her head, she forced herself to refocus. And if she was truly honest, she would have been as furious as

George had roles been reversed; had she been in his shoes. Furious and worried, too. She wasn't sure what she'd have done, perhaps not something far off his actions if she'd had those options before her. But the fact was: in the here and now, he cared. Deeply cared. Loved her. Was proud of her. Thought she was beautiful. Her, Susie Morris!

And that made George Silbury pretty much too good to be true.

George hung up the phone with a series of curses and started making his way to the kitchen. He paused in the doorway, the frown leaving his face as he took in Susie, sat at the table in his shirt. She had her own clothes here, yet she was in *his* shirt and on a primal level that more than worked. She was his. The beautiful, gorgeous, stunning, sexy, witty, highly intelligent, argumentative . . . sometimes infuriating woman before him – was his. And he couldn't wait to get his ring on her finger. Perhaps he'd have another attempt at that tonight?

He refused to dwell on the conversation he'd just had with Michael. He'd sort it.

'Good morning, sleepy-head,' he swooped down to give her a quick good morning kiss, but had trouble pulling away. *Her taste* . . . Addictive. Taking a deep breath he forced himself to move back. Grinning, he nodded towards the papers before her. 'Believe me, now?'

He took himself over to the coffee machine and

pressed the button to prepare them both a mug. Susie had evidently not got that far. Returning to the table, he pulled a chair up to sit beside her. That wasn't good enough. He pulled her over from her own chair to sit on his lap, where he wrapped her in his arms.

She still hadn't said anything and his grin broadened at her expression. There was no way she couldn't see how beautiful she was now.

'Thank you,' she said.

'Whatever for?'

'For last night. For making me feel beautiful. For having me. For letting me have you. I love you so much, George, although it feels so much more than that.'

'Do you have any idea how much I like hearing those words,' he buried his face in her neck. They got to him so deep. She was his. He was hers. End of.

And, dear God, let them live happily ever after.

She wrapped her arms around his neck and he wallowed in the feeling.

'The living room appears to be full of bouquets of flowers, for me,' Susie said, sounding confused.

George knew. And none were from him. He should have filled the whole damned house up with bouquets from *him*! 'I apologise they aren't from me, but I will make it up to you.'

'Who are they from?' She nestled into his neck.

'An army of admirers, no doubt.' He fully intended to find out *exactly* who made up that army and read every last card. Unfortunately, Michael had distracted him from that very task this morning. Attempting to sound casual, he said, 'There's sure to be a fair number from dress designers, too, who can't wait to get you into their frocks.'

'This is all beyond bizarre, George,' she said, shaking her head.

'And that from the girl who has yet to look out the window this morning.' He immediately winced at his words.

She went to stand up and he pulled her back down, shaking his head. 'You're not going to the window unless you want to be photographed looking X-rated in my shirt. And even if you wanted to be, I won't let you. I do not want every Tom, Dick and—'

He stopped himself and she met his pursed lips with a smirk. 'It's your own fault, you know. Where are they, by the way?'

'At the bottom of the front steps keeping the hordes away from the door.' Today there was no question their employment was rational.

'Well at least they are out of my hair,' she muttered.

George stroked her back and kissed the top of her head. 'Thank you.'

'The things I do for you, George.'

'I know.' He just wished she'd make their assignment easier. She'd allowed their presence on the basis they stayed 'the hell' out of her way. And he'd leapt at the compromise. But according to Tom, she'd made squeezing past people and through the smallest of gaps on the bus to and from school, an art form. They couldn't casually follow, so they would spend their journey at opposite ends of the bus to her. But it was better than nothing; far better than nothing. It meant they were there if, God forbid, they were needed.

'Is it that bad out there?'

'Mmmm.' He tightened his hold around her as he thought of the fifty or so people armed with cameras and that wasn't counting the television crews. 'But I promise it'll die down. Last night and today were always going to be the worst. You were fantastic, Susie. I was – *am* – so proud of you.'

'And me you. Your film was brilliant George. You were brilliant.'

He'd not watched any of it. He'd spent the entire time absorbed in the sensation of Susie being at his side, being able to finally cry from the rooftops. But her opinion mattered more than anyone else's. 'Thank you. That means a lot. I believe there's enough of me out there for a while though. I called Michael earlier and told him about cutting things down a bit. In fact, I've asked him to clear the next twelve months or so. Once this one is out of the way, I'm taking that holiday.'

Susie leaned back to look at him. 'You mustn't—'

'I want to, sweetheart.' He pulled her closer again. 'You know how much. We talked about this.

I'm not prepared to spend so much time in the States.'

She hugged him tightly. 'The idea of you being away is . . . horrid.'

He'd second that. Since they'd got their act together, they'd not spent a night apart. And that suited him down to a tee. 'Future projects will definitely be close to home.' He grinned. 'Just imagine . . . if you play your cards right during my sabbatical, my mushroom risotto could be on the table for when you get home from work.'

She gave him her adorable knowing look and the depth of heat in those eyes. 'If I play my cards right?'

Oh yeah. And he knew she was remembering, as was he, the game of cards they'd played a few nights ago . . . and the forfeits. 'You and I are clearly on the same wavelength, I'm pleased to see.' And they were. And not just in bed. Which he could really do with not thinking about at this precise moment. She'd added to her eyes, the drawing of small circles over his chest and . . . He shifted her slightly on his lap. Whether it was that profound connection they shared or simply that they were meant to be, he didn't know. But every second with Susie was a joy. Even if they were talking crap, or he was being told off for leaving the toilet seat up again, or for not wiping the basin out after shaving. She was exhilarating and being with her resulted in a higher high than he could have ever imagined. Nothing compared to it. It was just . . . right. Oh, they could disagree. And yeah, he could bollocks things up when his fears screamed at him. He instinctively tightened his hold around her. But what they had, what they shared . . . As things stood, it went so deep he couldn't imagine them parting . . . willingly. He closed his eyes, ignoring the shudder in his spine, and imagined a dose of rationality flooding his system. He reopened them and grinned. 'And I rather think our honeymoon is going to have to be in the summer holidays. Two weeks would never be enough.'

And dare he? He wasn't sure there was ever going to be a right moment to ask this. But he wanted it so much. He took a deep breath. He wanted the world to know. 'If you're happy with the idea – and only if you are – can I get Michael to announce something on the engagement? I've asked him to get something drafted . . . but only just in case. Only if you are . . .'

Her grin provided the answer and he let out an elated laugh.

'We'll have to tell my dad and my brothers first though.'

'Does that mean I finally get to meet them?'

Susie's grin broadened. 'We'll have to see what we can arrange. They will no doubt give you the Spanish Inquisition though, particularly my brothers. Dad is simply happy because he considers you might possibly love me.'

'I wonder what makes him think that?'

Susie reached up and planted a kiss on his cheek.

'With your brothers, I've got a plan. Josh, I'll talk cars with. Not a hardship; as you know, if I couldn't act, I wanted to do just what he's doing and be a mechanic. Craig, whose got a soft spot for my last female lead, I'll arrange an introduction!'

Susie laughed. 'That's bribery.'

'Call it what you like, sweetheart, but I'll do pretty much anything to get them on board.'

'Porsche's not going to be happy,' Susie mused and he felt her tense in his arms.

'She can go to hell! And now we're sort of public, how about you bring your class along to the set for a day trip? I can give them a walk around and I'm sure wardrobe would let them try on some clothes. Aren't you teaching them about the Georgian and Regency periods at the moment? They can even have a spot behind the camera if they want and can have a go at the clapper board and sit in the director's chair and . . . Hey,' he said, breaking off, concerned at the suspicious glistening of her eyes. 'Baby . . .?'

'Don't ever leave me. *Please.*'

'Never, ever, ever,' he vowed, wrapping his arms around her tightly. Into her hair he said, 'And one day very soon, you will believe me when I tell you that; no matter what your best friend managed to do to you a decade ago.'

Wrapped in each other's arms, it was Susie that finally broke the silence. 'I should get dressed.' She started up with her circling fingers again.

'I was thinking of taking a bath first though and wondered if you'd care to . . .'

George was abruptly snapped out of the very, very wonderful place he was at, as a po-faced Harry walked into the kitchen and deposited a manila A4 envelope on the table, before returning to the fray.

George forced himself to breathe, his lungs seemingly reluctant to take in air. He gave Susie a kiss on the head and attempted to sound normal, utilising his professional skills to the full. 'You pop up and run the water . . . I'll join you in a few minutes.'

Susie frowned. And there was no wonder. It didn't matter that he was an Oscar-winning actor. She'd always see through him. She studied him closely before glancing at the envelope and back to him. He went for an innocent look. 'Go on,' he said, easing her up from his lap and giving her a tap on the bottom. 'I won't be long.'

George watched Susie slowly exit the kitchen before reaching for the envelope. He held it in his hands for several moments before forcing himself to snap open the top. He took a deep shuddery breath, pulled the contents out, and made himself look.

His head instantly filled with the roar of white noise. They were a thousand times worse than Michael had let on. George closed his eyes for a moment, ordering himself to breathe and then forced himself to open his eyes again. He stared in horror at the image in front of him, before placing it with shaking hands on the table. He then focused on the next. And then the next. Each picture was worse, more heart-wrenchingly damning than the one before.

They were all now laid out before him. He sat and stared. Not able to believe this could possibly be happening. He needed to be sensible here. This couldn't be. But he wanted to scream longer and harder than he had ever screamed before and he didn't know that he'd ever stop.

'George?' Susie said from the doorway.

No. Not now. He couldn't see her now. He gulped and quickly started to gather the images up and put them back in the envelope. He needed time to get his head around things.

But he hadn't been quick enough. She was at the table and picking up the one remaining picture his shaking hands had struggled to grasp. He closed his eyes for a moment. Then made himself look at her, to watch her reaction. She looked confused, which told him nothing. And now she looked horrified, but that could mean anything.

Susie couldn't believe what she appeared to be seeing. It made no sense. It wasn't real. She knew that. So why was . . .?

'Show me,' she said, her voice grating over a now bone-dry throat.

George made no sign of moving, so she snatched the envelope from his hands and emptied its contents onto the table. She grabbed at the images, spreading them out before her, her movements becoming more and more frenzied. Image after image showed a man and woman in varying stages of sex.

'This makes no sense,' she said, shaking her head. 'These aren't real. How could they . . .? Why would anyone . . .? Where did they come from?'

'Michael. He's trying to stop them running in tomorrow's tabloids.'

The way George spoke made Susie look up. There was no inflection. His voice was completely tone-less. She'd never heard it like that before. Rather than reverberating so pleasurably through her, it stabbed.

'But George. These aren't real. You know that. Rob and I have never—'

'They are dated the Friday before last.' She needed him to stop speaking that way. It was so alien. 'The day I got back from Canterbury.'

She let the relief flood through her. 'Well, there you go.'

'The times on the pictures range from sixteen forty-six to sixteen fifty-nine.'

Susie covered her mouth as nausea swept through her. *He believed them!* He was sat with his head in his hands and his fists clenched so tightly in his hair, his knuckles were white. She shook her head frantically. 'These aren't real, George.'

'I know we hadn't made love at that point so perhaps you didn't think it mattered, but—'

'George! I have *never* slept with Rob. He's like

340

a brother to me! I was with no man for three years before you! I was already in love with you, for God's sake. Look at me, George. Look at me!'

He very slowly raised his eyes to meet her gaze – dull, lifeless – and they were . . . soul destroying. He turned away and Susie swallowed the bile that had reached the back of her throat. 'I didn't do this. You have to believe me. Tell me you believe me.'

There was a pause before he spoke. 'You've caught me at a bad moment . . .'

But he should believe her, unequivocally! He had to believe her! 'Why don't you *believe me?*' she cried desperately.

George moved his chair back, its feet scraping noisily along the hard floor. 'I need to sort this out with Michael . . . stop them going to press.' He stood and began walking to the door.

Susie clutched at the table for support. This couldn't be happening. She'd done nothing wrong. *Loss, desolation, betrayal.* 'You can't walk out of here, George. You can't walk away from this. We need to find out why someone would do this. I didn't do it. I love you!'

He paused in the doorway of the kitchen. There was a flicker of something in his eyes before he turned away.

Susie stood rooted to the spot, listening to the front door open, a mass of voices and shouting and then the door closing behind him. She didn't bother reaching for a chair. She let herself slip down onto the cold marble floor.

341

My dearest Freddie,

Wake me up please, I beg of you! For this must be my worst nightmare. I know not what else it can be. But a moment ago, I was so blissfully happy – betrothed to the one who owns my heart, feeling like a fairy tale princess upon his arm – and now it is as if my being has been ripped into two.

Mr Richard Barratt is the brother of my dearest friends and, with our having grown up in close proximity, a brother to me, too.

Whatever wicked gossip your sister has heard, it is simply that. Should you need proof, then name a day, a time, a place, and I shall duly account for all my actions. But I implore you to remember, Freddie – this is me, Hannah. Your Hannah and I have to believe that your faith in me is as strong as my faith in you and your words were only a momentary aberration. I have always believed in you, in spite of Miss Prudence Argylle's ongoing public comments.

I have remained true to you, Freddie. I could never not be, I swear.

Forever yours,
Hannah

CHAPTER 24

Susie wasn't quite sure how long she sat on the floor, but she had finally managed to make herself move, find her mobile and put a call into Rachael. She now sat at the table staring unseeingly at the images before her.

'Suse? Suse? Where are you? *There* you are. We came as soon as we could.'

Susie slowly looked up from the table to take in Rachael, Cassie and Rob. She determined to remain in control.

'Guys . . . there may be a little problem on Susie and George's cloud nine and . . .' Her voice broke and no matter how hard she tried, she couldn't recover herself. Hugging herself tightly, she finally managed to beg on a sob, '*You have to help me.*'

'They're not running it,' Michael finally said, hanging up the phone on his desk. George let out the breath he'd been holding and immediately stood. It had taken far too long to sort things out. He glanced at his watch: 9.00 p.m. The whole day had gone, but he'd had to stop the story. He couldn't have Susie go through that.

'What are you going to do?' Michael asked.

'Beg for forgiveness,' George replied, crossing the room.

He *knew* the images weren't real. His gut had told him that from the start. When Michael first mentioned it on the phone, he'd not for one moment considered there to be any truth to the story. Then he worried only about its impact on Susie should the pictures hit the press. It was *seeing* the images that rocked his world. Susie in the arms of another. Real or not. He'd lost all sense and reason.

'I may have stopped the story, but you can't still trust her after—?' Michael cut his words short at George's furious look.

Oh he could trust her. Did trust her. One hundred per cent. He just prayed he could restore her faith in him. It was the images that had rendered him temporarily . . . He'd never experienced anything like it before! He'd scared even himself with whatever was raging through him. It was beyond fury. He hadn't trusted himself to be around Susie. Certainly hadn't wanted her to see him like that.

And it had had to be 'Rob'. He'd kept seeing his hands all over her on the dance floor. He clenched his fists now and took a deep breath. He'd only just regained control. He was not going to lose it afresh.

He had to make things right. He couldn't damned well live without her.

'Porsche Sutter-Blythe – welcome!'

George froze in the doorway.

Michael had evidently turned on the television.

George's stomach nosedived. It was Sunday night and Porsche's turn on *The Jonathan James Show*. He should be with Susie! She should *not* be listening to Porsche on her own.

He frantically went through his options. But even leaving now, driving like a bat out of hell, Susie was going to be watching this without him. He'd *totally* screwed things up. How the hell had he let this happen? He heard the words, 'Well how fantastic do *you* think he is, Porsche?'

He had no choice. He walked back into Michael's office and prepared for the worst.

Susie sat on the edge of one of the sofas in George's television room, arms and legs crossed. She knew she was sitting defensively, but they were lucky she was sat there at all.

Watching Porsche Sutter-Blythe was the last thing she needed. She needed George. She needed this whole nightmare to be over. She bit her lip, willing herself not to give in to the urge to roll herself up into a ball and bawl her eyes out. That was another reason she was determinedly sat in her current position.

Rachael, Cassie and Rob were presently sat around the room on sofas and beanbags, with bowls of popcorn and peanuts on hand, as if it

345

were movie night. But they were making her uneasy, even with everything else going on in her head. Despite their efforts at appearing casual, they kept exchanging glances, and Rachael and Cassie were currently whispering urgently to each other on the sofa they shared. At least Cassie was now sat and not pacing around with her phone to her ear, partaking in sometimes heated conversations, as she'd been for much of the time since her arrival. Rachael momentarily raised her voice enough for Susie to overhear. 'They have to be stopped! You were right, okay. You were right! They don't just have the motives, they're acting on them! And what if the protection isn't enough? You'd have thought our not being involved would be an obstacle, but it's still repeating. There must be—'

And it wasn't just this. They hadn't seemed surprised at all when Susie had finally recovered enough control to relay what had happened between her and George. And she would never forget that look that had appeared on their faces. They had almost looked . . . haunted. Or at least Rachael and Cassie had. Rob had simply looked horrified. Once they'd recovered themselves, they'd then proceeded to dismiss all of her concerns about what had happened. They were confident George would return home with his tail between his legs, begging for forgiveness. That it was just the shock of it. That he was without doubt, a 'complete toss-pot for ever believing it. No matter what's going down here' (Rachael) and 'a fuckwit of a brother. How could he fall for it all over again? And if he doesn't start returning my calls he'll have hell to pay!' (Cassie). But they were confident he would come to his senses. Overly confident, she'd thought. Almost smugly so. Although that wasn't quite the right word because they didn't seem at all happy about it. It made no sense.

Susie narrowed her eyes at Rachael and Cassie now. They were up to something. As long as it didn't involve her, she was fine. But she had a horrible feeling it did.

Despite their presence, Susie had never felt so alone. And it wasn't the paranoia. It was George. She gulped hard. Without him, she was . . . It was pitiful.

And she didn't know how to make things right. She could attempt to account for her whereabouts at the given time; Rachael and Rob would support her and she'd certainly made enough of a scene in the dry-cleaners for their shop assistants to remember her.

But what if he didn't give her a chance? What if he still didn't believe her? And most significantly – why did she *have* to? He should have believed her. It felt like betrayal . . . and loss. And her brain was screaming. Had she lost him? She crossed her arms tighter around herself in the hope of providing some physical comfort. He wasn't around to zap the sensations! He was, predictably, their cause.

She shouldn't still be here. 'Guys, I'd like to leave,' she said for the umpteenth time. She wasn't strong enough to hear George's voice like that again or see that soul-destroying blankness in his eyes.

Rachael diverted her attention from Cassie. 'Suse, we've gone through all this. You're over reacting. He *will* be back. Trust me on that one. And anyway,' Rachael nodded her head in the direction of the door. 'Tom, Dick and Harry won't let you. Not without them. There's truck-loads of press out there.'

The theme music for *The Jonathan James Show* blared out of the giant flat screen television making Susie jump violently.

She instinctively hugged herself yet tighter. How could George leave her to deal with Porsche's venom alone?

'Let's just watch this and then talk again, okay? And don't look so worried. Remember, whatever she says you take with a *sack* full of salt. But you need to see it, to be prepared. It's all part of their sick game and . . .'

Susie tuned out Rachael's words. Rachael kept asserting Porsche and Michael were *baddies*, no doubt behind the photos, and that, whatever Susie might one day remember, she and Cassie were the *good guys*. Conversations with Rachael were getting even more nonsensical these days. She'd braved asking for more on Michael, breaking her cardinal rule about never asking Rachael for an explanation. Someone had manufactured those pictures and when she thought of her adverse reaction to the man, and his conversation with her on the bus . . .

'He's a baddie. They don't get any worse. Do *not* trust him! And Porsche is one, too. If you ever encounter them – run. Seriously, Suse – run. But not towards water, okay. *Never* towards water!' That's what Rachael had said, refusing to elaborate. Susie had known her rule was there for a reason.

When it came to Porsche . . . Susie already knew Porsche was 'a baddie'; she wanted George. She reckoned the woman was in love with him. She saw the way she looked at him. And then there were her words in the newspaper. And the *horse*! The horse was all down to Porsche. Not her. She refused to blame herself for that little incident. She'd have been absolutely fine if Porsche hadn't turned up to gloat.

As audience applause sounded, Susie tentatively focused on the screen and wished she hadn't. Porsche was dressed to kill in a miniscule red dress and matching killer heels. She had legs up to her armpits. The wolf whistles were not surprising and all of Susie's insecurities came flooding back. How could she ever compete with *that*? And George was a man. A full-blooded man at that.

Susie caught an appreciative sound from Rob, sprawled out on the beanbag in front of her. She so wasn't in the mood. She shot him a look that would have made the one given to Joseph Robinson on the coach appear angelic. She'd have kicked him, viciously too, if she hadn't needed to uncross her legs to do so, severely threatening her physical composure. She was comforted a little as a cushion, thrown by Rachael, hurtled across the room to hit him hard in the face.

'How are you liking England?'

'Well it's cold . . . but you people are just *soo* warm and friendly.'

Blurgh! Susie's disgust was shared throughout the room.

'You are here filming *Pride and Prejudice*. Elizabeth, the female lead of course, to George Silbury's Darcy.'

Audience clapping and whistling. Susie's stomach lurched at the mention of George's name. Oh God, she missed him. She missed him so much. How could things have gone so wrong? This time last night she was on his arm, feeling precious . . . whole. Now . . . The next question sounded.

'We had him on the show a couple of weeks ago. A sensational show I must say and a fantastic guy. Great to have him back in the country. How fantastic do *you* think he is, Porsche?'

'Oh. My. God,' from Rachael.

'Not good. Not good at all,' from Cassie.

Rob shifted his position to sit up, with his back against the sofa. 'This is going to be . . . *interesting*,' he murmured, turning to shoot a worried glance Susie's way.

Susie shut her eyes and tried to calm her rapidly

beating heart. She had a really, really bad
about this.

When she opened them, Porsche was play.
audience, raising her eyebrows before ret
her attention to the host. 'Fantastically fa:
of course!' And the floozy actually leant fc
to touch his knee . . . and Jonathan James g1
like a Cheshire cat.

'So how did you take being dumped, Por
Ooooooo from the audience.

'No. No. No!' from Cassie.

'Flaming hell!' from Rachael.

Susie felt sick.

'I'm sorry?' from Porsche.

'Well, George dumping you for one of our
Rachael groaned into her hands.

Cassie cried, 'He's got to stop provoking he1
can't do this!'

Rob let out a low whistle.

Susie silently wept.

Porsche cackled.

'Well, hasn't he?'

'I really don't think it would be appropriat
talk about our personal lives, Jonathan.'

Emphasis on 'our' Susie noted on a painful g
'George didn't seem to mind.'

Cackle. Cackle. Cackle. 'You're forgetti
Jonathan, that we are actors. We make films a
our contracts ensure we promote them. We do
in a number of ways. Some clearly more imagii
tive than others. George currently has a numt

351

of films out which he's promoting over here in England and . . .'

Oooooooh from the audience.

'Bitch!' from around the room.

Susie closed her eyes. She hadn't thought of that. Why hadn't she thought of that? That would explain so much.

George leapt up from his seat in Michael's office over-turning the chair in the process. He snatched the nearest thing at hand – a mug – and hurled it at the wall. Flakes of plaster flew as it shattered.

Susie would be watching this without him. What if she believed it? Despite all of his reassurances, she was still scarred by whatever the hell Rachael Jones had done to her a decade ago. And look how he'd behaved this morning!

George counselled himself to take deep breaths. He found a glass of whisky shoved under his nose from Michael. He shook his head. He was driving as soon as Porsche uttered her last word. He'd make it her last breath, the way he was feeling.

'Surely you're not saying George's emotional outburst, made while in that very chair, was a ploy for promoting his films? He was totally smitten and had my wife in tears at home.'

The audience clapped and cheered.

Susie closed her eyes, hoping to stem her own threatening tears. It had seemed so real. They'd been in love . . . hadn't they?

'He's a good actor, Porsche, but not that good. And the photos of them in the papers this morning would indicate they've really got something going there. That was another excuse for my wife to have a go!'

Audience laughter.

Had it all just been for promotion? But if an act – why her? *'Because you're Ms Ordinary,'* that sensible part of her brain jeered at her. *'What better promotion could there be?'*

Turning to the audience now, Jonathan James cried, 'One for the men! How many of you have suffered serious grief from your wives and better half's because of George Silbury's courtship of a certain woman we cannot name for legal reasons?'

Cheers and clapping and several hands going up.

The silent tears flowed now and Susie could no longer see the screen.

'Glad to see I'm not alone. If you're watching George – cut it out! We're mere mortals and can't compete on this romantic front. I hate to think what you're like at home together.'

Susie found herself being pulled into Rachael's arms. She wouldn't uncross any of her limbs. She just couldn't.

'Susie Moo, cut it out. You two are so made for each other and you can't possibly believe her. She's speaking crap.'

Susie shook her head, stiffly.

'Porsche, it's difficult to see what he said on this

show as anything other than a declaration of love for Susi . . . Ooops! Can't say that!'

Audience laughter.

Susie's hand went to her mouth and she took deep breaths to try and regain control. Oh God. How was she going to live without him?

'George refuses to confirm Susie is the girl he *didn't* get his horn out for. So, to the lawyers watching at home, please don't write a nasty letter. I'm very, very, sorry. And to George and Susie, of course. I beg not to be crossed off any wedding guest list you may be preparing.'

'As if.' The mutter was clearly picked up on Porsche's microphone.

'So, Porsche. You're saying all this is to promote his films. And what? You and him are in a relationship? I thought I was just being a bit naughty with the dumping stuff. He insisted his relationship with you has always been professional, despite all the gossip in the press.'

'Have you never heard of the saying . . . I don't know if you have it over here, but where there's smoke, there's fire? So where there's gossip, there's . . .?'

He'd never been hers. How could he have been? Why hadn't she listened to her head? It had told her.

'There's . . .?'

'I've said too much here already, Jonathan. I promised I'd keep the lid on things and play my part.'

Susie was only vaguely aware of the words now. She had no idea how everyone was responding in the room. She'd long shrugged Rachael's arms away.

'Is this just sour grapes, Porsche?'

'Well all I can say is, does she *honestly* believe we are "filming" until ten o'clock at night?'

That was it. Susie couldn't take any more. Somehow she found the strength to rise to her feet. Porsche still spoke, somewhere in the back of her head.

'George and I being seen together . . . publicly . . . would be *inappropriate* at this current time.'

Susie had to get out. She couldn't be here when he got home – *if* he got home. Susie and George's cloud nine had just blown away.

'Suse?' That was Rachael, sounding concerned.

'Susie? You don't actually *believe* her? She's delusional. She's in fantasy land. Michael could well be feeding her lies about George. None of it is true!' That was Cassie.

The phone rang in the background. She just had to get out of there. She turned, trying to work out the way to the door. She finally exited the room and headed towards the main door and . . . Tom, Dick and Harry. She really wasn't in the mood for them.

'GET OUT OF MY WAY!' she screamed at the top of her voice.

'Susie?' sounded from behind her and from an uncertain-sounding Cassie. 'George is on the phone and desperately wants to talk to you. He says it's all rubbish and is on his way home now. He believes you about the photos. He always knew they weren't real. He loves you. Talk to him.'

Susie spun around and focused on Cassie, lamely holding the phone out. 'Tell your brother, if he loves me, he can recall his dogs and let me out of his prison. NOW!'

Cassie slowly returned the handset to her mouth. 'George . . . Yeah. You heard. Okay.' Cassie ended the call.

'He's calling them off, but you have to give him an opportunity to explain, to apologise. He's no more than half an hour away.' She added, pleadingly, 'Please Susie. They're trying to separate you. Don't let them.'

Rachael, now at Susie's side, held out her coat to her, while saying to Cassie, worriedly, 'Save your breath. The cycle or whatever it is, is still to break.'

Talking to Susie now, Rachael said, 'Come on then. Back home. It was on the cards. I actually tidied up this morning especially for you, although I warn you, I've yet to brave the supermarket.'

My darling Angel,
Can you ever forgive me? It was a moment of lunacy! Indeed an aberration, but of the very worst kind. The thought of you in another's arms took me to the brink of insanity in an instant and you saw me thus. Whatever my

sister might say, I know you to be true. As I am to you, now and forever.

Miss Argylle's evil lies – and they are ALL lies my love – will be stopped. I am pursuing legal channels, but my fury is such that I would take extreme pleasure in throttling her!

I pursue you now to the Misses Barratts and pray you will receive me. Should you not, I will request they pass this letter to you.

I must have the opportunity to put this right. I beg of you not to deny me. Forgive me my idiocy, my sweetheart.

Your imbecilic Freddie

CHAPTER 25

'I'm going to my room,' Susie muttered on entering the flat.

'Hold up, Suse!' Rachael addressed her back. 'We should talk. You need to believe in George and realise nothing the bitch said is true, otherwise they've won and . . .' Her words trailed off before she cried, 'Cassie! I've got it! If we could break them up now, it couldn't end how . . . *No!* There's the Soul Mate thing! *Flaming Nora!* There's not a chance we can—'

Susie slammed the bedroom door, silencing the words. She had long stopped listening to Rachael and Cassie in any event. How could they possibly *know* she and George would sort things out? Thankfully Rob hadn't added to their nonsense, remaining quiet as he drove them here. The hug he'd given her though, before heading off to work, and his words, had so nearly shattered whatever composure she'd managed to put into place. '*Prove* to me there can be happy endings,' he'd said into her hair.

Susie moved to her old bed, picking up the empty cardboard box that sat on it, dropping it to the floor. She sank down in its former footprint, amidst her scattered belongings yet to be packed. She was so confused. George believed her? She clutched onto that. So he bloody should!

But there was Porsche. Susie's whole being cried out for George, urging her to believe in him. But her head? Oh, her head was a disastrous place to be.

Could this all be for publicity? Could he and Porsche be . . .?

She recalled how Porsche taunted her when Susie was on that killer horse. Susie had dismissed it then, but . . .? And Porsche was so beautiful.

But her gut cried out to believe George. He'd loved her. He really had. She knew that . . . didn't she? How good an actor was he?

Susie's instinct was to run, but she wasn't brave enough. How pitiful was she? While there was still hope, she had to clutch onto it for dear life because without it, without him . . .

She looked around at the contents of her bed and then at the near empty dressing table and the windowsill. The photo she was looking for, of her mum and dad, was no longer here. It had been taken over to George's on the very first trip. It currently sat in pride of place on the chest of drawers in their bedroom. George had suggested she order some copies, along with others, including the last picture she had of her mum, so they could be hung on the walls amidst his family pictures. She and George had been so happy. She had finally found home.

Blinking her eyes furiously, refusing to give into the tears, she visualised the image in that photograph now. The love between her parents sang out of the picture. It had been taken a couple of years before Mum first got ill. They'd been so happy. Dad was now a shell of what he once was. And there'd never been another woman since Mum. And it wasn't that he kept that sort of thing away from his kids. She and her brothers were constantly urging him to date. It was simply that he never would. His heart had died with Mum. Was that the future before her? She knew the answer to that. And it was terrifying. How had Dad managed to keep going? If he suffered just a fraction of what losing George would do to her. *Oh Dad. I never knew.*

Susie looked around the room, plucking absently at the duvet cover as she continued to fight back the tears. This wasn't home anymore. It wasn't where her heart was. She needed to call George. She needed to hear what he had to say. If there was any hope . . .? But first . . . she needed the loo.

Susie raised herself from the bed, and made her way to the door on legs that quivered. What was the chance of reaching the toilet without being waylaid by Rachael and Cassie? She opened the door as quietly as she could . . .

Hannah.

The name whispered through her. Susie's heart started pounding and that box in her head bled.

She clutched the door frame. It had come from Cassie.

'—and Hannah! I can't bear seeing them going through this. And what help are bodyguards with *this*? When is it going to stop? It *has* to stop! I haven't a clue what to do! These photos aren't enough to lock Michael away, even though we know he's behind them. And the drug use – it's not enough! Tell me it's going to stop. Please! This shouldn't be happening. For pity's sake, the photos shouldn't have been Michael anyway. It was *Kathryn* who fed the lies about Hannah to Freddie, yet it's still . . .'

Hannah and Freddie.

Susie collapsed against the door, slamming it noisily in the process, but somehow she remained on her feet.

Hannah and Freddie, Hannah and Freddie. The names were on a loop, echoing through her, all consuming in their intensity and in their demands that she acknowledge them. She wouldn't. She couldn't. She'd kept them at bay for ten years. She wasn't about to surrender to them now.

Hannah and Freddie. Hannah and Freddie.

She became vaguely aware of being pushed backwards. The door was moving and she was moving with it because one of her hands appeared to be clutching the handle for support. And then she faced Rachael and Cassie.

'Suse?' There was a momentary pause before Rachael murmured, '*Shit.*'

Susie made herself focus on a horrified-looking Cassie. She swallowed so her throat would allow her to talk.

'Hannah and Freddie?' Her voice was a choked echo of that whispering through her. Why would Cassie be saying those names? Why would anyone say those names? Had Rachael told her? She shook her head. She'd never told Rachael, Freddie's name. Why would . . .?

'Suse, sit down before you fall down. We'll talk when you're sat down.'

Rachael appeared to be moving her backwards and then down. Her bed. She was sat on the edge of her bed.

'I'm so sorry, I'm so sorry,' Cassie was saying.

Rachael crouched down on the floor before her, and held Susie's hands between hers. 'Can we do a rain check on this?' she asked gently. 'I think you've got more than enough to deal with here. You can't seriously be meant to know about this now.'

'Tell me!' It was the only way Susie was going to stop the names going around and around in her head. There had to be a perfectly innocent explanation for why Cassie used them. Then she could get them securely back into that box and battened down. Perhaps if she worked harder on the locking mechanisms she could get them locked away properly this time, never ever to see the light of day. She hadn't a hope with those, now constant, seeping emotions . . . but the memories themselves? Perhaps . . . Oh God, she was remembering something.

'Tell me,' she whimpered amidst flashbacks to Rachael's consulting room.

She saw George. No Freddie! No. No. No. No. She recognised him. No. Please God no. *Hannah* recognised him.

This couldn't be happening. Hannah and Freddie weren't real. They were never real. It had been her poor intoxicated brain. It wasn't real. She clutched her head and seemed to be rocking backwards and forwards.

It was all flooding back. *No!* It couldn't be.

Her face was being stroked. 'Suse. Just hear me here. George loves you. The bitch's words were lies and everything else can wait. Now you need—'

'I remember!' Susie wailed. 'I'm going mad, Rach. Tell me it didn't happen. Tell me I didn't call him Freddie. Tell me I wasn't Hannah. Tell me they weren't real. Tell me they never existed!'

George hung up on Tom. Susie was at the flat. He did a U-turn, ignoring the blaring horns that accompanied the process. He put his foot down. Speeding across a zebra crossing the roar of his V8 engine drowned out the expletives hurled at him by the pedestrians flinging themselves back onto the pavement.

He was going to sort this. He had to sort this. There was no way . . .

He frowned. There was something . . . He put his

windscreen wipers on to clear the screen of hail. It appeared he was finally remembering the consulting room. Amidst the confusion of images flashing before him, something was beginning to . . .

Hannah.

The name whispered through his being. It was somehow familiar. His heart raced. And . . . he'd been regressed? Had he actually been *regressed?* His frown deepened while his windscreen wipers automatically upped the tempo to keep pace with the hail and his speed.

He *may* have been regressed. It seemed pretty real at the time, but that didn't mean . . . For a moment there he thought he'd been someone called Freddie. And – wow! He couldn't help but grin at the memory. And no headache! He and Susie had really gone for it. He now understood exactly why his body had been unable to forget.

But . . . *Susie. Bloody hell!* He'd thought she was *Hannah?* He'd recognised her and she'd recognised *him? Freddie?*

'Shit!' George exclaimed aloud. He didn't believe such stuff, so why . . .? So why did Freddie and Hannah seem so familiar? Why were their names echoing around his head, demanding to be embraced as long lost friends? Why did he know they'd been in love? Deeply in love. Happy. So happy!

Actually it could be worse, George reflected. He wouldn't mind . . .

He slammed on his brakes and a horn blared somewhere in his head. He counselled himself to take slow deep breaths. He *couldn't* deal with this. He *wouldn't* deal with this. He would *not* believe this.

The pain! Freddie had lost Hannah. It was too close to his own fears of losing Susie. He wasn't going to accept this. Absolutely not.

George slammed his foot down on the accelerator pedal while fighting against the agony coursing through him – remembered and anticipated. He was not going to lose her. He was *not* going to lose her.

'Tell me they never existed!' Susie cried. Then she could go and get the professional help she'd known she'd needed for a decade. She'd been on the edge for so long. The problems with her and George had obviously sent her over it. And getting help would be bliss. She'd let all and sundry into her head now. Anything to stop what was ricocheting around it. And she had to have it stop. Because George could not have been Freddie. She could not have been Hannah. Because Freddie had betrayed Hannah. Just as she feared George had betrayed her with Porsche. Freddie had destroyed her. Destroyed Hannah.

Her head was like a broken dam. And there was no stopping the insanities rushing through the breach. Agonising memories. Agonising, insane memories that were not hers. That couldn't be hers, which she'd managed to lock away in a box now blasted to oblivion, but which . . .

Rachael's words abruptly intruded. 'All right Suse. The timing's so beyond crap, but you evidently need to hear this. Just know that whatever you remember, I love you so much and I'm here for you and . . . *Shit. Shit. Shit!* Look you *did* know George before and you recognised each other. What happened a decade ago was real. You *were* Hannah and George was Freddie.'

She'd known. She'd always known she realised on a sob. It had been there under the surface the whole time, but she kept it there. Suppressed. Locked away. And now? Oh God, she couldn't deal with the now. It somehow all made the most ridiculous sense. Their connection and how it had all seemed so right. How she'd felt she'd known him forever and . . . *the eye obsession*!

'But it's not bad. It really isn't. You guys are *meant* to be together. *So* meant to be together. You are Soul Mates and will move heaven and earth to find each other.'

Susie's brain no longer registered Rachael's words. It was awash with memories. They aren't mine, she screamed silently. And all that loss and betrayal. Hannah loved Freddie *so* much, but it hadn't been enough. She'd lost him. She knew she'd never be good enough for him. But he made her believe him. All his declarations of love, reassurances, promises for the future. But then he betrayed her with Prudence Argylle. It hurt so much. And now George had . . .

'It's why you were obsessed with George Silbury.'

Rachael's words were just sounds being added to the excruciating blur that was now her head.

'It's why you couldn't help but hurl yourselves into each other's arms. You have found each other again. You are drawn together like magnets. George has to be with you because you were Hannah. You have to be with . . .'

Susie's brain somehow snatched onto those words. *George* had *to be with her because she'd been Hannah.*

She made her eyes focus. Rachael was looking at her desperately and with such pain and concern in her eyes. Susie cried out, 'George *has* to be with me because—?'

'Do you see, Suse? Because he was Freddie and you were Hannah. Do you get it? He recognised you as Hannah and . . .'

She had the answer. She actually had the answer! If she embraced Freddie and Hannah, if she accepted what her body and soul were screaming at her, then she had finally found the answer to that constant, plaguing question: why me? Why would George ever choose me? She didn't even need to believe Porsche's assertions. Because she had it. The answer.

He had no choice.

George gave up on ringing the buzzer; nobody was answering. He let Tom, Dick and Harry at the door. It took one unified kick. He bounded up the stairs, letting them do their stuff on the next door. Indicating they remain at the building's entrance, he made his own way through to the flat.

He hammered on the door refusing to give airtime to Hannah and Freddie, despite their desperate attempts to be heard.

'Susie!' he yelled. He tried to rein himself in so he sounded less . . . psychotic? 'Susie, sweetheart. Please open the door. I need to put this right. Please . . .'

The door was unlocked and swung open. Cassie. George gulped. He . . . he . . . he . . . *Kathryn?* And . . . and . . . she'd . . . she'd killed . . .

'Sweet Jesus!' her words were agonised and snapped him out of wherever the hell he'd just been. He finally focused on her face. Cassie's haunted face. His sister, Cassie.

'Not you too!' she cried frantically, shaking her head. 'You remember? I promise I'm not bad now. It wasn't me, it was Kathryn. Please understand . . .'

George was not going to deal with whatever the hell was going on right now. He was going to sort things with Susie and then . . . He heard her.

'I need to go away,' she sobbed from somewhere inside the flat.

He was immediately through the door and crossing the room. Cassie kept trying to get in front of him and now Rachael was there and . . . and . . . *A maid?* He thought she'd been . . . The name was just there, but he couldn't . . .

He ground to a halt. Scenes were flashing through his brain. *Memories?* But not his! What the hell was going on?

Susie's sobs refocused him. The sound of her crying was killing him.

'Get out of my way. NOW!' he demanded.

'You need to listen to us first,' Cassie pleaded. 'I'm so sorry. For everything. But you and Susie have found each other again. Even death couldn't separate you. We're working to keep you together now, but Mic—'

He didn't have time for whatever crap Cassie was spouting. 'Get out of my way, Cassie. Nobody is going to stop me seeing my fiancé when—'

'*Fiancé?*' Cassie gasped, as she rocked on her feet. He instinctively reached out, but she'd steadied herself. 'Rachael. Did you . . .?'

'We're screwed! Totally screwed,' Rachael declared with conviction. 'It's *all* playing out!'

George had had more than enough of this. 'Out of my way or you both get plastered over the door.'

With that they moved aside and he was left with the door.

Susie stood braced against the farthest wall. She heard George out there, but didn't know how to face him. This was too painful as it was. Because none of it mattered any more. Whether he believed her. Whether he'd betrayed her with Porsche.

He'd only ever been with her because he had to be. He'd been compelled. It wasn't free will. He would never have *chosen* her. And she loved him too much to let him throw his life away on some ridiculous link to the past which had only materialised because of Rachael's insane mumbo-jumbo. Hannah and Freddie be damned.

And there he was in the doorway and she was sobbing again and couldn't stop. Freddie. He *had* been Freddie, but, oh God, now he was George and she loved him so much. Her whole being reacted to him. She battled the urge to run into his arms and be held against him and never be let go.

'Susie, sweetheart,' he said in a voice brimming with emotion as he closed the distance between them. It was no longer dead and expressionless. It sounded full of love.

She shook her head and her hands went up to stop him. He came to a halt less than a foot away and the distance between them was excruciating.

'Don't George,' she managed to get out. 'I'm going away. This isn't right and—'

'Isn't *right*?' he declared in complete disbelief, shaking his head furiously. 'You're NOT going away. You are NOT leaving me. You vowed. *We* vowed.'

He reached his hand out to touch the side of her face. She wanted the contact so much, to lean her cheek into his palm, but turned her face away instead.

'I believe you about the photos. I always believed

you. It was just seeing them. You should never have seen me like that and I will never forgive myself. And Porsche. It was evil lies, sweetheart. I'm going to sue her to kingdom come. I don't know what she's playing at, but clearly needs help. How could I ever be interested in her when I have you?'

He sounded so sincere. But it no longer mattered.

'Look at me, Susie. Look into my eyes and see I'm telling the truth. I've never lied to you and never will.'

She couldn't. She avoided eye contact. She had to. Looking into them would destroy whatever strength she was attempting to muster. He gently raised her chin while turning her face. His touch zapped that haunting loss and betrayal, but the relief was miniscule. She was losing George for real. Perhaps she knew now how dying might feel?

He moved closer because his breath caressed her face and his scent filled her lungs. 'Please, baby,' he begged in a voice so anguished it was impossible to resist. She tried so darned hard too.

And . . . Oh God. Their eyes connected and everything started slotting into place. The power of those eyes. And she knew he was telling the truth. It was plain as day. It was impossible to deny. But no matter how right this felt, it couldn't be. She wrenched her eyes away.

'Do you believe me, sweetheart? Tell me you believe me.' His mouth hovered just millimetres from her lips.

If she just moved forward a fraction she could experience him one last time. She could surrender to what her whole being craved. But she mustn't. She raised her hands and pressed them against his chest, forcing herself to push him back. She shook her head. 'I believe you, George, but us together isn't right. I'm going to—'

'Isn't *right*?!' He thought she believed him, so how the hell could not being together be right? There had never ever been anything so right. She had been Hannah. Incredibly, he knew that now . . . *Freddie's Hannah*. But this was Susie. *His* Susie. He'd never been more certain of anything in his life.

'I love you, Susie. And you love me. I know it. Tell me you don't love me. Go on! Tell me!' *And it will kill me Susie. Please don't.*

'It doesn't matter!' she cried. 'You only think you love me. It's all to do with Hannah and Freddie, don't you see? I had them locked away, but they were real, George. Real.'

Hannah and Freddie. So she was experiencing all this, too. This was doing his head in.

'You're only with me because of her. Hannah. You're not with me because I'm Susie Morris but because of some completely crackpot past that crashed into your life as soon as Rachael got into your head. The two are confused. But I'm going to put it right. I'm going to bow out so you can lead the life you should have been leading before she screwed you up and made you remember something you should never ever have remembered.'

She was talking rubbish and he couldn't take any more. He closed the gap between them and grasped her shoulders. 'Hannah you say. Yeah I remember too. And it's a hell of a lot to take in. But don't you *dare* insult me by saying I'm with you because of *Hannah*!'

Her eyes widened. He'd shocked her with his outburst. Good because he had to shock her out of this terrifying talk. If she thought he was going to let her walk away because they remembered what happened in that room, remembered what . . . what appeared to have happened in the past, she was insane. Even more insane than he currently felt.

Shaking his head he spoke more gently. 'I've only just remembered. Half an hour ago, Hannah and Freddie meant nothing to me. So explain to me why I'm with you because of Hannah? I fell in love with Susie Morris. You! And how could I not? And I've fallen deeper than I ever thought possible. But now I've found you, don't *ever* think I'm going to let you just walk away. And as for having me lead a different life? I don't want a life without you. Not because of the past, but because I can no longer live without you. Are you hearing me here?'

He was missing the point. He felt this way about her because of Hannah and because Rachael had . . .

'Tell me you don't love me!' he demanded again.

She couldn't do that. And he knew it. But neither

could they carry on something where he had no free will and . . .

'Are you only with me because of Freddie?'

How could he *possibly* ask that? Surely he knew how she felt about him, how this was destroying her?

'When you tell me you love me, is it Freddie you're speaking to? When you shout at me, is it really at Freddie? When we make love, is it Freddie you're thinking of and I'm just a body that you can use and—'

'*How could you?*' Susie cried, raising her arms to shrug off his hold on her shoulders and with the intention of pummelling his chest. She found her wrists grasped gently in his hands. How could he possibly ask her that? 'I love *you*!' she cried. '*You* George. You are everything and this is killing me. Freddie was someone Hannah loved, not me! You've always been George and—'

'So, explain to me,' he interrupted softly, moving closer again. 'Just why *you* can love me as George, and *I* can't love you as Susie?' He gently shook her wrists. 'What is different here? It works both ways. You aren't making any sense. And I know this must be doing your head in like it is mine, but Hannah and Freddie aren't us. Me and you are us! Freddie and Hannah were nothing to me when I fell hook, line and sinker for you. I didn't even know of their existence. So, tell me Susie!'

He was twisting things. And she was getting really confused.

374

'Tell me, baby,' George whispered, freeing her hands to so gently push a lock of hair away from her face.

She shook her head and the tears ran anew. She hadn't thought of that. She thought she'd found the answer to that question that kept replaying in her head: why me? But if she could love him as George, could he love her as Susie? She wanted to clutch on to it, but it was all so confusing.

'So you believe me about the photos and Porsche?'

She lamely nodded. She did. She one hundred per cent did and even her head wasn't doing its *betrayal* stuff.

'And you love me as George, not Freddie?'

She bit her lip and nodded again. He was George. *Her* George.

'Then what is the matter here? I don't know about you, sweetheart, but I'm really struggling with all this stuff and could do with a hug. I'm forcing myself not to take you into my arms and never let you go, but I need to know you want to be there. We can get through anything. I know we can. But we can only do that together.'

Susie raised her eyes to meet his and as they locked, he started breathing again. He drew her into his arms, clutching her to him so tightly. He would *never* let her go.

'I love you, George,' she sobbed, wrapping her arms around him, too. 'So much. It hurts so much. I'm sorry. I got so confused and thought I'd found the answer and then there was Freddie, and Freddie betraying Hannah, and everything Porsche said, and it all got such a mess and—'

'Ssssshhh,' he whispered, kissing the top of her head. She loved him. That's all that mattered here. Whatever else was going on, they'd sort it. Together. Nothing was going to separate them. He *had* to believe that.

Especially when right now his fear of loss had reached terror status.

He tightened his arms around her. It made no sense. It would appear he now had an answer as to why he'd been *haunted* by fears of losing Susie. Such pasts couldn't but haunt. Yet . . .?

Susie's hips moved against him and he needed no encouragement. As she pulled his head down his lips crushed hers in a demanding frenzy which she matched. Each and every uncertainty that had threatened them needed to be pounded into oblivion. Every one of his fears needed obliteration. She was his. His.

And he was going to reassure them both.

My darling Angel
No matter what they throw our way, they cannot separate us. Our faith in each other has survived these hurdles and, my sweetest darling Hannah, our love will conquer all.

Your Freddie

CHAPTER 26

'Have they stopped?' Cassie asked from the sofa, refusing to remove the cotton wool and earphones from her ears until Rachael nodded and gave the thumbs up.

'I had no idea.'

'No idea what?' Cassie asked, removing the final piece of cotton wool.

'Susie was a secret screamer.'

'How could you?' Cassie cried. 'I'm screwed up enough as it is without—'

'Six hours. Non. Stop. I don't get it. I thought a man needed to recharge after—'

'Stop! It beggars belief that you can focus on such things with what's going on right now and knowing what we have to tell them!'

'It's because of that I *am* focusing on such things! It's got to be the Soul Mate thing. It's just got to be. I really don't know it all. It's logical it carries on into the bedroom, it's just I had never really considered the details. No wonder I find my connection with Matey so frustrating! I—'

Rachael's words died and her jaw dropped open. George had emerged from the bedroom. Cassie slammed her eyes shut as tight as they could possibly go. 'George?' she managed through her screwed up face. 'Spare us. *Please.*'

George cursed, and evidently disappeared, because when Cassie braved opening up her eyes a crack, he was reappearing with jeans on. He sent an apologetic look their way, before heading to the bathroom. Cassie now narrowed her eyes on Rachael. She still sat, jaw hanging. She snapped her fingers in front of her face.

'I'm a woman,' Rachael declared, after a single blink of her eyes, 'and just how else am I meant to react to George Silbury in the—' She now blinked furiously and turned to Cassie to declare, 'The stupid thing is he doesn't hit those parts of me I thought he would. It's got to be because of Matey, which I must say I find very reassuring. But Flaming Nora, Cassie, I *can* appreciate what's before me! He's stunning! A total work of art. In fact he's—'

Her words abruptly stopped again as George reappeared.

He glanced their way and hesitated outside the bedroom door. After a quick curse and a hand through his hair, he abandoned the bedroom and strode past them into the kitchen. 'I need some answers,' he announced, weighing the kettle in his hand before placing it back on its stand and switching it on. 'Coffee and answers.' He turned to face them now, leaning against the worktop, arms crossed over his bare chest. 'You two are going to tell me *everything.*'

George took in their uneasy demeanours; in fact Cassie looked ill, but he was not going to be swayed, despite the sense of dread that now sat like a brick in the pit of his stomach. *And* despite Susie's no doubt sound advice. Before falling asleep, she'd warned of attempting to get explanations from these two.

But he didn't have a choice. They definitely knew things he and Susie didn't. There hadn't been a hope of his sleeping. His fears were in overdrive . . . and something felt alarmingly wrong. Incredibly he didn't think it was the past life stuff, no matter how mind-screwing that was. He and Susie could – *would* – work through that together. They'd already started. There was something else . . . And he very much hoped, with the fuller picture, he'd be reassured.

He turned his attention from Cassie, whose look was doing nothing to lessen his concerns, to Rachael.

'How about you start with that Soul Mate stuff you were spouting when I came out of the bedroom?' He couldn't quite believe what he was asking here, but in for a penny in for a pound.

She visibly paled. No wonder with what he'd overheard.

'Before we move on to . . . to . . .' George knew he was frowning. He sighed and rubbed his forehead. 'To whatever the hell else is going on here, because there's something, I just know it.' He forced himself to look again at his sister. 'Tell me about the horse . . .' George's voice trailed off. *The horse.* Unsettled didn't begin to go there. And Cassie had been avoiding him.

Several minutes later, George slowly smiled. He liked this one. He was so pleased he'd asked about this. So pleased he'd braved talking to them both. This he'd accept. And why *couldn't* he? If he was having to believe in past lives, why not Soul Mates?

'It could be worse. It kind of explains a lot of things and . . . You know? I can live with Soul Mates.' *Happily* live with Soul Mates. 'I'm not so sure about the labelling . . . or the *cherries*, but . . .'

He shook his head pointedly at Rachael, clearly about to interrupt. On the basis of the last several minutes he knew exactly what she'd be interrupting with. 'I am not satisfying your curiosity as to our sex life! Do *not* ask me again. And don't even go there,' he warned, as she opened her mouth again, '*Even* in the name of science! You've sold me on this one, okay, so I suggest you quit while you're ahead.'

Not that it had been a hard sale. He *wanted* to believe in Soul Mates. *Needed* to believe in them. It was comforting. To be frank, he'd currently believe in faeries if it allowed him the promise of more than one life with Susie. And it confirmed what he'd always known: they were meant to be together. *Yes,* he'd – he watched Cassie and Rachael exchange a look – *grab* hold of this one.

Because it was impossible to shake that feeling that something far less comforting was afoot.

'As for the other . . .' Cassie's voice, uncharacteristically high, fizzled out.

George sitting next to her on the sofa, leant forward, putting his elbows on his knees. He felt sick. This was all in his head, it had to be. It hadn't been a good day. He was getting himself all worked up for nothing. And this would have absolutely *nothing* to do with that damned sixth sense!

He looked up as Cassie's silence continued. She seemed to have been rendered mute and slowly shook her head. The expression on her face . . .

Rachael moved over to perch on the arm of the sofa nearest to Cassie. Gently touching her shoulder, she murmured, 'We'll do this together.'

Redirecting her attention to him, Rachael asked, 'How much do you remember?'

George closed his eyes. He knew she was talking of Freddie here and . . . too damned much! And this was nuts. He now had a whole new set of bloody *memories* and had a horrible feeling it was getting bigger with each breath he took. Certainly looking at these two hadn't helped on that front . . . *Kathryn* and *Tessa*? That had been her name.

And the memories of Kathryn were *not* good. And then there were the flashbacks: horrific, agonising, irrepressible. No wonder he and Susie were haunted by loss.

But the betrayal stuff that had so troubled Susie . . . she'd been wrong. The flashbacks were making that painfully clear. So wrong. Freddie hadn't had the chance to put the record straight, but George would. And perhaps that would make all this easier on Susie? She'd been haunted by betrayal for a decade. Perhaps it would help with her insecurities, with reassuring her he—?

'Kathryn was . . .' Cassie had evidently found her voice in at least some form. It was enough to pull George from his reflections and he didn't let her continue.

He shook his head and reached out to clasp her hand. 'She wasn't you, Cassie.' He knew that much and realised now how it must have been screwing her up. This all had serious screwing-up potential. And how selfish was he? He hadn't stopped to think how Cassie might be feeling. Finding out you were *Kathryn*. He wouldn't wish that on his worst enemy.

He squeezed her hand. 'The past is the past. Kathryn Montague is not you, so not you. Frederic Montague isn't me. Susie isn't Hannah Marsh. Rachael isn't Tessa . . . I don't think I ever knew her surname.' He spared a glance at Rachael to apologise. 'And thank God we aren't!' He grinned in an attempt to get a smile from Cassie. 'I'd have to hate you if you were Kathryn.'

But it was impossible to keep that grin on his face. Internally he shuddered at the idea of living the agony that had become Freddie's life. And he evidently once had. The remembered pain was excruciating, but imagining how he might feel losing Susie, as Freddie had Hannah? He roughly pushed the torturous thoughts away. Swallowing hard he continued.

'Whatever happened in the past between those people, is just that: the past. And dwelling on it really can't be healthy. Cas? God, Cas, is this what has been getting to you? Why you've been avoiding me? Tell me you didn't think I'd blame you? You can't possibly be held accountable for stuff that happened hundreds of years ago when you weren't you! I think no differently of you. I never could.'

Cassie closed her eyes, shook her head and clutched his hand.

'You mustn't dwell, Cas. We have *our* lives to lead. And despite all this crap, the present is good. In fact, it's bloody amazing. And the future is going to be more of the same. Come on, Sis! I grant you finding out about Kathryn couldn't have been good. But think about it. I'm getting married and that pretty much guarantees Mum's preoccupation, so she'll be out of your hair for . . .'

George's voice trailed off and that brick in his stomach instantly became replaced with a breeze block; one that descended at great velocity knocking all the air out of him on impact. Cassie had turned towards him and her face was . . . Jesus, she looked like someone had died. And her bottom lip was . . . *trembling*? Cassie's bottom lip did *not* tremble. Except when he was being a shit as a child and then – George swallowed painfully. Now was not the moment to explore that thought. Was *this* why he'd so disliked Cassie as a kid? Had he recognised her as Kathryn and until he'd known her as Cassie . . .? He'd been right about horses . . . and *water*. He'd always hated the stuff . . . and *now*? Knowing what he now did courtesy of the excruciating flashbacks . . . The idea of Susie near water . . .

George wasn't quite sure how much more of this he could take.

'Cassie?' he managed to rasp out, refocusing on her. 'What can possibly—?'

'I'm so sorry, George, so sorry. This is all my fault. And you *should* blame me. I don't know how to stop whatever has been set in motion. How to stop them! I just don't know. I'll do anything. And I mean *anything*. I never ever meant for this to happen. And I know I'm going to have to tell you, but have no idea *how* and—'

Rachael calmly interrupted. 'Why don't we start with Porsche and Michael before we tackle that? Leading with that would . . . Look, even I struggled with it.

'Porsche and Michael are clearly upping the anti, even without our help this time around. But despite what they're doing, the cycle *has* to break. It has to. Too many things are different this time around. I don't care how many of us are around, how many things are repeating – it has to break. It should have already broken. No, it should never ever have been there in the first place. Because it can't happen. But it is. I'm not even going to add Fate into the equation because they *will* have their own fate. They have to! There's no way they could have got muddled up. We need to forewarn, avoid and . . . wait . . . patiently and without panic . . . for it to break. And it will. It so will!'

George looked at Rachael incredulously. Of course he'd been getting into a state. Rachael *bloody* Jones was on the scene!

George only had to look at what Cassie had become since meeting the woman to see how hazardous to health she was. Look what she'd done to Susie a decade ago. Susie had known. Her advice had been plain as day. 'Don't talk to Rachael about this. She'll do your head in and, at the end of the conversation, you won't know which way is up. And absolutely never ask her for an explanation. You'll do it once and never make the same mistake again.'

Michael and Porsche? Cycles breaking? Fate? Susie had warned him of Rachael's unnatural preoccupation with the latter. Shaking his head he turned to share his incredulous gaze with Cassie. But she . . . She'd reverted to that haunted look of hers. The one that seemed to indicate crap was going down.

No. The one she wore regularly since starting to hang out with Rachael Jones!

And Rachael was continuing. 'They're the baddies, George. We're the goodies. We *were* baddies but are good guys this time around. They're still bad. Rotten to the core I'd say, and seemingly determined on separating you and Susie just as they did

385

in the past. And they don't seem to need our help this time. Cassie's found out all this stuff on Michael and, just as then, it's all down to money. And then, of course, there's Porsche. She so wants you and, more likely than not, Michael has been feeding her lies because even she can't be that stupid.'

Rachael slid off the end of the sofa and patted Cassie's leg. 'Shuffle up!' When there was no response she forced herself into the small gap between Cassie and the edge of the sofa. 'Cassie, why don't you tell him what you found out about Michael?'

When she was met with silence, Rachael continued, 'Fifteen million pounds worth of debts. Gambling, terrible property investments, and his expensive little drug habit isn't helping. And some of the low-life characters he owes money to . . . even Cassie didn't like digging deeper on them. Although she did in the hope it would reveal something that would get him locked up, but so far zilch. But it's safe to say he has never needed his cut of your earnings more. We reckon he's worried you'll do fewer films now because of Susie, whereas of course, were you with Porsche he'd no doubt be looking to become her manager too and end up doubling his income rather than seeing it shrink. It's hardly like you'd want to take time out to spend with the witch. In fact you'd probably want to work *more*. In films she *wasn't* in! On the other side of the world! For months and months on end! It's a no-brainer decision for him really

386

when he needs the money. Susie – Porsche, Susie – Porsche . . .'

George held up his hand and shook his head. Enough was enough. His brain was already struggling with the challenges of the day. The last thing it needed was to listen to another word uttered from the mouth of Rachael Jones.

He'd wondered about Michael's financial situation. He knew about the drugs but . . . but . . . *'Goodies and baddies? Michael and Porsche?* What do *Michael and Por. . .'* George's words trailed off on a frown . . . He was experiencing a nagging . . .

'George?'

Cassie was clearly speaking again. He held his hand up. He needed some time here. He needed to try and make sense out of what his brain was trying to tell him.

Porsche and Michael seemed . . .

'This is *so* impressive!' he heard Rachael cry, and he felt Cassie's hand on his knee.

He closed his eyes and took a very large gulp. 'Have you anything stronger than coffee?' he managed to finally ask.

'You recognise them too!' Rachael exclaimed, heading into the kitchen area. 'The memories must be coming at you like juggernauts. I didn't expect you to . . .'

But George was engulfed. Memories consumed him. He saw Freddie make mincemeat of Matthew Argylle's evil, smug face after he suggested he make Hannah his mistress. He then saw himself give Michael two black eyes for suggesting he get Susie out of his system and what he should do to do so. The memories were interspersed, playing over and over.

Rachael's ongoing words sounded far away and he only half heard them. 'I've never met them, but Cassie identified Michael as Matthew Argylle and our dear darling Porsche as Prudence.'

George clenched his eyes painfully tight. Freddie was hearing Prudence Argylle's vicious lies and innuendo in a crowded ballroom. Then George was listening to Porsche's venomous voice utter her fabrications on the show last night. It flickered and was back with Freddie.

Prudence had lured him into a room and . . .

Not this one again! This was the one that wouldn't stop playing and . . . Hannah saw them together. She thought the kiss Prudence engineered was real.

And then Hannah was fleeing.

It was dark. Freddie couldn't find her. George's fists clenched tightly into his hair. He didn't want to see any more. He knew where it was going.

He willed it to stop but . . . *Oh God* . . . He was pulling Hannah's body from the lake. She lay lifeless in his arms. He reverently moved her hair from her face and wiped her cheek of mud. He covered her face in kisses, all the time desperately begging her to wake up and rocking himself backwards and forwards, backwards and forwards.

'Oh my angel, my dearest, darling angel.'

Backwards and forwards. 'Why did you lose faith in me, my love? I was true to you. How could I ever not be?'

This time though, rather than the scene petering out, it morphed into one of his own memories.

It was the consulting room. Susie was in his arms, drenched, muddy and . . . looking half-drowned. 'Why did you lose faith in me, my love? I was—'

'Enough!' George cried, leaping from his seat. He started pacing furiously around the room, tugging afresh at his hair. This was going to send him over the edge. He had to find a way to stop the horrific flashbacks – they weren't even his! Yet some of them *were*. And that was terrifying him because there were similarities. And he didn't want there to be any similarities between the past and the present, between Freddie and Hannah and him and Susie. Freddie had lost Hannah.

A glass appeared before his face. He focused enough to take in Rachael holding it out to him. He took it and swallowed its contents in one. And gagged. *Baileys?* A whole glass of *Baileys?* He shuddered and shoved the empty glass back into the waiting hand and wiped away the moustache from his upper lip with the back of his hand.

But it had snapped him to some kind of sense.

'I've just realised,' he growled, pointing an accusing finger at Rachael. 'This is all down to you! You screwed Susie up a decade ago and have left her struggling with the aftermath, you've

389

messed with my sister and now you're torturing me. And yet it's me you chose to call psychotic. *You* are the dangerou—'

'I may have mentioned "*repressed* psychotic tendencies". I never called you psychotic though! It was mean, granted, but I was working to get you two together. It was either that or explaining about Freddie and Hannah and you weren't ready to—'

'Guys this really isn't the time,' Cassie said, wearily. 'We've got to find a way to stop Porsche and Michael and perhaps if we work together, we've some kind of chance of—'

George spun around to face his sister. 'You know, I've had enough. You're both as bad as each other. What has happened to you? So Porsche and Michael were the *big bad* Argylles in the past. I get that, okay. But so what? *Get over* it. It was the past! It has *nothing* to do with who they are today, just as with you and Kathryn!

'I don't want to know anything more about the past. Susie and I will sort things from now on in. We'll reassure each other. On a desert island' – *minus the water* – 'as far away from the two of you as possible.' *Make it Australia.*

He shook his head and let out an exasperated sigh. 'You need to look at yourself long and hard though, Cassie, you really do. Look what's happening to you. And have a go at *listening* to yourself. You aren't sounding remotely . . . For God's sake, the past is the past, but you've managed to get yourself to a point where you're confusing it with the present. I know this does your head in. I *know*! But . . . Look, when I'm a little calmer, on a day other than today, I'll help you, okay? Help you sort things out in your head. But . . . I'm sorry . . . Tonight I've had more than enough of . . . Tonight I need . . . I'm . . . God you've done it. The two of you have managed to completely do my head in!'

George turned and headed towards the bedroom, shaking his head and muttering as he went.

'You have to listen to me about Porsche and Michael. You must—'

He pointedly shook his head and continued walking.

'History is repeating itself, George. That and the letters is how we knew about the horse. I'm so sorry.'

CHAPTER 27

'George, *please*! There is nothing you can say that will make me change my mind. I'm coming to Leicestershire with you. Full stop. And look, there's the "Welcome to Leicestershire" sign.'

Susie pointed out of the passenger window of George's car at the road sign they were now zooming past. 'Thank you, I'm very pleased to be here.'

She turned back to George to say, 'You are going to have to get used to it, you know.'

It was the Easter holidays, no school, time she could spend with George. He'd tightened his grip around the steering wheel and taken his eyes off the road to look at her and there was that dreadful look in them again. The one she knew he tried so hard to keep under wraps, but which nevertheless kept making an appearance. She was never going to forgive Rachael for this.

'I'll be filming the lake scene, Susie. The *lake* scene. Do you have *any* idea what that is doing to me?'

'George,' she said more gently. 'How many times have we covered this? I'm not going to drown in the lake, or anywhere else, no matter what my ex-best friend might say. And anyway, even if I wanted to go paddling – *not that I do*,' she added hastily on seeing George's alarmed glance, 'just how am I supposed to get anywhere *near* the lake? You've got Tom, Dick and Harry on full red-alert mode. How I ever thought they couldn't get any worse!

'But you need to know, and I'm sorry to be harsh here, but I've just about had enough of this now! We've discussed this over and over and I think you're reassured and then you reveal a stereo-typical, Hollywood-bimbo-actor-like tendency that is not remotely . . .'

Susie paused as George turned narrowed eyes to her. 'Don't let me stop you,' he insisted, through gritted teeth. 'Pray continue.'

'History *repeating* itself?'

'I don't believe history is—'

'That's what you keep saying. Lulling me into thinking you are neither certifiable nor halfwit . . .' She chose not to complete that sentence because of the extreme flexing and un-flexing of George's hands around the steering wheel. 'But then you seem to lose all sense of rhyme or reason and go on and on about not wanting me around water, not wanting me anywhere near Michael and Porsche, how you should have pulled out of the film and—'

'I should have pulled out of the film! I should have sacked Michael and we should be in Peru!'

'See? *See* what I'm saying! And I wondered when you'd mention Peru. I saw you googling for the driest places on earth last night! You have to snap out of this. I don't know what else I'm supposed to say or do to reassure you. It is coincidence! Coincidence! History does *not* repeat itself, love. You *know* it doesn't. In your lucid moments, you *know*. . . And if that simple fact isn't enough, Rach is involved. Rach!'

Rachael was going to regret ever having been born when Susie finally caught up with her. No wonder she'd been in hiding. How dare she do this to George! It was eating away at him and . . . his nightmares. His nightmares were terrible. And Susie had no idea what she could possibly say, or do, to stop him worrying like this.

Susie gentled her tone again. 'I've humoured you on the Soul Mates.' Their eyes met. 'I want to believe in it too, love, I really do . . .' She couldn't allow herself to be distracted from the task in hand here. 'But history *repeating* itself? It is *the* most ridiculous thing to have ever come from her mouth. It even beats Matey! And to think she's sucked your sister into this, too.'

'I don't think history is repeating itself,' George declared. 'It's a ludicrous idea. I can't – *won't* – give any credence to it. And you don't need to warn me about Rachael *bloody* Jones, or my sister, come to that. I get it, okay? It's coincidence. I know it is. Definitely know it is. Totally know it is. But it doesn't mean, I'm going to tempt fate and—'

'Oh my God! You mentioned Fate! That's one of Rachael's too!'

'Susie! You know what I'm trying to say here. While I won't – *don't* – believe it, it doesn't mean I want to see you near water, near Porsche, or near Michael.'

His look silenced her intended interruption. 'That has nothing to do with who they were in the past or history repeating itself, and *everything* to do with what they're up to now. The facts remain: you can't swim and they *are* evidently trying to split us up!'

'But they can't! Don't you see? We're onto Michael, and we all agreed keeping him on is the best way to watch him. Keeping your enemies close and all that. We've always been onto Porsche, and there is nothing, absolutely nothing she can do, or say, now that will make me believe her delusional lies. So exactly what are they supposed to be able to do to split us up? Why should we hide? Why—'

'The horse, Susie! You think it's safe to be—'

'We've talked about this,' Susie said gently, reaching over to lay her hand over his tightly clenched, now white one. 'Oh, George, Michael was not involved and—'

'We don't know that though, do we?' George ground out, removing his right hand from the steering wheel to scrub across his face. 'He would have had access to the props . . . to the gun!'

'All right, all right, let's look at it this way then.

Even *if* history were repeating itself, they *still* can't touch us! Things ended up how they did last time because there wasn't trust. Don't you see that? Hannah, no matter her love for Freddie, ultimately didn't trust him. He didn't betray her, with your input I can see that, but *she* betrayed *him*. If she had only believed in him things wouldn't have ended how they did. She wouldn't have been running around that lake at night, not caring whether she lived or died . . . And Freddie wouldn't have—'

Susie broke off the sentence, unable to continue. Hannah hadn't just betrayed Freddie. She'd killed him. He'd ended his life rather than continuing without her. According to George, Cassie even had the letter Freddie wrote before he threw himself into that same lake that had claimed Hannah. The letter had remained hidden in their hole in the tree for decades. It was so tragic. She and George had shared so many tears over their 'memories', but neither of them was prepared to re-read the words. And the tragedy had all been Hannah's doing, all because she hadn't trusted him.

'Susie?' George said gently. 'You can't blame Hannah. Everyone and their dog seemed to be working against them, manipulating and feeding them lies. And seeing Freddie and Prudence together was damning. Freddie shouldn't have been stupid enough to get himself into such a situation. Believe me, he blamed himself for that. And she was so young.'

Susie met George's eyes. 'You know I trust you, don't you? One hundred per cent.' He held her intense look, before darting his eyes back to the road, and rapidly correcting his steering.

'I did before, too, if I'm honest with myself,' Susie continued. 'My heart did. But since you filled me in on things, since I now know Freddie didn't do the dirty . . . well, I don't fear betrayal at all!' Susie suddenly realised what she'd admitted and decided a caveat was needed. 'Having said that, if you *ever*—'

George managed a laugh – oh this was better – and stretched across to give her a kiss on the cheek. 'You've nothing to fear there. And I trust you, too.'

'As long as we trust each other we *are* invincible, George. Do you see? We don't need to run. We don't need to hide. We can sing from the rooftops. As long as we trust in *us*, then there is no chance *at all* history can repeat itself. In fact, Michael and Porsche can screw themselves! And it's liberating. I want you to be feeling it, too. It's an incredible sensation. We will *not* lose each other. I've been haunted by loss and betrayal and insane eye obsessions for ten years, but now, for the first time, I can—'

'Insane eye obsessions? Whose eyes were you obsessed with?' George growled.

Susie stared at him. He was jealous! It made her feel all gooey inside. How could he think she could possibly have been interested in someone else's eyes? They hadn't met, she supposed, but she realised now, once she'd seen . . .

'*Whose* eyes?'

She grinned. She couldn't help it and it got broader as the furrow in George's forehead deepened.

'You've got beautiful eyes, George,' she ventured.

'Susie!'

'Oh yours, for heaven's sake! Your eyes do something to me and have done for a decade.'

'But I haven't known you for a decade.'

'Hence the "insane" bit,' she murmured.

'Susie?' George prompted when she didn't continue. 'Susie!'

'All right! Ever since I saw you in *Dalek Zombies*, I've—'

'*Dalek Zombies?*' he groaned.

'Rach had just done her freaky regression thing . . .'

He looked at her too intently for someone who was supposed to be driving. 'And . . .?'

'The road – please! And . . . I thought your eyes were . . . beautiful.'

'In *Dalek Zombies*? Weren't they bloodshot or something?'

'They were beautiful. You're going to think I'm nuts, but—'

'Sweetheart, I'll never think you're nuts. You are the sanest and wisest person I know.'

Under the circumstances she was glad he thought so. She beamed at him.

Grinning lopsidedly, he continued, 'Not hard, of course, when you see what I'm surrounded with. Cassie, Michael, Porsche, Rachael blo—' He broke off on a chuckle as Susie thumped him on the shoulder.

'Owww! I was serious though. How the hell you managed to keep your sanity living with that woman, I've no idea. Anyway, how nuts can it be with what's been going on lately?'

A most valid point. 'I thought they were beautiful, but also . . .' She sat back in her seat and shut her eyes. She'd never ever told anyone this and admitting it to *George*, even with the Freddie and Hannah thing, it still sounded crazed.

'Susie?' he prompted, gently.

She clenched her eyes more tightly shut. She had no choice here. 'I thought I was going mad because whenever I saw your eyes it was as if . . . as if they were trying to tell me something. Every time I saw you on the screen, or in a magazine, or *even on the side of a bus*, I got this feeling that . . . Well, like I said, I thought I was going mad.'

There was silence. A long silence. Too long a silence. Susie winced. There had been a very good reason for not telling him this. She braved turning her head to open her eyes a crack.

George had his seat belt off, was turned in his seat and was staring at her. Confused, she opened her eyes fully, shot a look out of the windscreen and saw that they had arrived at the hotel. She hadn't even realised they'd left the motorway, let alone stopped.

'I told you it was insane,' she groaned. 'Even now, knowing what we do.'

He slowly shook his head, not removing his eyes from hers. 'You're telling me you had a reaction to me for ten years – *ten years!* – and you did *nothing* about it?'

'I should have got help, I know. I told you it was mad, but I promise I'm not—'

'Susie!' he cried, reaching out to cradle her face in his hands. 'I'm not talking about getting help. I'm talking about getting *in touch* with me! How could you have let ten years go by? Ten years in which we could have been together.'

Susie shook her head now. 'It wasn't like that. How could I possibly know we'd hit it off, that we had . . . *history*! I just thought it was about losing my mind.'

'No,' he rumbled, shaking his head forcefully. He moved his face closer while one of his hands unclipped her seat belt. 'It was about you being *mine*.' His lips were against hers. '*Always* mine.'

Oh she was.

Hand in hand they walked past the fountain and across the crunching gravel towards the hotel reception. George swallowed hard as Susie slowed. He attempted to keep her moving, but she was resisting his tugs on her hand, and was now giving the fountain her full attention.

And *perfect*! *Bloody perfect!* She had turned, keenly taking in the wider grounds and . . . He started to rub his forehead. He hadn't spotted the pond off the main driveway . . . but Susie evidently had.

She snatched her hand from his and faced him. 'George?' she asked, in an overly calm voice, not at all an appropriate accompaniment to the hurricane storminess of her eyes. 'Why are the water features boarded up?'

And what the hell could he say? He decided to say it how it was. 'It's sensible. It's better to be safe than sorry. I challenge *anyone* in my position not to do the same! And I'd do it all over again!'

She stared at him long and hard, before she slowly shook her head. She then spun herself around and started marching furiously towards the hotel.

His actions *were* sensible! History repeating itself? It was coincidence. He had to tell himself that if he had any hope of keeping his sanity here. But what if it wasn't? What if . . .? And then there was that little matter of what felt ominously like a sixth sense. He knew history didn't repeat itself. He *knew* that. Yet past lives existed so . . . he could *not* take the risk. *Would* not take the risk. Not where Susie was concerned.

Rachael *bloody* Jones's most recent words replayed over in his head. 'Do what you must with the lake,' she said. 'Just know, if history is repeating itself and she's fated to drown, there's nothing you can do about it. And really it could as easily happen in *a bath* than in a lake. There will be no cheating it.'

George sprinted into the hotel.

Oh my angel, my dearest, darling angel
I am coming for you, my love. With or without breath, I will allow NOTHING to part us. Know I was true to you, how could I ever not be?
Be ready for me.

Yours forever, Freddie

CHAPTER 28

'Remind me why you're here?' Susie asked, moving her eyes from the lake in front of her to look from first one, and then to glower at the other.

'He's my brother. And until this has stopped . . .' Cassie's words died away.

'*Lake* scene?' Rachael declared, as if she couldn't believe the stupidity of the question.

'How did you get in here?' Susie narrowed her eyes on Rachael. 'Surely security knew better. I'm assuming you got my voicemails? Only you would be stupid enough to appear before someone who wants to—'

'George sorted it,' Rachael interrupted, pointing to her security pass. 'I told him I wanted to patch things up with you and, after I solemnly vowed not to talk to you about "*history repeating itself*", he rolled over. He thinks you still love me and miss me and wants to see you happy. So I'm *officially* here. And I do miss you, Suse.'

Susie took a deep controlling breath but knew her eyes were glinting. She missed her, too. But this wasn't just about Rachael lying to her for a decade, which she had by not telling her about Tessa, or even about her not revealing what happened in her consulting room. It was about what she'd managed to do to George.

He wasn't even sleeping. And when he did, he'd wake screaming, heart pounding uncontrollably, drenched in sweat, and it would take hours for Susie to calm him down, reassure him she was there. To attempt to convince him, all over again, history did not repeat itself. George asserted he didn't believe it, but his subconscious and his actions spoke far louder than his words. And nothing Susie could say or do seemed capable of relieving him of his fears.

Rachael continued, 'I couldn't, of course, tell him I refused to miss him emerging from the water all wet, clothes clinging . . . Never thought I'd say it, but eat your heart out Colin Firth.'

Susie's eyes narrowed to slits and she found herself needing to consciously take very deep breaths.

'Although,' Rachael said innocently, 'I must ask. Why are we so far away from the lake?'

Susie shut her eyes. Breathe in. Breathe out. In. Out.

Rachael knew damned well why they were so far from the lake. And it was all her fault! Just like the bath! All that was presently off in her and George's lives was down to Rachael. Or at least that's how it felt.

Not that technically only being able to have baths

with George was unpleasant. She concentrated on stopping the tingling hot flush she could feel spreading. But she liked having baths on her own! It was her right!

And after all the issues Rachael had caused, she dared to stand before her talking of watching George come out of the water all wet and . . . *Her* George.

'Looks like Slutty-Blythe is going to have a far better view than you. And I bet his clothes cling in all the right places. Not that you'll see that right back here. Unlike her.'

'Rachael,' Cassie growled.

'Trust me,' Rachael murmured. 'I know what I'm doing.'

Susie snapped her eyes open and scanned for the bitch.

Yes. There she was. No more than ten metres away from the way-too-small-from-this-distance George and in prime viewing position.

'I never thought you'd be someone to do what a man told you. Or to let that witch catch an eye full.'

'What are you doing?' Cassie hissed. 'You know *exactly* why she's back here and there can be no better reason! How can you possibly—?'

Susie stopped listening.

As if Porsche had sensed Susie's eyes on her, she had turned, held her look – if the raised hairs on the back of her neck were anything to go by – and was in the process of . . . smirking! Oh,

Susie was sure it was a smirk, even from this distance. How dare she? How bloody dare she?

Rachael and Cassie had evidently stopped arguing to observe the interaction. 'Look away,' Cassie instructed quietly.

'I have no intention of cowering from her,' Susie replied, giving the impression of calm. 'He's mine. And there's nothing she can do about it.'

'Unfortunately, she doesn't seem to have grasped that. There's no point in winding her up. You need to stay away from her. And . . . you should know my brother is watching.'

Susie immediately looked away to focus on George. Oh my love. He was looking straight at her. She knew that for sure because she felt their eyes connect and then there was that injection of neat need she simultaneously received. But she could tell from his body language he was stressed. Even more stressed than his normal stressed-out status at present.

He'd obviously just witnessed things. Like Cassie, and indeed Rachael on earlier occasions, he insisted Porsche and Michael should be avoided like the plague and was not remotely approving of Susie's less passive inclinations.

Susie smiled ruefully and placed her right hand over her heart. George did the same, before he bowed to her, all the time keeping his head up, their eyes locked.

She should still be angry with him – the bath, the desecration of water features, Tom, Dick and

406

Harry in Duracell mode – but it was impossible. She knew why he was doing what he was. Damn Rachael!

'How attractive can a human male get?' Rachael muttered. 'There is something seriously wrong here. You end up with that and, in the very best case scenario, I end up with Puss in Boots!'

Perhaps there was some justice in the world, Susie thought . . . before she saw red.

Porsche had moved over to George. She was clearly attempting to talk to him, having to nearly jog to keep up with his long strides. But she'd cornered him at the water's edge and he'd had to stop to listen to her.

And she had her hands on his arms!

'Are you going to let her get away with that?' Rachael exclaimed.

'Oh God,' Cassie murmured.

Rachael continued, 'She's no doubt coming on to him in a way only one of the most beautiful women in the world can. I wonder . . . does being a Soul Mate male automatically qualify one for sainthood status or does temptation still come into play?'

The last thing Susie heard as she marched determinedly in George's direction was Rachael saying, 'I guess we're going to find out. Don't look at me like that, Cassie. She's safe. And she's going to be even safer after this. It's a means to an end. She might hate me right now, but believe me I'm acting out of love. There's a little bonus thrown in, too. I get to learn a bit more about Soul Mates. There are evident gaps in my knowledge and I can't help but worry just how big they might be.'

Susie had had more than enough of Porsche Sutter-Blythe to last her a lifetime. Make that two! Prudence Argylle had forced her attentions on Freddie and now Porsche was daring to do the same with George. George's lawyers were clearly not hands on enough. And whereas George might not feel able to deal with the woman as she deserved, Susie damned well could. In the absence of forks – fists and nails would do.

'Ooommph.'

Susie felt like she'd rushed into a brick wall and found herself temporarily winded. In fact a brick wall would have been less hard.

She kept her glower fixed on Dick standing before her with legs apart, arms crossed over his chest, as she was hoisted backwards, Tom on one arm, Harry the other. How could she have forgotten them?

Susie found herself deposited at her starting position. And she was seething. She wasn't sure who to rant at first. Yes she was. Rachael.

She hurled herself around, hands on hips, only to find the object of her livid focus, otherwise distracted.

Rachael was looking towards the lake. 'Oh. My. Giddy . . . Aunt!'

Susie spun around to face the lake.

And she just knew her mouth was hanging open but . . . *And he was hers?* How was that possible?

But he shouldn't be out in public like this. Definitely not. If she could drag her eyes away from him, past Rachael – she gritted her teeth – she knew for sure, every single female member of the crew, and more than a few men, would be goggle-eyed and equally open-mouthed. And that included the bitch! Her fists clenched tightly at the thought.

And why was he wet? Soaked in fact. And he *hated* water! Oh George! Why was his previously billowy Darcy shirt, several top buttons undone, now sticking to every part of his torso? And his breeches or whatever they were called . . . She gulped and forced her eyes to return to his face.

She imagined a water droplet falling from the floppy dark locks over his forehead, trailing down his nose to its tip and . . . the closer he was getting, the less she required imagination. And then there were the drips travelling down that indented central line of his chest. Warming against his skin on their downward journey. Getting hotter and hotter . . . as they went down, down . . . down.

Oh God. And she thought she'd had an injection of neat need earlier.

'How good am I?' Rachael murmured. 'Susie has demonstrated it's not just the male in the Soul Mate species that reacts to protect their mate. George, by entering the water he so hates in order to escape Slutty-Blythe, has given serious clout to his Saint George labelling. His dash out of the water, and march in our direction, furthermore provides a most delectable demonstration of his need to keep his mate safe. And indeed, by provoking Susie into breaching the Tom, Dick and Harry perimeter patrol, I've undoubtedly ensured the recruitment of an additional battalion of re-inforcements to protect her. Hopefully, within a setting that features no lake because her being here is insane! That was the goal of this little exer-cise. But, holy moly. Just look at that!'

It was taking Susie far too long to absorb Rachael's words. Her brain and body being somewhat distracted by the approaching George and— *Shit!* He didn't look happy. She was meant to be doing everything in her power to reassure George, to not add to his worries, no matter how unfounded she considered they were. And now look what she'd done.

Rachael's words finally hit home. And Susie's fury was such that she managed to snatch her eyes away from George, and fling herself around.

'You cow! You total utter cow! You deliberately provoked me! I will *never* forgive you if he recruits any more bodyguards. You *know* how I feel about them. How could you. *Stop* looking at him! Look at *me*! I want you to be looking at *me* when I—'

And he was there. Oh God he was there. She didn't need to track Rachael's following eyes to know he was right behind her. Her body was reacting to his proximity, the steamy warmth, his scent. He couldn't possibly be any closer without touching her.

'A word. Now.' It sounded way too calm, way too quiet. But the accompanying fanning of his breath over the skin of her ear . . . She shivered all over.

'I'm . . .' She took a deep, albeit tremulous breath and attempted casual. 'I'll just finish Rachael off if you don't mind. Then I'll be right with you.'

'Now!' George growled into her ear. She found her arm hooked into his and they were walking. Fast.

'Don't think I've finished with you Rachael!'

'He *does* smoulder. Rob was so right . . . although I *really* shouldn't be thinking of Rob right now. Do you think . . . Matey is missing me?'

'Out.' George somehow managed to get past his lips as he addressed the occupants of the large tent he steered Susie into. It was the underlying tone of his so quiet voice that ensured every last one of them scarpered.

He released her arm and stood staring at her, forcing himself to take control of his breathing, while the last straggling evictees scuttled away.

She met his eyes head-on, not flinching from what she saw there, and he felt himself slowly calming, his breathing becoming slower and less ragged. Although his heart rate didn't seem to be slowing down much.

She broke the silence but not the eye contact. 'I'm sorry.'

George swallowed, talk presently beyond him. They stayed like that for several moments before he managed to get another word out. 'Why?'

Not why she was sorry, but why she had nearly killed him by marching towards the water like that. All he had been able to imagine was holding Susie in his arms, lifeless . . . as Freddie had held Hannah.

'I'm sorry. I couldn't stand seeing her all over you and—'

'You think that makes me feel *better*?' He rubbed his hands furiously through his wet hair. 'Have you any idea what you just did to me? You can't have because you wouldn't have done it if you had. You're meant to be staying away from her. But instead . . . instead . . . instead you . . .' He broke off to take more calming breaths.

'I'm so sorry,' she said.

He just stared at her. How could anyone survive feeling this deeply for another person? It was pure agony because what if you lost them? How the hell were you supposed to be able to cope with the fear of that?

'You promised me you'd honour the perimeter. You promised me you'd steer clear of Porsche and Michael. You—'

'I think you'll find I didn't promise to steer clear of that bitch. I distinctly recall changing the subject and—'

'Susie!' He was shaking his head. 'It's no good. You're going home. I can't have you around a lake like this. Around Michael and Por—'

412

'You can't do that!'

'What the hell else do you expect me to do? It's an impossible situation and—'

'You'd send me away? You'd want not to be with me? You'd want to—'

'Of course it's not what I want! I want *you*. Every second of every day. Even now. When I'm so furious with you I might just kill you myself. But I can't take this.'

I seriously can't take this. I need you locked away somewhere, with trusted armed guards. Somewhere where I know *you can't come to any harm! Because God help me if something happens to you.*

'I won't leave. Whatever you say. Just so you know that.'

He'd known she'd say that. He looked at her pleadingly. 'What if I need you to?'

'It's not going to happen. That's not what you need anyway.' She took a small step forward, closing the gap between them.

George gulped. 'Fine. I'm pulling out of the film then. I should have done it before. I never wanted this film anyway and with everything—'

'You're not pulling out, George. We've talked about that. We are not running.' She shook her head and put her hand on his wet shirt, palm resting over his heart. 'You're trembling,' she exclaimed, immediately looking concerned. 'God, you're freezing. Oh George. What are they doing making you do a water scene in March?'

Was he? Probably. Whether he was cold or not

hadn't crossed his mind. And currently, her hand on his chest was sending sizzling hot sensations right to his groin. Not that his groin needed any extra stimulation. Susie was before him, his senses full of her. And then there was that primitive stuff his whole being was crying out for. He took her hands, the one over his heart and the one currently running so distractingly up and down his side, and held them away from his body.

'Towels. You need towels and . . .'

He shook his head. 'We need to sort out what I'm going to do with you because—'

'Can we just look at what happened rationally for a moment? I walked forward a few feet and—'

'More than a few damned feet! What the hell Tom, Dick—'

'Okay. I walked forward a little way. But that was it. I encountered the wall with the nasty boils on top, but that was it. That's all that happened, love. I was nowhere near the water. I was nowhere near Porsche. There was zero danger.'

He could feel himself frowning as he tried to go back over events, but all he could recall was that rush of terror. Susie heading towards the lake. Susie about to drown. Intermingled with those horrific flashbacks. But when she said it like that, it didn't sound . . . In fact . . .

Bloody hell! He was like this . . . because she'd taken some steps *forwards*?

'Don't you think this is all getting a little out of hand?' She retrieved a hand from his to gently

414

stroke his face. She moved her thumb to follow one of the darkened areas under his eyes which make-up had yet to tackle. 'You're worrying so much. You're not sleeping and that can hardly be helping. But together we are invincible, George. We are. I *promise* not to do anything like that again. Let's get through this together, yeah?'

She always succeeded in calming him down. Reassuring him. Making him believe for *a moment* there was nothing to worry about. But his fears invariably resurrected themselves.

He angled his face to kiss the palm of her hand. At this precise moment he needed to absorb himself in her . . . *sink* himself into her.

'And do you honestly think I'm going to leave you alone up here with the rampant Porsche? You worry about me around her, but it's *you* she wants and is hell-bent on getting. If anyone's in danger here, it's you. There's definitely no sex scene with her is there? You won't be . . .'

George couldn't help the incredulous chuckle. He rested his forehead on hers. 'How good an actor do you think I am? And don't be so sure the kiss will happen either.'

'You might not have to kiss her?'

He looked into those stunning eyes of hers. 'My favourite option is changing the ending.' He watched her eyes widen. 'I'm lobbying Francis and he hasn't ruled it out.'

'You can't change the ending of *Pride and Prejudice*!'

'I've a new take on it.' He moved his lips to brush against her neck. God she smelt glorious. 'It wouldn't take much re-editing to turn it into a Gothic – or Regency – Horror, even.'

'A . . .?'

He grinned against her skin. 'Think about it. All that simmering pent up stuff going on with Darcy. It could be more to do with his need to kill, than to rut. I'm looking to have Darcy throttling Elizabeth in the final scene.'

He moved his head back to take in her mirth. She took his face in her hands. 'I love you so very much George Silbury,' she said with a giggle, before breaking off with a frown. 'You're still so cold!'

'Then warm me up, sweetheart. Warm me up.'

CHAPTER 29

'*Flaming* . . . Oh *Flaming* . . .' A gulp replaced the rest of Rachael's words as she entered the former ballroom of George and Susie's eighteenth-century country-house hotel, now home to a highly contemporary party, evidently in full swing. She'd not a hope of missing the gargantuan 'Congratulations George and Susie' backdrop, resplendent with love hearts. It was a far cry from that crooked strung-up banner you'd get down the local, but provided much the same effect – if you multiplied it by a thousand.

No provocation they'd agreed. *No* provoking Michael and Porsche. *No* making them feel compelled into action! George had even told Michael to scrap his release on the engagement. That things between him and Susie were moving too fast. And that he was to fill George's forward schedule up because *work* was his priority!

A loaded food tray hovered before Rachael's face. She scooped up a handful of . . . mini cupcakes? She rotated them in her hands suspiciously before shaking her head incredulously. They were iced with 'George 4 Susie' and 'Susie

4 George' – Hollywood – or was it footballer-wife – style?

'Whose deranged idea was this?' she spluttered.

Cassie, at her side, was silent, completely and utterly silent as she took in the extent of the celebration taking place. There were hundreds of revellers and evidently not just film crew, but also the A to Z of the A list. 'Dear God,' she finally managed. 'It . . . it—' She broke off, looking frantically around the room, seeming to see things afresh. She then stared at Rachael aghast while she struggled to get the next words out between her intermittent gasps for air. 'We're in a ballroom! A ballroom! *That* night . . . That *God awful night*! . . . A ball . . . that became a celebration of their engagement!'

'Cassie . . .' Rachael said feebly. 'We are in so much . . .' But she had got distracted. They could *not* be serious? A life-size ice sculpture in the style of Rodin's *The Kiss* depicting the happy couple!

'We can thank the studio,' Cassie choked. 'I couldn't get much sense out of George when he called. And no wonder! They'd just sprung this on them – an impromptu surprise party – and he was beside himself, trying to remain calm but failing dismally. Apparently Francis the director overhead George telling Graham of the engagement and *this* is the result! George needs us to help get Susie *the hell* out of here!'

'This is *impromptu*?' Rachael said, then in an urgent hiss, 'Michael in deep cahoots with Porsche at three o'clock.' She turned slightly, so Cassie could see for herself.

'God only knows what they're saying. I have such a bad feeling,' Cassie said.

Rachael would second that having taken in the wild look in Porsche's eyes and the way she knocked back a full glass of champagne in one, and immediately started on another.

'It's different,' Rachael murmured. 'We might be in a ballroom celebrating their engagement but it's different! Remind yourself of that. Comfort yourself with that because that's what I'm frantically doing right now.'

'*We're out of time here!*' Cassie said desperately. 'We've got to *do* something! We'll get Susie out of here but . . . but . . .' She held Rachael's eyes and said in an anguished whisper, 'If the only way to stop this playing out is to remove Michael and Porsche from the equation . . . *permanently* remove them . . . then I'll do it. I'll do it Rachael. I'll do *anything* to stop this ending how it did before!'

'*We'll* do it,' Rachael corrected, meeting Cassie's now determined look with one of her own. 'We're out of options. If it comes to it, *we* will do it. But . . .' She shook her head. 'You're forgetting we are out of the equation this time around and it's still playing out. Removing Michael and Porsche is no guarantee. Not if it's Fate. Not if it's destined to repeat no matter the obstacles. Then it will happen whatever we do.'

419

But they *can't* have the same fates! They *can't*! *Please* don't let it be that!

Rachael took a deep fortifying breath and continued, 'Look, the cycle might break tonight. It *has* to break tonight!' She attempted to repress the panic that was sounding in her voice. 'Things are *seriously* different! We're onto them, so there can be no luring away and there's Tom, Dick and Harry, too, thank God. And we're not near the lake and everything in the hotel grounds is boarded up. George saw to that very efficiently. Though I'm amazed he's not had her locked away somewhere . . .' Rachael re-met Cassie's eyes. 'We need to get her locked away, Cassie!'

Cassie nodded. 'Let's get her out of here. And if he won't lock her up, *we* will. Both of them if necessary! And then we'll tackle Michael and Porsche . . .' She swallowed audibly. 'With where we're at right now, it's the only way. And I'm up for it. I really am. I'm up for *anything*!'

'Anything?' Susie asked, emerging to stand next to Cassie, glass of champagne in hand. She shot a look at Rachael that promised revenge at the first opportunity. 'That sounds fun. Can I join you? Because I've finally got my get out of jail card. Tom, Dick and Harry are currently indisposed, stomach bug or something. I should feel guil . . . *pity*, but it's such a liberating sensation, I can't bring myself to feel anything but glee! I am going to make the most of it.'

Susie ignored the look of horror on Cassie and

Rachael's faces. It was too similar to that which George continued to display in his unguarded moments. The three of them were managing to completely freak each other out.

She made a face of her own at George's words sounding in her ear, interrupting both her thoughts and her liberty.

'Reinforcements are already on the way.'

She shook her head self-pityingly, but nevertheless couldn't resist leaning back into the arms that wrapped themselves around her waist and surrendering one of her hands to be held in his.

'It had better be an army. When do they arrive?' a pale-faced Rachael pressed.

Susie glowered at her.

'Not nearly quickly enough,' George murmured before muttering, 'they would appear to be stuck in a twenty mile tailback on a motorway that has just been closed.'

Rachael's face paled further and Susie didn't need to look at George and Cassie to know what theirs would be looking like. Give her strength! 'You are so ex, Rachael, I can't tell you. But at least by morning it won't only be me that sees you for what you really are. You see, I know what you're all thinking – *know* it – but nothing, absolutely *nothing* is going to happen tonight. *Ooooooo. Spoooookkky*. An engagement party in a ballroom. *Oooooo*. Must mean Susie's going to drown in a non-existent lake in the grounds! Tonight you will be exposed, Rachael. And the only other thing I want to say to you is this. If you *ever* again look at—'

'It meant nothing! I was provoking you and you know it. Although I *can* appreciate beauty. And I'm not going to apologise for that, but that's all it was. Even seeing him starkers didn't press those particular buttons although there was definite appr— *Ow!*'

Cassie had pinched her arm. 'Why?' Rachael demanded. 'Just . . . *Why?*'

Rachael had seen George, *starkers*? *Her* George? As in nude, unclothed, in the all together? George had tensed behind her. She turned around in his arms and narrowed her eyes up at him.

Rachael – *Rachael!* – had seen his naked body, and he hadn't thought to *mention* it? She watched his face flitter from one expression to another: grimace; frustration; pasted on smile that would win no academy awards; long-suffering . . . oh *please*; nonchalance – he'd get booed off stage for that one; and . . . ah, we were back to the grimace.

'I was en route to the bathroom the other night and—'

'And you didn't think to *tell* me? Why wouldn't you tell me? Why would I have to hear this from *her*?'

'It wasn't important. I completely forgot about it.'

Susie stepped back out of his arms. 'Wasn't *important*? How would you feel if someone . . . *saaaay* . . . *Rob* saw *me* naked?'

George's face paled and each of his features hardened. That was a red rag to a bull and she knew it. 'That man . . . *that* man . . .' He didn't seem able to form his sentence.

'Not a nice feeling is it, George?'

'You cannot possibly compare Rachael to . . . to . . . I would have told you but, believe it or not, I've been somewhat distracted of late! It was – *is* – so insignificant an occurrence, I—'

'Not quite so insignificant seeing *me* naked was it, darling?'

Everyone froze as Porsche Sutter-Blythe's words, partially slurred, whispered over them. She continued strutting past as she added, 'I recall you being most attentive.'

'Oh boy,' Rachael exhaled.

Susie concentrated on her breathing. It was games. She knew it. But there was something about George's stance that . . . She went over in her head the films in which George and Porsche had co-starred. There had only been two, she was sure of it. And if she was not sorely mistaken, there had *not* been nudity in either. So why . . .?

'It's not as it sounds.'

'You are not seriously telling me, she's been *naked* around you?' Susie hissed. 'Not when it couldn't have been on set. Not when you have assured me you've never ever had a thing going with her. Not when you haven't *told* me!'

'Can we go somewhere to talk about this?'

'No!' She flung off his arm, which had crept

around her waist. 'You'll use your physical arsenal to wheedle your way out of things. That woman – *that* woman – reveals she's been in your company, minus her clothes, and you haven't told me about it? Why? Why would you not tell me? What else am I going to find out here? That you *have* in fact had a thing going with her?'

'Susie! There was nothing deliberate about it. It happened years ago and—'

'You see I can't help but think if she hadn't mentioned this tonight you would never have told me. And it makes me wonder what else you aren't telling me, and *why* you aren't telling me. It doesn't instil trust, George. I tell you everything. Even the eye obsession and you have no idea how hard that was. How many times have we talked of her? How many opportunities have you had to *mention* it? It . . . it . . .' *It bloody hurt. And her damned head had started up again!*

'Sweetheart . . .'

Susie repeatedly batted his hands away.

'Let's go and—'

'No! Ever since we got here you've been trying to herd me out of the room and I'm suspicious of your intentions.'

She watched all three share a look. Oh yeah. She could just imagine what they had up their sleeve. And she wouldn't put rope past them! They'd all lost it. Completely and utterly lost it. She was currently going nowhere with George. How dare he not tell her! How bloody dare he! And why? *Why* hadn't he?

'I want to dance.'

George stood at the bar watching Susie slow dance with Francis, the director. He made himself loosen his hold on the glass in his hand, not completely convinced the glass could take it.

A chuckle sounded at his side and he glanced around. Graham. Returning his eyes to Susie, George took another swig of whisky.

'Let me guess. She's not currently talking to you and is dancing with all the males in the room to demonstrate her displeasure?'

George snapped his head around. *All* the males? He hadn't thought of that. Francis was enough and he was old enough to be her father. He darted his eyes around the room, glaring in turn at anything in trousers before groaning. She wouldn't do that to him, would she?

And *tonight* of all nights.

George fought afresh the rising tide of panic which had been threatening to consume him ever since they'd walked into the room to cries of 'Surprise!' They'd been here for less than an hour, but it felt like eternity.

He continued self-counselling. History did *not* repeat itself. This was all just coincidence. And come on, Porsche wasn't going to ask him to dance in order to lure him away and he wasn't stupid enough to be lured away in any event. He'd never get caught in a honey-trap and Susie would never believe it anyway! Sorted.

But damn the plaguing flashbacks to that crowded ballroom! It felt as if they were trying to tell him otherwise. It was no good. He had to get Susie out of the room. If she didn't come to him willingly in two minutes flat, he'd have to resort to more desperate, physical removal measures. Cassie and Rachael would help him.

Graham chuckled again. 'Jeannie did it to me once. No twice actually. Get used to it, mate. It's a sign of affection I tell myself. Shows they care.'

George's snort must have been audible.

'Why else would they want to make you jealous? It works too, doesn't it?' Laughing now, he continued, 'I saw you try and cut in earlier.'

George hurrumphed at the memory.

'You hitting the club after?'

George shook his head, as he looked at Susie. 'We're going to have an early night.' He'd never been more determined about anything in his life.

'Good luck with that one. I'd say . . .'

Graham's voice fizzled out to be replaced with a whistle of air escaping his mouth. 'I think your worries are over, mate. In ten seconds she'll be off that dance floor and by your side . . . if not in your arms. You might care to thank me for not abandoning you here. Ten, nine, eight . . .'

George turned to Graham who was now wearing an 'I am a saint' look upon his . . . *And Porsche*

426

was at his side! George took in a strangled breath. If she—

'May I have the pleasure of this dance?' Porsche asked.

George stared at her outstretched hand as his heart pounded. He had to get Susie out of here. NOW!

Coincidence, he countered. Coincidence, coincidence, coincidence, he told himself over and over. This wasn't necessarily . . . And . . . *She couldn't possibly think he would say yes?*

Her audacity was staggering. How much clearer could he make things? How many more times was he going to have to say no? How much more blatant could he make his avoidance? And there were even solicitor's letters. Words and actions. He was doing it all. What the hell else was he supposed to do? Other than completely flip out, that is. And that was an option he was having to work seriously hard to repress. She'd be publicly humiliated, which in turn would provoke her and . . .

He watched Porsche rest her hand on Graham's shoulder to keep her balance. She was drunk. A sober Porsche was bad enough. A drunk one he *knew* he couldn't handle. She'd been drunk that night seven years ago when nudity had indeed entered the equation. He'd gone about things wrongly then. He must have done.

'I believe it's the leading lady's right to—'

'Have her head kicked in?' Susie's dulcet tones interrupted from George's side.

In other circumstances George might have been amused. But in the here and now amusement didn't quite go there. He wrapped his arm around Susie's waist and pulled her closer. He held her tightly and he wasn't going to let go. They were out of there.

'If you'll excuse us Porsche, Graham,' George said, taking in the venomous look Porsche fixed on Susie.

He was attempting to steer Susie but she wasn't budging.

George took a very deep tremulous breath. Not only was she not budging, she was meeting Porsche's look with one that . . . She couldn't make it more provoking if she tried! She wasn't meant to be doing this. He knew she gave no credence whatsoever to history repeating itself, considered their faith in each other made them invincible. But no one was invincible and tonight . . . *tonight*! And idiotically, he'd managed to put that faith to the test by not sharing with her his and Porsche's past. God almighty! If she didn't start moving . . .

'George, there you are!' Cassie's cry was overly bright. Her look mirrored his sentiments. George's *outside* demeanour was hopefully award-winning. She positioned herself on Susie's other side.

'Porsche Sutter-Blythe!' Rachael whooped, sweeping in between Susie and Porsche, breaking their eye contact. 'I must have your autograph. I must. I must. I must!' She bounced up and down as she searched through her handbag for something to sign.

'Perhaps later,' Michael's dry voice sounded, immediately snatching George's attention. George's whole body went cold. He observed him place an arm protectively around Porsche's shoulder and whisper in her ear before moving to steer her away.

Michael smiled at him over the top of her head, one that didn't show in his eyes. He mouthed, 'Too much to drink.'

George managed a curt nod, tightening his hold on Susie further. It was instinctive around Michael. *If he'd fired that gun!* And then there was Susie's desire to pursue Porsche. He could sense it.

Only after he had tracked Michael and Porsche leaving the room did George start breathing again.

'Give me one *sensible* reason for my not being able to have it out with her,' Susie ground out.

Sensible? He very much doubted there was one.

'Lawyers,' he finally murmured, but was way past feeling any satisfaction at providing an answer to a near impossible question. He bent to her ear to say, 'After your little performance there, I'm taking things to the next level.'

Turning to steer her towards the room's exit, he caught Cassie's eye. They were all struggling with occurrences here – apart from Susie. He let out a ragged breath. Cassie moved her hands and he guessed she was indicating she'd keep tracks on Porsche and Michael. He nodded. Rachael simply mouthed, 'Get her out of here. And locked up!'

After saying a quick goodbye to Graham, Susie let herself be steered away. 'You are not locking me up anywhere and I am only going home if I want to. And that depends on what you have to say about Porsche naked! Know this. The only reason I'm coming with you now is because I can see how freaked out you are and I can't bear to see it. Not that you remotely deserve my sympathy and understanding here.'

'Thank you,' George said, and it was heartfelt.

CHAPTER 30

As Susie entered their room realisation hit: it *was* all coincidence. Oh thank God! She'd always known it. But now George could finally stop worrying.

If history *had* been repeating itself she and George would not now be in their room. He would have been lured away from the party by Porsche. Yours truly would have been encouraged to stumble upon them by Tessa – *Rachael*! Oh, they had so much unfinished business. And then, of course, she'd have ended up drowning in a lake. The fact they were nowhere near a lake, and the one on the film set miles away, hadn't made a jot of difference to George, Cassie and Rachael in full freak out mode.

George could start sleeping again. That haunted look in his eyes would disappear. He'd tried so hard to disguise it, but . . . History was *not* repeating itself. She could prove it! And yes, that childish part of her actually felt like going *na na nanana* while she performed a victory dance. She'd save that for Rachael.

If it wasn't for the nude Porsche revelation, Susie

would now be in a deliriously happy mood. But by not telling her about the incident in question, George had somehow managed to reawaken that part of her head that had whispered betrayal at her for a decade. And it wasn't proving simple to shut back down again. There would be a reasonable explanation. She *knew* that. But why hadn't he *told* her?

'I should have told you about Porsche,' George said, collapsing on to the bed and putting his head in his hands. 'I swear to you nothing happened and will tell you all about it on the way home. Because we are leaving.'

Okay. Not remotely adequate and . . . they were leaving?

'I'm pulling out of the film. And I won't be dissuaded this time,' he said, shaking his head. 'There's not a hope I can survive that again.'

She wanted to argue, talk some sense into him, but then she remembered the moment she spotted Porsche, hand held out to George as she asked him to dance, and . . . they had *that* scene to do. The script would have them kissing, she just knew it.

And she didn't want George around Porsche at all. It was nothing to do with the latest nudity revelation – it *wasn't!* – but everything to do with the fact Porsche wanted him. And there had been that look in her eyes tonight. She hadn't been all there. Porsche was dangerous all right, but to George, not her.

432

'Okay,' Susie said, lowering herself onto the side of the bed next to him.

George raised his head. 'Okay? You aren't going to argue here?'

'No,' she said, shaking her head.

'What am I missing?'

'Nothing. But I expect one hell of an explanation from you.'

'And you'll get it. I promise.' A hand tenderly brushed back strands of her hair. 'Along with a vow from me that I will never again be such an idiot as to not tell you everything.'

Okay. That was an improvement. And his eyes looked so sincere. 'I'm not going to dissuade you at all. I'm happy we are leaving. But George . . . history isn't repeating itself.'

'Susie . . .'

'No, just hear me out. It *is not* repeating itself. And I can prove it. You've broken the cycle. Porsche asked you to dance. Instead of accepting, albeit reluctantly, as Freddie did Prudence, you never danced with her, never got lured away. Instead, side-by-side we left the room, turning our back on what happened in the past to Freddie and Hannah. And as a result, we are here now, in this room, very much alive, very much together. It's history, George. Literally. You've consigned it to history. You've broken any cycle there may have been. It's over. Freddie and Hannah are history. Me and you are now.'

George was staring at her.

'Think about it.' Her hands were on his shoulders now, gently kneading them. 'Just think about it.'

He closed his eyes and let her continue kneading. She could feel his muscles loosening with each depression of her fingers. Suddenly his arms were around her and she was enfolded in his tight embrace.

George moved back to cradle her face. He seemed to be trying to find the words, but was struggling.

'It's all right.' She laughed. 'I'm right, aren't I? I'm right?'

He started laughing too, and the sound was incredible. 'I always knew it was coincidence,' he said deadpan.

'Yes, yes, you did,' Susie played along.

His forehead lowered to hers and she could feel his heart racing against her chest. And she held him. This was over, it was finally over.

'I'm sorry, sweetheart. I'm so sorry,' George said.

'Hey,' she said, shaking her head. 'Don't apologise. I get it, okay? And you tried. I loved you all the more for at least *trying* to use your head. The results were dismal but . . .'

'I deserved that.'

'Yes you did. But I do get it. You guys were feeding each other's fears. It was like tales around a campfire. I wanted to bang your heads together. The lot of you have been pretty much unbearable. But now we might both manage a full night's sleep!'

He moved his head back slowly and she could feel the atmosphere change. Oh his eyes . . . She would never get used to what they could do to her.

'Is that what you were banking on?' he asked so, so quietly, all the time leaning closer again and, joy of joys, she found her back lowering to the bed as he pressed forward. At each point his body made contact with hers, she was ablaze. God this man was beyond hot. He whispered over her lips, 'I'm going to have to re-educate the future Mrs Silbury on how time is best spent in my bed. And I believe I might just need to reacquaint myself with every–'

A harsh rap on the door had them both cursing.

'Ignore it,' Susie pleaded against his lips.

Grinning and against hers, he breathed, 'I fully intend to.'

But the rapping was now persistent, and Susie could hear Rachael's voice. 'Come on you two, open up!'

George rolled over onto his back. 'She isn't growing in my estimations!' he snarled, before getting up from the bed and moving to the door.

Susie had just raised herself from the bed when Rachael burst into the room, with Cassie in her wake.

'It's broken!' Rachael cried. 'It's broken!' Before Susie knew it she was wrapped in one of Rachael's hugs. And this one was tight. Really tight. 'It's finally broken! You aren't going to die. Not quite yet, anyway. Oh Suse, I love you!'

Susie couldn't help but return the hug. 'I love you, too,' she murmured, realising on a grimace that there wasn't anything Rachael could do that would ever change that. Not that they wouldn't still be having words.

Looking over to George she saw he was in a similar clinch with Cassie, although it seemed she was also emotively beating his chest. He met her gaze with an accompanying eye roll. Susie started giggling, she couldn't help it.

Rachael, finally loosening her grip, stood back, wearing a grin ear to ear. She was also swiping tears from her eyes. 'Porsche left straight away to head back to wherever she is staying and Michael disappeared off in his car a few moments ago. It wasn't repeating! It *couldn't* have been. It was all just down to so many of us being around again. Cassie and her flaming history repeating itself concept, I always said it was similarities.' A choked sound escaped Cassie. '*Anyway!* We need to celebrate life, the universe – the history not repeating one – and everything. You two up for it?' She glanced from Susie to George.

They both started shaking their heads, but George's head movement was interrupted by the sound of his phone.

'I think we'll pass,' Susie said, as George cursed.

'Text message from Francis,' he said in explanation. 'Everyone's hit the club, but he's calling them back. I'm needed on set.'

'It's past eleven o'clock!' Susie pointed out indignantly.

'He does this sometimes. About this stage in a film, too. He gets something in his head and he needs it done instantly. But his timing's not bad.' He shot her a rueful glance. 'The sooner I tell him I'm pulling out, the sooner we can be out of here. And I need to tell him this face-to-face.'

'You're pulling out? What? Of the film?' Cassie asked, evidently shocked.

'Absolutely,' he replied. 'I refuse to be around Porsche and Michael a moment longer.'

'I'll come with you,' Susie said.

George shook his head. 'Nope. This one I need to do alone. You celebrate with these two.' He grinned at the face she pulled. 'Or you could make a start on the packing?' His grin broadened further at the look now upon her face. But his humour abruptly turned to a frown. 'Although actually . . .'

'George?' she prompted as his frown deepened and his words died away. She moved to him and he wrapped his arms around her distractedly.

'With Tom, Dick and Harry out of action, perhaps it's best if you stay in the room. At least until the reinforcements arrive? In fact you could all celebrate up here . . . use room service to order whatever you want?'

'We can order *anything* on room service?' Rachael clarified.

'Anything,' he confirmed.

'Well, let's party then girls!' she cried.

'George?' Susie prompted, for his ears only.

'Sorry,' he said. 'I'm probably being overly cautious but stay with these two, yeah?'

Susie slowly nodded, knowing she was frowning herself now. 'Be careful, please.'

George raised his eyebrows.

'Porsche will be there.' And she didn't like that idea. Not one little bit.

He grinned and shook his head. 'As soon as I've spoken to Francis, I'll be back.'

With a last kiss on her forehead he headed for the door.

CHAPTER 31

'I reckon there'd be more atmosphere in the bar,' Rachael observed, after draining her latest glass of room service champagne. 'And peanuts. I forgot to order them. *And* music. In fact, I spied a jukebox down there earlier. This is meant to be a celebration.'

'George suggested we stay in the room,' Cassie reminded.

'She'll be with us and anyway there's plenty of security around downstairs should the press make an appearance. What do you think, Suse?'

'I'm in,' she said, with no hesitation at all, getting up from the bed and heading to the door. There wasn't enough up here to distract her from her worries about George. She was finding them particularly hard to shrug off right now. 'I wonder how much longer he'll be?' she voiced, as the three of them swept through the lobby and reception area towards the adjacent bar.

'Why are you so worried about—?'

'Hey!' a shout sounded behind them, cutting off Cassie's words. Susie spun around in surprise.

'So George didn't get the early night he was hankering after, then?'

'Graham?' Susie couldn't help the frown.

He grinned, shrugging his hands into his jeans pockets as he sauntered over. 'Plenty would take that look personally.'

Susie shook her head and forced a smile. 'Sorry. Just didn't expect to see you.'

'I thought I'd give the club a miss. Not much fun when tee-totalling it.'

She shook her head again. 'Weren't you needed?'

'Is this insult Graham night?'

She shook her head more forcefully and grinned. 'No, I just thought you'd be needed on set.'

He looked at her blankly.

'The text message. Francis calling you all back,' she prompted, determined to ignore that plummeting sensation in her gut.

Graham shook his head. 'Know nothing about it. And he'd have a riot on his hands if he pulled that stunt tonight.' Having retrieved his phone from his pocket while talking, he scanned through his messages.

'There's nothing here,' he said, before heading towards a seriously-worse-for-wear party of five who had yet to work out how to enter the hotel through its sheer glass door. Ouch. That would have hurt.

'Mac?' Graham said to one as he opened the door for them. 'You know anything about going back to set?'

'No sireeeee! And that's not funny.'

'You've not had a text from Francis?'

He shook his head dramatically.

'Have you seen him?'

'Big F? I most certainly have. He was giving us all a lie-in, but flipping out because he couldn't find his phone.'

'Who's still at the club?'

'Everyone! Bar lover boy, of course, and we all know what he'll be . . .' Mac's words died on spotting Susie. She moved her hand in a little wave. 'Sorry,' he mouthed, before attempting to control a series of hiccups. 'The bitch is obviously above being there, too, but she'd have been a no-show after her total flip-out anyway.'

'Bad?' Graham's tone indicated flip-outs might not be uncommon.

'The worst! You should hear Evie go on about it.' Mac started calling, 'Evie? Evie?'

Evidently Evie had been one of the party who had got themselves into the lift and had just mastered closing the doors behind them. Whether they'd get themselves out of it again was another matter.

'Evie normally takes it all but tonight she got seriously spooked. She said she's never seen The Demon-atrix like it.'

Susie made a mental note to remember that way of referring to Porsche.

'She completely trashed that all-singing, all-dancing pad she's in and was going on and on about betrayal and if she couldn't have him, nobody could.'

Susie's skin prickled and her heart raced. Rachael and Cassie were suddenly close at her side.

'And we know just who she was speaking about there.' Mac's attempt at whispering the last sentence didn't work. 'Evie fled. Said it wasn't safe to be around her. Michael what's-his-name sour-face turned up, said he'd get a doctor out. Evie reckons Porsche will get dosed to the nines, if not straight-jacketed.'

'So no one, as far as you know, has had to head back tonight?'

'Nope! And nobody is capable of . . . Sorry. The bog! The nearest—?'

Graham turned a green-looking Mac in the right direction and gave him a shove towards the right door, before rejoining them.

Susie sighed and shook her head. She would not let herself worry. George had most probably got the wrong end of the stick. 'Thanks, Graham. I'd better call him.' She found Cassie's phone plonked into her hands.

'He's so not himself at the—'

'No!' Cassie gasped.

'Crap!' Rachael exclaimed.

Susie looked up and—

'What's up?' Michael asked, as the hotel's glass door swung closed behind him. He didn't stop walking until he was standing in front of them.

Before Susie, Cassie or Rachael were fit for

442

purpose, Graham started explaining to him about George heading back to the set.

Michael raised his eyebrows a fraction. 'Porsche headed that way, too,' he said casually.

He then wished them a goodnight and went to reception where he immersed himself in a tête-à-tête with the receptionist.

As George's phone clicked onto voicemail yet again and Susie resorted to leaving yet another garbled message, she told herself to remain calm. Facts. She'd look at the facts and not let her emotions get the better of her. George had been lured to a deserted site, and the bitch, who'd completely lost it and spoke of nobody having him but her, was headed his way.

She hadn't a hope of remaining calm! Terminating her message with a desperate, 'Call me! Urgently!' she leapt from the seat Cassie and Rachael had deposited her in, only to find herself yanked back down.

'Sit down!' they hissed in unison. Susie looked from their hands, wrapped around each of her wrists, to their faces: freaked out.

Oh God! They weren't back to this? Please *no*!

'I know this looks bad,' Cassie continued with deliberate calm. 'But this is not what it purports to be. You do know this is not some clandestine meeting between Porsche and George? That—'

'Of course I do!' The thought hadn't even crossed her mind . . . until now. And then there was naked

443

Porsche. *Betrayal* . . . She ordered her head into silence. She could *not* lose sight of what was happening here. George was in danger.

'They are deliberately trying to lure you to the set, to the lake, to—'

'For God's sake – open your eyes! This is not like last time. Can't you see that? This time George is in danger, not me!'

'George can look after himself,' Rachael stated. 'It's you we've got to stop drowning. So you are going to come back to the room with us, right now.'

'And we're going to check in on Tom, Dick and Harry en route,' Cassie added. 'We'll wait with them until the reinforcements arrive.'

'You *what*?' Susie exploded, frantically trying to release her wrists from their grips. Why couldn't they see what was happening here? 'We can't abandon him! Why can't you see it? It's as plain as day. Porsche has lost it. Completely lost it! You heard what was said: if she can't have him *nobody* can! And instead of getting medical help, she's lured George away and— Oh God! What if she's armed?'

Cassie blanched.

'You guys keep reminding me how dangerous she is, and I believe you. But not to me! George hasn't slept in days thanks to you two. He's not at his best and is too much of a gentleman to thump her when needs be. And he's not going to know how volatile she is. He's not going to know what we know. He'll have no idea how to handle her . . .'

Susie felt the tears roll down her cheeks. She couldn't help it. She was terrified for George. Through blurred eyes she watched Cassie and Rachael stare at each other.

'You've been helping George with his misguided need to keep me safe. Yet now, when it's George in danger – *real* danger – you won't help *me*? Not only that, you are physically stopping me from going to *help* him?' How could they not help? And they couldn't seriously expect her to just sit back and leave Porsche to it? George would not have abandoned her and there was no way she was going to abandon him. She couldn't do it. Wouldn't do it. She'd move heaven and earth to help him. He was her life, there was no two ways about it. *Loss* . . . And she was *not* about to lose him! However this played out, she was going to George.

'We don't know Porsche is going to be there,' Cassie finally said.

Susie shook her head. 'But we don't know she isn't. And . . . And . . .' Snot dripped from her nose and she couldn't wipe the blessed thing because they were still holding her wrists. She sniffed noisily, but it didn't ease the problem. 'I'll tell you this now. If something happens to George tonight,' *Loss* . . . 'I *will* find a lake to throw myself into. I swear, as God is my witness, that I will—'

'Stop!' Cassie cried. 'Stop! Stop! Stop!'

'And then you really will have history repeating yourself, won't you?' Susie murmured.

'I'll go,' Cassie said. 'I'll go and check that—'

'You are not leaving me on my own with her!' Rachael fumed. 'I wouldn't put anything past her right now.'

'I'm not being left with anybody! I am going to help George and there's nothing you can do or say to stop me. I've managed to escape from—'

'Once!' Rachael snapped. '*Once* you got away from Tom, Dick and Harry.'

'That's what *they* say,' Susie clarified. 'And just who do you think put them out of action tonight?'

Cassie and Rachael simply stared at her.

Susie had to concede that she'd not expected the laxatives to make them vomit too, but . . .

'How could you do something so . . . *stupid*?' Rachael finally fumed. 'So beyond stupid and—'

'Tonight of all nights?' Susie added sarcastically, knowing full well that would be the next line. 'Because history *is* not and *does* not repeat itself. And I couldn't take any more! And I had the opportunity. So what is it? Are we going to go and help George together, or are you going to force me to go there alone? Because I will.'

And it was so simple she suddenly realised. Looking at them through narrowed eyes, she said, 'If you do not agree to my terms in ten seconds flat, I will start screaming this place down. Security will force you to release me, and then I'm gone. I'm going straight to him, alone if needs be, because . . . because . . .' She sucked back the tears. 'I won't have him face Porsche alone, not when he's going to need all the help he can get. And if *anything* happens to him, I swear that I will—'

Susie found her left wrist released by Cassie, who then turned to Rachael.

'For the record – Soul Mates? I *hate* them! *Despise* them! All sense goes straight out the window! If I *ever* encounter one destined for me – put me down! I mean it. Just put me down!'

CHAPTER 32

As the headlights of the taxi going in the opposite direction passed them, George frowned. Where was everyone? It had become evident only one small Portakabin had lights on. 'Stop over there,' he instructed the driver, while pointing towards the lit window.

It had taken an age for the hotel to secure a taxi and he'd thought he'd be one of the last to arrive. But then again, getting everyone out of the club was neither going to be quick or easy.

Settling up with the driver, George bounded up the steps and opened the door.

Empty. He moved into the room and sat down on one of a dozen or so chairs grouped loosely around the Formica table in the centre of the room. He spotted a kettle and mugs. He got up, switched the kettle on and then returned to his seat.

He took a deep shuddery breath as he sat back in the chair. This nightmare was finally over. It had all been coincidence. He took some more deep breaths. He was torn between elation and the need to start bawling out of sheer bloody relief.

Instead he frowned as he had another fruitless rummage through his pockets for his phone. He wanted to check on Susie . . . just in case. His gut was taking a while to catch up on the facts. It was to be expected, though, the last few weeks had been . . . horrific. But the sooner it realised there was no need to panic, that Susie was safe, the better. He couldn't wait to shrug off this incessant fear.

When had he last had his phone? He'd definitely had it at reception when he was waiting for the taxi, but had got distracted as the receptionist pushed mounds of paper in his direction for him to autograph for all her friends. He'd put it down. Had he picked it up again?

He couldn't remember.

'You came!' Porsche's voice gushed as she entered the room through a door he hadn't noticed. 'He said you would. Oh George . . .'

George thrust his chair backwards and leapt to his feet as Porsche, slurring her words, rushed towards him. She was wearing a long coat, with not much else underneath if the intermittent flashes of bare flesh were anything to go on.

George scooted around the table, putting it between them. He took several calming breaths for the benefit of his pounding heart and attempted to introduce reason to the equation. The others would be here any minute. History was no longer repeating itself and even if it were, Susie was safely back at the hotel. This was therefore nothing more sinister than a highly unpleasant interlude he'd have to survive. *Okaaaay.*

The kettle boiling behind him clicked off. He'd start by making coffee. That would occupy him for a few minutes by which time the others should have arrived and he wouldn't have to look at Porsche in the meantime.

'Coffee?' George murmured the question, adding coffee to a second mug to which he now added water.

'Coffee?' she shrieked.

George spun around. It wasn't the word, but its banshee-like sound and . . . her eyes were wild, her face contorted.

What the hell?

As she sped full throttle towards him George decided to go with instinct. He abandoned the coffee and got himself to the other side of the room, that table and chairs again between them proving their weight in gold.

What was the matter with the woman? *She* was screaming at *him?* George felt his anger rise. After everything she had said about Susie, her lies and innuendo. The terror he'd felt earlier tonight came flooding back. All his fears and frustrations provided fuel.

'*Coffee?*' she screamed again. 'You turn your back on me and say – *coffee?*'

He should have seen the mug coming. He gasped and instinctively leapt back, not as a result of the mug slamming into his chest but because

450

of the boiling hot liquid that now seeped through the cotton of his shirt, burning his skin. He tugged and tore at the shirt, determined to remove the source of the ongoing burn. As he wrenched it off and stared at his red angry chest, he turned his black angry eyes on Porsche.

'Why?' he yelled. 'Why would you . . .?'

'I'm sorry. I'm sorry. I didn't think. Let me have a look and—'

His hands immediately raised in a halting gesture. 'Stay away from me. Stay. Away.' If she came any closer he would not be held accountable for his actions.

'I didn't think. It was you talking of coffee when . . .' Her eyes glinted. 'You've fallen for her, haven't you? I've done everything you asked of me. Played my role perfectly. And you've gone and fallen for her! Mike says no. You're just choosing your moment.' She screamed, 'But I can SEE it!'

George saw the second mug coming. He ducked and side-stepped to the left to avoid further boiling splashes reaching his legs. They'd already taken a hit earlier but he was not removing his jeans. He didn't even want to be shirtless around her. With that thought, he un-scrunched his now coffee-stained, but no longer scorching, shirt and slipped his arms into the holes, while all the time keeping an eye on Porsche's movements.

Only now did Porsche's words sink in. His look turned incredulous. 'You are not seriously asking me whether I've *fallen* for Susie?'

'Oh George . . .' Was that relief, elation – what the hell was that in her voice? 'Thank God! I should have listened to him. It's just tonight you looked—'

'Of course I've fallen for her!' he roared. 'I love her!' Provocation? Oh yeah, but he was stuck in a room with a hysterical, delusional Porsche whose words were equally as disturbing as her actions. She *was* going to hear it and grasp it! And Susie was safe at the hotel. And any minute now Francis would appear. George would say his piece and they'd be gone.

'What *exactly* has "Mike" said to you?'

'Susie, I have a feeling I shouldn't be doing this.' Graham spoke as he turned the car out of the hotel driveway. 'Whenever you ask something of me, I suffer at George's hands. The horse was—'

'I'm sorry. You *did* blame me?'

'Of *course* I did! But why do I think he's not going to be happy with this turn of events?'

'Blame me again. We think Porsche has lured George to the set.'

She didn't need to say any more; he cursed and put his foot down.

The phone clutched in Susie's hand, vibrated: George's phone. The hotel receptionist had handed it to her on the way out. He'd apparently left it there earlier. At least that provided an explanation for why he wasn't returning her calls. It didn't mean he was incapacitated, that Porsche had— She took deep calming breaths. She couldn't let her fears take hold. If she lost it here she'd be a useless, blubbering wreck. But the idea of George . . . She swallowed hard. He was going to be fine.

Focusing on the phone, which had now lit up, Susie stared. It was a text message . . . from Porsche.

As Susie continued to stare at the screen, Cassie, at her side, reached across and clicked the receive button.

'I'll be there in five. Delayed a bit this end. Our usual spot?'

Betrayal . . .

No! Porsche was sick. This was her playing games all over again.

Susie found the phone snatched from her hands by Cassie, who in turn started scanning through the messages.

'You can't do that!' Susie protested.

'Just watch me,' she replied, distractedly. Moments later she slanted the phone away from Susie so she couldn't see the screen.

Why did they keep doing this to her? What hope did she have of keeping her head in check when they did things like this!

She found herself asking, 'There's more isn't there? Give me the phone.'

'Don't be ridiculous.'

'Give. It. To. Me.'

'I'm not handing it over. Yes there's more but . . .

Rachael . . . they've got hold of his phone somehow. They must have done.'

'The receptionist,' Rachael murmured from the front seat. 'Michael was talking to her earlier.'

'Oh for goodness sake, I'm a big girl. Let me see it,' Susie demanded.

'Soul Mates don't cheat on each other, Suse. It's a physical impossibility.'

'Like Matey? Who's forever at Rob's heels? You can't even entice him to the flat on his own to be fed!' Susie immediately regretted her words. 'I'm sorry. I didn't mean that.' And she didn't. And she trusted George . . . She was sure she did.

'How about you just let me see the text from Francis?' Susie cajoled of Cassie. 'Does it say where on site they were to meet so we know where George would have been heading?'

When Cassie didn't respond she prompted again.

'I think . . . I might have deleted it by mistake.'

Susie attempted to swallow over the lump in her throat. There had to be one. 'Cassie?'

'I've done something by mistake.'

She was lying. But there had to be a text from Francis, or at least from whoever was purporting to be him. It was why George had had to leave her tonight on the evening of their engagement party. Why he'd rushed off . . . insisting he needed to go alone.

Betrayal . . .

'They've got hold of his phone!' Cassie said again, defensively.

'I don't pretend to know what's going on here, but you don't honestly think George would cheat on you?' Graham asked, astounded. 'Ignore the gossip, that's all it is. Playing around with texts would be right up Porsche's street. I've never believed the flowers are from George whatever Evie might say. I'm convinced she's far enough gone to send them to herself and pretend—'

'Shut up!' Rachael growled ferociously from the front of the car. Cassie sank down in her seat.

'What flowers, Graham?' Susie forced herself to ask.

'Flowers?' George spluttered. 'You think I sent you flowers!'

'You bastard!' she screamed, eyes flashing disconcertingly at him from the other side of the table. 'You *did* send me flowers, damn you!' She kicked and threw over all the chairs in her vicinity. 'Even today!' she spat, now placing her hands palm down on the table and leaning across in his direction. 'Today! On the day we cele- brated your engagement! And you dare say you love that blimp when all the time you're telling me how beautiful I am, all the things you can't wait to do to me, how you think of me all the time. How after the publicity stunt we'll be together!'

'I've never said that to you!' George cried. 'Did Michael? Is that what he told you?' Placing his own hands on the table he looked Porsche right in the eye. 'And if you ever, ever refer to Susie like—'

'Why are you doing this to me?' Porsche suddenly wailed, moving back.

And in that split second he caught a flash of pain in her eyes. In fact it was in her whole body language as she proceeded to pick up a chair, position it upright and . . . crumple into its seat.

She appeared vulnerable; as he'd once thought her. And she still was, he realised. And Michael had used it, evidently feeding her lie after lie after lie. Just as in the past.

George didn't know what to say or do. He just shook his head and said quietly, 'When have I ever spoken such words to you? I haven't done any of this, you have to believe me. I wouldn't. I wouldn't do it to you. I wouldn't do it to anyone.'

'So what are you . . . saying here?' Porsche asked shakily, albeit with her chin raised in the air.

He was going to kill Michael for this. 'I'm saying . . .'

'Because this sounds to me like you're trying to wheedle your way out of things!'

'Porsche! Will you just *think*? I have never said any of those things to you and when have I *ever* given you the impression I feel that way? I've been actively *avoiding* you because of the things you've said about Susie and the lies you've been spouting. My solicitors have even sent you letters.'

'Mike said—'

'Whatever Michael has said is crap! I sent no

flowers. The letters from the solicitors were real. And on my instructions! I have avoided you because we have to work together and I haven't trusted myself not to throttle you! I love Susie. Whatever the hell "Mike" has said, I am going to marry her and spend the rest of my life with her.'

Porsche lowered her head to her visibly tremulous hands. And George felt like shit. She was hurting, plain as day. He'd had no choice. But she should have bloody known. If it hadn't been for Michael, she would have done!

He sank into the chair opposite her, rubbing his eyes. 'I don't know why Michael's been doing it. He seems to have his own agenda. His financial position is desperate and he doesn't . . . *approve* of Susie. He does, however, approve of you and—' George caught himself rubbing his damned forehead and stopped on a curse. 'And he's often tried to match us up.'

'You expect me to believe he would do all this to—'

'He thinks I'll cut my work down if I'm with Susie. And he's right. It's my own fault. I always told him I would when I found the right woman.'

'Yet he doesn't think you'd do that with *me*?'

Bloody hell! And that was another shriek. He chose his words carefully. 'You're in the business. It's different. He probably thought he'd get to manage you, too.'

'He is!' She looked at him horrified. 'As of next month.'

'Well there you go. With you his income doubles, with Susie it dwindles to next to nothing.'

George rose from his seat and started pacing. 'That's the best guess in any event. But I don't *know* why he's done it, just that he has! And as well as saying all this stuff to you, he's warned Susie off and manufactured photographs and God knows what else.'

'The horse,' Porsche said, shaking her head. 'I didn't know how it would pan out – I promise. I can't stand the—' She paused, before continuing, '*Susie,* but I never imagined it would end up how it did. I hadn't a clue Michael planned on using the gun. I promise you that.'

Michael *had* used the gun! He *had* used the gun! Porsche went to speak, but George held up a hand which he forced himself to unclench from its fist, to buy himself some time to cool down. Dear God when he got his hands on Michael! Because he would. He'd make damned sure of that. He took several deep deliberate breaths and moved to lean heavily against the counter of the kitchen area. There he made himself slowly release the other fist, still clenched at his side, rather than give in to the urge to pound it against the counter. Jesus, he wanted to speak to Susie, to hear her voice.

'I used to think you were my knight in shining armour,' Porsche suddenly announced. Her voice was artificially bright as she fiddled with her fingernails and pointedly avoided looking at him.

'Why?' George asked with an accompanying frown.

'How you came rushing to my aid.'

'It was no more than anyone else would have done,' George said, cringing as he recalled the situation she'd been in. Naked, pissed and out-of-her-head on God knows what; in the corner of an 'exclusive' club to boot. She could hardly stand, but men were all over her.

'From that moment you were . . . special to me. I don't know why I'm fessing this. Perhaps because things can hardly get any worse . . .' Her voice broke.

George moved away from the counter to sit himself down again. He had no idea what to say.

'Perhaps because I want you to understand why Michael seems to have played me . . .' She looked at him afresh, a spark of hope in her eyes. She shook her head again in response to his look and said acidly, 'Because he evidently has! And he knew, of course. He saw it whenever I looked at you.'

The man was beyond a bastard. His only saving grace was that perhaps he'd thought he and Porsche might eventually get together? Had under-estimated how he and Susie felt for each other? But that was clutching at straws. George had trusted him. He'd been his manager for eighteen years! How did that reflect on him?

'I'm not special, just ask Susie.' George winced the moment the words were out of his mouth. He watched her roll her eyes.

He tried again. 'I did what any man would have done and don't deserve your . . . gratitude.'

She shook her head. 'You think? Similar things happened before and since. Believe me, your reaction was not the norm. You looked after me. Made me feel better than I deserved to feel. And from then on in, all I wanted to do was age.'

'I'm sorry?'

'You said no that first time because of my age. Seven years on I'm not seventeen anymore. I thought finally I may have become acceptable.'

He spluttered. He had not said no because of her age. That had definitely been one of the reasons he'd used to lessen the rejection . . . and in fact it *would* have been a no because of her age, but . . .

'I never meant to give you that impression. It wasn't just your age. You had no idea what you were doing and it wouldn't have been right to take advantage of you. And I'm not the one for you. I've said no since—'

Porsche snorted and rubbed her eyes. She looked at him for a moment and then looked away to speak. 'You've never actually said no since, George.'

Oh come on. Yes he had. He could think of half a dozen times. He was . . . sure he could.

'You made light of things, changed the subject, but you don't say no. Yet, I was finally getting the message . . . until Mike picked up the phone and said you wanted me to be your Elizabeth.'

What the hell!

'You didn't . . . did you?'

George slowly shook his head.

'And then soon after filming began . . .' She took a moment before she could continue. 'All the flowers started arriving with *your* notes.'

When he'd met Susie and Michael had got panicked.

'I'm sorry,' George murmured. For Michael and for him. He'd evidently never known how to handle Porsche, inebriated or sober.

Graham turned the car engine off outside the only building presently displaying lights.

'You can stop trying to open the door, Suse,' Rachael announced smugly. 'The child lock is on. Graham, you are charged with keeping her in here. You'll need to get in the back, too. George *may* kill you for bringing her here. However, he *will* torture you grotesquely before killing you – repeatedly throughout eternity – if you let her out of this car. We are seriously talking about life and death here. And not just yours.'

'Where are you going?' George asked, as Porsche got up from the table and started heading towards the door.

'Fresh air, a walk; anything to clear my head. And I'd like to deal with my . . . rejection . . . and humiliation in private.'

She opened the door and . . . it was dark. There was a lake. She wasn't sober. And she was fragile.

461

She was hurting no matter how much she played the bitch.

'It's not safe,' he found himself saying.

'What do you care?' she asked, walking out the door onto the platform at the top of the steps.

He followed. The chill in the night air made him shiver in his wet shirt, hanging open to his waist. He couldn't let her go off in this state.

He reached his hand out to her. 'I care.' Bizarrely it wasn't a lie. He certainly cared enough not to want to see her floating face down in the lake. None of this was her fault; it was Michael's.

'What would little Susie say about that?'

'*No* talk of Susie,' he ground out.

'Fancy a spot of skinny-dipping then?' she asked, jiggling her body around and flashing what she wasn't wearing under her coat.

He shook his head. 'Come back inside.' He grasped her hand and pulled her back towards the relative safety of the cabin.

She giggled as the momentum brought her up against his chest. He hissed at the pain of her making contact with his raw skin. *And* at her contact. He immediately went to put distance between them. But a cry pierced the night.

'You SHIT!'

CHAPTER 33

'George?'

Was that *Cassie?*

'Cassie?' he called out, attempting to see into the dark.

'You total *shit!* I so don't know it all! You were meant to make her *happy!* I should never have lured her to . . .' George didn't hear the rest. *Rachael Jones.*

White noise instantaneously filled his head. George catapulted himself down the steps, his feet avoiding contact with most.

Susie could not *be here . . . It had stopped. It had damned well stopped!*

He encountered Cassie first. With his hands on her shoulders, he begged, 'Tell me she's not here. *Please* tell me she's not here!'

She stood staring at him as if he'd grown horns since the last time she'd seen him. 'How can you be half-clothed and saying—?'

He ran towards the car he could make out behind them, bypassing Rachael Jones who was screaming at him, not that he heard a word.

He tripped over something on the ground and

463

crashed against the open car door. His hands, finding purchase at the base of the wound-down window, kept him on his feet as his momentum slammed the door shut. He dared a glance into the car, lit by the internal light. Empty.

He attempted to calm his rampaging heart. That was good. Just because Cassie and Rachael were here, didn't mean Susie . . . . He bent to the ground to see what he'd tri— *Graham?*

He was rolling around clutching his privates. He grabbed him by the collar. 'Tell me Susie wasn't with you!'

'She's in the car with Graham,' Rachael Jones snapped. 'But we're leaving now and taking her with us and you will never—'

Her words froze as she spotted Graham.

'She's not in the car!' George roared.

'She flaming well is, not that you're getting anywhere near—' She'd reached the car. 'Noooo!'

Cassie was at her side. It took her a moment to take in the situation before she cried, 'Oh God! Oh God! No!'

Susie ran blindly.

There was no conscious thought other than if she perhaps went far enough, quickly enough, she could outrun it.

A broken sob escaped from somewhere. She stumbled and her ankle jolted painfully. She couldn't see where she was going. It was pitch black. But her tears would have blinded her day or night. *Loss . . . desolation . . .*

Betrayal . . . She welcomed her old friend back. Why hadn't she listened to her head? It had known. It had *always known* George would destroy her.

'Turn on the car lights!' George cried. 'And torches. We need torches!'

He couldn't lose it here. He couldn't give in to the terror. *Oh dear God help me!*

Nobody was moving and he went to Cassie and Rachael, standing motionless and staring blindly. 'This is your fault!' he screamed at them both. 'The least you can do is help me find her. Help me NOW!' And then he was begging, 'Please!'

He shook his head trying to get a grip on himself. He took deep breaths and attempted to clear his mind of everything but what he needed to do to find Susie. But the flashbacks were coming thick and fast, entangling with his consciousness. He painfully tugged at his hair in an attempt to clear his head, but they wouldn't budge. *Not now Freddie, please not now.* He had enough of his own fears and anguish in the here and now and needed no reminder of how the night could end.

'Torches,' he managed to mutter. He raised his voice, 'Torch—'

'We're onto it,' Cassie finally said, squeezing his arm before rushing away. They were going to help. He glanced up at Porsche, standing immobile halfway down the steps.

'Get security. Get Todd and Herb up here now. Get them to call anyone, everyone. We need a search party!'

She slowly shook her head. 'Don't you think this is extreme? If I *must*, I'll explain there was nothing to—'

'You don't remember!' he cried, shaking his head. And why should she? 'She's going to drown in the damned lake if . . .'

His voice broke. He couldn't go there. He spun around and flung himself to the ground, hauling Graham up.

'Graham, you have to help me! I need every last piece of lighting equipment and the floodlights! I need it trained on the lake and all around it. You see Susie anywhere near it, you do whatever is necessary to stop her going in. Do you understand that?'

'We understand,' Cassie said at his side, shoving a lit torch at him. 'Go and find her.'

The path forked and as a branch crashed down on the route before her, Susie lurched to the left, taking the less trodden path.

Her head saw nothing but George and Porsche . . . together. The scene played over and over. He was half-dressed, Porsche in *nothing* but a coat. Susie had wound down her window . . . heard his words . . . 'I care . . . No talk of Susie . . . Come back inside.' Porsche was giggling and in his arms . . .

There had been no meeting with Francis. It had been a lie so he and Porsche could meet. It had *all* been one huge lie.

She couldn't believe a word he had ever said to her.

As she ran, she ran in tandem with Hannah. The flashbacks to Hannah's heartbreak and flight, merging with her own. Oh Hannah. Kindred spirits when it came to betrayal, because George had lied about that, too.

George called her name. She forced her legs to move faster.

'Susie! Susie! You can hear me, I know you can!' George cried, crashing through a bush at the perimeter of the woods to momentarily scan the area around the lake. She wasn't there.

The whole area was now floodlit and people were spread out intermittently around the body of water. Cassie, Rachael and Graham had been rejoined by Porsche and with her Todd and Herb. On being spotted, Herb jogged towards him.

'Here,' Herb called, throwing a walkie-talkie which George fumbled to catch. 'We can keep in touch with these. Just press that button right there. The others are on their way. Nobody will get anywhere near the lake.'

George made himself focus on what was being said and look at what was being pointed out to him. He then returned his gaze to the lake. Porsche. He couldn't trust her. But Cassie evidently

467

had that covered because she stood at her side. He dove back into the woods.

George began running again, but on a changed course as debris blocked the path he'd been intent on following.

'Susie!' he cried afresh, shaking his head against the memories of that night and attempting to block Freddie out, but it was as if they were merged. Each step was his and Freddie's. Each desperate thought an echo of the other. This was *not* going to end as it had before. 'SUSIE!' he roared with all his physical might and with all of his and Freddie's combined anguish and fears.

He attempted to get more of a grip on himself and paused to lower his hands to his knees and to breathe through the panic. 'I need you to *think* here, sweetheart,' he cried out in between gasps for air. 'I know what it must have looked like, but *remember. . .Please* remember. Remember Prudence and Matthew and now Porsche and Michael. It wasn't real. I swear to you, it wasn't real! This is *me, George* and I will never lie to you. Ever . . . We're invincible remember, you told me that! Our *trust* in each other makes us invincible.' Taking several gasps of air he stood upright and bellowed, 'Well where is it Susie? Where is your trust?'

George paused to listen for any response or signs of movement. His heart pounded in his head and the white noise shrieked. He heard nothing else bar the torrential rain that had now started to fall.

★   ★   ★

468

The only sounds Susie heard were her own sobs. And Hannah's. And the pounding of her heart that still seemed to beat. *Betrayal* . . . And then she was slipping, her feet were out from under her and Hannah was tumbling with her. The only pain they felt as they continued to fall was in their one beating heart. *Loss* . . . *desolation* . . . But it *would* stop. Finally it would stop . . .

'SUSIE!' George roared as he heard the splash. *Susie* . . . He hurtled in the direction the sound had come from, leaping over fallen trees and ploughing through undergrowth. It had come from deeper inside the woods. It wasn't the lake. There was other water! *Where?* Dear God, *where?*

'SUSIE!' he screamed. 'SUSIE!' It was dark and he couldn't see a thing. All his torch was illuminating, whichever way he swung it, was vegetation and more damned vegetation and rain that was now falling in sheets. He made himself pause to listen. Was that another splash? He couldn't be sure but he changed his course. He reached into his pocket for the walkie-talkie, but he must have lost it somewhere along the way. 'Don't you dare drown on me! If you die, I'll die. Do you understand that Susie? Do you understand? I'll be in there right behind you! You are *not* leaving me!'

He blindly wrenched brambles away as they tore through skin and clothes. Then he was slipping and sliding downwards on the now muddy ground.

★　　★　　★

Susie clutched on to the overhanging branch for dear life. She couldn't risk going under again. What the hell was she doing in the water? She *hated* water! And this stuff was freezing and up to her neck. She repositioned her feet to get a firmer foothold as they started to slip out from under her.

She heard him. Oh George. She was so going to do her best not to drown. But what was he talking about coming in after her? He hated water, too and if he had any idea how cold it was in here . . .

She still didn't know how she'd got here. It was as if she'd been on automatic pilot, not completely sure of what her body was doing, where it was taking her.

She winced as that image of George and Porsche flashed into her head. For a moment there she'd seemed to lose her senses, completely overwhelmed by what she saw before her, the words spoken. She gritted her now chattering teeth. Evidently her senses were back. She wasn't sure she'd needed quite such cold water to bring them back. Or that initial immersion. Surely one of the two would have been enough? She shook her head. The idiot man. The stupid, stupid, idiot man. How on God's earth had he managed to get himself in that situation – *again*?

It wasn't real. She knew that. This was George. *Her* George. She trusted him. She adjusted her hold on the branch above her head as her grip had been slipping. She saw again the truth and sincerity in his eyes as he reassured her after Porsche's performance on the show. He couldn't lie to her. She'd know. And there'd been love in them too, so much which travelled throughout her being along that special internal highway that existed only for him. There may have been nagging doubts there for a while . . . Events had *definitely* been playing to her insecurities. But she *did* trust him. She really did. Whereas she absolutely did *not* trust Porsche. The scheming witch.

Bloody hell, though. She had to find her way out of this water. Was it a lake? She hoped it wasn't because they'd have a field day with that one. A pond would be that much more preferable. But not as preferable as a puddle she reflected as her feet began to slide out from under her again. She had to remain calm here and get out of the water without killing herself in the process. She needed to find George before he ended up doing something really stupid.

Even more stupid than letting Porsche into his arms.

The black vegetation all around blew in a squally gust and her face was stung by lashing rain. How much worse could this night get? She took a deep breath and took a tentative step forward. And was instantly submerged.

Oh God! She thrashed and flailed, momentarily managing to get her face above the water to take another breath, but her hands couldn't find the branch. 'George!' she spluttered before going under again. Oh God, *George*!

'SUSIE!' George screamed. *Susie* . . .

He sped into the water, determined to keep his momentum going, but the water swallowed up his speed as its icy temperature did his breath. He was wading forward. Freddie was wading forward. They pushed towards their target, but it was taking too long; the black ominous depths, thick and dragging.

Too late. Too late.

Freddie's desperate thoughts were as one with George's own. His footing was lost and he found himself within icy clutches. *I am not too late!* He managed to break free and was back on his feet and surging onwards.

George ditched the near useless and now flickering torch, the water too much for it. His eyes had adjusted to the night in any event. He kept them fixed religiously on the splashing up ahead. As long as she was splashing . . . He swiped his eyes repeatedly to clear his blurred vision. But it was futile . . .

Freddie's tears were relentless and the accompanying sounds of his sobs, torturous.

But George knew they were his, too.

George shook his head frantically. He was losing the terrifying battle with Freddie's flashbacks. They were merging with the present and – *the splashing had stopped*!

She wasn't floating face down in the water, her dress all around her. She wasn't! He silently screamed. She was. . . .

'I've got you, sweetheart, I've got you,' he choked out as his desperate lunge forward found Susie just as her head disappeared under the surface again. His arms wrapped around her as he raised her out of the water. Clutching her to him with one arm, the other held her head and face so gently against his shoulder.

But it was as then.

Freddie's agony was his own.

She was still.

Her skin, cold and wet.

Her eyes closed.

His breath came thick and fast.

He reverently smoothed away smears of mud from her pale cheek.

He moved sodden strands of hair so gently away.

He covered her cold, still face in the gentlest, most tender of butterfly kisses . . .

He rocked her backwards and forwards in his arms. *Oh my angel, my dearest, darl—*

But there was warmth . . .

Now there was warmth. *Susie . . . Oh dear God, Susie . . .* Warmth trickled over the skin of his hand upon her cheek. Silent tears he realised as he followed their tracks with his lips. And now . . . *now* she moved. She *moved*, nestling her face into the palm of his hand.

Susie . . .

He felt her heart beating so strong and fast against his own. Felt her warm breath against his skin.

The feather-light touches of his lips became desperate, frenzied open-mouthed kisses as the full force of his emotions found their release. And she was responding in kind.

Her eyes opened. They connected. His whole body shook and he couldn't find his voice.

His mouth found hers and her taste provided him with the laced adrenaline shot he so needed.

She was alive. Oh God, she was alive. And now so was he.

'Never let me go, my love. I beg of you,' she sobbed, clutching on to him tightly as her arms wrapped around his neck.

I'm never letting you go. Ever.

He was wading out of the water with her in his arms. His legs were trembling, but he had to get them out of there. As they reached land, George's shaking legs crumpled. He clutched her even more closely to him if that were at all possible.

She's safe, Freddie. Now *she's safe.*

He was kneeling upon the ground. He had her face cradled between both of his shaking hands. He stared into her eyes, getting yet more of that fix and reassurance he so needed.

'You idiot. I've not told you that yet have I?' It was half sob, half rasp.

He shook his head as he attempted to calm his heart, still not ready to release those eyes, that connection providing him with his life fuel. 'No. But tell me again. I need to hear your voice right now.'

'Idiot. Idiot. *Idiot man*!'

'More please. More.'

'There's more. But . . . but . . . tell me this is a pond!'

'It's water. That's all you need to know, baby.' His forehead dropped to rest against hers.

'A lake wouldn't be—'

He temporarily silenced her words with his mouth. She was alive. Dear God she was alive. Not that he could see himself ever recovering from this. Ever getting enough reassurance as to that fact. He scooped her up into his arms and stood. The primal stuff mercilessly screaming at him would have to wait. She was freezing and her teeth chattering. He had to get her dry and warmed up. If she caught pneumonia he'd—

'It's over, George. It's over.' Her warm breath whispered against his neck.

He swallowed hard. 'How about you try to convince me of that in Peru?'

Rachael moved into the coppice of trees to the side of the lake. 'Suse?' she called. She'd heard a noise and definitely had one of her feelings. It was a real ring-a-ding-ding one, too. She prayed it didn't mean something awful has happened to Suse. That Fate had—

She tripped. And was slipping and falling down

a slope of some kind and— 'Crap!' The cold water hit.

She so wasn't a fan of history repeating itself! And how could she have possibly known there was a body of water just here? *Deep water.* She couldn't get a foothold at all and there was nothing for her flailing arms to grab on to. *Cold water.* So, so cold. She struggled relentlessly against its downward pull.

Was Suse okay? Oh God. Please let her be. She'd failed her that night, too. Tessa had followed. She'd seen Hannah plunge into the lake. She'd gone in after her and tried to help, but her skirts had got tangled around her legs and weighed her down and—

Why had she decided to wear a long maxi dress tonight? The exact same thing was happening to her now and it had seemed to trip her up.

She closed her eyes. The pain in her lungs. She didn't think it had been painful last time. Hadn't she just felt herself sinking into . . . oblivion? Or perhaps she'd simply chosen to forget the pain? Flaming Nora. This time . . . oh crap it hurt.

She tried to move her legs but they weren't cooperating. The fog in her head was becoming a blanket. She needed to breathe . . .

The cold water engulfed her inside and out.

But she wasn't falling any more. Why wasn't she falling? And there was a touch. A blazing touch that spread warmth through every atom of her body. She embraced it, wallowing in its familiarity . . . Oh my God how good did that feel? It felt so much more than . . . life. Was this heaven? No, that feeling was too sinful for heaven, but . . .

'Breathe, Rach! Damn you, breathe!'

Rob?

She was on her side, emptying her lungs of water. She felt crap. But there was that touch again. It made all the pain go away. Oh God, that *touch* . . .

She was on her back and staring up into Rob's traumatised eyes. Water dripped from his hair and his lashes.

'Rach?' He gently moved a strand of her own sodden hair from her face and as his shaking fingers brushed her skin . . . How could a single touch be soothing, comforting, *heavenly* . . . yet hotter than hell?

'Rachael . . .' His voice . . . There was reverence in the way he said her name but its sound was a caress, inside and out. It reached so deep.

His eyes . . . His incredible *eyes*. It was as if they were connecting . . . As if invisible strands were winging their way through her instinctively finding their home.

Before slotting into place.

'You,' she whispered.

EPILOGUE

Rachael slowly lowered the newspaper to the kitchen table.

'Well?' Cassie asked, returning with Rachael's coffee and her mug of tea, before curling up in the seat opposite her.

'The picture's good,' Rachael said.

'You can't be talking about the one of me on the byline?'

'No.' Rachael picked up the paper again. 'Although that one's good, too. Sophisticated, sexy and learned all at the same time. I'm talking about my newspaper ad. I'm really proud of those little Casper-like ghosts. It took me an age to get them perfect. It does look good, don't you think? And it's most definitely effective.'

Cassie had no intention of answering the question Rachael had posed. She took a long sip of tea instead, before raising her brow and saying, 'Bearing in mind I found myself unable to use a single one of your quotes without it having an adverse impact on all I was trying to say, or indeed having it reflect detrimentally on your whole profession, I thought including the picture—'

478

'You flatter me, Cassie!' Rachael said, with a huge grin before refocusing on the article before her. She pondered, 'I get why you didn't use the names of those involved, but there's also no mention of history repeating itself or Soul Mates, other than in my ad, of course – which I thank you for big time. In fact, while it's a departure from your normal exposés, it reads like a morality tale! I mean this here: "*While practitioners talk up the healing benefits of regression, if you have nothing to heal and you value your sanity, it comes with risks. There is merit to learning from the past. Many a psychologist will tell you that. But some of our past can be buried for a reason. It deserves to be buried. Deep. Forgotten. And its resurrection can wreak untold havoc on the present . . .*"

'Actually, on reflection, this is a cop out!' Rachael declared. 'You don't even *confirm* the existence of past lives. This talk of our past could relate to what we did three months ago! Although it raises definite questions, it's what you *aren't* saying; that you've not dissed "Past Life Regression" in your trademark fashion, which is the giveaway. I don't get it. You can prove the existence of past lives. Soul Mates, too I'm reckoning. Then there's history repeating itself for want of a better name for what seemed to be happening and—'

'I'm not ready yet,' Cassie murmured, twiddling with the handle of her mug. 'As I told my editor after he read this and his jaw dropped. I gave more away than I intended . . . I'm totally off form . . .

479

and, of course, he wants more. But I'm taking some time out. A holiday, a sabbatical, I'm not sure yet. I need some recovery time. It's all been . . .' She shook her head and raised her eyes to meet Rachael's. She asked so quietly, 'It *has* stopped . . . hasn't it?'

'Well it's a week on and I'm still here. Susie, too – if you can call being shagged witless by George in Peru, *here*.' At the expression that had evidently appeared on Cassie's face, Rachael dropped her flippancy and said softly, 'We've discussed this Cassie. It *has* stopped. I'm sure of it. The cycle stopped that night and fates clearly weren't mixed up. It's over.'

'Why didn't you tell me that Tessa died that night too? If Rob hadn't had that premonition—'

'It wasn't a premonition apparently. More . . . a really powerful sense that he needed to be there and he couldn't budge it. He's been experiencing some serious déjà vu, too. It's all rather fascinating—'

'If he hadn't turned up when he did you could be dead! Don't you think you could have *mentioned* it? Kathryn had no idea. She just thought you'd run off, leaving her in the lurch. She had no idea you'd drowned that night, too!'

'It didn't seem relevant. How were we to know it was repeating for us, as well?'

'We *were* still manipulating,' Cassie said, shaking her head slowly. 'Plotting where George and Susie were concerned. For a different end, but we were still doing it, just as we had in the past with Freddie and Hannah.'

'I know. I was even finding out what Susie was flaming well up to so we knew her every move! And just as Tessa was so near yet so far to her Soul Mate, circumstances got in the way for me and Rob. While history was repeating itself, we couldn't get our act together and recognise each other for who we were. Because Tessa and Richard never did. The fact we have now is why I *know* it's stopped.'

Cassie couldn't help but look and sound flabbergasted. 'Tell me that's not the get out clause for the Soul Mate queen not spotting her own Soul Mate when he was right there in front of her!'

Rachael shrugged her shoulders. 'It's true though. While I may have been a little . . . *confused* to begin with – and had incidentally been reading my *Little Book of Buddhism* beforehand – once history started repeating itself, we didn't have a hope. It was an impossible situation. Just as in the past, circumstances had to get in the way. Bless him. Rob apparently experienced that *wow* moment just as I did. Only mine got focused on Matey as he jumped into my arms. If I'd only looked up and seen Rob standing in the doorway, rather than focusing on Matey, I would have *known* that what I was feeling was towards him and not his cat. But then that's where Fate comes in. History couldn't have repeated itself then you see. And it was meant to do that.'

'*Meant* to do that? We were all meant to go through hell for what reason? Actually, you know what, I really don't think I want to know.'

'You are sounding more and more like Susie every day. It's a compliment. The fact we can talk like this to each other is good.'

Cassie shook her head. 'You are so not normal. And I know by saying that, I'm not insulting you. Quite the contrary. . . I'm on to you by the way. I've got you sussed. You hide behind all your flippancy. You use it as a defence mechanism.'

'Don't a lot of people? But nope, I'm not normal. Never have been.' Rachael shrugged her shoulders as she took a prolonged sip of coffee. 'Perhaps it *is* a defence mechanism. I've never really thought of it before. With what I *know*, always have done, even as a child . . . it's perhaps best that people don't always think I'm serious? I could have gone one of two ways, I suppose. Silent and brooding and keeping my mouth shut, which I think my father would have preferred or— Well, I didn't go that way! Lives are too short . . . Even when history has stopped repeating!'

Cassie met Rachael's grin with a snort and a shake of her head. Life would have indeed been short for all of them, bar Rob, had history still been repeating. Hannah, Freddie and evidently Tessa had been followed into their early graves by Kathryn only a matter of months later.

Cassie sighed. 'It may have stopped repeating,

but I doubt George is going to re-emerge from Peru until he's identified where Michael is.'

'I know. And Susie is determined to get back for the start of term. It will be interesting to see whether she persuades him or not. Michael won't be a problem now though. George is a lost cause as far as he's concerned and there's no reason why he'd have another shot at Susie. Porsche might still have a go in the press, of course, but I doubt she'll be so bad. And she's no danger anymore.'

'When Michael does re-emerge, he's going to have to stay the hell away from George. George would honestly kill him given half a chance. Let's just hope he doesn't reappear with a foreign heiress on his arm.'

'Foreign heiress?'

'Matthew ended up with one. If Michael did that I'd have to start asking myself if it was all repeating again and—'

'There's bound to be similarities, Cassie.'

She made an incredulous noise. 'Don't start on that again!'

Rachael laughed.

'Why though?' Cassie now asked. 'Why did it all happen? Why, what, how? I still don't have the answers! Perhaps it's because of that I don't feel ready to write about it and—'

'Not everything in life can be explained.'

'Oh shut up! You just don't know the answers either!'

Rachael smirked. 'No. Not yet. But I really want to find out. Are you game?'

'I'm sorry?'

'Well, as I see it, all I need to do is to introduce another pair of Soul Mates to each other during a regression and—'

Cassie choked on her tea before staring at Rachael in horror.

'I was joking! Flaming Nora, Cassie – I'm left of centre, remember?'

'Don't ever think about doing that! I mean it. Never, ever do that again!'

Rachael shrugged. 'It's not as if I knew I was doing it. Although I did have an incredible ring-a-ding-ding feeling beforehand, I must say. Do you know though? Rob categorically refuses to be regressed, despite all I've told him about Richard and—'

'Can you *blame him*?' Cassie cried. 'After what we've just been through? And why would he ever want to remember his life as Richard Barratt? He never married. He lived to a ripe old age, but all alone. And according to what Susie recalls from her time as Hannah, Richard was obsessed with Tessa and tortured by the sense of obligation he had towards his sisters and the fact that he couldn't act on what he felt towards her. Clearly it wasn't just Tessa feeling the attraction.'

'It's so sad that we didn't get our act together back then,' Rachael said. 'Not that circumstances would have been in our favour. We clearly weren't meant to be. Rob has never believed in happy endings, you know? It's understandable why now. All those years alone and . . .' She shook her head and said determinedly, 'I'm totally going to obliterate that one! Anyway . . .' She refocused on Cassie. 'No I don't have the answers as to why it all happened. Although I can say for sure that the number of us around from that one lifetime was not good. Not good at all. We were all impacting on each other. Add into that some similar motivations and personal characteristics . . . I don't know how the hell that was allowed to happen. I reckon we are back to Fate. Everything happens for a reason.'

'You know, I can't *possibly* let you use Fate or history repeating itself as a get out clause for not sussing Rob. How *the hell* didn't you spot who he was? You were spot on with George and Susie, yet got that so beyond wrong!'

'It's so hard to explain,' Rachael said. 'When Matey was around it was *always* with Rob in tow. What I was feeling was down to Rob's presence, not Matey's, not that I had a clue as to that of course. And like I always said, it never felt right anyway. It all felt so frustrating, and no wonder. It was particularly frustrating when it was the case of just me and Rob, with no Matey around . . . That's when things got really tricky. I couldn't help but feel the physical side of things then. I've always felt good around Rob. More than good, secure – the lot. But I only allowed myself to feel so much. I didn't want to betray Matey, so I allowed myself to feel what a really good friend might because that would be acceptable. But when it came to the physical side of things . . . Well, I was flaming well losing the battle, no matter how hard I tried! I had to try and stop myself feeling it though because it wasn't right! Or at least I didn't think it was right!'

'You got it so wrong,' Cassie chuckled.

'Yes! I got it wrong! Happy now? But history repeating itself and Fate played a major part, too! Honestly, we weren't *allowed* to get our act together! And the Dalai Lama himself didn't help. His little book . . . And I didn't realise the importance of touch then either. We hadn't touched until that night when he got me out of the water. Rob says he didn't trust himself to . . . touch me.' A stupid grin had appeared on Rachael's face. 'But, *anyway* . . .' She was blushing now too and shook her head as if to get focus. 'Right! Well, obviously Tessa didn't identify who Richard was either. Not that I'm surprised there. There was the attraction, big time. And jealousy. She couldn't stand his friendship with Hannah. But she wouldn't have been able to label what she felt. And she and Richard didn't even talk let alone . . . *touch* . . .'

Cassie had heard enough. And the sounds coming from Rachael's bedroom indicated Rob was getting himself up. Cassie had seen the two of them together in recent days and didn't think she could stomach that again for a very long while. 'I need to get going,' she said.

'No. Stay!' Rachael cried. 'We've still got things to talk about and I've a proposition to put your way.'

She was most definitely going. And quickly. 'Another time,' Cassie said, gathering her handbag from the table.

'Seriously, Cassie, we need to talk. I've had this fantastic idea . . .'

Cassie was already walking to the door. She sped up.

'You're taking a sabbatical or whatever you want to call it and thanks to your article, business has never been so good. We'd make a great team. You would be *phenomenal* at all the research for the "Soul Mate Recovery" business, which I just absolutely have to go ahead with now. I would of course do the—'

Cassie stopped in her tracks and turned to stare at Rachael who was now looking at her eagerly. 'I'm sorry?' Cassie asked.

'You could do the research,' Rachael clarified. 'I haven't thought the details through yet, but I'm reckoning there's got to be some. You could use the opportunity to find out everything there is to know about Soul Mates in the process, in preparation for your pending knock-out article and—'

Cassie shook her head rapidly. 'No, not to the research bit which is incidentally ridiculous, but to the bit about going ahead with the "Soul Mate

Recovery" business because of my article and it being good for—'

'It's incredible, Cassie. My phone hasn't stopped since about seven this morning when the paper must have hit the stands. There are so many messages from people wanting my services and—'

'How?' Cassie demanded, walking back to the table. 'How? I don't—'

'My ad. In your article. Everyone wants me to help them find their Soul Mate and—'

Cassie was beyond confused. 'But how did they *find* you? How would they know where to call? How—?'

'My details. My number. The ad?' Rachael said as if she couldn't believe she was having to explain it.

'No,' Cassie said adamantly, having closed the final distance to the kitchen table, and snatched up the paper. 'No. The telephone number and name are blanked out. I made very, very sure of—' *Nooo!*

'It's not blanked out,' Rachael said smugly. 'Oh I am so meant to do this. This is Fate at his best! Thanks to the article I now have a mass of potential subjects for Soul Mate Recovery. I reckon that's what this has all been about, other than Suse and George, and me and Rob getting together, of course. I reckon I'm meant to fill in the gaps in my knowledge of Soul Mates and match them up along the way. Then when I know it all, I can recover and match up even more! Without all this happening, I'd have thought I knew it all and I may never have got my arse in gear with the business. Me and you wouldn't have become friends. The article would have never appeared like this . . . I'm reckoning one of those people that has left a message is going to be lucky enough—'

'You can't do this!' Cassie cried, her horror most evident. 'You *can't*! And why *the hell* are people responding to your ad? They are broadsheet readers! They're meant to be intelligent. And I *warned*! They're not meant to—'

Rachael was shaking her head and grinning. 'Come on, Cassie. Admit it. My ad was not only incredible, but incredibly effective, too! So . . . the partnership? Are you game? Think of what you could learn. We might even find the answers you're still seeking. And you never know . . . and how wonderful would this be? . . . I might be able to lead you to your very own Soul Mate!'

Cassie felt sick. She'd been rendered speechless and found she couldn't get a word past her lips. And she needed to let go of the top of the chair she was presently clutching and make her way out of the room. But she suspected that clutch was presently holding her up.

'It's Fate, Cassie. Don't you *see*? *Everything* has been leading to this. Two life times – *at least* – have been leading to this. We are *meant* to do this! I have *the king* of all ring-a-ding-ding feelings right now.'